FINDING
MERCY

KAREN HARPER

FINDING
MERCY

HARLEQUIN®
entertain, enrich, inspire™

PLEASE RECYCLE • THIS PRODUCT IS RECYCLABLE

Recycling programs
for this product may
not exist in your area.

ISBN-13: 978-0-7783-1484-4

FINDING MERCY

For questions and comments about the quality of this book, please contact us at
CustomerService@Harlequin.com.

www.Harlequin.com

Printed in U.S.A.

For all the Kurtzes
who enjoy Ohio Amish country:
Margaret, Ruth, Barb, Bev and her friends.
And as ever, for everything, to Don.

Prologue

April 12, 2011

Alex Caldwell was sick to death of having to hide like a hunted animal trapped in a borrowed lair. How had his well-planned life imploded so fast? From a great career with a corner office forty stories up overlooking the Hudson River to a room in a one-floor Georgia motel with a single, curtained window. From skiing vacations in Vermont and golf in the Hamptons to running in place in front of a TV. From lobster and steak dinners to carryout and fast food that was all starting to taste like cardboard.

Damn his mentor and former boss Marv Boynton and his under-the-radar schemes that had brought down SkyBound, Inc., along with Alex's career and hopes! He couldn't stand just hiding and waiting for the trial to start anymore. The Atlanta spring weather shouted to him, and he was going out for a run, no matter what his government watchdog said.

"I'm going to jog a couple of times around the building," he told Jake, who was slumped against his headboard, staring like a zombie at a cable news show.

"Not on my watch, you're not. I know you're going stir-crazy. You think this is my idea of a great assignment? But you're a precious commodity, Metro Man, and—"

"I asked you not to call me that. Use my name. It may be all I have left."

"You should've taken the offer on the witness protection program. At least you'd be stashed someplace you could see the light of day. We're both getting bugeyed looking at these cable news shows, looking for more on the big man's case. You'll hear soon enough when they're ready for you. 'Sides, you snore, and I'm missing my beauty sleep."

"You should talk. I finally made some earplugs out of toilet paper so I don't have to listen to you at night too."

As ever, they tired of sniping at each other, and their conversation trailed off. Alex could think of more than one comeback, including that Jake was no beauty. Jake—no last name permitted—was balding, nearly sixty, with such big shoulders it seemed he had no neck. He had a gun but no personality. A former private security firm employee, he'd been let go recently and had taken a job protecting witnesses. As long as Alex refused to go into the federal WITSEC program, he was evidently stuck with the man until he could testify against his former boss for economic espionage—with the Chinese, no less. His whole life, his climb up the ladder, sabotaged by his decision to step forward as a whistle-blower—one, evidently, who needed protection until he could testify, or so the feds claimed. He was tempted to wear a disguise and go back home to Manhattan. Five weeks of this, no date for the trial yet, and he was going stark, raving nuts.

In a rage silent but for grunts, he did sit-ups and ab crunches on the floor until he broke out in a sweat and his belly muscles screamed as loud as his desperation. Then he realized Jake was snoring. Since he was asleep…

Alex got up slowly, not turning the volume of the droning TV either up or down. As he tiptoed toward the outside door of the motel room, he caught a glimpse of himself in the mirror. He looked bad, too thin, almost gaunt. He'd lost his tan. His usual great haircut was shaggy, his once clean-cut skin scruffy with beard stubble. He was down to his last pair of clean chinos and a cutoff sweatshirt.

He had to get the hell out of here, even for a few minutes. He wasn't going to risk being traced by doing anything stupid like calling a friend or either of the women he'd been dating—man, he'd like to import either Marci or Anita right now.

Despite being thirty-two years old, Alex felt like a kid sneaking downstairs early on Christmas morning. Holding his breath, he slowly turned the dead bolt. Jake got to make phone calls—he'd made a private one last night. It really irked Alex to be a prisoner. But he knew the WITSEC program would be worse. There you gave up not only your past but had to create an entirely new present.

Jake snored on, though it didn't sound deep or regular. Alex opened the door and sucked in a big breath. He took a step out and savored it all. Fresh air! The sound of traffic on the nearby beltway, lined with tall buildings. The splashes of colored flowers in the distance on the hill and in a bed near the motel sign. Open sky with puffs of cumulous clouds and a jet gliding overheard, probably from nearby Dobbins Air Reserve Base or even the huge Atlanta airport. Freedom!

Shaking in anticipation, Alex closed the door quietly behind him and began to walk fast. Just a couple of times around the building, he told himself. Atlanta was hilly with rich, red soil, so different from the flat concrete of Wall Street or even the manicured grassy spots in SoHo. Different too from his grandmother's terraced lawn overlooking Nassau, where he'd wanted to hide out before the feds nixed it.

Filling his lungs with breeze, he broke into a trot, then a run. He turned a corner, passed cars and U-Hauls parked early for the night. He read license plates from up and down the Midwestern states…Indiana, Michigan, Ohio, what he used to think of as flyover country when he traveled to L.A., heading for Hong Kong.

He turned another corner, kept going, faster. Just get this waiting over, be further deposed, prepare his testimony with his lawyers, then make it through the trial, all the publicity. Find a new job, maybe start a new career. Save some money again, decide on which woman to pursue. "If you can't decide, man," a friend had told him, "the answer is neither of them."

His muscles felt the burn now, his lungs expanded to take in good air, despite an idling black pickup spewing CO_2 at the far end of the parking lot. The sun felt so good on his shoulders, so much better than the night that had become his friend. Even with Jake accompanying him, he could duck outside only for a few minutes to gaze up at the vast, black night.

The feds were being paranoid, he thought. He'd complained of overkill but had been told their precautions were so he wouldn't be "overkilled." They'd regaled him with stories of witnesses who had been kidnapped or killed, tortured, some whose bodies turned up and some who just vanished.

Shutting all that out, Alex spotted one of the maids across the parking lot, going from room to room with her cart of mops and brooms. She was either really pretty or he was getting desperate for female companionship.

He ran on. The next time around, the black pickup was still there with its motor running. Its side window was down and the driver was holding up some kind of mirror that snagged a piece of sunlight. No, not a mirror, maybe binocs. A telescope? Or maybe...

A crack resounded, echoed off the building behind him. Stucco and shards of shingles spit at him. He lunged forward and hit the concrete walk on his belly as a second shot sounded. It shattered the window he'd just run past.

Shooting at him! But how—no one knew where...

Somewhere a woman was screaming, then Jake's voice. "Stay down! Gun. Gun!"

The pickup roared away. Jake, cursing, hauled Alex to his feet by the waistband of his slacks and shoved him toward their car, pushed him into the backseat on his face, slammed the door, got in the driver's seat and roared away.

"That's it for me!" Jake shouted as he sped up, then made a screeching turn. "You don't play by the rules, and somehow they found you, Metro Man! I'm delivering you to the Atlanta cops and then I'm outta here! For them to track and find you, someone wants you bad. I'd bet city hall you got a nice expensive contract on your head!"

Alex felt shaken to his soul—bullets…hit man…contract. Traced hundreds of miles from Manhattan. He hated and feared having to become someone he wasn't, but he couldn't live like this or else he was going to die like this.

1

June 20, 2011

Ella Lantz's field of lavender, edging toward full bloom, stretched as far as her eyes could see. But, she admitted, peering out from under her bonnet brim, that was only because the humped, wide-set rows of the fragrant purple plants went up the hill and disappeared from sight. She had almost an acre of the sweet stuff and, as *Grossmamm* Ruth put it, with no man or marriage coming down the pike, her little garden of Eden here in Eden County was her future.

With her curved hand sickle, Ella cut an armful of the earliest, hardy English lavender, then rushed down to where her widowed brother, Seth, was loading the wagon with his household goods. Beside him in the wagon sat Hannah Esh, Ella's good friend, whom he was going to marry this Friday, in just four days.

Even though Amish weddings usually avoided the farming months, everyone agreed they'd waited a long time. Their borrowed wagon was filled with the rest of Seth's furniture, which was going into storage in the

Troyer barn until his and Hannah's house was done. Meanwhile, the newlyweds were going to live in the big Troyer house while Seth would build first his and Hannah's home, then one for the youngest Troyer son, Josh, and his wife, Naomi. So many weddings, Ella thought, but none of them hers. Both Naomi and Hannah were her friends, and she wanted to send enough lavender with Seth to scent the Troyers' house, then later the wedding itself at Hannah's family home.

Ella was grateful to the Troyers for hiring her oldest brother in these tight times. And, she was getting a house of her own in the bargain. Seth was giving her his two-story home on this property. She planned to live upstairs and make the downstairs into a lavender workshop and store where she could oversee a small staff to make potpourri, candles and soap.

"Here, for Mrs. Troyer," Ella said, and lifted the big bundle of blooms up to Hannah, who cradled them across her knees. On the wagon seat between her and Seth perched three-year-old Marlena, Seth's little girl, who adored her new mother-to-be. The child smiled and waved down at her aunt Ella, who had helped to care for her since her mother died two years ago.

One of the four big Belgians hitched to the wagon snorted and stamped a huge hoof. They were anxious to be off. Ella knew Seth and Marlena were only going four miles away, but she would miss them. Suddenly, the small home she was inheriting here seemed miles from the big Lantz farmhouse where her parents and two younger siblings lived.

"Oh, they smell so good!" Hannah said, sniffing the spiky blooms with their purple tips. "Remember, I'll help you when I can at your new store."

"When you can won't be much," Ella told her with a playful punch on her leg. "Not with taking care of Marlena. Besides, you have a lot of catching up to do since you've been helping Ray-Lynn manage her restaurant."

Ray-Lynn Logan was their *Englische* friend who owned and operated the Dutch Farm Table Restaurant in the nearby little town of Homestead. The kindly woman, who was recovering from an accident and a coma, shared ownership of the popular eating and meeting spot with Jack Freeman, the county sheriff and Ray-Lynn's close friend. Hannah had been living with Ray-Lynn for a while, after Ray-Lynn's accident, and would stay with her until her wedding.

"Gotta go now, Ella," Seth called down to her. "Enjoy the house. If you need help building the shelves, just let me know."

"Oh, *ya,* I'll just get on your waiting list, you mean!" she kidded him. She smiled through her tears and bit her lower lip as he giddyapped the horses. To lose little Marlena from her care made her so sad… Before that last wagonful of Seth's household goods rattled down the gravel driveway, the rest of the Lantz family, who had helped him load, came out into the front yard to wave goodbye. Ella wondered where they'd disappeared to while she'd picked the lavender.

Her parents, Eben and Anna, waved goodbye as did her sprightly grandmother Ruth, age 80, who lived with them. *Mamm* and *Daad* shouted advice in their *Deutsche* dialect as if Seth and Hannah—and their only grandchild, Marlena—were leaving for the ends of the earth.

Abel, age twenty-six, Ella's second-oldest brother, not wed yet, who farmed the fields with *Daad,* looked sad. He would miss their oldest brother too. Barbara, sixteen, and Aaron, fourteen, the youngest, who was aching for his running around *rumspringa* time to begin, both turned quickly away and headed back toward the big farmhouse. Ella, at twenty-four, was the middle child of the five of them. She'd felt that way too—stuck in the middle, not quite companions of the two oldest boys or her two much younger siblings. That was probably why she'd made two close friends over the years—Hannah and Sarah, who had gone to the world and been shunned.

Ella was surprised to see an outsider watching from the porch as everyone hurried back inside. So when had he arrived, and where was his car? Who was he? Maybe that's why everyone had disappeared inside for a while.

Yet she hesitated to follow her family back inside the house. Despite living with so many people, she often chose to be alone, especially when she felt the drowning darkness swirling toward her. No good to have someone see her that way, especially since an Amish girl, who trusted in her faith to pull her through, couldn't escape its clutches. Going off on her own when that inner darkness came, she'd managed to keep her terrible secret from even those closest to her. Ever since she'd almost died ten years ago, she'd felt not only blessed but cursed....

"Ella, come here!" Her father's voice pulled her from her agonizing. "Something for the whole family to hear!" Holding the porch door open, he windmilled his arm. As she hurried toward the house, she saw her mother's white face in the window, peering out at her—or else watching the road, even though Seth's wagon was out of sight. What was going on? It surely had something to do with that stranger.

Taking a shortcut down the row with her late-blooming French lavender, she broke into a run.

Alexander Caldwell was really a wreck. This area reminded him of an old Clint Eastwood Western rerun. He saw horses and buggies, people in hats and bonnets, big barns and farmhouses with no phone or electric wires, no satellite TV dishes. And he was to be a part of all this, he marveled, as the black buggy clip-clopped along at such a slow speed he could actually see what usually blurred past beside the road. Hopefully, somewhere up ahead, Gerald Branin, his link to the outside world, was laying the groundwork for this huge deception that could mean life or death to him, especially since the shooter in his attempted Atlanta assassination had not been caught.

Gerald, his WITSEC manager, had sounded so certain that the heart of Amish country was the best place for him to hide out until the trial. This was a one-eighty from his own life in Manhattan. This was Podunk, the boondocks, the sticks, aka Homestead, Ohio, in Eden County. Soon enough his testimony at the trial would splash his name across the country and the world. But since the attempt on his life and at the urging of his lawyer, Logan Reese, he had finally admitted he needed to hide out. The feds had convinced him to try Amish anonymity.

He could, he thought perversely, envision the headlines now: *Former NYC Exec Exposes Corporate Espionage by CEO of Tech Firm Skybound, Inc.... Investors Left Devastated and Furious... Chinese Businesses In-*

*volved... Atlanta Assassination Attempt Financed by—
Why, You Name It: Alexander Caldwell's rich and
powerful former boss? The Chinese who want to shut
Caldwell up to avoid sanctions? Irate investors? Place
your bets on who would most like to shut the whistle-
blowing witness up for good.*

"Best put that hat back on," Bishop Joseph Esh, who
was driving the buggy, told him. "It's to wear, not bend
in your hands. Make you harder to pick out among our
people, *ya,* it will."

"Oh, right," Alex said, smoothing and replacing it on
his head. He couldn't get used to his Amish hairstyle,
either, or the lack of zippers on his broadfall-style pants,
the suspenders, or the five hundred dollars Branin had
given him in small bills, when he was used to credit
cards. No smartphone, which he missed horribly. Like
an idiot he kept lifting his wrist to check his Rolex for
the time when he didn't and couldn't wear a watch—
and did time even matter in this place? At least he was
playing a younger, unwed man, so he didn't have to
grow a beard. This elderly man had a long, white one.

"I do appreciate everything, sir," he told his host.

"*Sir* is too worldly. Bishop or just Joseph is good
for me. Be careful not to talk much in front of strangers and just nod when we speak the *Deutsche* but for
those few words I told you. Too bad you got to use lies
to protect the truth. Learned it the hard way myself,
but the ends sometimes justify the means. You got your
story straight?"

"Yes—*ya.* My manager rehearsed it with me, so I
won't rattle my bio—biography—off again. I guess this
has never happened before, that your people have sheltered a kind of fugitive."

"Nope. Did it because we owe FBI Agent Lincoln Armstrong a favor for helping solve a crime in these parts and your man Branin is a friend of his. And because Armstrong canceled a money debt my daughter Hannah owed him. I would take you in myself but too many people in and out of a bishop's home. We all— you too, I know—hope this won't last long."

"That's for sure. I'd like to get this over, sanely and safely."

"Life is precious, each one. You got a lot to live for. Enjoy and treasure each day. We all do."

Bishop Esh turned the buggy onto another curving, hilly road with a metal signpost that read *Oakridge,* and a hand-lettered one under it with an arrow. *Lavender Plain Products, No Sunday Sales.*

"We *what?*" Ella heard her brother Abel ask *Daad* as she hurried into the kitchen where her family and the stranger were gathered around the big table. She took off her bonnet, draped the tied strings over the back of her usual chair and sat. Pieces of shoofly pie and raspberry iced tea were at each place. Abel went on, "Take in an *Englischer* and say he's our cousin? But why, *Daad?*"

Daad shot Abel a sharp look. Ella could tell their worldly visitor wanted to answer but deferred to their father.

"Partly in thanks," *Daad* answered, "for what Agent Armstrong did for the Eshes. The bishop asked us to house this man we will call our cousin Andrew Lantz from Intercourse, Pennsylvania, though he is really an *Auslander* from a big Eastern American city. Andrew will work with us, work the fields. He will be with us until at least late summer, maybe longer. We will not question him about his true identity or his past. He is a good man. Now Mr. Branin here will say a bit more before our guest arrives."

Ella noted *Daad* frowned at Aaron for rolling his eyes at the mention of Intercourse. She'd heard Aaron and a couple of guys from his buddy group snickering over the name of that town before. Ah, those almost-ready-for-*rumspringa* years, when Amish teens enjoyed running around and trying worldly things. She should have cut loose more, but after her accident, she was so afraid of doing anything wrong, of setting off the darkness again.

She studied the *Auslander*. Mr. Branin was a short, wiry man whose red hair was fading to gray and creeping up pretty high on his forehead. He had sunglasses sticking out of his pocket, both the pockets and glasses sure signs he was an *Englischer*. He was dressed half fancy, half country in a white-sleeved shirt with jeans and running shoes. He wore a gold watch and wedding ring, which stood out here. He leaned forward with his elbows on the kitchen table as he talked, gesturing so much he almost punched Barbara in the face and she scooted back in her chair.

"I know it won't be easy to pretend a stranger is part of the family," Mr. Branin said. "But when the bishop brought me here a while ago in his buggy, he assured me that you and your people will take good care of this man. I must admit this is a radical placement for a witness, and I want to assure you that Andrew Lantz has done nothing wrong. Sometimes this program is forced to protect criminals who are informing on worse criminals, but that is not the case here. Andrew is helping our country at great risk to himself—a risk we will eliminate by hiding him here in a world so different from his own. Among your people, we appreciate that even the photographing of faces is not permitted."

"And," *Daad* said, "the new owner who bought the county newspaper, so far at least, is not like those big newspaper people, always poking into our privacy."

"Good," Mr. Branin went on. "And I assure you, I'll make a visit every once in a while." He looked from face to face and, evidently, since he hadn't been introduced to Ella before, nodded at her. "Sometimes you may be aware of my presence, but sometimes not."

Ella thought that sounded funny. Was this man going to hide in haystacks or up on the hill above her field? She sure didn't need someone spying on her, especially if she had to go off alone. She took a drink of iced tea and tucked into her piece of pie. For a moment, silence descended, but for the clink of forks on plates and Aaron's fidgeting and shuffling his big feet under the table.

"Someone's going to have to tell Seth," Ella said, her pie halfway to her mouth.

"I told him and Hannah first," *Daad* said. "They will keep Andrew's secret too."

"But the others," she plunged on, ignoring Mr. Branin's frown, "the neighbors, the church…"

"We have been helped, and we will help in turn," *Daad* said. "We will be the Good Samaritan to this wounded man."

This *wounded* man? Ella thought. She'd sure like to know more about what had happened to the outsider they were taking in.

Bishop Esh's words seemed to cut to the core of things, something Alex had always admired in mentors and bosses, even Marv, whom he was going to betray—as his boss had betrayed everyone who'd trusted him and SkyBound.

"It's like you been banned from your people for a while, and we understand that." The old man went on, "And to tell the truth as you have about a sinner, at cost to your own safety—that is also why I said yes to the witness protection people. *He makes me to lie down in green pastures, He leads me beside the still waters...* that is why too. As the Lord shelters us, we ought to shelter others."

Alex could only nod. He kept telling himself he was Andrew Lantz now, the Pennsylvania cousin of the family he would stay with and was about to meet. Gerald Branin, the WITSEC Deputy Marshal Inspector in charge of his case, had grilled him about his fake background but had not told him much about the Amish family who would take him in until the case came up in federal court in Manhattan. Five children, he'd been told, four of them still at home. As an only child, that would be a challenge, but maybe it could help to keep him from missing his friends so much. What he wouldn't give for a good, noisy bar crawl with his buds right now.

Again he surveyed the rolling hills with fertile fields of nearly knee-high corn guarded by tidy farms and barns. It was pretty, he had to admit that, like stepping back into a Currier & Ives painting. He watched other buggies pass with a nod or a wave on this narrow road. Everyone seemed to know the bishop's buggy—which looked like all the rest to him—and many called out a greeting in the German dialect.

When the bishop turned the buggy down a long lane, Alex saw a pale purple field of flowers marching partway up a high hill. The unearthly beauty of that—and that scent in the air amidst the buzzing of bees as the bishop reined in—seemed so foreign. As tense as Alex felt, the peaceful scene calmed his heart.

"I live just next farm over yonder," Bishop Esh said, pointing. "Three of us church families close together here—Kauffman, Esh and Lantz—with a real nice pond in the center. You just walk that field there, come have a meal with me and my wife, tell us how you're doing. Better make it after Friday, though, big family wedding with my daughter marrying the oldest of the Lantz sons. All kinds of things going on. You're invited too."

"Thanks. That's kind of you. I appreciate all you've done."

At least living with these backward, simple people would be a break from the high-speed chaos of his life, Alex thought. He usually lived fast and hard—he'd even been tempted to try an extreme sports vacation once, but he'd chickened out. Since he didn't know the first thing about horses, barns or crops—or much about the Amish—maybe the next couple of months would be pretty extreme.

"Wait—maybe that's them now," Mr. Branin said, and jumped up to look out the window. "Mr. Lantz, that's the same buggy that dropped me off here, isn't it?"

Daad looked out the window as *Mamm* had been doing off and on, when Ella thought she was just yearning for Seth to bring little Marlena back. "*Ya,* it's the bishop—them," *Daad* said with a nod.

Ella leaned back in her chair, but it wasn't worth it to crane her neck. Just get the man here, greet him kindly, then *Daad,* Abel and Aaron would keep him occupied, she thought. She had loads of work to do getting her new place ready and tending her crop, so she'd be too busy to help much. Her sister, Barbara, usually helped her tend the lavender but she was living with the Kurtz family ten miles outside town, since they had six children and the mother was ailing. Ella missed her younger sister, but Barbara would be back for Seth's wedding. Everyone expected Barbara would be the next Lantz bride, because she was closer than ever to her come-calling friend, Gabe Kauffman.

"I see he's tall and thin, this Andrew Lantz," *Daad* said. "Can't tell his hair or eye color from here—hope he's not got dark eyes and hair. Harder to fit in among our people."

"Ah, no," Mr. Branin said, sounding nervous now. "Dark blond hair and blue eyes, though you can't tell it with that hat yet." He hurried to the back door behind *Daad.* With a single, small black suitcase in his hand, the stranger appeared on the threshold behind Bishop Esh.

Though Ella had heard *Daad* describe the *Auslander,* she was surprised to see he was a whole head taller than the bishop. His square chin had a little cleft in the middle of it under his firm lips. He put his bag down but kept rotating his hat brim in his hands, clean-looking ones, no broken nails or bruises. *Daad* introduced each of them in turn by name as they stood at their places around the table. She realized she'd been rudely staring.

"Next, Ella, middle child, eldest daughter, keeps the lavender field, sells her goods, yet a *maidal*—not married."

Did *Daad* have to introduce her like that? Not only as a *maidal,* but *sells her goods and not married yet?*

"Ella." The stranger repeated her name as he had not the others. His gaze, sharp blue as winter ice, snagged hers and held a moment. His voice was deep and in just the few words he said, she sensed how lost he felt. He looked sturdy, though, with the muscles he'd need to help around here. His chest swelled his shirt and his upper arms filled out his Amish coat, which was just a bit too short at his wrists. His trousers fitted him just fine, though. He had new running shoes; so clean and white they stood out.

"Welcome, Cousin Andrew," she said, as the others had before, and then the introductions went on until *Mamm* sat him down and fed him and the bishop pie and iced tea, while Ella and Barbara bustled around to help *Mamm* prepare a light evening meal. They would feed him up good, unless his working around here kept the weight off.

More than once, when Ella darted a quick glance his way, their guest—Andrew—had those sharp blue eyes still on her. Later, when she placed his roast beef and gravy sandwich in front of him, she said, "Things are upside down today, first dessert, now the main course."

"I appreciate both," he said directly, quietly to her, then addressed everyone in a louder voice. "I mean to pitch in and help any way I can, though I've got to admit, planting a memorial tree after 9/11 is about as close as I've come to farming."

"Oh, *ya*," *Daad* said, "9/11, when the country was attacked and so many people died. Whatever is in the evil and sad past in your life, Andrew, we will keep you safe here."

Ella was amazed to see tears shimmer in Andrew's eyes. His lower lip quivered. He looked just the way she felt when she was afraid of the drowning darkness she had shared with no one and never could. She fought the desire to put her hand on his shoulder and began to serve the others.

2

That evening as dusk descended, Ella worked late in Seth's house. No, it was *her* place now, she reminded herself as she carried cartons of lavender products in from her work shed. Kitchen cabinets and counters, two long tables and planks on sawhorses would have to do for shelves and work areas until she could get everything built the way she wanted. She hoped to buy a still someday so she could distill the precious lavender oil. At least she'd finished stitching her dress to attend Hannah at her wedding. She'd been thrilled when Hannah asked her to be one of the side sitters, special friends of the wedding couple.

From dowels overheard, Ella hung the remaining bunches of last year's dried flowers by the rubber bands around their stems. Instantly, the kitchen and living area, even the two small first-floor bedrooms, gave off the familiar, delicate smell. Sometimes she was so used to the scent that her nose went numb from it, but it was deep in her mind and heart and she could imagine it. The kitchen here bothered her, but not because it was so small. On its wooden floor, Seth's wife, Lena, had died of an aortic aneurism, something she'd carried inside since birth and no one knew about.

Ella lit a third kerosene lantern to keep away sad thoughts. Her black mood had been lurking lately, probably because Seth and her little charge Marlena had left. Ella guessed worldly people would call her malady an off-and-on depression. Secretly, from books in the book mobile, she'd looked up the problem, but she still just wasn't sure what to call it or how to best cope with it. She hoped it wasn't what she read about bipolar disorder. Mostly, she just hid out when it hit her. You'd think nearly drowning would make every second of life that followed full of relief and joy, but that cold, grasping whirlpool seemed to pull her under sometimes, as it had then.

At least the hard work of producing her small number of Lavender Plain Products kept her focused outside herself. Now her family's new houseguest gave her lots to think about. Since she'd moved her things into the previous unused upstairs here, "Cousin" Andrew was being given her bedroom. How strange to think of an intriguing mystery man sleeping in her once private place.

She decided to go back to the farmhouse to get the refrigerated items Hannah had brought her from the restaurant for her generator-run fridge. It had been so kind of Ray-Lynn and Hannah to think of a sort of housewarming gift for her, and she was going to give both of them scented candles when she got settled here.

But as she stepped out on her back porch, she saw a figure jogging down the lane from the house or barn. In the gathering gloom, she could see clean white shoes.

Those, and the fact no one Amish went jogging, told her who it was. His quick steps spit gravel in a regular rhythm. But it was almost dark, and even buggies should stay off the roads now.

Earlier, she'd seen *Daad* take Andrew for a tour of the barn and the fields—back to the pond too, a place she always tried to avoid. Then she'd seen *Mamm* showing him around their big garden, pointing out and naming flowers and vegetables as if he were from another planet. It was pretty obvious to them that their adopted cousin had no idea of how to garden or farm. But *Daad* and the boys would teach him. She sure could use his help weeding her lavender beds, but she hadn't dared say so.

Ella headed for the farmhouse. Since her brothers had carried her bedroom furniture to her new place after supper, maybe this would be her last trip tonight. Trail bologna, Swiss cheese, some of Ray-Lynn's delicious baked goods; she'd seen how much Andrew had appreciated their food... *Ach,* she had to stop thinking about him so much, just because he was new and different. Too much happening around here at once, but maybe that would help her keep her head above water— she always thought of it that way....

She was almost to the farmhouse when she heard a long squeal of car brakes, then a crash. Not far down the road! What if a car had hit a buggy? It happened too often, and who came out the loser then? Little Marlena's maternal grandparents had been killed in a buggy car crash in the area that sound came from—the direction Andrew had run.

What if a car had hit him, jogging in the dark on the road?

Not even taking time to call for help inside the house, she lifted her long skirt and broke into a run in the same direction he had gone.

When Ray-Lynn Logan heard the screech of brakes and the *bang!* she stopped her van right in the middle of the road.

She'd given her restaurant manager, Hannah Esh, the day off to help her fiancé, Seth, get settled at the Troyer house and to help her family prepare for her wedding day. Ray-Lynn had promised she'd pick her up after she closed the restaurant, and bring her home. Hannah had been living with her ever since Ray-Lynn's concussion and coma, though of course Hannah was leaving this week to begin her new life as Seth Lantz's wife and little Marlena's mother. After her accident—which was really an attempted murder—Ray-Lynn had lost a couple of years of her memories, and that was about how long she'd had the restaurant. Worst of all, she'd forgotten her entire relationship with Jack, the county sheriff, which they were trying to rebuild—a relationship she still wanted to work, thank goodness. As appealing a man as Jack Freeman was, that kind of love—romance—she could not just fake.

But she was certain of what she'd just heard. Her accident had been at night too. She shouldn't have driven out after dark even now, but she had to learn to cope again, to be normal.

Sweating, shaking, she knew she couldn't just sit here in her new van in the middle of the road, even a usually quiet, country road in Amish country. She hit her emergency blinkers, fumbled for the cell phone in her big purse and punched in the easy-dial for Jack's private number. He'd know it was her from the caller ID. He had to answer! Good! No recording. He was picking up.

"Honey, you home?" he asked before she could say a word. His voice sounded so good. "I had a domestic outside of town, didn't get a chance to call you yet, but—"

"Jack, I'm in the van on Oakridge just before Troyer Mill Road, going to pick up Hannah! I—I'm not hallucinating, but I just heard a car hit something—it's wrecked—I'm sure of it."

"What direction from there?"

"Before the covered bridge, but past the Amish cemetery, not too far from that pond in the woods. I'm afraid to go look."

"Keep clear of it. Go on back to the bishop's house and wait there. I'll check it out right now."

"But Hannah will worry about me. You know she does."

"You can explain to her later. Just do what I said, and I'll look into it."

He punched off. Yes, she should do as he said, but what if she could help someone the way others had helped her? The old Ray-Lynn, the one who was so outgoing, feisty and strong—she had to get her back so she could be the woman Hannah and Jack both assured her had made him fall in love with her. How could a take-charge man like Sheriff Jack Freeman ever love a wimpy, wishy-washy, scared little rabbit? Ding-dang, she still had to recover her old self!

She turned on her brights, put the van into Drive and headed down the road toward where she'd heard the crash.

* * *

Alex's first reaction when the car roared down the road toward him was to dive out of the way, not even be seen. At least the roar hadn't included gunfire. Since Atlanta, he'd been paranoid about loud sounds, about vehicles backfiring or even speeding up. If there was a contract out on his life, did he just have to fear guns or could someone try something else? A car accident would look a lot more natural than bullets in the brain.

Praying his location had not been compromised again, he leaped off the narrow road. The speeding car had barely missed him as it vaulted up and over the next hill ahead—and then the crash.

At least the ditch where he'd landed was dry, but when he got to his feet and tried to climb out, he realized he'd twisted his left ankle. Idiot! He'd been so desperate to run for a while, savor the safety and freedom of this place. Now how was he going to get to that wreck, get back to the farm and the Lantzes?

He had to go up and over a hill to see if he could help. When others came, he'd have to fade away, try to cut through the woods past the pond Eben had showed him on his tour this evening.

Alex limped up the hill, which seemed endless. A sharp pain stabbed his ankle with each step. What else bad could happen to him? His past in ruins, his life endangered, probably a price on his head. But he couldn't just leave someone who might be hurt or dead. As much of a jerk as the driver had been to speed on these hills, Alex couldn't leave someone in need, no matter if his own hide was in danger.

Running footsteps behind him. What if this was a setup? Someone tried to flush him out with the headlights, tried to hit him, but he'd jumped aside, now they'd make sure...

He hunkered down just off the road—no ditch this high on the hill—and saw a person running toward him. A woman? Her light-colored apron and the white cap Amish women wore seemed to glow in the dark. His eyes had adjusted after staring into the headlights of that car.

He stood and limped onto the berm of the road. The woman running toward him stopped. "Andrew? Oh, thank the Lord, you're all right! I heard that car crash like it hit something."

"I sprained my ankle getting out of its way. Can I lean on you? I'm pretty sure the crash was just on the other side of the hill."

"Oh, *ya,* sure. Is it bad? If it hurts too much, I can just go see. That crash was loud. Surely someone else will come. They didn't hit a buggy, did they—or if you didn't see it, only heard it..."

He could tell she was nervous too, and not only because of the wreck. Did she not want him to touch her, put his arm around her shoulders? Ella was pretty, the lavender lady, with the white-blond hair and pale blue eyes. She had a great bod her Amish garments could not quite hide and an almost angelic face, framed by that stiff white cap. Unlike her mother and grandmother, Ella had her feelings written plain on her face, emotions that flitted past and changed. He'd been upset to hear he was being given her bedroom, but Mrs. Lantz had assured him that Ella had already planned to move to the small house on the other side of the garden and her big field.

"Okay, sure, lean on me," she told him, stepping

closer. Strange that, just as he reached his arm to touch her, the new moon popped over the horizon behind her head. Its sickle shape didn't give them much light but, in the midst of his fear, it seemed strangely like a celestial smile.

At the bottom of the hill, the side of a small, red sports car was wrapped around a big tree. And the hood of the car was evidently on fire. As they trudged toward it together, their awkward gait—Alex was now half hopping, just putting pressure on his good leg—reminded Ella of a three-legged race.

When they got there, they both gasped. It looked as if the red car itself bled strings of blood. No—Ella saw it was spools of shiny, red cord that had been thrown out of the car.

"Stay back," Alex ordered her, and took his arm from her shoulders. "I'll see if someone's still inside."

"You can't—your ankle. I'll check."

"No! If that fire spreads, the gas tank might blow!" he shouted, and made a grab for her. He missed and only snagged his fingers in her prayer *kapp,* which pulled off and yanked her long, pinned-up braid free. The weight of it slapped between her shoulder blades as she ran. She was pretty sure she heard a couple of curse words from Cousin Andrew.

He was right about a possible explosion. She smelled gas. She'd have to hurry. Passenger side crunched in. Driver's door open. No one in the car, maybe got out, but to where? Been thrown out?

"No one here!" she started to shout back to Andrew, but he'd come up right behind her. He tugged her back so hard by an elbow that she almost flew off her feet.

She banged into him. He fell back, but she balanced them before he pulled her away. His face, lit by the fire, looked like a mask of anger. What was this man really like?

"Get back, I said! You could be killed if that blows!"

Limping, he managed to drag her across the road and shoved her into the ditch, just as the car went up in flames with a big boom! Clinging together, they huddled in shallow water among grass and weeds. The light and heat slapped them, a hundred times worse than an open oven door or roaring fireplace log. Light all over—no, that was headlights up on the road. Someone was here to help! And here she was in Andrew's arms, clinging to him.

Ella clambered up and out of the ditch, dripping wet, her snagged braid spilling her hair loose. Despite the headlights in her eyes, she could see someone was getting out of a van.

"Ella? Ella, you okay? It's Ray-Lynn. The sheriff's on his way. What happened? Whose car?"

"Don't know, but he didn't burn up with it. I went to get him out but he was gone."

"We've got to find him, like you and Hannah found me, saved me. I— Oh, who's that?"

"This is our cousin, Andrew Lantz from Pennsylvania, visiting us for a while. We were— We both heard the crash."

Ella could see Andrew was already searching among the charred trees along the road, using a Y-shaped branch he'd found for a crutch. "Here!" he shouted to them. "He's back here!"

They ran to him, bent over a prone form. It seemed one unwound spool of the crimson cording pointed right at him. A young, dark-haired man lay sprawled half in the ditch on this side of the road. When Andrew turned him over to see if he was breathing, they saw he looked Asian. Andrew gasped.

"You know him?" Ray-Lynn asked.

"No—just surprised. Chinese, I think, and here—in Amish country."

They could hear the sheriff's siren coming closer. Andrew's head jerked up, turned toward the sound.

"It's all right," Ray-Lynn said. "Just the sheriff. He'll call the authorities for help, and we can tell them what happened."

Ella took off her apron and covered the unmoving man.

"He's breathing, has a pulse," Andrew said as he rose and moved away.

Ella bent over the injured man while Ray-Lynn walked away to flag down the sheriff. He jumped out of his squad car with a bright flashlight. Ella saw him give Ray-Lynn a quick, one-handed hug and whisper to her, though his words carried on the wind.

"Don't you let this flash you back to your own accident. You done good, honey, you and Ella and— Where'd that Amish guy go?"

Ella looked around as Ray-Lynn filled the sheriff in, and he came over to look at the unconscious victim. Unless Andrew had dived back into the ditch, he was nowhere to be seen, and with that sprained ankle. Then in the scarlet reflection of the sheriff's pulsating light bar, she saw he was crosscutting the field that led toward the pond and the more distant farm, moving jerkily with that homemade crutch.

Like a real Amish man, was he just humble, not

wanting to take credit for helping to save someone's life—if the car's driver lived? Or was it because he had his identity to hide and even the sheriff could not know about his being in that protection program? Or, she thought as the new, local newspaper editor, Lucinda Drayton, pulled up, was Andrew just making sure he wouldn't be interviewed or photographed?

Ms. Drayton slammed her car door and ran toward the sheriff shouting, "What happened?" Ella would have to tell Andrew that the new editor was real good about not showing Amish faces. Didn't he know he'd have to talk to the sheriff later?

Sheriff Freeman told Ms. Drayton, "Don't know much yet. That license plate's almost toast, but I'm gonna call in what I can see of it. We got an injured man on the ground. Squad's coming."

He walked back to his car and bent inside it to get some sort of telephone from the seat. Ray-Lynn knelt by the victim, and Ms. Drayton started photographing the still-smoldering wreck. In the reflected headlights, her short, sleek silver hair looked like a prayer *kapp*.

Ella walked over and told Ray-Lynn, "I can answer the sheriff's questions tomorrow, but I've got to get back right now."

"I can take you home, but it will be a while. Where did your cousin go?"

"He's new—shy, too. I've got to go see if he's okay," Ella said, and hurried away as she heard other sirens coming closer. Even though Andrew was hiking toward the place she never wanted to so much as see again, she cut through the trees the way he had, toward the pond.

3

Ella hurried to catch up with Andrew, but he had a good start on her, even using his makeshift crutch. Whatever he was hiding must be bad if he didn't even want to meet the sheriff.

She wasn't planning to go near the pond now, just skirt around it, but she needed to be certain he'd make it back to the farmhouse. She'd get *Grossmamm* Ruth to tend to that ankle with a poultice or a wrap.

Oh, no, he was making straight for the water. It was all worse in the dark, with the trees hunched over it, because it had looked like that when she'd met her best friends Sarah and Hannah there that night so long ago. Back then, Ella had been the wildest of the three, planning pranks, urging the others to sneak out at night. Scolding her once, *Mamm* had called her a daredevil, but even that bad name hadn't stopped her adventures.

That night, they'd taken off their clothes to keep them dry and, stripped bare, had gone into the cold water.

"Ooh, goose bumps already!" Sarah had said. "I'm gonna get out and just sketch the scene."

"Of us naked?" Ella had challenged, and they'd all

giggled. "Just swim around a little and you'll warm up. Hannah's not complaining."

"It's 'cause my teeth are chattering too hard!" Hannah had cried, chin-deep in the pond.

And then, somehow, amidst the laughter and the kidding, the kicking and the splashing, it happened. In the middle, where the coldest water came in from a deep stream that fed the pond, it seemed an evil, icy hand reached for Ella and pulled her around and down.

Had she put her own head under? In their horseplay, had she inhaled or swallowed water? Later, she could never remember. It was black and wet, and she held her breath, but her air was gone and a darkness like death sucked her in. She struggled, but it was too strong until someone grabbed her long hair and pulled and then...

The next thing she remembered was lying on the bank, spitting up water, shaking, gasping with her friends bending over her. Later, when she could breathe and talk, she begged them not to tell her parents what had happened—what had almost happened.

But she was changed after that. Hannah and Sarah knew it. Ella admitted it. Her parents saw it as an improvement. The daredevil had drowned and a more careful Ella was born that night, fearful the Lord had scolded her, shaken her.... Ever since, she'd lived with the curse of the sudden, drowning moods that she hid from everyone, however hard that was in such a tight community. Oh, they knew she was moody, a bit of a loner, a hard worker tending her lavender. But they never knew she carried with her the burden of the blackness, the wet, drowning fear of...

"Ella? I thought you'd stay with them." Andrew's voice jolted her. She saw pale moonlight sliced through the opening in the trees enough for him to see her too. He was sitting on the bank of the pond with one leg in it. "Your dad showed me this pond and said the water was cold. I needed to soak my ankle. I should have soaked my head for getting in that mess my first night here, but I'm glad we could help whoever that was. I think he's going to live."

"I pray he will," she called to him, staying put at the edge of the clearing, leaning back against a big maple as if glued to it. No way was she getting closer to that water—or to him again. "You reacted like you knew that injured man."

"No. Just surprised to see an Asian man in Amish country, which was stupid of me. I—I used to know some Chinese, and that's what I think he was, American-Chinese, of course." His voice had a slight tremor to it. "I didn't expect him here, that's all."

She wondered if Andrew had been a travel agent. Or what if he was a spy against the Chinese and that's why he had to hide out? No, that was crazy.

"Is the cold water helping your ankle? My grandmother is good at tending to things like that. I can head home and bring a buggy closer so you don't have to walk far."

"I think I'll be able to make it with this crutch. I apologize for leaning on you earlier."

"Oh, that's fine. We all have to do that—lean on each other. You know, you still might have to answer some questions from the sheriff. The woman who owns the local newspaper showed up too. She's pretty nice, though, not like the man who owned it before."

No answer from him but a huge sigh. Silence. Just

an owl's *whoo-whoo,* wind rustling the leaves overhead and the ripple of the water where he moved his foot in it.

"You can tell me if I'm out of line," he said, not looking at her now, "but are you afraid of me? Or is there some rule about not getting too close to outsiders or to men for unmarried Amish women?"

"Oh, no—not like that. I'm just—wary of the water."

"Oh. The pond. Your dad said it's deep. You mean you can't swim."

"I used to. Liked it, even, but not now." She almost blurted out more. She had a strange urge to confide in this stranger when she'd not even told her own family. Nor had she shared her near drowning with her come-calling friend, Eli Detweiler, though they were once, briefly, betrothed. But Eli would not—could not—give up his liquor after *rumspringa,* and there was no way she was going to trust him to be her husband and the father of her children—or to know the deepest, fearful secret of her heart.

Wide-eyed, drawn to Andrew but not going closer, she watched him stand unsteadily. He still had his makeshift crutch. She almost ran forward to help but stayed put. He kept his shoe and sock off; they dangled over one shoulder. It was even a big step for her to be this close to that water, looking at its cold, pale face.

"I'll run ahead and bring *Daad* back with the buggy," she said, and started across the fringe of the clearing. "I can drive it through the Kauffman farm, then I'll call for you."

"No, don't walk all that way alone in the dark," he insisted. "It's bad enough for me to be out here alone. Since you said it's okay for us to be close, I can make it with this crutch and you."

It's okay for us to be close... His word snagged in her mind. A while ago he'd said, they had to lean on each other. *I can make it with this crutch and you.* She'd wanted someone to trust and tell her deepest fears to for so long, someone strong to rely on. Since Andrew wouldn't be here long, maybe she could confide in him, and then he'd be gone and she could go on alone....

She shook her head to clear it, then remembered her *kapp* was gone and her hair was loose and wild. When she turned against the breeze, her tresses, silvered by moonlight, blew in her face. Though an Amish woman only unbound her long, uncut hair for her husband in their marriage bed, Andrew limped closer, his eyes taking her all in.

"Yeah, I suppose I'll have to speak to the sheriff," he said as they started off together, away from the pond. He didn't touch her this time, and they moved slowly. "But I'm pretty sure Mr. Branin hasn't informed him yet about my being undercover here. And the last thing I need is a newspaper interview."

"Maybe I can help, at least with Ms. Drayton at *The Home Valley News.*"

"You've helped already, just by being here, by caring about what happened to me."

He turned slowly sideways to stare at her. Up this close, with his face etched by moonlight, she could see how thick his eyelashes were, see the little squint lines at the corners of his blue eyes and the worry line on his broad brow. Suddenly self-conscious, she pulled her hair back behind her head, twisting and knotting it into a horse tail. When her gaze locked with his, she nearly stumbled, and it was he who reached out to briefly steady her.

Lightning leaped between them, something unspoken but understood. They both had secrets. They both had a new friend.

Alex was not used to being fussed over by women. By anyone. Yet the fact that Ella and the woman she called *Grossmamm* Ruth were tending to him was strangely comforting. It made him miss his own grandmother, now lost to him by her dementia.

His father had always tried to make him grow up too fast, which turned out to be a good thing when he lost both his parents in a boating accident when he was thirteen. Until he was eighteen, he'd lived off and on with a New York City legal guardian with vacations with his grandmother at her place in Nassau—lovely but lonely. She was being tended there now by a full-time caregiver and wouldn't recognize him even if he did visit.

His first instinct when the feds convinced him he might have a price on his head was to hide out at her place, but they'd told him that could endanger her too. Gerald Branin had said they'd seen WITSEC cases where a hit man used a close family member to flush out or coerce their target.

"Ow!" he clipped out as *Grossmamm* Ruth, massaging his ankle, hit a sore spot.

"Good!" the silver-haired lady said. "So that's the exact spot of the sprain. We tie the ice bag there, but you keep drinking that good dandelion tea, keeps swelling down real good."

Obviously, this dear old woman's favorite word was good, or *goot,* as she said it, even in English. "Ella, you pour him more tea," she said. "And please get him some more of your *daad's* good honey with the comb on a biscuit—good for what ails you."

She was bossing Ella around too, but she seemed to take it. He'd known a lot of kids growing up who didn't get it that rules and regs from a parent—with consequences—mean they cared, they loved you, wanted you safe. Damn, he hoped he would be safe here among these kind and good people.

He was yearning for a cup of Starbucks java but he downed the weak, strange tea. It warmed his insides anyway. Ella warmed him too, and that presented a problem.

"Now," Ruth said, "no more using that tree limb crutch you found. I got a good hospital one you can use. But, *ach,* even with that, you'll not be going into the fields with Eben and the boys tomorrow, not for a couple days. I gave my ankle a bad twist our last winter in Florida, on the Lido Beach. Made me so mad—I could not walk in the sand and wade the waves."

"In Florida?" Alex asked.

"Oh, *ya.* My husband and I, we had a nice little house down there in Pinecraft, right by Sarasota. You think the Amish can't take trips, enjoy warm weather in the winter?"

"I've just never heard of Amish snowbirds," he said.

"*Ach,* these old bones did not like the winter cold, even though there's always work to do here."

"That's why I want to help," Alex insisted, still trying to deal with a mental picture of fully clothed, black-clad Amish like *Grossmamm* Ruth on a south Florida beach amid the bikinis and Speedos. "I'm already enough of a burden."

"You go help Ella with her bed—right out the back door."

The way the old woman had put that—Ella's gaze met his. She actually blushed, her fair skin turning rosy from her throat to her cheeks.

"Help me weed my lavender bed," she put in quickly.

"I know what she means. If I can kneel and not put weight on this foot, that's fine."

"My sister Barbara usually works with me but she's helping another family out. You'll get to meet her at Seth's wedding though. I think Barbara will be staying home after that, so you wouldn't need to help me for long."

Ella's father came in the back door from outside. "I walked the field to tell the bishop all that happened," he told them, bending to take off his muddy shoes before coming into the immaculate kitchen in his socks. "The sheriff was there, coming here next to talk to Ella and Andrew. The bishop says we should tell the sheriff the truth about you, have him keep the newspaper editor and others away from you, best as can."

"I'd rather leave it for Gerald Branin to tell him— procedure, protocol, he said."

Eben shrugged, then nodded. "Then you are only Cousin Andrew Lantz until we get the say-so, but the sheriff always been straight with us. And you tell the bishop when next you see him."

A sharp knock rattled the back screen door and "Sheriff Freeman here!" resounded through it. Alex wondered if the sheriff could have overheard any of that. Sure, he'd been called to the accident scene, but he seemed to materialize out of the blue—the darkness— everywhere. No, that was unfair, Alex scolded himself.

He was just paranoid, not trusting anyone with a gun, even a law-and-order guy.

The phone call his guard Jake had made in Atlanta the night before someone tried to kill him had been eating at him. Could the call have been to sell him out? Neither he nor Branin could figure how the would-be assassin had found him. When Alex had sneaked out to go jogging, Jake sounded like he was snoring, but it was a different sound from those he made at night. Could he have been faking it, setting it up for Alex to sneak out while the assassin awaited? And then, of course, he rushed out to help so it would look good. Could a man so deep asleep wake up and get outside that fast?

And that car last night—could someone have sat in a vehicle, waiting for Alex—Andrew—to go out alone? Was that speeding car sent to kill him and just went out of control? The black pickup sitting in the Atlanta motel parking lot had looked harmless enough. Even the glint-eyed reflection had not panicked him at first.

Who to trust? Very few in the outside world—but he did trust these people who had taken him in.

After talking briefly alone to Andrew, Sheriff Freeman called Ella into the living room. She could see why he didn't want to question them together, but she wished he would have. That way she could help Andrew seem more Amish, maybe cover for him a bit, because she knew he hadn't told the sheriff who he really was.

"Standard procedure to talk to witnesses separate, Ella," he said when she sat down on the other end of the couch from him.

"We weren't exactly witnesses to the wreck—only about as much as Ray-Lynn was."

"Right, after the fact. I'll talk to her too."

"I hope seeing that didn't bring back bad memories of her own accident."

"She seems pretty steady. Still can't thank you and Hannah enough for getting her help when she was hurt. She's getting some of her old spunk back. Now, isn't it a little strange for your cousin Andrew—anyone Amish—to be out for an evening run, especially with all the exercise the men get in the fields?"

"He just arrived and hasn't started to work the fields yet. Then with the sprain he got, jumping out of the way of that car, it will be a few more days before he starts to work with *Daad* or the boys."

"Yeah, thank God he wasn't hit. By the way, the driver/victim regained consciousness en route to the hospital. Broken bones, some question of spinal injury when he was thrown clear. He was lucky he was thrown, though. If not, he would have fried in the wreck. We've contacted NOK—next of kin. His address was actually local, though I'd never seen him. Moved in recently from New York State. You know any reason that would upset your cousin? Andrew looked kinda green at the gills when I told him that. He's from Pennsylvania, right?"

"Yes, from Intercourse. Lots of Amish, lots of Lantzes there."

The sheriff led her through telling him how the wrecked vehicle began to flame, then blew up. How Andrew found the driver, turned him over.

"Which he should not have done, but I'm giving him a pass on that because it was natural to want to learn if the guy was dead or not," he said, still taking notes. Ella saw she'd been gripping her hands in her lap and tried to relax her cramped fingers. The sheriff was writing on his notepad, so maybe he hadn't noticed how nervous she was.

"They talk a little different in the eastern Amish enclaves, don't they?" the sheriff said as he looked up straight at her. "Andrew doesn't have the same kind of—excuse me for putting it this way—accent as your people here."

"There are some differences," she said in a rush, trying to answer him in a way that wasn't a lie. Would he be angry when he heard they hadn't told him the truth about Andrew? Mr. Branin should tell him soon. Why hadn't he already? "A lot of back-and-forth, long-distance relatives," she went on, "even marriages, but each area has some things unlike and special. All kinds of varied people come into Amish country, like that man who got hurt."

"Yeah. Samuel Lee. Word is that he's here to open a luxury spa and retreat in our area. Now, that's a good one. What next? I hear it's out on Sweetgum Lane near the Yoders' dairy farm and the old Troyer Mill. All right, I've gotta go now. Thanks, Ella."

Feeling bad they hadn't told him the truth about Andrew, she stood and walked out with him. Andrew still sat in the kitchen with his foot up on a kitchen chair with *Grossmamm* Ruth keeping an eye on him. *Mamm* had come downstairs and was dishing out strawberry shortcake for everyone. After quick goodbyes—and the sheriff's giving Andrew another steely-eyed stare—Ella walked him to the back door even before *Mamm* could ask him to stay for shortcake.

As he went out, Ella called to him, "Sheriff Freeman! Just a minute. Let me cut some lavender for Ray-Lynn if you're going to question her. I know she has trouble sleeping sometime and, with this going on tonight, it will help her, one of the best things lavender does. I will just take a minute."

Her hand sickle was in her new workshop, so she grabbed *Mamm*'s pruning shears by the back door and darted out to the closest end of the English lavender beds. As she'd come into the kitchen, she'd overheard *Daad* agreeing that Andrew could help her weed for the next day or so, stay on his knees and off his ankle. That possibility and the familiar, heady scent of her plants stretching up the hill, made her feel she could fly. Despite the terrible events of the night, her dark mood had lifted. Yes, with Andrew there, even the nightmare of being near the pond hadn't pulled her down.

She cut a good armful of the fragrant, flowering spikes and handed it to the sheriff.

"I oughta have this all over my office and the jail," he said as he put it next to him on the passenger seat of his cruiser. "Keep me calm with all the bad stuff been happening 'round here. Thanks, Ella, for Ray-Lynn and me. Night, now."

As he pulled out, the yard, the lane, the road went dark again. Only the kerosene-lantern-lit house and the slice of moon sailing high gave wan light. Starlight—so distant, such tiny specs in the big dark ocean of sky. She spun to look up at her lavender beds, marching toward the hill and up. It was the perfect site for the crop, with the much larger hill and its woodlot above, which sheltered the flowers from winter winds and where *Daad* kept his beehives so the bees would work all the gardens in the area.

And she saw, reflected, atop the hill, a large, staring eye, pale and lit from within.

She started toward the house, still looking back and up. Had she imagined it? She saw nothing now. Had a camera light popped, like when English folks tried to take verboten images of her people? Could Ms. Drayton have come by to follow up on the story of the car wreck and— No, she'd come to the door, wouldn't she? Hunter with a night-vision rifle? Binoculars?

Whatever it had been, it wasn't there now. She rushed inside and closed the storm door but decided not to upset everyone. What if it was just some strange reflection of light off one of the tin pans she had hanging high to keep birds away? What if it was a cluster of early lightning bugs?

Out of breath, she told everyone, "I gave the sheriff some lavender for Ray-Lynn."

They turned to her, including Andrew, as *Daad* said, "You can use Andrew's help with the lavender for a couple days, *ya?* We'll get him out in the fields soon enough."

"Oh, *ya, danki, Daad.* Andrew too," she said with a nod their way.

Patting the plastic ice pack on her patient's ankle, *Grossmamm* put in, "You just be sure you take good care of his ankle, Ella."

Ella bit her lower lip, uncertain whether to laugh or sulk. She was too old for *Grossmamm* to scold. Ella felt exhausted, yet energetic too. And she'd just take those tin pans down so they didn't reflect moon or lantern glow and get her all het up over nothing.

4

It had rained some overnight. Ella had heard the pat-
ter on her roof, a gentle rain, but she still hadn't slept
well. Her first night in her new house...the car accident...and Andrew. Then too, when she'd drifted off,
she'd dreamed she'd seen a huge glowing animal eye,
watching her from the blackness.

She shook her head to pull herself back to the here
and now. "I guess you can tell which are weeds, *ya?*"
she asked Andrew as they surveyed her lavender from
the bottom of the hill after a hearty breakfast with the
family. *Daad* and the boys had set out for the fields already. *Mamm* and *Grossmamm* had headed into town
in the family buggy to help Mrs. Lantz with wedding
preparations. For now, it was just the two of them.

"Of course, I can tell the flowers from the weeds,"
he said, sounding a bit annoyed. Maybe he had not
slept well either on his first night in a new place, in her
old room. "It's just going to be a question of getting to
them since the lavender's so tall and I've got to manage this crutch."

"If I don't keep after them, they'll be taller than the

crop, though part of the height is because I have to build up the beds with crushed limestone and ground oyster shells."

"No kidding?" He turned to her instead of surveying the plants. "Where do you get oyster shells around here?"

"At the mill that has chicken feed. They use ground shells as grit in the feed. I'll need to buggy there later to get some more, if you want to go along. It will look funny, though, with the man just sitting there and the woman handling the reins. One of the boys should teach you."

"Or you could show me while we drive."

"While we buggy," she corrected him. "Like we say, 'He buggied over to see me.' Even in English, you've got to learn some of the talk."

"So," he said, frowning and looking around again, "you've got quite a cottage industry going here."

"*Ya,* and now I've got the cottage for it. I'm going to turn the house into a workroom and store instead of just delivering things here and there."

"Instead of buggying things here and there, you mean," he said with a grin, then sobered again. "Your fledgling enterprise impresses me. You know, only two-thirds of small businesses survive their first two years and fewer than half make it to four years, but growth is the answer. With the right packaging, branding and promotion—financing too—your Lavender Plain Products could really turn into something with expanding market opportunities. Your dad could do the same for his honey and the honeycomb he sells on the side."

"Our businesses already *are* something," she said,

hands on her hips. "In your other life, did you own a company that sold something?"

"Not exactly. So, tell me more about the lavender. I take it with all the mulching, the roots don't like water."

"Right. The saying is, 'Lavender does not like to get its feet wet.'"

His eyes lit and, thinking he must like the way she'd put that, she smiled back. They stayed that way a bit too long, as if they were suspended at the bottom of the hill, lulled by the buzz of the bees, the scent of the flower, like in a dream.

"I was just thinking," he said, "the lavender's mistress doesn't like to get her feet wet either. You wouldn't come near that pond last night. So no wonder lavender grows so beautifully for a beautiful gardener and in Eden County, no less."

Her stomach did a funny flip-flop. A worldly compliment. And he'd called her *mistress*. Should she explain that her people only valued inner beauty? Her family had one mirror in the whole house and that was turned to the wall and mostly unused. But she said, "Sadly, there was a serpent in the Garden of Eden. Besides, I think of myself more as a farmer, of an important crop too. Lavender does lots of things, all good."

"It smells great, that's for sure. I didn't mean to imply you haven't done a good job with all this." They started up the hill to where she'd left off with her weeding yesterday. The two tin plates she'd left hanging up the hill were knocking together in the breeze. For sure, one of those must be what had made the reflection she saw last night after the sheriff left.

"Lavender does more than smell good," she told him, suddenly anxious to keep their conversation on her work and not herself. He kept stealing glimpses at her. "It can be used in recipes too, all kinds of yummy things like muffins, jellies and jams, chocolate, breads, teas and honeys. I plan to hire some friends to make those products to sell when I get the store going."

He was frowning now at some inward thought. What had she said to set him off? She wished she could read his moods.

"You won't believe this," Andrew said, "but I had a lavender-infused drink not long ago."

"Of course, I believe it. Lemonade?"

"Actually, a martini."

"Oh. Liquor. I couldn't go worldly with my sales. You have a lot to learn about us and our ways."

"I want to, so I'll get busy here. The bees won't sting me, will they?"

"Not if you let them be themselves and don't try to take over what they do best."

"I hear you loud and clear, Ella Lantz. Okay, boss, I'll get to work."

She watched him lean on his crutch, put his weight on his good leg and start to pull weeds. Though she just tried to accept the way things were, she was aching to know what he was hiding from. Had he left loved ones behind? A woman? A family? Even children? How she would hate being forced away from her life here. That thought chilled her and she shivered.

Ray-Lynn had carted her bouquet of lavender into the restaurant because it cheered her up. She put it right on the table where folks came in, near Ella's products she sold, under the front door sign that spoke of both her love of her Southern roots and of her adopted neighbors, the Ohio Amish: Y'all Come Back Now. *Danki!*

Jack was sitting in the back booth, facing the front door as he always did when he was here so he could keep an eye on things. Keep an eye on her too, she knew. Both he and Hannah had told her that Jack and she had been dating for a while and had been getting very involved before her accident and coma, whatever *very involved* really meant. She was embarrassed to ask Jack and wondered how much he really knew of her—had seen of her, in the flesh.

She was finally getting up the courage to ask him how intimate they had been and what he really wanted from her. They were business partners—she had the legal document that explained that—but had they been bed partners, too? Evidently taking the high road, good guy that he was, Jack had not pressured her on resuming where they left off—and just exactly where was that?

Today he looked not only bleary-eyed from getting little sleep after that car wreck last night, but she could tell he was upset by something the stranger who had joined him was saying. Jack, tall and imposing in his uniform, even sitting down, seemed to dwarf the outsider, a compact, balding man, maybe in his late fifties, with graying, reddish hair and a creeping hairline. He reminded Ray-Lynn of a rumpled professor and kept gesturing as he talked. Ding-dang, they looked at odds, but they were keeping their voices down, leaning forward over their empty plates, as if they'd like to leap over the table at each other. When she'd refilled their coffee cups, she had overheard only that the guy's name was Branin, nothing else.

She went over with their check herself. Although

Jack owned half of the restaurant, he always insisted on paying. She should, she thought, carry the big bouquet of lavender right over to them and plunk it on their table, since its smell was supposed to calm people down.

"...still say I should've been told up front, not after the fact..." she heard Jack mutter.

"We had to get him placed," Branin said. "Since the Amish were willing and we had a go-between, it happened real fast..."

They stopped talking and looked up at her. "You two gentlemen need anything else?" Ray-Lynn asked, and put the check on the table.

"We're doing fine," Jack said. "Thanks, Ray-Lynn."

She and Jack exchanged one of their "see you later" looks and she walked to the next booth and chatted with those patrons while keeping an ear cocked. Branin was saying, "Sorry I tracked you down here. Your office dispatcher told me where you'd gone. I appreciate your inviting me to join you for breakfast, Sheriff."

"So, you staying in the area for a while? Don't you have to get back to D.C.?" was the last thing she heard as she saw new patrons come in and went to seat them.

D.C.? Washington, D.C.? Having to put up with that FBI Agent Linc Armstrong from Cleveland a while ago was one thing, but D.C.? At least her car accident and coma had not hurt her curiosity, even though it was said that was what killed the cat.

When Ella saw that one high patch of her hardy Hidcote lavender had their flower heads about one-third open—which was ideal picking for sachets—she decided to take a break from weeding, get her hand sickle and cut some. The morning breeze and sunshine had dried out the foliage and flowers well enough for cutting.

"You are allowed to take a rest, you know," she told Andrew as she started past him down the hill. "I'll be right back. Oh—look," she told him as he stood and stretched his big frame, "a car just turned in the lane."

She could tell he tensed right away. "It looks like the same make of sports car that was in the wreck," he said. "A white one, though. Do you know who it is?"

"No, but sometimes customers see my sign down the road and just stop by. It's all right. You can stay here."

Since no one was at the farmhouse, she walked down to the driveway. It was a stranger, a woman dressed fancy in a pale blue linen suit, white silky blouse and gold jewelry that glinted in the sun. Her hair was sleek and black, collar-length, with flat, straight-cut bangs. The ebony sheen of it in the sun looked so unusual in this area full of fair-haired folks. Just like the young man in the car wreck last night, she looked Asian.

"Hello," the woman said, nodding. "This is the Lantz farm? Sheriff Freeman told me on the phone where to find it. I'm Connie Lee, Sam Lee's mother—the man whose car went out of control last night."

"Oh, *ya,* how is he doing?"

"Back injuries, two broken legs, but at least they don't think he'll be paralyzed. His father's with him, and we're having him flown to the Cleveland Clinic, but his long-term prognosis is good. I understand that you and your cousin were the first to reach him and risked your lives to be sure he was out of his burning car. I can't thank you enough. I wanted to give you this token of our gratitude," she said, and reached in her purse for a white envelope.

Ella's eyes widened, not in the surprise at a gift, but because she glimpsed a gun in that purse. A small one, gleaming silver. She tried to keep calm. Amish women might not deal with firearms, but lady *Auslanders* evidently did.

"Unless that's just a thank-you note, we are glad to have helped but nothing else is needed," Ella told her.

"Oh, but—a donation for your church then."

"It is not our way, but you could donate to our church's Help Haiti fund—in your son's name."

She drew the envelope back. "Haiti? Yes, that was a mess there. How nice of your people. I need to rush today, but let me just mention the other thing then, something that has nothing to do with the accident. My husband, Chang, and I are from New York City, and we're going to open a luxury spa here in the Home Valley. You know, clients can come for few days or a week, get out of the rat race, lose weight, find peace and quiet. I believe Sheriff Freeman said you are the one who sells the lavender."

"Yes, Ella Lantz. I'm currently expanding my shop and products."

"That's great, because we want to decorate our new spa with country decor, kind of Amish chic. We were thinking of calling our own products we use here the Skinny Spa line, but we'll probably repackage things as the Sweetgum Spa line, since that's the road we're building on. Great buzzword for anything today, you know—*skinny*. You might want to consider that for your products line. We'd want to purchase and sell for you things like lotions, essential oils, spritzes, scented candles, body candles…"

"Body candles?"

"Right. People love them. They burn with a fragrance, then leave a puddle of warm liquid we use for massages. Well, more later, as I'll be back and forth, but we are so grateful that you helped save our Sam. He'll eventually be running the Sweetgum Spa, and I'll be sure you and your family have unlimited free beauty packages."

"That's kind of you," Ella told her, but it just showed this woman knew next to nothing about Amish anything. "Skinny" products and Amish chic decor around here? No way.

"So, where is the man you were with?" she asked, evidently as an afterthought as she squinted up the hill into the sun. "He seems to have disappeared, but if he's your cousin, I'd like to thank him in person."

As if she expected no answer to that, Connie Lee headed for her sleek car, which still had its motor running. She got back in, slammed the door, backed up and drove down the lane.

And the woman was right. Andrew was nowhere in sight on the brow of the hill. Wasn't he overdoing hiding himself? He was only Cousin Andrew now, not whoever he really was. At least since he'd seemed eager to lend advice about organizing her business, he'd probably be happy to hear there would be a new demand— an expanding market—for her lavender.

She headed toward her house. Surely, with his sprained ankle, he hadn't hiked higher up the hill. He'd no doubt reappear when he saw the stranger was gone. She got the hand sickle, which she kept good and sharp, picked up a big basket and started back outside, still thinking about Connie Lee, her husband with the strange name of Chang and injured son, Sam. Was that really Samuel, a good biblical name? And in Connie Lee's world, was that little gun just what this sharp blade was to Ella, a part of her she didn't even think as a weapon? Because, in Amish country, what could she be afraid of?

Ella startled and almost cut herself when she glimpsed a man standing right outside her kitchen window. Oh—Andrew! But what…why?

Ella hurried outside and around the corner. "Were you hiding there while she was here?" she asked him. "Did you hear anything she said?"

"I saw she looked Chinese, like the driver who wrecked his car," he said only, not looking at her, but staring at his feet. His crutch rested against the side of the house.

"What is it? What about the Chin—"

"Never mind. But look at this," he said, pointing at the damp soil beneath her window. "I came down the hill and watched from around the corner to see what was going on and noticed footprints in the ground, pointing inward. See?"

"*Ya,* well, it rained last night and a couple of days ago. Seth did me a favor and cleaned these windows outside, so that's probably why the prints."

"Would he have cleaned every window? Because I've almost made it all the way around now and there are the same prints."

She went with him. He was right. And, for sure, not Seth's prints, not those of any Amish man, she reckoned, because they were pointy toed with a distinct separate heel, like maybe cowboy boots.

"Not Seth's," she said, shaking her head. "Not even Amish."

"And recent. Maybe made last night, with the rain and all. Let's go see if they're at the farmhouse too."

They were, around all the lower windows, which Seth had not cleaned. The hair on the back of Ella's neck prickled. Could this be related to that huge eye she imagined on the hill?

"What about the sheriff?" Andrew asked, his voice urgent.

Again, she agonized, what and who was this man hiding from? Despite the fact she was sweating, she shivered. Maybe the prints had been made by someone who wasn't used to mud, so in the dark he didn't think about leaving a kind of calling card.

"I—I think the sheriff just wears black shoes," she told him. "And why would he come here and look in after being here last night?"

"Maybe he knows there's something fishy about me—but why your place, too, unless he thought I'd be living there and that you were still here in the farmhouse? Can you think of anyone around here who wears boots? That woman wasn't wearing boots, was she? They could be a woman's."

"Andrew, she was at her son's bedside in a hospital last night. She says they're moving him to the Cleveland Clinic, so—"

"I'm sorry to involve you in my problems, and if I thought there was one moment of danger for any of you, I'd leave."

"And go where?" she challenged.

Their eyes met and held as happened far too many times. Ella gripped the hand sickle hard in her hand. For one moment, she thought she should tell him about the reflection she'd seen on the hill last night, but it surely had been one of those tin pans catching wayward light. She didn't want him to be more upset, or to think he'd have to leave.

"Let's tell my father about these prints, and we'll keep an eye out," she said, longing to comfort him. "My sister Barbara has a come-calling friend from the next farm over, so I'll ask her when she gets home if it could be Gabe, but he must know she's not here."

Ella reached out her free hand to touch his arm. The man was so tense he felt like a carved piece of wood. "Don't fret," she said. "Let's just sniff some lavender, okay? It's supposed to be as calming as it is stimulating."

"Sniff some lavender," he repeated with a little shake of his head. He sighed, and his shoulders heaved as if he was trying to force himself to relax. "As for stimulating," he told her, "I find peaceful, pacifist Amish country very stimulating."

His eyes took her in again. What a shift of moods. The man was teasing, almost flirting now—wasn't he? How she wished she understood worldly ways better.

"So tell me everything our visitor talked about," he said as he leaned on his crutch and they started back up the hill side by side. "Did she seem to have a foreign accent?"

"There's something about you and the Chinese," Ella blurted, when she'd meant to keep her own counsel.

"Have you ever heard of the 'Don't ask, don't tell' policy, Ella?"

"No. Meaning keep my nose out of it?"

"Truth is, I like your nose—and quick mind—but the less you know, the better."

"I have heard of the 'inquiring minds want to know' policy."

"You are so honest and open, and I can't be either, not now at least. Can you trust me enough that we can still be friends—as well as boss and slave, of course."

She could not stop her laughter any more than she could stop wanting to be around this mysterious man. Whatever danger he was in, he was dangerous too—at least to her usually careful and controlled secret self.

5

Ray-Lynn stood with her sack of two turkey sandwiches, dill pickles, slaw and raspberry iced teas in the sheriff's office, waiting for Jack to finish a phone conversation. Lately her attempts to rebuild a relationship with him seemed destined to be overhearing snatches of his conversations with others. Only this time, she knew who he was talking to.

Standing at the back of the reception area near the short hall to his office, she'd figured out he was talking to FBI Agent Lincoln Armstrong, who had helped him solve a murder case here in town. Meanwhile, Ray-Lynn kept up sporadic chitchat with Doreen, the sheriff's day shift phone receptionist and dispatcher. Doreen was only twenty-two and fairly new to Homestead, so at least, Ray-Lynn thought, here was someone who didn't know more about her recent past than she did.

She and Jack had arranged to have lunch together today in his office. At least it was past the noon rush in the restaurant. She wished Doreen would quit chattering so she could hear Jack better.

"Have you seen the new deputy who came over from

Wooster?" Doreen asked with a roll of her brown eyes.
Her reddish-tinted hair—a much wilder color than Ray-
Lynn's—was in tight ringlets that bounced as did her
full breasts. "He's absolutely gung ho about working
here—and absolutely darling," she said in a stage whisper. "Winston Hayes, but goes by Win, and he is a win-
ner! Not married, either."

"I heard he was coming but haven't met him."

Ray-Lynn could tell Jack was giving Agent Armstrong a bad time. "So why did you recommend to Branin sending someone who was a hit magnet to the Home
Valley?" Jack demanded. "That's a fine way to say
thanks after what we been through around here lately!"

Now what in tarnation was a "hit magnet," Ray-
Lynn wondered.

"And now that you've taken early retirement," Jack
went on, "forget coming anywhere near Hannah. She's
marrying Seth this Friday. Yeah, that's what I said, so
just keep clear."

Wow, Ray-Lynn thought, cocking her head to concentrate on his voice while Doreen rambled on about
Win Hayes. Linc Armstrong had retired from the FBI
he seemed to love so much? She dare not tell Hannah,
because she'd also have to tell her where she got the
info and no way was she admitting to eavesdropping
on Jack Freeman, even if she was desperate to know
everything she could find out about him—about them.
Drat her memory loss. She had to keep calm; she had
a lot to be grateful for, to look forward to and live for.

"In other words, Win's really a good name for him,"
Doreen was saying in her southern Ohio twang, which
could not hold a candle to a real Georgia drawl. "He's
built real muscular, a little short for a guy—like maybe

my height—but he's got big ideas. I can tell, he's going places, wants to be a sheriff someday. Does he ever look great in a uniform! I get the vibe of you're-safe-with-me, but he gives me the shivers at the same time, know what I mean?"

"I do indeed," Ray-Lynn said as she heard Jack hang up. "Nice chatting with you, Doreen." As she went down the hall, Jack swept open the door of his office, which had been ajar.

"Hey, didn't know you were here!" he said with a smile.

"It's one-thirty. Actually, after. I was waiting in the main office with Doreen."

"Wish we had time to drive out somewhere nice, 'cause it's a pretty day, but I 'preciate your bringing this here," he said, ushering her in and closing the door firmly. He gave her a hug and a quick kiss. Would he guess she'd overheard him? If so, it wasn't her fault. "Too much going on for us to really connect sometimes," he muttered as she took the food items out of the sack and placed them on the edge of his desk.

"And that's something I want—feel I'm ready for," she said as they sat in his two guest chairs. He had repositioned them in front of his desk so they were facing each other. Jack reached over and put a big, warm hand on her knee.

"I'd like that, honey. I been trying to give you some space and time, but you bet I'd like that, picking up where we left off."

She almost blurted out the question that had been haunting her: But where did we leave off? Were we sleeping together? Talking marriage? The Ray-Lynn who was rebuilding her memories and confidence after her brain trauma wasn't ready for any of that, was she? Because she needed to know where they'd been to trust where they were going.

"Let's do dinner soon," Jack said as he unwrapped the sandwich she'd made for him herself in the restaurant's kitchen. "Not around here unless it's a private picnic somewhere really pretty. You know, my new deputy—"

"Oh, yes, I heard about him just now from his fan club groupie Doreen," Ray-Lynn said, thinking he was going to talk business now.

"Yeah, real ambitious, doesn't quite know yet that he doesn't know much. But I'm glad to get the extra manpower with the crimes we've had around here lately. He was fairly new on the Wooster force but volunteered to come here when he heard there was an opening— likes smaller towns and rural folks, he said. Anyhow, I was going to say, Win told me that if you stand on the hill above Ella Lantz's lavender field, the scent is great and there's a stunning view of the valley. How about we do wine, cheese, a loaf of bread and thou up there some evening as the sun sets—maybe tonight, if I can get away. It's short notice, but how about it? I'll take a radio, bring a blanket, just like in the old days."

"You know the old days for us are new days to me, Jack. But it sounds wonderfully romantic."

"That's what I mean it to be. I think we're more than friends again. We've rebuilt that a different way from what we did the first time, but now we can move on by going back."

He looked so intent. His sandwich was halfway to his mouth, but he seemed not to know it, and she saw that as a great compliment.

* * *

Ella knew Andrew needed some horse skills, especially hitching and handling a buggy. She was disappointed when *Daad* told Aaron at midday dinner that he should take an hour and give their guest his first buggy lesson. She'd been planning to take a back road through a field to the mill today and teach Andrew herself along the way. Though it wasn't her regular day for it, she'd also planned to make lavender deliveries to Amanda Stutzman's Plain & Fancy B & B and to the Dutch Farm Table Restaurant in town, all excuses to show Andrew around a little more. And, she admitted to herself, just to have more time with him. She had never been so passionately curious about anyone in her life.

Daad called to Aaron as he and Andrew headed out the back door, "Harness up in the barn, so no outsider can see you teaching him." *Mamm* and Ella got up from the table and began to clear dinner dishes while Aaron walked out to the road to get the mail. "So," *Daad* said, turning toward Ella, "what do you think about those footprints Andrew spotted? You got a secret come-calling friend who's too eager?"

"I'm not seeing anyone. I don't know what to make of those prints, made by Western cowboy boots, I think. Maybe Aaron's ready-for-*rumspringa* friends came after him or were playing a prank. Some of them don't have much sense about sneaking out."

Amidst the clink of flatware and dishes, *Mamm* put in, "Though you've changed your ways, that's the pot calling the kettle black, my girl. I believe you and your friends used to sneak out once or twice."

At that, Ella kept silent. She'd been pleased she'd somehow thrown off the black mood that was threatening her yesterday, and she didn't want it circling back. Just because she couldn't teach Andrew to handle a horse and buggy, just because he couldn't go with her to get ground oyster shells from the gristmill today, so what, she tried to buck herself up.

Also she didn't say anything back to *Mamm,* because it would be a lot worse for her if her parents ever learned she'd almost drowned on one of those nights she'd sneaked out, had suffered the attacks of black moods ever since—and had never told them one thing about it. Shouldn't someone Amish just be able to trust in the Lord for healing? It should work to just pray fears away. A good Amish soul would confess to the bishop or the entire church to cleanse her conscience, yet Ella was certain that would not change a thing for her. In a way, she felt afraid of life now. The sampler *Grossmamm* Ruth had on her bedroom wall upstairs seemed like good advice, but it just didn't work for Ella: Do Not Fret. It Only Causes Harm.

"You're a real pretty girl, Ella," *Daad* said as he rose from the table. Ella looked up, taken aback by the worldly compliment. *Daad* continued. "And since you go here and there delivering the lavender, sell some to outsiders, talk friendly to them, maybe you attracted the wrong kind of attention. What about a secret admirer, someone you might not even be thinking about? Should *Mamm* go with you today to the mill?"

"You mean like I'm being stalked? No one like that, *Daad,* really," she said, and began washing up the dishes with such a vengeance that the warm, sudsy water swirled in the sink and made waves. "Sometimes,

I wish there was someone for me—but not one who peeks in windows. I'll be fine going to the mill on my own, just fine."

As Ella started out to the barn to hitch her horse Fern to her buggy, two of Aaron's buddy-group guys pulled into the lane at a good clip. They were in a fancy courting buggy one of them must have borrowed, because at fourteen, they were both too young to own one. Two more bug-in-their-beans pre-*rumspringa* boys who were feeling their oats already, Ella thought. They couldn't wait for their running-around time, couldn't wait to court a girl.

"Hey, Ella!" Mose Raber, a distant cousin, shouted. "Where's Aaron? We got to show him this buggy!"

"He's in the barn. I'll send him out!" she called back. Since Andrew seemed to want to steer clear of people, no use to get these excited kids chattering away at him too in their *Deutsche* dialect he wouldn't understand. What if the bishop hadn't been able to tell everyone in the church yet that they were harboring an *Auslander* for a while?

Ella was surprised to find that Aaron was teaching Andrew with her horse and buggy. "We knew you were going to the mill, so we thought we'd hitch up for you while I show him," Aaron said.

That kindness didn't sound like Aaron lately—or had Andrew suggested that? "*Danki,* but I can do it. Besides, Mose and Sol are outside to show you a courting buggy. It's okay if you go out to say hi. I can show Andrew."

Could it be, she thought, that the Lord had set this up with perfect timing? Andrew might not be going with her to the mill, but she had him to herself again. How she wished he'd tell her something about his real life.

"Aaron said your horse's name is Fern," Andrew said, interrupting her thoughts as he patted her mare's flank.

"Right. See the little leaf mark on her forehead, like a fern? What else did he say?"

"That you always curry her before hitching up, but he'd skip that part right now. And that she used to be a champion pacer and could do almost eight miles an hour instead of just six, like the slower horse your dad lets him use."

"Speed," she said, giving Fern a few quick strokes with the curry brush. "Both my brothers like fast buggies, new leather and speed. I do too, and if I blow Fern a kiss she goes even faster."

He smiled. "I'll remember that. The love of speed sounds universal to me—something the Amish have in common with the world."

"I know what universal means," she replied, trying not to sound testy. "You had to leave behind a fast car, I bet."

"Not a sports car, though. I went for a black BMW—corporate image."

He had actually told her something personal. "Oh, I see."

"I don't mean to talk down to you, but I suppose you think I'm speaking a foreign language sometimes."

"Like you think about us, I guess. And never the twain shall meet, my grandfather used to say."

"But we are meeting, and I want to learn your ways. I admire much about your life."

"Okay, then," she said, tossing the curry brush onto a hay bale. She hoped Andrew didn't notice she was blushing over a compliment as simple as that. She stroked Fern hard with the palms of her hands a couple of times where she'd brushed her, whispering, *"Ser gut, ser gut, mein Fern."*

She picked up some of the tack Aaron had already taken from the pegs along the wall near the stalls. "Here's what to remember to harness a horse and hitch him or her to the buggy." She named the different parts of the tack while she used each, then reviewed. "Collar around neck, breast strap between forelegs, crupper under tail…"

"That under-tail stuff can be dangerous, right? Got to watch out on that back end."

She turned to look directly at him for the first time since she'd started harnessing. "You mean, what we call horse apples? Mostly, that happens when they're grazing in the field or especially on the road. It's one of the things some English hold against us, that and they say these steel wheel rims on the buggy cut into the asphalt. But we have a right to be there too, and we put up with fumes and noise and the danger of being hit or run over."

"I never thought about outsiders disliking the Amish for anything. Do they harass or retaliate against you? Could that be a reason someone would be looking in the windows—to plan something against your family?"

"There have been a few hate crimes. Some folks blame us for being pacifists, for turning the other cheek, not serving in the army, and they take advantage of that. You know, I'll tell Aaron to ask around to see if anyone else has had people looking in their windows. It could be just someone curious. Okay, here now, let's back her up to the buggy. These long, narrow hickory pieces attach the horse to the buggy and keep her in line with it."

As he helped her, he said, "I was surprised to see the bishop's buggy had a foot brake. I mean, can't you just tell the horse to 'whoa'?"

"Going fast enough, the buggy could slide into her. Did you notice all our wagons and buggies have reflective orange safety triangles on the back? Headlights too—a high-and low-beam switch on the floor with the battery under the seat. Now, whatever is keeping Aaron?" she asked, taking a step back when he came closer to peer into the buggy.

"I'm learning a lot from you anyway. So, does it matter which side the driver sits on if two are in the buggy?"

"Sure, rules for everything, though this is not in the Ordnung. That's the big church rules, moral things. But, *ya,* the woman always sits to the left of her husband or any man in a buggy."

"Sounds good to me. That means the man is always right—right?"

She turned to him with a little laugh. He still bent so close to look inside the buggy that her bonnet brim bounced against his cheek. Again, that strange, silent but oh-so-loud force crackled between them. They breathed in unison. His lower lip dropped slightly. Even in the dim barn, she could see her reflection in his narrowed, blue eyes.

"Guess what?" Aaron's voice startled them apart as he hurried back into the barn. "That courting buggy cost Mose's older brother almost twelve-hundred bucks! It's got emerald-green carpeting! His father was against it, but he saved up 'cause he wanted it so bad! Oh—you did it without me," he added as Ella climbed quickly up in the buggy and bent to take the reins.

"That's okay, Aaron," she said. "Let Andrew hitch the other one himself and you just watch this time. And then take him for a ride but just up and down the lane."

"I know what to do. You, *Grossmamm, Mamm* and *Daad* don't have to tell me everything!"

"*Danki,* Ella!" Andrew shouted after her. *"Ser gut, ser gut!"*

"She can be really bossy," she overheard Aaron say as she blew a kiss to Fern to speed her up—or was it a kiss to Andrew?

As Ella headed home from the mill, the early afternoon sky clouded over and the wind picked up. The weather was important to her people, a big topic of conversation, but she hadn't heard it was going to storm. She could feel the extra weight of the buggy from the four big bags of ground shells, or else she would have giddyapped Fern faster. To avoid getting caught in a downpour, she turned onto a farmer's lane that was a shortcut home. It was only wide enough for a four-horse hitch or big work wagon, but if she met someone coming the other way, she could easily pull off on the grassy edge of the cornfield.

Her thoughts on Andrew, she didn't hear the motor vehicle behind her at first. Too much of a smooth sound, not loud like an English farmer's tractor or planter. She craned her neck and tried to look back through the thick plastic window, which she hadn't rolled up today. It looked like a big buggy at first but it was a van, a black one. It seemed to have dark-tinted windows. She knew how impatient English drivers could be. She'd better pull off and let it pass. But why would a vehicle that probably wasn't local be on this cut-cross lane? There was nothing back here but corn and a couple of wood-lots.

You might know, it began to rain. She didn't stop to unroll the plastic windshield in front of her and blew Fern a kiss to get her to a place up ahead, which looked like a good pull-off spot. Most drivers in Amish coun-try were considerate and polite—at least the ones who weren't out drinking, like Sam Lee might have been, or who weren't taking the hills fast because of the roll-ercoaster-like thrills.

Thunder rumbled even as the van's engine behind got louder, *vroom, vroom,* like it was going to leap at her. The vehicle came closer, bumped the back of her buggy! Didn't they see the sign that read Slow-Mov-ing Vehicle? The van's lights had been on low but now bright headlights popped on. Another bump, harder. The buggy jolted. She was nearly to the pull-off spot—or should she just keep going? No way she could escape, however fast Fern could go.

Rain pattered on her bonnet as Ella leaned out and looked behind, even extended an open hand as if to say, "Keep back! Stop!" *Ya,* the windows of the vehicle were tinted so dark she could not see the driver. The wind-shield wipers whipped back and forth hard. Her heart pounding, she threw herself back inside the buggy.

Though she wasn't to the best spot yet, she swerved Fern to the right onto the grassy fringe of the field. Rain thudded on the fiberglass frame of the buggy like loud drums. She twisted around to stare out through her back plastic window. To her dismay, the car stopped, backed up and turned in too, this time shoving the buggy al-

most into Fern. Thank God, she wasn't on the edge of
a treed ravine like the one that had almost killed Ray-
Lynn when she plunged over it! But that would-be killer
was in prison. Out here in the open, exposed, no one
around—what did this person want? Just to scare her?
Or worse?

Don't fight back...turn the other cheek, she recited to
herself. Should she leave Fern, get out and run through
the field? The plowed soil and rain would make for slow
going. The van couldn't follow but a person could. She'd
be a sitting duck if someone had a camera—or a gun.
Some terrible attacks on the Amish she'd heard or read
about increased her panic: some drunk English teens
turned over a buggy with a woman inside; an Amish
boy throwing tomatoes at cars was shot to death. The
only thing she had to fight back with, without really
fighting back, was four bags of ground oyster shells.

When lightning crackled and struck something
nearby, Ella nearly jumped out of the buggy. Had it
hit a tree in the woodlot? If it struck again, what was
taller out here in the open, the buggy or the van? Metal
would attract the bolt, wouldn't it? No one emerged
from the van as it just sat there, rumbling low with the
front windshield like a huge eye just staring at her. She
should have told *Daad* and Andrew about that light she
glimpsed on the hill. At least there was no more bumping or shoving. What did that person want?

She fumbled on the floor for her jackknife and slit
the string stitching at the top of one of the big plastic
bags. If someone got out and came around to hurt her,
she'd fling ground oyster shells at them, in their eyes,
get out and run across the corner of the field into the
trees, lightning or not. Surely, this could not have any-

thing to do with their hiding Andrew. No one around here knew who he really was, did they? So how could anyone have found him? This had to be about something else, about her. Like *Daad* had suggested, was she being stalked?

The van hulked behind her like a big beast, its hood and front bumper tight against her buggy, as if playing with its prey. She was certain her wheels would sink in the soil if she drove straight ahead into the field.

While thunder rumbled again, this time more distantly, she dug out fistfuls of the ground shells and dumped them in her lap, ready to throw. Sweating, praying—*Oh Lord, please take care of Your own*—she waited. Then came a deep *honk-honk!* of the van's horn. Ella jumped. Fern snorted and startled. After another hard bump of the buggy, the van backed out, turned and drove away.

Despite the rain, Ella scrambled down from the seat, spewing ground shells and dust from her apron. She was going to get that license plate at any cost, tell Sheriff Freeman. Maybe the sheriff would know if others had been harassed this way too.

But the license plate was draped with a big dark cloth that dragged behind in the mud. It looked like an Amish woman's cape, black as ravens' wings. For a moment, she thought she glimpsed a face in the big, tinted back window, but it looked too thin—the white barrel of not a gun but a lamp? A telescope? Her grandfather had one they used to watch the stars through from the hilltop, years ago.

As the van disappeared down the lane at the end of the field, Ella heaved a frustrated, furious sigh and broke into tears she'd been holding back. She crunched through the wet oyster-shell grit and scrambled back up into the feeble protection of the buggy. At least the spilled feed would mark the exact spot so she could tell the sheriff where to look for tire tracks or anything to identify the van.

"Thank you, Lord, for Your protection," she whispered as she picked up the reins and backed Fern and the buggy out onto the road. One of the buggy wheels seemed wobbly, but she had no choice but to head home. She was wet and chilled but that wasn't why her hands were shaking so hard she almost flapped the reins. She reached behind into the small back seat and storage area for her cape.

It was gone, not on the floor, nowhere, but she knew she'd left it there when she went into the mill. And she knew now what was being dragged to death in pieces through the mud behind that black van.

6

After a dash through the woodlot, where she was afraid the van might appear again, Ella emerged onto Oakridge and headed straight for home. Now only the rattle of a bent back wheel pursued her until she heard the piercing shriek of a siren behind her.

She gasped when she saw a black vehicle. She stuck her head out to look back. Thank heavens! Only an Eden County police car. It must be the sheriff! She reined in, then realized it could be a trick. It wasn't the sheriff's car—no markings—nor did she recognize the short, muscular man who emerged from it, but he was wearing an officer's uniform.

He must have realized her unease, because before approaching her he called out, "Winston Hayes, ma'am, the new Eden County deputy. You don't have a fluorescent safety triangle on the back of your buggy. It's the law. Some Amish been protesting that and even went to jail over it in Indiana."

She looked at the back of her buggy. Not only was the safety sign gone but the back was scuffed and dented. Obviously, the van had knocked it off somewhere. She'd rather tell Sheriff Freeman what had happened, but she couldn't pass over it with this man. Deputy Winston Hayes flashed his badge at her. Looking very sure of himself, he stood so erect. He was built strong, almost stocky, but was only tall enough to look her straight in the eyes—though she couldn't see his eyes since he wore reflector-type sunglasses, despite the fact that the sky was a stormy gray. In her line of view, right behind his head, he'd left his light bar flashing. It made it look as if pulsating colors sprang from his head.

A buggy went by. She recognized the folks who stared but went on.

"Well, then?" he prompted, frowning.

"A black van bumped into the back of my buggy about a quarter hour ago, and I didn't realize the sign was gone."

"Yeah, sorry," he said, whipping off his glasses and bending closer to the damage, then brushing his hand across the scuff marks. "Your left wheel rim's askew too. Can you give me a description of the vehicle?" he asked, taking from his jacket pocket a small device that must be a cell phone, but one he typed things into with his thumbs.

"I'm not sure of the make. Tinted windows so I can't describe anyone inside. And what's scary is they had their license plate blacked out."

"Someone with malice aforethought," he muttered, straightening and putting a hand on his gun belt. "And this was where, ma'am?"

"I was taking a shortcut through the fields between Troyers Mill and here. I intend to tell Sheriff Freeman about it. I'd like to head home now."

"Which is where?" he asked, his thumbs busy again

on his little machine. A car went past; it slowed and people stared.

"I live at the Lantz farm, 400 Oakridge Road. I'm Ella Lantz."

"Oh, yeah, the lavender farm. You and one of your brothers helped the guy in the wreck the first day I was here. Sorry for being so curious, but I'm trying to familiarize myself with your people. So, three brothers still at home?"

"No, Seth just moved out to the Troyer place. That was my cousin who found the accident with me."

"Oh, yeah, that's what the sheriff said. So your cousin is living here now?"

How much had the sheriff told his new deputy? she wondered. And why did Andrew even figure into this? A police officer trying to get his feet on the ground here or not, this man was being too nosy about Andrew. After deadly persecutions of the Amish in Europe years ago, it wasn't her people's way to trust government men, lawyers or law officers. After all that Sheriff Freeman had been through with the Amish community here, he was the exception. Besides, as bedraggled and upset at Ella was, her hackles went up in her desire to protect Andrew.

"I'll be sure to get another safety sign, Officer Hayes," she said, hoping to change the topic. "We have one in our barn. I got caught in the rain, and I don't want to catch my death of chill, so I'd like to head home. I plan to talk to the sheriff soon."

She edged away from him toward her buggy. He was frowning now. She got in, hoping he didn't call her back or ask another question. But he let her go—that is, if she didn't count the fact he followed so close behind

her in his black cruiser all the way home that it brought
back the panic of the black van. She fought hard to keep
an attack of the drowning darkness at bay. When she
turned into the farm lane, he sped away.

"I don't need to be scolded like a child, *Daad!*" Ella
protested at her father's reaction to her telling him what
had happened.

The rain had stopped drumming on the barn roof.
The men had come in from the fields, but only *Daad*
was still here when she buggied in. Though wet and
shivering, she'd told him right away. He'd wrapped her
in a horse blanket and unhitched Fern for her while
she talked.

"Then don't act like a child, going out on your own
after those footprints around the houses!" he said.

"Those weren't targeting me anymore than the boys!"

"Ach," he went on, shaking his head so hard his
beard wagged. "My fault for not insisting you take
someone with you. That theft of your cape from your
parked buggy at the mill, and then dragging it behind
the van—what next?"

"I'm going to talk to the men who were working
there, see if they can describe or identify someone who
might have been near my buggy so I can follow up—"

"No! No. For all we know, it could be one of those
men who followed you, been watching you—looking
in windows. All right, you want to tell Sheriff Freeman
what happened, fine. His deputy will probably tell him."

"But I intentionally didn't tell the new deputy everything. Especially when he started asking questions
about our family and Andrew."

"A new man, trying to learn the territory, that's all.

Police are too nosy anyways, always were. But you cannot go out without one of your brothers with you until we find out more!"

"*Daad,* I have a business to run, and Abel and Aaron are busy in the fields with you. I can see why I shouldn't take Andrew with me, but—"

"But why? Someone is stalking you, I still think so, *ya,*" he said, starting to wipe Fern down with an old towel. Their raised voices obviously didn't bother the horse, who was already munching from the feed trough.

"I mean," Ella said, forcing herself to speak more slowly and calmly, "Andrew should stick close to home to keep himself safe."

"And have people wonder if he's sick? Folks would start talking about it and lots of others would get curious about him. He's going to attend Seth's wedding, so he'll be on display then anyway. Besides, I think he has cabin fever already. It's a hard time, his waiting to do the right thing, waiting to get his life back again. I didn't ask, but wherever they were hiding him before, I think something bad happened."

She almost blurted out, *You mean he was stalked?* but she kept quiet on that one. Was her protective father suggesting he trusted her going off alone with a worldly man? Her mind raced as she watched *Daad* hang Fern's tack on the wall pegs. He immediately started to hammer her bent metal wheel back into place. She pulled the blanket tighter around her wet shoulders.

"You mean," she said, having to talk louder again over the din, "you think I should take him with me when I leave on deliveries or errands? You didn't even want me to show him how to hitch a buggy."

"Never said that, just wanted to give Aaron more

responsibility. You should take Andrew and visit just once to your places that sell the lavender. Tell them for a while they need to come here to pick things up."

"But I've promised them I would make deliveries and included that in the price. All six of my vendors are busy women, and I'm hoping to expand. *Daad,* I'm twenty-four and am self-supporting and have my own home now, so—"

"That's a problem too," he said, stopping the hammering and turning to her. "At night, for a while, you should not sleep alone in that house, but come back inside with us."

"But you just gave my room to Andrew."

Daad sighed and put down the hammer. His shoulders slumped. His anger seemed to ebb from him. "We will set it up for Andrew to sleep in your *mamm's* quilting room, since the three men in one room would be too much."

"I can sleep in the quilting room."

"Must you always argue with your father, girl? You think Andrew would go for that? I see him as good man and not only because of what Mr. Branin told me about him."

"Here I thought Andrew was the one who had to be guarded, be worried about—not me."

"With the sheriff's help, we will find out who is bothering my girl, *ya?*" He put an arm around her shoulders, and they walked toward the barn door together. "And maybe it is not as bad as we fear, but you just let me explain to your mother."

"I know it probably doesn't mean much, but I thought I saw a light on the lavender hill the other night," she said as they walked out of the barn and he slid the wooden bar across to close it. "I was pretty sure it was a reflection off one of my tin pans that scare the birds away."

"Not a flashlight?"

"No, unless the battery was bad—dim. It was single, like an eye that opened and blinked shut."

He put her between the runners of the sleigh they had put outside, propped up on its end against the barn so they could fix the bottom of it. He moved away from her and, hands on his hips, stared up the hill, then looked toward the house.

"I'm going to walk to the phone shanty and call the sheriff to come out," he said.

"After I dry off and change clothes, I'm planning to take Ray-Lynn Logan her weekly lavender products into the Dutch Farm Table and also stop at the gift shop and B and B. I can ask Andrew to ride with me and see the sheriff then."

"*Ya,* I guess, if you stay on the main roads, with others around from now on. And no asking those men at the mill if they saw someone take your cape. Pranksters, I pray, just that."

She was glad to see no one in the kitchen, because she knew she must look a drowned cat—though it jolted her to think of it that way. Despite all she'd been through today, she had a hopeful heart. Blessedly, none of the feelings of impending doom that so often plagued her when something went wrong hovered over her head. However independent she'd been these past years, maybe she felt better because she liked the idea of Andrew taking care of her, just as she'd watch out for him.

* * *

Ella made sure Andrew heard her entire story before she asked him to accompany her for her deliveries that afternoon. He'd already agreed to move into the smaller quilting room. Abel and Aaron had moved his bed there and were muttering about having to move Ella's bedroom furniture back into the farmhouse after just taking it in the other direction.

Andrew had said he'd like to go along in the buggy. They sat companionably close as they headed toward town three miles away. She didn't know how he felt, but she felt good just to be with him.

"Want to handle the reins?" she asked.

"Always," he said with a tight smile as he took them from her. Their fingers touched. His were strong and warm, smooth too, not like a farmer's or a carpenter's. She showed him how to hold the reins, wrap them a bit around his hand.

"I guess 'always' means more than it sounds like," she said. "You were an important man—are still—if you can get things settled at home, right?"

"Some would think so. Also an ignorant man. I got taken in and in over my head. Now I'm trying to make amends. Do the right thing, as they say."

"I admire you for that. I know all about making mistakes. I almost married a man who couldn't give up his drinking. It was a blessing I had the courage to pull out, even though I'd said yes. Hold the right rein a little tighter, not all that slack."

"You need a rearview mirror."

"Some buggies have them. I just never saw the need—until earlier today."

"Being followed like that is one of my worst fears."

"I can't begin to imagine what you've been through or still have to face. But maybe what happened to me today gives me a little hint of how hard it's been for you. Do you think a lot about what you've left behind—what you're missing—besides your car to impress your corporation?"

"You are a smart and very persuasive woman, Ella Lantz. If I were my enemies, I'd send someone like you to get me to confess all."

"You're teasing."

"Yes and no. All right, I know a lot about you, so let's play something like twenty questions—or ten. You tell me things you think you know about the other me, the real me. As long as you're correct, you can ask another question."

He smiled at her, a bit prideful, she thought, but she was grateful to have the chance to learn more about him.

"You're from a big city, but not one in Ohio," she said.

"That's two questions, clever Ella, but yes and yes."

"You're not married."

"How did you guess that? I could hardly wear a wedding ring around here, not an Amish man."

"Because on your left ring finger, there is not a hint of white circle, but on your right hand, where you took off a ring, there is."

"I think the sheriff and that new deputy should be asking you for help."

"Don't change the subject or think flattery will get you anywhere, not with the Amish," she told him. "For us, cooperation, just like we have now, and not competition is the best way to live."

"Which means we are worlds apart. You should see the dog-eat-dog environment I came from. And, you know, this stay here has really been lucky for me."

"Not lucky—blessed. Blessed by God. Okay, here's another guess. You believe in God but you hardly ever think about Him anymore, because you've been too busy. You think you can solve your problems your way."

He turned to look at her as they clip-clopped along. He'd been turning his head away a lot and leaning out to look behind them. "I'd say that's fair," he admitted. "Until everything blew up in my face and what I was facing was the ruin of my dreams and maybe even death."

She gripped his left wrist. "I know. That changes things, doesn't it? Then you need something and someone to lean on. Oh, I have my questions too about life's troubles, but I never think that the Creator of the world—of these hills and fields and my lavender—doesn't have the answers. Last night I saw you go outside and look up at the stars, even though you were hobbling. You felt the strength and power out there in the vastness, didn't you?"

"Sure. Yeah, I believe that. But I also know we've got to use what we've been given—gifts and time and talents—to do our best and accomplish something in life. I've said it before, but I mean this—I really admire your people and your family, so close and supportive, despite some pretty strict rules."

"We're almost to town. One more guess about you. Your company had something to do with the Chinese—maybe you've even been to China—but you're worried they might be after you now."

His eyes widened in surprise. His nostrils flared; he

sniffed sharply, but he only shook his head and didn't answer. As they headed into the fringe of town with more intersections, she took the reins back from him.

"So much for that game," he said. "I don't want you involved in any way."

"But by coming along today and telling my father you were willing to help keep an eye on me, you *are* involved, so I am too. All right, you don't want to say more, that's fine. So, whatever big city you are from, this is lovely, little Homestead," she said with a sweep of one hand at Main Street.

She pointed out the Dutch Farm Table Restaurant and told him the pizzeria was partway down the block and the two fast-food places were at the very end. Pulling Fern into the hitching post in front of the sheriff's office, she gestured here and there. "That's the volunteer fire department, the string of shops, Kwik Stop food store where we usually get our groceries, the pharmacy and hardware store. And that's the newspaper office, down there near the only traffic light in town."

"A one-traffic-light town! Never thought I'd live in one, though I did see one once in Scotland."

"Oops, something personal slipped out. You'd better guard your mouth, Mr. Modern Andrew Lantz."

The corners of his taut mouth crimped in an almost-smile as he intently studied her mouth. She wet her lips with her tongue. His eyes widened, then he turned abruptly away. "And my heart," she was amazed to over-hear him whisper as he grabbed his crutch and climbed carefully down to tie Fern to the hitching post.

The sheriff invited them both into his office at once. Before they even sat down, Ella said, "I want to apologize for not telling you who Andrew really was before, but we were sworn to total secrecy until Mr. Branin filled you in."

"Which he did in his own good time. I understand, Ella. Like my Dad used to say, 'Loose lips sink ships.' Go on and tell me about the incident yesterday. Is there more to it than what you told Deputy Hayes?"

Ella told him about the "incident," including the theft and misuse of her cape, which she hadn't shared with the deputy.

"Did you see the way it was dragged behind the van as a threat?" the sheriff asked, frowning.

She wasn't sure what he meant. "I— No. You mean like a threat they would drag me? I think it was just a stranger or strangers picking on an Amish girl who was alone—easy game to scare. They stole my cape, then to be sure I didn't get their license, they covered it with what they had at hand but not—not like a message or a threat."

"I don't mean to upset you more, Ella," the sheriff said, sitting forward in his chair so that it squeaked. He folded his hands on his desk over the papers there. He glanced from Andrew to her. "I just gotta look at all possibilities. I haven't had any similar incident reported."

"You know our people don't like to deal with officials, don't like to complain or make reports like that. We handle things on our own. Maybe no one's been telling you, that's all."

"True. I'll send my new deputy out to look for the spot with the oyster-shell feed you dropped and the buggy's safety triangle. He may be able to spot something to help us ID the vehicle. Also, I'll check out who could possibly own it, if it's local. Besides checking vehicle records, I'm gonna ask around about who has vans like that locally, especially with those tinted windows. In the sunny South, that's fairly common, but can't say I've seen it much here. If it's from outside the county, taking in the whole state or country would be a needle in a haystack. My deputy and I will keep our eyes peeled. I'm real glad to have your report on top of what he told me. It's great to have him out in the field, so to speak, so I can have more time for people, Amish and English."

The sheriff turned toward Andrew. He sat, leaning intently forward in his chair with his crutch against the back of it. "Have you been with Ella in her buggy before today? Any way whoever followed her could have thought you were with her, then saw you were not and so drove away?"

Ella saw Andrew grip the wooden arms of his chair. His knuckles went white, but his voice was steady.

"No—today's the first I've been out with her. Sheriff, if I thought for one second Ella or the Lantzes or any of the Amish were being targeted or harassed because of me, I'd leave."

Ella jerked her head around, trying not to look upset.

"Ella," the sheriff said with a nod, "you tell your father Deputy Hayes and I will keep a good eye on your place for a while, even at night, though you all probably won't see us. Does your family own the top of the hill behind your house and lavender field?"

"No. The end of the lavender field is the end of our property line. Why do you ask?"

"Just 'cause at the top of that hill and in the large woodlot there are vantage points where someone could spy on you."

"I—I've only told my father this, but I did see a sort of reflection up there the night you questioned us about the car accident. But I'm pretty sure it was moonlight off a tin plate I have up there to scare the birds."

"You should have told me," the sheriff said.

"And me!" Andrew added.

"I said, I could explain it away," she insisted, looking from one to the other. "We can't live our lives fearing a bear behind every tree—well, you know what I mean. The next day, I was pretty sure it was just that tin plate."

"Okay, okay," the sheriff said. He seemed to be calming down better than Andrew. "And, on a happier note, I was going to ask permission to take Ray-Lynn on a picnic up there—for the great view of the valley."

For the first time since they'd been in the sheriff's office, Ella smiled. "Oh, that sounds lovely. You can see the sunset just great from there, and I don't think it's supposed to rain again for a while. Just be careful not to walk too far along that hill, because not only does it get steep with a couple of hidden rain wash holes, but there are six hives of honeybees up there, which take care of my lavender. *Daad* gets some honey from them too."

"Well, I'll remember all that. Just one more thing. You said you thought you saw the long-range part of a camera or telescope in the back of the van."

"Something like that."

"Okay. Just wanted to check. Now, if you wouldn't mind waiting outside, I'd like to talk to Andrew for a minute."

"Oh, *ya,* that's fine. I'll just carry Ray-Lynn's lavender products over to her."

"And don't you go telling her about a picnic. That's a surprise."

"And a lovely one, very romantic, a perfect place to get betrothed."

"Now, never you mind," the sheriff said, kind of shooing her out the door with a wagging index finger. "You and your buddies Sarah and Hannah don't need to do any more matchmaking for the two of us than you already have."

Putting her own index finger over her mouth as if her lips were sealed, Ella went out and quietly closed the door.

Alex wondered if the sheriff was going to tell him to stay away from Ella, give him some sort of lecture about getting too close to the Lantzes. How could he not respond to a family that took him in and to that sweet, saucy woman?

"Now that I've been filled in on what's going on, I've been doing some homework on the situation—your case," Jack Freeman said, keeping his voice low. "Even if you tried to explain to the Amish about SkyBound, Inc., I doubt if they'd get it about international GPS and satellites and the Chinese commies paying your boss for our technology. I really don't grasp it all. But there's something that is in my bailiwick. Have you given a thought to the fact that guy who almost hit you was of Chinese heritage?"

"I have. I'm glad to see you've got my well-being in mind, but it doesn't comfort me to have you think Sam Lee's a possible enemy too."

"Yeah, but a long shot. His family's spas are on the up-and-up. I checked them out. They got a small chain of them, real nice, real expensive too. But one more thing."

Alex held his breath. Of course, Gerald Branin had given the sheriff a heads-up on the case and he had technology at his fingertips. That made it all the more amazing that Ella had come up with the Chinese connection on her own.

"Here's my point," the sheriff went on. "Whatever Ella saw in the back of that van that blocked her in, either a long-range camera or a telescope, could point to someone being spied on. Then that reflection she glimpsed on the hill—who knows?"

"You just admitted it's a great view from there, but being spied on? If you get any hint of that—and it could tie to me—I'll be out of here, for my own safety, but for the Lantzes' too. I don't want anyone getting hurt."

"Keep me apprised, okay? I don't think we need to panic, but you see anything, I can arrange for you to have a cell phone. And I'd better tip off your friend Branin. I have his cell number, and he said he'd be in and out of this area, sometimes incognito."

"No thanks about the cell phone. It was part of the deal that I would become a member of the Amish community, honor their ways while I'm here, and I want that." The sheriff rose, so Alex did too.

"The so-called plain people aren't plain at all, Andrew. They're complicated as heck, but it doesn't take long for some of us to want to do anything to protect and help them. Just don't get in too deep, you know, with any single person."

That assumption and advice made Alex angry, but the man was probably right. He didn't need personal complications, especially when he was in a rush to get out of here as soon as possible. Or now, was he?

7

Before supper that evening, while it was still light, Ella worked alone in the lavender shop. She didn't feel alone, though. *Daad* was in the barn, putting another safety sign on the back of her buggy. Andrew was weeding about twenty yards away on the hill, and *Mamm* was taking clothes off the line on the other side of the lane. Ella knew she'd better quit and go help her with supper, but she wanted to finish up here before dark.

She did feel a bit lonely now that little Marlena wasn't toddling around. She imagined she could hear her high-pitched voice and feel the tugs on her skirt. It had been almost like having her own child. But she'd see her Friday. Despite the tension Ella had felt ever since Andrew arrived, the anticipation of the wedding bucked her up.

Every so often, she stooped to look out the window to watch Andrew bend over to pull weeds high up on the hill. He was getting really smooth at handling himself with just one crutch, though she hoped *Grossmamm* didn't see him balancing like that. In a couple of days, he wouldn't even need it. Ella's eyes kept drifting to his tight bottom as he leaned over.

She forced herself back to spooning last year's dried lavender heads into small quilted bags and tying them shut with lavender ribbons. These were her most popular and least expensive sachets. To each ribbon was attached a little tag with the hand lettering, *Lavender Plain Products*. But, she thought, if she did begin to work with that fancy new spa run by the Lee family, would that mean making things that weren't so plain and simple? Body candles to produce warm, fragrant wax for a massage? Obviously, the person would have to be partly or completely naked...and then to have a stranger rub warm, sweet-scented wax...

She shook her head to clear the image of Andrew stretching and bending over. He had his sleeves rolled to bare his upper arms and his shirttail had come out to expose a strip of tanned back, so unlike the white skin of Amish men....

"So what would he think of a massage?" she said aloud to the empty room.

"You talking to yourself lately, Ella?" came a masculine voice behind her. It wasn't Andrew's—or an Amish voice. She gasped and turned.

FBI Special Agent Linc Armstrong blocked the light as he opened the screen door and came in. She hadn't seen him for almost seven months. He looked as thin and edgy as ever, and he'd grown out his hair from its usual finger-width cut. Holding a white envelope in one hand, he wore a red knitted short-sleeved shirt with something sewn over its pocket. Oh, a little alligator. That was a good emblem for him.

"Agent Armstrong. You startled me."

"So I did. Just Linc Armstrong now. How's your guest doing?"

She decided not to answer that, even though she'd learned this man had a part in placing Andrew here.

Instead, she told him, "The bishop and my father think you more or less recommended us to host him."

He shrugged. "I thought of Bishop Esh's family first, since I knew Hannah was out of there, living with Ray-Lynn Logan. But the bishop needed privacy since so many of your people come to him for counseling."

"And the Eshes needed time to help prepare for Hannah and Seth's wedding. It's this Friday."

"That's why I'm here. I mean, not for the wedding, but to ask you to give Hannah this." He extended the white, square envelope toward her, but she didn't move around the table to take it. Instead, she gripped the back of a chair and didn't budge, though her mind was racing. *Daad,* Andrew too, would be upset that an outsider could corner her alone like this with them nearby. It was obvious he had not driven a car down the lane. He must have walked in across the front yard so no one at the back saw him coming. Besides the fact she didn't like the man, it unnerved her that he'd seemed to just appear out of nowhere.

Standing her ground, she told him, "With all that's happened between you and Hannah, I wouldn't feel right about giving her a personal note."

"It's a wedding card and a gift certificate for the Brand Amish furniture store near Homestead, so she can pick out something she and Seth want for their house when it's finished. That's all and that's it."

"Oh."

He sailed it onto the kitchen table, just missing her

big wooden bowl of dried lavender. "You always were too protective of her, Ella." He frowned, and his voice hardened. "I can see why you pushed Seth at her, but—"

"I didn't. It was their decision all the way."

"Yeah, well, maybe." She could tell he was angry but trying to hide it. "Decisions, decisions, right? I guess you didn't hear I've retired early from the FBI."

"No. I thought you loved it."

"Maybe I learned there were other things to love. Yeah, I took early retirement. I've gone into a private security firm with a couple of friends. The FBI just didn't love me anymore, and it didn't help that Seth and Hannah solved the graveyard murder instead of me. So, will you give that to her for me?" he demanded, pointing at the envelope.

"I'll give it to her and Seth together since you said it's for both of them."

"Ella Lantz, always on the straight and narrow. Well, take good care of your cousin Andrew. I'd hate to see that go wrong, the way other things have around here."

His voice and harsh expression grated on her composure. His words almost seemed like a challenge or threat. He glared at her. For a moment—maybe just because she'd been harassed earlier today—she felt afraid of him, but he turned away. Was that because he heard Andrew thudding up the porch steps on his crutch?

"I saw you have an English visitor, Ella," Andrew said. "One who appeared without a car, *ya?*"

She was glad that Andrew was trying to sound Amish. He had even mastered the pace of their English words pretty good. The two men stared at each other. They were about the same height.

"That's because I left my car down the lane and

walked in," Linc told him. "Great country for walking—right?—though I heard about your little accident. I'm Linc Armstrong, a friend of Gerald Branin's," he explained, finally extending a hand, which Andrew shook. "I'm just here to ask Ella to deliver a wedding gift to her brother and his bride."

The man had evidently said everything he wanted to, because he walked out, just when—now that Andrew was here—she was wishing he'd stay and the two men might talk a bit about Andrew's witness situation, so she could pick up more about it.

"Kind of a brusque guy," Andrew said.

"He doesn't like me much. He thinks I swayed my friend Hannah Esh against him and toward Seth."

"Hannah and him—an outsider? I didn't know. And is he right? Did you sway Hannah?"

"She always loved Seth, but it's true that Linc Armstrong had his eye on her. Anyway, I don't think she could have been happy with an *Englischer.*"

"But you said earlier your friend Sarah is happy with one, despite the fact you were against that too."

They stared at each other with the wedding card and her lavender on the table between them. "And she's been put under the ban because of that," Ella argued, her voice rising. "She can't be at Hannah's wedding, can't so much as sit down to a meal with her family. She can receive things from their hands but they cannot take things from her or visit her."

"That's pretty harsh. So I won't meet Sarah and her *Englischer* husband at the wedding? And the wedding is one of your and Sarah's lifelong friends, but she's not invited?"

"That's what I said! Keeping the way things should

be—it's difficult at times but necessary for the protection of our people."

"Protection. Well, I wouldn't want to mess with that. As your grandfather said, Never the twain shall meet. But that's a shame, isn't it? I'll wait out here on the porch for you to go into dinner so you don't get any other surprise English visitors—just old Amish me. *Ser gut und danki, Ella.*"

The undertone in his voice—even his few German words—sounded sarcastic and angry. Either he agreed with Linc Armstrong that she'd been wrongly judgmental, or he was just upset someone had been able to sneak up on her when she was alone. Or what if he thought she meant that the two of them shouldn't get any closer? *Ach,* for sure, like he'd said, that would be a shame.

But when she started out onto the back porch to make amends, Andrew wasn't there. He must really be angry with her. But no—there he was going back up the hill, shading his eyes against the late-afternoon sun. He was still limping a bit, but she saw he'd left his crutch on the porch and was staring down the lane toward the road.

As if she could read his mind, she realized what he must be doing. Dashing back inside, she hurried to a window at the front of her house and looked out toward the road. Linc Armstrong was nearly to his car; it was dark blue, not black and not a van.

Trembling, Ella leaned against the wall next to the window. Must they suspect everyone? Well, she'd told Andrew that her visitor didn't like her very much. But he was a former FBI agent. Could he want to harass and hurt her just because she'd urged Hannah to give Seth a second chance? Who else out there hated her and why?

* * *

Ray-Lynn was even more thrilled with the impromptu picnic than with the fabulous view from this vantage point. Holding hands, she and Jack had taken a walk atop the hill, admiring the valley from all sides, though they'd steered clear of what Jack called potholes, several small, grassy sinkholes where someone could fall and might tumble all the way down. From a safe distance, they'd looked at the stacked white boxes that were the neatly kept beehives that Eben Lantz tended. Best of all, they'd cuddled and kissed.

Now Jack was looking through his binoculars while she poured the Merlot he'd brought. She was touched that he'd brought delicate, slim-stemmed goblets clear out here. For once, he'd arranged everything, including bringing an old transistor radio tuned to an easy-listening station.

"Doggone!" he said, sitting up straighter. "If that isn't Linc Armstrong down there, getting in his car. He's driving away from near the Lantzes' driveway! Just earlier today I told him on the phone to give me a heads-up if he was in the area, but I assumed he was in Cleveland, when he must've been nearby."

"He better be here on FBI business and not to look for Hannah."

"He's not FBI anymore, took early retirement. And I told him to steer clear of her. He's doing some kind of private security work now, pays a lot more, he said."

"I don't care what he's doing. After what Hannah told me about the graveyard murder investigation, all she'd need is former Agent Armstrong suggesting she try a professional singing career again or messing with her feelings. Jack—wine."

He put the binoculars down and took the glass from her. He clinked it with hers. "I guess a lot of brides get the last-minute jitters, but is she shaky about the wedding?" he asked.

"No, rock solid in her feelings for Seth."

"Sounds good to me," he said, stroking her cheek with the curled backs of his fingers. A sharp sizzle swept down from there to her lower belly. Even though she couldn't recall the early days of their courtship, she bet he'd always affected her this way.

She had to smile that the song on the radio was "The Second Time Around." Momentarily content, they sipped their wine and settled back against one of the big oaks at the fringe of this lofty woodlot. She knew how hard it was for him to mentally leave his job, even when he was off duty. She understood that and could live with that—live with him.

"I can see someone—or something's—been here recently," Jack said, indicating the smashed grass on the brow of the hill just ahead of them. "Maybe deer lying down or lovers—other lovers."

"Is that a hint?"

"Wouldn't mind, but I'd rather roll out of a bed we shared than down this steep hill," he said with a slow, lazy smile.

"One of my Amish waitresses at the restaurant told me this brow of the hill used to be called Lover's Leap."

"Don't like the sound of that. What's the deal?"

"She said that a couple of decades ago an Amish girl and an English guy who shared a forbidden love jumped off into the ravine near the pond below when they couldn't marry." Even though Ray-Lynn could not recall her plunge down a treed hill, she shuddered at the thought, and Jack put his arm around her.

She cuddled against his ribs. She could tell he had something to say but was holding back, so she decided on a careful approach. "Jack, all of this is great. It's a real treat, having you bring the food."

"Lasagna, bread and salad from the pizzeria, though you deserve much more. Much more from me too, honey, but I've been biding my time." He put his wineglass down on his binoculars case, then took hers and balanced it there too. "I know I'm a busy, distracted man, rough around the edges, Ray-Lynn. I was so afraid I was gonna lose you, first because you could've died, then because you didn't remember me—that is, the way we were. But you were worth waiting for a second time."

"The way I hear it from Hannah and Ella, I waited for you the first time. You know what I mean, played a little hard to get. But now that past has been so difficult for me to get back."

"Ray-Lynn, I've been real patient and will wait longer if you want me to. We don't have to do things the same way as before, but..."

"The same way as before..."

"Well, yeah, I mean, we both had keys to each other's places and stayed the night sometimes, after we fell in love, that is."

"Jack Freeman, I believe that is one of the best, clearest things you have ever said to me. I can't thank you enough for giving me the support, the space, and the time to fall in love with you all over again."

"Then how about not only being in love again but maybe making love again?"

"*Maybe* sounds a bit wishy-washy to me, especially coming from you. I really think your take-charge attitude should come into play here," she said, and punched his chest. Ray-Lynn felt so high she could soar right off this hill. She was starting to get her old self back, she was sure of it, the teasing, even a bit of temper. It was so lovely here, and this man was so precious. "The sky's the limit," she said with a sweep of her arm toward the clouds.

Jack stretched out on the blanket and pulled her tight against him, then under him, though he kept his weight off her. Then he shattered the remnants of her poise with a moving, probing, devouring kiss. She clung to him, giving back as good as she got, so grateful for his touch and love. But one thing still gnawed at her: he'd mentioned making love but not a future.

They came up for air, breathing hard together. "Let's finish this food fast—before it gets any colder and I get any hotter," he said, sitting up and pulling her up too. He reached for their glasses, then froze.

"What is it?" she asked, trying to see around him. "Not a snake?"

He kept staring at their wineglasses in the matted grass, then reached for something just beyond their goblets.

"What is it?" she repeated as he pulled a round, slightly concave black plastic item from the grass.

"You ever see this before?" he countered, studying it closely.

"No. Is it a cap that fell off the salad dressing or something?"

"Bushnel, it says, but it's too big to have come off my binocs. I'll bet it covered a telescope lens."

"Wow, that would give a great view of the valley! You're frowning. What's the problem?" She could tell he had shifted back to sheriff mode.

"Hopefully, nothing. But as soon as we eat and hike down to where we left my car, we're gonna have to stop by the Lantzes for a sec. Then I plan on breaking the law, speeding to get to your place. You're sure Hannah's gone home, and we can have your house to ourselves?"

"Absolutely—she moved home until the wedding. Jack, I understand about your job, really. What's with that telescope lens cover?"

"Not sure, but I'm gonna find out."

It was barely dark when a knock sounded on the front door of the farmhouse. Coming up the stairs from the cool basement where she was storing the loaves of bread she'd made for the wedding, Ella heard the sharp *rap-rap-rap*. No one used the front door, so it worried her. She quickened her steps through the kitchen and dining room and into the living room, where *Daad* peered out the window, then headed for the door.

"*Ach,* bad news?" she heard him mutter to himself, and then she saw why he'd said that.

Deputy Sheriff Winston Hayes, whom her father must not recognize, stood hat in hand on their front porch. Did the deputy intend to check that she had put the safety triangle on her buggy as she'd promised? She saw his cruiser sitting partway down the lane.

"Good evening, Mr. Lantz," he said. "I'm Winston Hayes, the sheriff's new deputy. I know your daughter—hello, Miss Ella—was harassed today, and I just wanted to be sure the guy who parked on the road and drove away earlier wasn't the same one. I would have stopped then, but I was on another call."

"Ella?" *Daad* said, as he went out onto the porch, so she did too. It was very unlike her father not to invite someone in, but when it came to law enforcement around here, only Sheriff Freeman had passed muster with the Amish, and that had taken years.

"No, not the same man at all, but thank you for keeping an eye on things," she told Deputy Hayes. "I realize you're new or you would know him. That was the FBI agent who helped the sheriff solve the graveyard murders."

"Oh, wow, glad I didn't jump him," he said with a sudden smile that lit his handsome face. "I saw he didn't have a black van, but the fact he didn't drive right up to your place bothered me. Just trying to be helpful. The sheriff and I are pledged to serve and protect, and we realize you've all been kind and brave enough to take on an extra responsibility."

She assumed he meant Andrew. But *Daad* said nothing, so neither did she. At least the sheriff trusted his new man enough to tell him to keep a special eye out for them here because of their guest.

"Glad you're all doing okay," Deputy Hayes said in the awkward silence. "By the way, the sheriff had me check out the site where you were accosted. I found the oyster-shell grit on the ground you told him about. You didn't mention it to me."

He stared at her for a moment, so she assumed she was being subtly scolded. "But no sign of your safety triangle anywhere along the road. So anyway," he went on, pointing off into the distance, "I see there's a phone shanty down on the road, so you just call nine-one-one if anything else comes up and that will get us day or night."

As Abel came to the door and looked out, Deputy Hayes's head jerked around, then turned sharply away. Without another question, the deputy stepped back, put his hat on his head, turned and walked off the porch.

"I think," she told *Daad* and Abel, "the sheriff is keeping a better eye on us than we realized, since we have our guest here. That makes me feel a bit better for us—safer."

Yet she shuddered as she followed *Daad* back into the house.

8

Ella did her best thinking when she was working, so she was banging around in the big kitchen after dark that night, making a double batch of Lavender Surprise Muffins. The recipe called for one-and-a-half cups of lavender, but the surprise was lemon curd.

Her parents were working a jigsaw puzzle in the living room, and the boys were both upstairs. Andrew was sitting in a rocking chair on the front porch, just enjoying the peace and quiet, he'd said. Truth be told, he was probably worrying and watching the road.

She would like to be with him, but these muffins were one of her contributions to Seth and Hannah's wedding feast just two days away. For the Eshes to feed almost two hundred people took some doing, and the groom's family provided the smaller, evening meal. *Daad* had prepared ten jars of his special honey with the comb in it. Ella had already made and frozen six loaves of Cherry Lavender Nut Bread and had stored dozens of these muffins. But she was making extras so that Andrew could taste something with her lavender in it for breakfast tomorrow. At least Ella's other preparations were pretty much under control; namely, her attendant's dress was made and presents purchased. Strange, though, how Andrew's arrival had distracted her a bit from the wedding, and a family one at that.

Also, Ella kept going over in her mind what the sheriff had said about finding the telescope lens cover he'd shown her, *Daad* and Andrew. It had been found on one of the spots where the family had looked through *Grossdaad's* telescope at the stars years ago, though that clean lens cover could not have been that old. Anyone could stargaze from that lofty spot. The trouble was, they could spy on her family and Andrew too.

The sheriff had said he'd seen Linc Armstrong leaving their property and he'd asked why he was here. He had mentioned that Armstrong had suggested to Gerald Branin that this Amish community would be a good place for Andrew to stay for a while.

Ella startled when she saw headlights slash across the lawn outside the window over the sink. It was a small car that looked ghostly white in the dark. Oh—it might be the vehicle Connie Lee, the spa lady, drove.

Mamm and *Daad* hurried into the kitchen, and *Mamm* peered out the window. Ella told them, "I think it's the mother of the man who was in the car accident, the one who wants to buy lavender products for their family's new spa." She heard the front door slam, Andrew's voice in the living room, then Aaron's and Abel's. Her brothers might have come downstairs to see a sports car up close, but Andrew had probably come in to avoid being seen. He'd disappeared off the hill fast enough on Connie Lee's first visit.

With *Daad* behind her, Ella went to the back door. It was Mrs. Lee, coming up to the back porch steps.

"Would you like to come in?" Ella asked, hoping the woman didn't still have a little gun in her purse. "I hope your son is doing better."

She came in, and Ella introduced her parents. The front door banged again, and she heard Abel and Aaron's voices outside, but not Andrew's. "I hope you don't mind if my brothers look at your car," Ella added.

"Of course not. Yes, Sam's doing as well as can be expected with two broken legs and some spinal injuries. Thank God, he isn't paralyzed."

"*Ya,* thank God," her father put in.

"Please, you come sit in the living room, and I'll serve some pie," *Mamm* said.

"Oh, no, thanks. As someone who owns a spa, I must watch my figure, and Amish food can be deadly for waistlines. I just came to talk to Ella about placing an order for lavender products, so sitting here will be fine." She pulled a chair out for herself at the kitchen table. Hadn't she read somewhere, Ella thought, that the Chinese were polite and proper in social situations? Anyway, this woman seemed all-American, like some of the tourists in town who just pushed their way in.

Her parents went back into the living room, and Ella sat kitty-corner at the table from her guest, who pulled a list from her purse, one that looked made from snakeskin.

"I've drawn up a wish list I'd like you to go over," Mrs. Lee said. "I think it will go a long way with our spa guests to use local Amish products. In addition, I'd be happy to stock your things in the gift shop we'll have on the premises. I especially wanted to ask you about lavender spritzers, since they use alcohol for the coolness."

"Rubbing alcohol like for a sore muscle massage?"

Mrs. Lee's sleek eyebrows shot up. "No. Drinking alcohol—vodka, to be exact. You'd need to stock vodka, infuse it with lavender essence."

"I must admit, spritzers and body candles are new to me, Mrs. Lee. I can ask the bishop about the vodka since it's kind of for medicinal purposes, like dandelion wine, only not drunk this time."

For once, the woman seemed at a loss for words. Finally, she said, "Please call me Connie, Ella. Well, this is going to be an interesting partnership and a big learning experience for both of us. I've been reading up on lavender while just sitting around by Sam's bed. What an interesting history, way back to King Tut's tomb, Cleopatra's charms and Roman warfare—sprinkled in the streets to cover the smell of blood, no less."

"It isn't in the Bible, but legend says that Adam and Eve took lavender with them when they were banished from the Garden of Eden."

"Folklore, I'm sure, but lavender's aromatic and medicinal properties—useful to help with depression, too, I read—is all good. Here, I'll leave you with this monthly list of what we'll need and let you decide what you would set for prices, then we'll talk again. I'm driving back to Cleveland tonight, back and forth to the hospital there—the Cleveland Clinic is really not a clinic at all, too big, but names can be deceptive. Oh, here, I wanted to mention one more thing."

From the depths of her purse, she drew out not only her car keys but a small package wrapped in silver paper and tied with shiny crimson cording. Ella recognized it at once as the same material that had spilled all over the road at the scene of Sam Lee's accident.

"That's a very pretty package," she observed as Connie extended it to her.

"It's empty, because I know you won't take gifts, but I just wanted you to see how important packaging is and how your products will be presented. Spa products in our line all have this signature wrap. We import this red cord and could supply you with yours. Appearances are sometimes more alluring than what's really inside, you know."

She stood and tugged at the long sleeves of the bright pink blouse she wore under a white leather jacket. "Well," she went on when Ella stood too but said nothing else, "I'd better give your brothers an inside look at my car before I go. I take it your father's not interested. How about that cousin of yours who helped save our Sam? Is he still here? I'd love to take him for a ride. I swear, I'd *give* him the car if he weren't Amish, for what he did for Sam, but I got your message that you don't take gifts for good deeds."

Ella followed Connie Lee outside. Abel and Aaron were looking over every inch of the car. Connie said to them, "Get your shy cousin Andrew out here too, and I'll let you all sit behind the wheel!"

"Oh, he's busy with something," Aaron put in, not sounding a bit convincing. There it was again, Ella thought: it could be because the woman was grateful to Andrew, but her interest in him seemed a little too strong.

After Connie Lee let Aaron and Able sit behind the wheel, she got in her little car and drove away. Ella hurried back in the kitchen and went over the list. Talk about expanding her products line! She could hire several Amish women to help produce these products, including getting someone to make her own soap in her own shop, something she'd wanted to do for years.

She covered her cooled muffins with plastic wrap, but before she could go looking for Andrew, she saw him walk past the kitchen window outside. She barely made him out since the window gave back her own reflection like a dark mirror. Had he been out there all the time, observing Connie from the dark? If he was worried about his safety, where was he going?

She dimmed both kitchen kerosene lanterns so she could see out better, then went to open the storm door. The June night air was laced with the scent of lavender. Andrew had gone away from the house, and it appeared he was walking up the hill, without his crutch. Surely, he didn't mean to continue weeding in the dark or climb clear up to the woodlot hill to look around. When the sheriff and Ray-Lynn had stopped to show them the lens cover, Andrew had closely questioned him about the lay of the land up there and had been warned about both the beehives and the sudden drop-offs.

Ella went out after him, quietly closing both doors behind her. Realizing she didn't have her bonnet on, she almost turned back, but instead, picked up her pace. She wanted to look for her grandfather's old telescope in a wooden chest in the barn loft—at least, that's where it used to be. She'd told the sheriff she'd let him know if it was a Bushnel brand or not. Maybe she could take Andrew with her, make *Daad* feel better about it because he'd told her not to go anywhere but to bed or the bathroom alone. Right now she was hardly alone with Andrew just ahead of her.

As her eyes adjusted to the darkness, she noticed

again he was barely limping, though he climbed the hill slowly. "Andrew!" she called as she hurried behind him. "You aren't going higher just because of what the sheriff said about finding that lens cover, are you?"

He turned and waited for her. "Not in the dark," he said, sitting on the wide grassy strip between her mounded beds of English lavender. "I don't need to stumble into bee colonies or sinkholes. I like to look at the stars, and the minimal light pollution out here makes the gazing great."

She could feel his eyes on her. Sitting down about three feet away from him and wrapping her arms around her bent knees, she said, "You were probably reminded about the stars when the sheriff asked about the telescope. I came out to check in the barn to see if our old family one is still there."

"You shouldn't even go in there alone. But let's do this first."

He flopped onto his back with his hands linked behind his head. *Let's do this first* obviously meant look at the stars, not lie down together, but she lay back too. The grass was cool, the wind gentle and so sweet. She could hear him breathing hard, probably from his exertion due to climbing the hill. The sweeping, stunning black cup of sky lit by bright pinpoints kept her silent. But then she saw an arc of light skitter across the heavens above them.

"Oh, look, a shooting star!" she cried, pointing.

"No, that's what I've been watching for. I had to estimate the time because I don't have my wristwatch."

"Then what is that? I see now it's a steady light, in a straight line. And it doesn't twinkle."

"It's a man-made satellite."

"Like people get TV from? I've heard of that."

"Yeah, a communications satellite. They go from east to west, and military ones go north to south. They do rotate, though, so their brightness can vary even if they don't twinkle."

She felt awed. The hair on the back of her neck tingled. "You know all about that," she whispered.

He sighed. "Yeah, I do—used to. The industry changes pretty fast."

"The company you worked for—it made them or watched them?"

"Both. Do you know what the game of golf is?"

"Oh, *ya,* there's a course off the road near Charm. Real pretty hills, lakes and little beaches, but kind of fake too, all trimmed and raked."

"The company I worked for started out making what are called GPS range finders for golf. The GPS stands for global positioning satellites. In this case, they sync—link up—with satellites in the sky to supply exact locations and distances to the little holes where the ball is supposed to go in."

"Wow! All that for a game to put a ball in a hole! But you're not with the same company now?"

"Not exactly. The company branched out in big ways, and I did too. No, I'm not with them anymore and never will be. But I've got to admit, I'm still fascinated by watching satellites, knowing their names and life expectancies."

"Like a person. Well, I suppose people who put those up there think they're as clever as the Lord who made the heavens and earth. Just tell me some of their names then, the man-made ones."

"*Delta* will be visible tonight but much later. The

Agena is due and the International Space Station, as well."

She sat up and turned to look down at him. "Do the Chinese have them too?"

He sat up, his elbows on his bent knees, his arms dangling but his hands in tight fists. "They make spy satellites," he told her, his voice hard and cold now. "Not that we don't too. But some of theirs have secret pay-loads and cloud-piercing radar. That's like special eyes that can see through the clouds. And they can disable our satellites, communication or military, if we don't watch them, stop them."

"They have telescopes up there and cameras to take pictures of things this country doesn't want them to know about, I'll bet."

He just stared at her. She could see his mouth had fallen open a bit. "I'm an idiot," he muttered. "I'm so hungry to talk about my old self, the things I knew and loved, and you are so appealing and open and hon-est and smart… Forget I yammered on about all that, okay?"

"Only if you assure me that you think *the heavens are telling the glory of God and the earth shows forth his handiwork.*"

"I do, Ella Lantz. Really. I feel like there's time to think and feel things here. In just a few days, I've come to love this area and the people, and I'm grateful to be invited to your brother and your friend's wedding."

"You love it here?"

"I love the peace and quiet and strong beliefs. How close your family is. How your grandmother fusses over me and, when I called her Mrs. Lantz, how she corrected me to call her *Grossmamm* Ruth. And how kind you've all been—you most of all."

She had an overwhelming urge to hug him, to smooch him. She had to get out of here now.

"Hey, what did I say? Where are you going?" he demanded as she jumped to her feet.

"Into the barn to see if my grandfather's old telescope is still there. When you mentioned my grandmother, I remembered I'd told the sheriff I'd check on that, see what kind it was and all," she threw back over her shoulder as she brushed grass and lavender off her skirt.

"Wait up! I'm walking better but not running down hills. Ella!"

She both wanted to wait for him and flee from him. She'd never felt like this with any man, and it scared her more than the idea of anyone looking down at them from the hilltop or a black van or even from a man-made satellite.

"You know, honey, I don't mean to rush you into anything if you're not ready," Jack told Ray-Lynn and put his wineglass on her coffee table next to her bobblehead dolls of Scarlett O'Hara and Rhett Butler. Ray-Lynn's *Gone with the Wind* collection was one she'd had for years, so at least she'd remembered that after her head trauma.

They sat tight together on the couch in her living room. "You've been really patient and loving," she told him, putting her goblet down too. "I'm so sorry I don't remember our first courting days, but you've given me a second time to treasure."

He put his hand on her knee and squeezed it. "I know

you're the kind of woman who expects commitment, and you've got it. You say the word, you think you're ready for forever, I am too."

She cuddled closer, holding to him, wishing she knew herself—her real, previous self—as well as she felt she knew him now. But this Ray-Lynn—the one the two of them, with Hannah's help, had rebuilt from the disastrous wreck of her memory—was ready to move on. "Me too, Jack—forever, with you."

Tears glazed his eyes but he smiled. "Just gotta promise me you won't make me look at that movie of yours every week," he said, "not even every month, sweetheart. Three time's the charm. I got *Gone with the Wind* memorized. So how 'bout we do a scene from it right now?"

"Like what?" she said, smiling at his teasing tone. "At least we don't have a Civil War to face."

"Got a war 'gainst crime going on here off and on, but I know you understand how I got to fight that. No, I was thinking 'bout another scene."

"If you're going to leave, maybe the scene where Rhett and Scarlett parted when he was going off to war, and he gave her an amazing kiss, I hope."

"Nope," he said, standing and pulling her to her feet. "I know I'm jumping the gun—though I'm asking you to marry me—but it's the one where he carried her up the stairs to a wild night in bed." He stooped a bit and swept her up into his arms, bouncing her once to get a good hold.

"Why, I do declare," she said in her best Southern accent, "though you have already swept me off my feet, I do give a damn about your avid attentions, Sheriff Jack

Freeman! But don't you hurt your back! I can walk up those stairs just fine."

But he didn't listen as he carted her upward to the landing, turned and climbed the rest of the way. But deep within, Ray-Lynn still had fears. That something would happen to him, that she'd lose her memories of all this as she had before. Words from the novel swirled through her mind where Rhett carried Scarlett up those stairs, up into darkness again, darkness that was all around.

Ever since the local rash of barn arsons, Ella had stopped using lanterns in the barn, though *Daad* and the boys still did. She usually just grabbed the big flashlight she kept inside the door. But the boys must have moved it from its right place, and she had to fumble for it in the dark. Yes, there it was.

Even before she turned on its bright beam, the familiar sounds of the barn calmed her a bit: the horses snorting and stamping, the *whoo-whoo* of the barn owl in the loft that kept the mouse population down. But Andrew's footsteps behind made her nervous again.

"Ella, don't go darting off like that, because I can't keep up yet. My ankle's better but not back to normal."

"Sorry," she said only, and lit the way for both of them. With this man around, nothing was back to normal. Would it ever be, even when he left? She had the strangest urge to share with him, as she had no one else, that the barn was one of her havens when she had her terrifying attacks of the drowning blackness. But better she keep that a secret, as well as how he made her go all hot and shaky.

She heard him close behind her as she went over

to pet Fern. "You'd best wait here," she told Andrew, "because I have to climb. The wooden chest in the loft is where the old telescope will be. Can you—can you wait in the dark?"

"I'm tempted to go up with you. Can you see the stars through the drop-down straw storage opening up there?"

"Hay and straw aren't the same thing, city boy. It's a haymow and the spring supply of it is almost gone."

"I know I have a lot to learn," he said, his voice low, almost a whisper now. "This is a whole new world, one that—that fascinates me."

He reached out and brushed away a stray tendril that had come loose from her *kapp*. She nearly swayed into him. It took every shred of strength she had to move toward the ladder to the loft, but he reached for her hand, tugged her back and turned her to face him. He took the flashlight from her fingers, clicked it off and put it on the edge of a feed trough. And then it happened.

9

Andrew pulled her gently but firmly toward him and touched her lips with his, as if just taking a taste of her. Lightning jolted through the barn, through her body. His kiss was soft, but his hands were strong on her waist. He tipped his head. She could tell that much in the dark because he breathed now on her cheek and not her nose. He was breathing fast, faster, but so was she.

"If you tell me to stop now, I will," he whispered, his voice raspy. "Otherwise, I won't stop for a while. However long I have here, I will never forget you, Ella enchanted. That was a movie title once, I think, and that's the way it is for me with you, so—"

Not only did she not stop him, but she looped her arms around his neck. Oops, he was taller than she remembered and she hit one of his ears, knocking off his hat. But that hardly mattered, nothing did but being close to this man.

His mouth came down hard on hers, mastering her, making her want to give in to him desperately. His mouth was a bit open, so she opened hers. His tongue teased her lips, invaded, sleek and smooth. She tightened her arms around his neck, and his hands held her waist like iron bands. How angular and flat he was—his stomach and hips, so unlike the places she was soft and round. She was getting dizzy, she couldn't breathe and it was all so wonderful and so—forbidden.

They came up for a breath, and she managed a ragged "I can't," but she knew she didn't mean it. Yet this is what she'd scolded and judged her friends for, being taken in by an English man. Now—right now—she finally understood and forgave Sarah for running off to the world with Nate. At least Hannah had resisted Linc Armstrong's lures and snares.

"Can't what?" he asked, when she'd almost forgotten what she'd said. Chills raced down her spine, but she felt hot all over, weak-legged. Despite her dress and apron, she could feel her breasts pushed to his hard chest as if there was nothing between him. He had startled, no doubt surprised that Amish women did not wear bras.

He propped her up, pressing her against a barn beam and kissing her again, then twirling her around and holding her with his hands on her waist and then slowly, gently kneading her bottom right through her skirts. Alarm bells went off in her head, louder than a police car siren, louder than a shout…

She gasped and tugged away, breaking the kiss she needed and wanted.

"What was that—who?" Andrew asked as they heard the voice again.

"*Daad,* outside, calling your name, not mine."

He muttered something and pulled away. He fumbled for the flashlight a moment, then put it in her hand. "Go up in the loft and check for the telescope," he whispered. "And fix your cap and hair. I'll go see what he wants, say I'm waiting for you down here because I didn't want you in here alone. Now! No, wait, shine that flashlight on the floor until I find my hat."

She still fell stunned by the heat of him, by her own runaway emotions. Ella enchanted, as he'd put it. But she did as he said. What he intended to tell *Daad* wasn't a lie. She hesitated partway up the ladder as Andrew called out, "Eben, we're in here. Ella's in the loft looking for her grandfather's old telescope."

The barn door creaked open. "A visitor for you, Andrew," *Daad* said, "one you can trust. Mr. Branin is here, walked in not looking like himself, but it's him. Ella," he called out louder, "what did you find up there?"

"Just a second! Still looking!" she called down and scurried the rest of the way up the ladder. She saw the big old trunk, once *Grossdaad*'s tool chest. Gideon Raber had been the master barn builder who had taught Seth all he knew.

Ella lifted the heavy, dusty lid and shone the beam of light inside. Thumb-tacked to the inner top of the chest was a big map of Sarasota, Florida, where he and *Grossmamm* used to spend their winters in the small Amish colony called Pinecraft. So few outsiders realized that Amish families, especially the elderly, took a bus to visit Florida.

She saw, nicely laid out, his collection of seashells she used to love to handle, including her favorite, the big pink-and-white conch. She'd held it to her ear many times, imagining she could hear the roar of the distant ocean in its depths. When she was young, she'd pictured herself swimming there, but after she nearly died in the pond, no more. Yet she had saved every postcard of the palm trees and beaches of south Florida her grandparents had sent home, and it all enchanted her—Ella enchanted, gazing in this treasure chest once again. She also saw an old leather carpenter's apron and a few tools; Seth used most of them now. But nothing else.

"Not here!" she called down.

"*Ya,* it is!" *Daad* shouted up. "Saw it a couple weeks ago. Too big to miss. Even thought about getting it out but got too busy. The boys don't have it—unless Seth took it with him."

"That must be it, but he's got a few things on his mind besides that."

She played the light around the area, but nothing looked out of place, nothing missing. "I'll be right down!" she shouted, but took time to smooth her hair and repin her prayer *kapp.* She still felt shaky all over, even in the pit of her belly. The Amish woman and English man had done what was verboten together, and she'd loved every minute of it.

She was ready to go down when she heard Andrew's voice, not below in the barn, but floating up from outside through the haymow drop-down door, which was propped open in this mild weather. And a strange voice, Mr. Branin's, of course, then Andrew answering. They must be huddled against the barn in the dark.

Andrew: "Yeah, working fine except it seems someone might be watching the place. The oldest daughter, Ella, has been followed and harassed, but even the sheriff and his deputy aren't sure why or by whom. I'm hoping it's not related to me."

Mr. Branin: "I'll hang around for a few days, though don't expect to see me. I'm pretty good at playing the invisible man."

Andrew: "So I see, with that Amish getup. Gerald,

I don't believe they can find me again—not here—but if anything else weird happens, I'm out of here, however much they've made me feel at home. Bad enough I'm in the bull's-eye, but I could never forgive myself for collateral damage."

What did *collateral* mean? Ella wondered. And she'd just die if—*when* Andrew left.

Mr. Branin: "Listen, just stick it out, and I'll tell Linc Armstrong to stay away. He's a malcontent lately, and he doesn't need to be upsetting your hosts by horning in, Alex—Andrew."

Alex? Mr. Branin had only thrown in *Andrew* after he'd made the slip. Alex. So was Andrew's real name Alexander? The only one of those she'd ever heard of was Alexander the Great, maybe some important Roman or Egyptian. But she had to admit, whether that was their guest's real name or not, she thought this Alexander was pretty great, and not just at kissing. Even *Daad* admired how he had given up his own life to do what was right to testify against someone evil—maybe someone who made spy satellites.

Their voices were fading now, but Ella heard Andrew give Connie Lee's name to Mr. Branin. She was sure of it now: the Chinese were after Alex/Andrew's former company or him because they wanted information on building a spy satellite, and, of course, he'd refused. So should she turn Connie Lee's deal down or try to find out more about her to help Andrew?

Wishing the two men hadn't walked away, Ella scurried down the ladder.

The next morning, still feeling starry-eyed in more ways than one, Ella helped *Mamm* pack the food, including her lavender breads and *Daad*'s jars of honey she was taking over to the Eshes in her buggy. Then Ella drifted out toward her house to prepare lavender-scented candles to light for the evening wedding meal tomorrow. It was going to be an exciting day, Andrew's first time with many of her people. Right now, since his ankle was better, he was helping Abel hitch the team of four big Belgians that pulled the plow.

No one seemed to have guessed that she and Andrew had been smooching last night, except maybe *Gross-mamm,* who had taken Andrew under her wing and still had eyes sharp as a hawk's. And she'd told Ella that her cheeks were bright pink and, since she'd been out after dark without her bonnet, was she forgetting to wear it during the day so she was getting sunburned?

Inhaling the scent of her lavender, treasuring the mild morning and her memories of last night, Ella fumbled for the house key she had tied on a plastic coil around her wrist. But when she looked up and saw what hung from the back door of her house, she stopped short and gasped.

Someone had nailed a torn, bloody-looking scarecrow with a painted, grotesque, grinning face to a crude cross made from long spikes of lavender. She recognized the scarecrow as one stored in the barn, though its face had been disfigured. *Ya,* someone had been in the barn, taking things from there. The scarecrow was wrapped in something dirty and torn—her cape she'd last seen draped over the license plate of that black van!

And the cross no doubt from her lavender! Her mind jumped to a use of the herb in the past, one Connie Lee had not mentioned. During plague times in Europe, a cross of lavender nailed to a door was supposed to ward off disease and evil. But someone evil had done this!

Her lavender was once a symbol of love, but she shuddered now to see the perverted, clever threat here, one surely aimed at her.

Had this been done by a person who knew something about lavender? Because of the scarecrow nailed to a cross, was someone mocking the Lord, mocking Amish beliefs? Surely, Connie Lee had not sneaked back after her visit last night to put this here. If so, wouldn't Gerald Branin have seen her, if he was lurking around, disguised Amish and thinking he was invisible?

And who could have been sneaking into their barn for the scarecrow—and maybe the telescope? Who had cut her lavender? It looked like the Munstead variety that grew at the very top of the field where no one could see it from the house. When she was younger she'd never liked to work the plants up that high because the next high hill seemed so loom over her, so foreboding.

She started to run for *Daad* or Andrew, but for the first time in weeks, she felt it coming, the black sickness that tried to drown her. It coiled around her, squeezing the breath from her chest, pressing in on her forehead. Her stomach roiled; her vision got grainy and wavy. Someone would see her and think she was crazy. Here it was a bright morning, the day before the wedding, and she was going to lose control, lose herself…

Gritting her teeth, panicked, she ripped the cross and crucified scarecrow off the door, unlocked it and ran inside. She slammed the door, threw the hideous thing on the floor, kept going. Hide in the basement? She'd done that before, but darkness was already closing in around her, and it was doubly dark down there. The bathroom upstairs? She could just say she felt nauseous if anyone came looking for her.

Holding her sides, Ella thudded up the stairs, bouncing off the walls, hitting her hip against the banister. She ran into the bathroom. Thank God, the morning light came in. She closed the bathroom door, then, leaning against the corner of the tub, she curled up sideways on the hard tiled floor, gasping for air. She couldn't breathe! She couldn't think. She couldn't fight the drowning currents of dark, deadly fear.

As Abel giddyapped the big work team away—the Budweiser horses had nothing on those big babies, Alex thought—he actually wished he was going out to work in the fields with him. It was a great day, and, despite the allure Ella had for him, he didn't want to spend more time weeding lavender, or even working in the barn at tasks he'd volunteered to do.

But along the road and out in the open fields, sitting up on the wagon seat or plowing, he'd be an easy target. Abel could be injured too. At least he'd be busy tomorrow at Seth Lantz's day wedding. He hadn't even met the man yet, but he'd heard plenty about him from his family, and Ella had filled him in on the bride— the bishop's daughter, Hannah Esh, one of her two best friends. The other one, Sarah Kauffman, she'd said, had been banned from her people when she "went to the world and married a modern," and she missed her a lot. At the wedding, Alex would finally face the entire Amish congregation, but he was yearning for men's work today.

He knew next to nothing about farming, but it seemed so honest, so clean to him, despite the sweaty, soiled clothes and the dirt under their fingernails the Lantz men had when they returned. Wouldn't they flip

out if he told them he used to get an occasional mani-
cure? That seemed really stupid to him now. So much
of what he used to value seemed frivolous here in this
solid, slow-paced place. New York and SoHo seemed
far away. How had he ever put up with working all day
in an enclosed office suite, even a luxurious one with
lofty windows? Compared to these soft, rolling hills,
he was sure the tall buildings of home would suffocate
him now.

He glanced over at what he'd come to think of as the
lavender shop, since Ella wasn't living there now. Was
it his presence that had triggered the attack on her? Did
someone who liked to harass the Amish think she was
easy game? Or had some idiot taken a perverse liking to
her? He should talk: though he'd not been here a week
yet, he was really attracted to Ella, even when he knew
it was wrong of him to so much as touch her.

Despite that, he walked over to the lavender house
and knocked on the back door. It was studded with four
nails, some with tatters of black cloth and straw—or
was it hay?—clinging to them. Now why had she done
that to her door? "Ella! You need any help carrying
more stuff in from the shed?"

No answer. He looked in the back window. The narrow room just inside was a small sunporch or mudroom,
but he could see beyond to the kitchen. No Ella, though
he was certain she'd been heading this way.

He turned back and scanned the lavender field, his
gaze racing up to its crest where pale purple herbs
stopped partway up the hill. If he hadn't been tracked
to Atlanta and shot at there, he'd hike all the way up
right now to look around, but he didn't need his ankle
acting up again either.

He opened the back door and shouted in, "Ella?"

Why was it unlocked if she wasn't here? He went in and nearly stumbled over a big, stuffed doll. No—a scarecrow, disfigured and ugly, attached to a lavender X with a black cloth for a background. A woman's Amish cape? The one Ella had lost?

"Ella, you in here?" he shouted, running into the living room, then checking the two small first-floor bedrooms. She had said Seth and his little girl had lived entirely on the first floor. "Ella!"

He pounded up the stairs, saw the bathroom door was closed, but she surely would have answered if she was in there. He peeked in the bare room she had obviously meant to make her bedroom. A chest of drawers sat there and a treadle sewing machine on a wooden table. Of course, her bed was still over at the farmhouse.

The second small bedroom was empty but for cartons and boxes, jars and bolts of cloth, all smelling of lavender—of her. His heart beat so hard it nearly shook him. He'd need to look in the closets and basement. He opened his mouth to call her name again. But then he heard it, a whining, a moaning. It almost sounded like a cat or kitten closed in somewhere.

Yeah, she had to be in the bathroom. Had she suddenly taken sick? Had someone hurt her? He rushed to the door and put his ear against it. Sobbing? Wheezing?

"Ella, it's me. I'm coming in."

"Noooo."

"Are you sick?"

"I'm fine."

"I'm going to get your mother," he said before he remembered she'd left for the bishop's house.

He turned the doorknob, slowly, carefully. The door

was not locked. He opened it a crack. "Ella, tell me what's wrong, or I'm coming in."

He prayed—actually prayed—that his kissing and caressing last night had not upset her this much. She'd seemed normal at breakfast. An Amish woman—was he nuts? And in the volatile position he was in? He was betraying his hosts, playing with fire. He should leave her alone, be kind and polite but not touch her again.

He strained to identify the strange sound she was making. Panting, like a dog. He opened the door farther, wishing the room had a mirror so he could look at her without going in. A foot sprawled on the floor, her foot. Had she fallen and hit her head?

He stuck his head in and gasped at the sight. Her hair loose like a golden curtain, Ella was sprawled with her head buried in her arms by the claw-foot tub as if some dreadful, white-bellied animal stood over her. She lifted her head then, her eyes huge on him, her frantic face white and wet with tears.

He rushed in, bent over her, unsure whether to touch her, hold her or run for help.

"Ella, tell me. What is it?" he demanded, his voice breaking.

"It's all around me, dark and cold," she cried, reaching out to grasp his wrist in a fierce grip. "I can't breathe. I'm going to drown."

10

Ella was not only surprised but stunned. Never, in all these years had she let someone see her like this. But this man had barged into this room and into her life. His mere presence as he sat on the tile floor beside her and lifted her into his lap began to pull her back from despair.

"Ella, your skin's damp with sweat but cold as ice." He cradled her, rocked her. "What happened? Are you sick?"

"It—it happens sometimes. I don't let people see, don't let my family know—my weakness."

"Set off by that scarecrow downstairs? It had your ruined cape on it too. Was it nailed on the back door?"

She barely nodded. Like a child, she clung to Andrew. At least she wouldn't drown now. The black waters were receding, not pressing into her chest or stabbing into her nose and throat. How had her prayer *kapp* come loose, her hair free over her shoulders?

"I knew someone once who had panic attacks," Alex whispered, his lips in her damp hair.

"What's that?" she whispered. "Panic attacks?"

"You have the signs of one. You shouldn't have kept it to yourself. You can get counseling and help—"

"Mental help?" she asked, surprised at her own feeble voice when she felt life flowing back into her limbs. "Andrew, I'm Amish. I tried to pray it away but can't. It's my sins still in me from the night I nearly drowned."

"Drowned? When? Where?"

"In the pond, sneaking out at night with Sarah and Hannah years ago. They saved me. I made them promise not to tell. I was disobedient—I lied. And I've been defiant and dishonoring my parents ever since by not telling them."

"You never shared it with anyone until now?"

She shook her head, then rested it on his broad shoulder. "Of course, Hannah and Sarah know I nearly drowned, but not about my—my attacks. I can't control them, thought I'd been better lately. I didn't even get sucked into the blackness when that van trapped me. But—that thing nailed on the door—from our barn, with my cloak that got dragged…dragged to death."

"Stop that talk! We'll tell the bishop and the sheriff. At least we know now it's the same idiot who tormented you before. If someone was on the hill to cut your lavender and in the barn to take the scarecrow, maybe he took the telescope too. I should leave the Home Valley, go hide out somewhere else, but maybe this is not tied to me. Besides, you might need extra protection."

"I'm all right now," she said, and reluctantly pulled away from his embrace and scooted off his lap. "It always passes, but at the time, I'm so frantic I just can't fight it, and it seems like forever."

She gathered her loose hair into a horse tail, twisted it and found some scattered hairpins on the floor to fasten it into a tight bun. His eyes were huge as he watched her. Somehow, her *kapp* had gotten in the tub, and she retrieved it. Her arms ached from swimming so hard, trying to keep her head up in the surging water....

No! she scolded herself. She was not in real water. It was only that black nightmare. Now she had a lifeguard, and she couldn't bear to let him go.

"I promise you," she told him, "I'll tell the bishop and the sheriff, but not until after the wedding. I don't want to rile things up with law enforcement again or upset Bishop Esh when he's father of the bride. I don't want to ruin tomorrow for Seth and Hannah. And I'm still going to ask the bishop and Sheriff Freeman—and you—not to tell my parents. Please don't tell *Grossmamm* Ruth. I'll tell them when I can, when I'm ready."

"All right," he said, standing and lifted her to her feet. "But you've got to get over the idea you're being punished for some longtime sin. And I hope you don't think what we shared last night was wrong. As for panic attacks, they just happen to some people—even to saints, I bet."

She shook out her skirts and smoothed her apron. "There are no saints anymore, only people, some of them evil, and that's the problem." Finally, her voice sounded more like her own. She was thinking now, not just panicking. At least there was a name for the blackness she'd fought for so long. Not bipolar, not mental illness, and others had it too. A panic *attack*. That sounded like someone or something outside herself was the enemy, not something within.

She told him, "We'll need to keep the scarecrow and lavender cross safe until we take them to the bishop and the sheriff."

"I'll lock it all in the basement here, so we don't upset your parents and the boys. Ella, does it usually take some sort of shock or crisis to bring on an attack?"

She nodded as they went out into the hall and downstairs. "Some surprise—something that upsets me deeply," she tried to explain. With her legs still wobbly, she descended slowly, hanging on to the banister, when she'd rather hang on to him, but she had to be strong. She could not, *could not,* fall in love with this *Auslander,* however much she needed and wanted him. Look what that had done to Sarah: gotten her put under the *bann,* forbidden to be at the wedding, even to sit at the same table with her Amish friends, her own family. What if that happened to her?

In the kitchen, they stared down at the bizarre scarecrow and tattered, dirty black cape so ruined compared to the sweet-scented lavender cross. "I hope and pray," Alex muttered, "that someone this sick is only into mental torment and not physical harm."

"*Ya.* We are not going to let him—or her—ruin tomorrow, not on my dear brother and best friend's wedding day."

"Andrew, you sit over here with me and the boys," Eben Lantz told Alex as the Amish stopped milling around and began to take their seats for the church service and wedding ceremony. Alex was amazed how well behaved even the little children were. He was grateful that people had been kind. He almost felt he belonged. Though their German dialect swirled around him, they spoke English to him and obviously tried to make him feel at home. Ella, since she was a kind of bridesmaid called a side sitter, was with the women, but both Abel and Aaron had been introducing him to people in this shifting sea of the Home Valley Amish church members with everyone dressed in their Sabbath best.

"We'll take the back row," Eben explained, "in case you need to get up and move around. The church service will be almost three hours, *ya,* then the short ceremony itself."

Three hours and in German, Alex thought, but it would give him a lot of time for people watching. Man, he wished he'd paid more attention in his high school German I class before he switched to Spanish because he heard it was easier.

It turned out he could study the women best, because the men sat facing them on the other side of the Esh barn. Amazing a barn could smell this good, all swept and scrubbed. It was a pretty new one, he'd been told, built by a barn raising of the brethren headed up by Seth. He'd really liked Ella's oldest brother when they'd met today. The bride, Hannah, looked radiant as the betrothed couple left with two elders for some sort of premarital counseling before returning later to take their vows.

But his eyes sought out Ella. She still looked a little pale after her panic attack yesterday, but he knew the tears shimmering in her beautiful blue eyes were those of joy for her brother and her friend. She looked almost angelic with that pale blond hair, parted and pulled back under her white prayer cap as if it were a halo. It was almost as if she'd stepped off a Christmas card. He thrust away the image of her with her hair wild and loose, covering her shoulders, smelling of lavender. He shifted on the hard bench. That woman really got to him, and it wasn't just because he'd been without one for so long.

His SoHo neighbor had been right: If you aren't sure which of the two women you're dating you prefer, you don't like either of them half enough.

"Good to have you with us today, *Cousin* Andrew," the elderly Amish man on the other side of him said with a nod and a little smile.

That's one thing he'd learned this week: the Amish were not austere at all, but had good senses of humor.

Eben thrust a book called the Ausbund into his hands. "Our hymns," he said, opening it to the page from which everyone began to sing in harmony, no parts. Oh, *ya,* he should have known it would be total togetherness. And had he just actually thought the word *ya* instead of *yeah?*

The service gave him a lot of time to think. He had to admit he'd never had a close family, not even a friend who wasn't a competitor or rival somehow, for better grades, for a starting spot on a team, for a promotion. Way into the service, when he started to doze off and his head bobbed, you might know he saw *Grossmamm* Ruth giving him a sharp look from across the way, as if he were her own grandson. It made him miss his grandmother, but it made him care more for this strong, old woman too. *Ya, ser gut.*

For a guy whose favorite movie was once *Wedding Crashers,* Alex thought the solemn and sedate wedding of Seth Lantz and Hannah Esh was moving to behold. It was a combination of simplicity and complexity to someone who knew so little about the Amish, but who wanted to know everything.

Ella was surprised to see that Bishop Esh departed a bit from the usual ceremony after the marriage vows had been exchanged. Hannah and Seth had come back in with the elders and stood before them all, hand in hand. Their eyes were only for each other and Ella had to admit, she longed for a love like that. But with whom among her people? Because, unlike Sarah, she could never leave her family or her faith.

"This new husband and wife have asked me to read a short passage from the Book of Ruth," Bishop Esh announced. "Hannah is our wedding singer and Seth our *vorsinger,* song leader, and, of course, no one can sing at his or her own wedding—but they are singing in their hearts. So, from a song our Hannah has gifted us with at many weddings, I read to you and for them,

> *'Entreat me not to leave you,*
> *Or to turn back from following after you;*
> *For wherever you go, I will go;*
> *And wherever you lodge, I will lodge;*
> *Your people shall be my people,*
> *And your God, my God.*
> *Where you die, I will die,*
> *And there will I be buried.*
> *The Lord do so to me, and more also,*
> *If anything but death parts you and me.'"*

Ella tore her gaze away and glanced at Andrew. It was her secret that he was really Alex, that he knew all about lights in the night sky made by men to adorn—and to defile—God's heaven. He was looking straight at her, his eyes surely as intense as the newlyweds' mutual gaze.

When they were dismissed and everyone congratulated Seth and Hannah, the congregation skirted the big garden and trooped across the lawn toward the Esh home for the dinner reception. Ella walked with *Grossmamm* Ruth, who was going at a good pace for her eighty years. Ella supposed she should have been running ahead with Hannah's friends, especially the other side sitters. How she wished that Sarah could be here. Years ago, she, Hannah and Ella had made more than one vow that they would all be together on their wedding days.

Abel rushed past, trying to catch up with his girl, Nancy Troyer. That might be the next Lantz wedding, after Barbara and Gabe's. Then Andrew and *Daad* came along, walking with some of the church elders.

"Andrew!" *Grossmamm* Ruth said, and motioned him over. "I want to tell you something more from the Book of Ruth, my favorite one in the Bible because it is named so good—ha!"

His face lit. "Are you going to lecture me about staying awake and proper manners for Pennsylvania cousins?" he asked.

"Now you just listen," she told him, shaking her finger at him. "Your own *grossmamms* are not here to keep you on the straight and narrow, so you listen to this one."

She drew Andrew apart from the crowd, and Ella stopped to listen too, even though she saw Ray-Lynn drive in. She was the only *Englischer*—besides Alex whatever-his-name-really-was—invited to the reception, and she wanted to greet her to make her feel at home. And wasn't that exactly what *Grossmamm* was doing for Andrew? It comforted her to know that both her father and grandmother liked and trusted him.

"Here are the words for you from the Book of Ruth

and *Grossmamm* Ruth," the old woman said. "It goes something like this. You have left the land of your birth and have come to a people whom you did not know before. The Lord repay your work, and a full reward be given you by the Lord God, under whose wings you have come for refuge. And I add my own words, you are welcome by our family and our friends."

For a moment Ella thought Andrew was going to cry, or even hug the old woman, when her people did not show affection in public but to little ones. *Grossmamm* patted his cheek and went on her way, leaving him standing near the porch steps.

"I have to get inside, but I want to welcome Ray-Lynn first," Ella told him, and fled before he could see she had tears in her eyes too.

Gabe Kauffman, who was head hostler, taking care of the horses from the sea of buggies out back, appeared in the living room and tapped Ella on the shoulder after the big meal. He looked upset; he'd gone ashen.

"Ella," he said, raising his voice a bit in the happy hubbub when he looked as if he'd like to whisper. "Someone asking to see you out back."

Her eyes sought Andrew. He was having a good time with some Amish men, and working on a big piece of wedding cake, so he hadn't sent Gabe for her. "Who is it?" she asked, but the boy just gestured to her and moved away.

Well, she told herself, with all that had happened to her, she wasn't going outside unless she knew who wanted to see her. She hurried to catch up with him, nearly bumping into one of the women working in the kitchen. "Sorry!" she said, and managed to reach Gabe on the porch steps.

"Gabe, wait! Who is it?"

"It's my sister," he whispered. "It's Sarah. Out behind the barn. She parked at your farm and walked in over the field, has something she wants you to give to Hannah. She says please, she knows you're not to take things from her hand, but she needs you."

"You come too," Ella insisted, and picked up her skirts to break into a run. "Why can't she just send the gift in with you? Is Nate with her?" she asked, out of breath already.

"No. Alone. He's away somewhere. The thing is, I think she's sick."

Ella peeked around the side of the barn. Sarah, indeed, her hair shoulder-length, her clothing worldly, of course. She wore a long denim skirt with a big blouse— a big blouse, because she was pregnant! And *ya,* she looked like she was in bad pain.

11

Whoo-eee, Ray-Lynn thought. She was stuffed with delicious homemade food, always her problem at Amish events. She just had to get up and walk around a little. The chicken, mashed potatoes and gravy, and especially Ella's delicious lavender-laced breads and muffins, had made her feel she'd just eaten a Thanksgiving meal! And she was going to ask Ella's father if the restaurant could start serving his honey there. She and Jack had admired his beehives up on the hill, and there was nothing like including another local product on the menu.

Just after the cake was cut—three layers but not tiered, of course, since that would be too worldly—Ray-Lynn excused herself and stepped out on the front porch. At once she noticed two things. First, this was evidently the hangout for the dating-age Amish young men. They seemed more interested in two courting buggies they'd brought around in front than in the girls inside the house who were oohing and aahing over the bride and groom. And secondly, two police cruisers were parked side by side down the road a ways with Jack and his new deputy having a parlay.

Even from this vantage point, she could see that Jack was upset with the new heartthrob of his office staff. He was gesturing, pointing. Deputy Hayes nodded, got in and drove away.

Jack saw her coming across the lawn toward him. "You having a good time?" he called to her.

"Eating myself silly," she yelled back, and kept walking closer until she got to the log rail fence along the grassy berm of the road. "It's great to see Hannah and Seth so happy. They deserve it."

"You like weddings, maybe we can plan one of our own," he said, coming closer.

"A small, private one, except for a big reception shindig at the restaurant?"

"You been thinking about it, too, honey? Like they say on the soap operas, we've got to talk."

"What in the world would you know about soap operas?"

"My mother used to watch *As The World Turns* and *One Life To Live*. If I was home sick from school with a cold or strep throat, I'd see them with her." They clasped hands across the corner of the fence, and he leaned in for a quick kiss. "She'd baby me, fix me my favorite foods. Memories…" His voice sounded rough as it trailed off.

"Which I wish I had more of around here, but we're making new ones. I should have brought you some food but I just came out for a breath of fresh air, which you always are," she told him.

The big man actually wiped a tear from under his left eye. Would wonders never cease? she thought. Just when she thought she knew Jack Freeman, new layers peeled away, just like with an onion. "Meanwhile," he went on, "how're things going in there, other than the food? You met the Lantzes' Pennsylvania cousin yet?"

"No, but he's a good-looking guy. And, I swear, having gone through a lot with Hannah mooning over Seth and Sarah longing for Nate—not to mention my own *slight* attraction to the town sheriff—I recognize the warning signs. He and Ella can't take their eyes off each other. But what was the problem out here with the guy with the new shiny star?"

"He thought since there was a big gathering here, he'd just park on the road to make sure everything went smooth when all the buggies started to leave. I tried to tell him that's not how the Amish operate. Police protection, like weather vanes, show a lack of trust in God's ways—too prideful. He's curious as can be about the Amish, but his tendency is to stamp in with both feet, and that's not gonna get him anywhere except in the doghouse with them—and me."

"I'd better get back inside. Love you," she said, and leaned over the fence to give him a peck, which he turned into another real kiss.

"Love you, too, honey," he said. "Since I got Superman on patrol, I'm going back to the office to catch up on some darn deskwork. Hey, one more thing. Talk about this area getting more diverse, despite the big Amish population. You hear that Chinese couple from New York are gonna open that fancy spa retreat out on Sweetgum?"

"You mean the parents of our favorite speeder and wrecker of cars, Sam Lee? His mother Connie's been in the restaurant, but I haven't seen Mr. Lee."

"Well, I met him—Chang Lee—today and could hardly keep a straight face. The guy must be pretty new to this country. When he heard he was going to visit the Midwest, he got all decked out in a cowboy outfit—I mean, jeans, checkered shirt, fringed leather vest and Western boots, no less!"

"Oh, right. The wild Midwest! No ten-gallon hat?" she asked as they shared a laugh.

"It was probably in their fancy little car. I think they're gonna be a hoot around here. Well, gotta get going. Enjoy, now."

After kisses from Jack and even so much as a brief mention of their own wedding, she sure would.

Ella was aghast. Not only because Sarah had dared to set foot here today and had a wrapped wedding gift she'd put on the ground, but because she looked as bad as Ella usually did after a panic attack. Could it be her friend suffered from that, too?

"Sarah," she cried, running to her. "You're pregnant!"

"Yes—but not why I'm—here," she gasped out. Her face was contorted with pain, and she panted between words. "Nate's away at a convention—in Washington, D.C. I wanted to bring this gift—just get it to Hannah, but...but this huge pain...I think the baby's trying to turn over and got twisted and it hurts. I—ah," she moaned and fell onto all fours in the grass.

Gabe stood on one foot, then the other, his fists pressed to his mouth. *Bann* or not on her friend, Ella knelt in the grass beside her and put her hands on her shoulders. "Gabe," Ella said, trying to support Sarah as she gasped and writhed, "go get your mother and tell her why, but don't tell anyone else yet. Go!"

The boy turned and ran. Sarah sat on her haunches

and tried to knead her belly. Ella could see it moving. "Can you help me turn the baby?" Sarah cried. "I can't lose her, Ella. Six months along, not enough yet. I've been fine. I don't know what's wrong. I walked, didn't run over here, and felt just fine. Oh, it hurts. You know my mother lost two before she had the four of us, twisted birth cord and then…"

Ella had never heard that, but why would she? Here she'd blamed Sarah, scolded her for going to the world and wedding Nate, but now, with their child at risk, Ella wanted nothing more than to help her, no matter that Sarah was under the dreaded *meidung*. Ella moved one hand from her friend's shoulder to put it over her belly.

Yes, the baby was moving inside her—struggling. Ella pictured it drowning in the sea of water in there. "But which way to push?" she asked. "I don't want to hurt it."

"Her—a girl," Sarah said. "I had a—a sonogram. Why—the moment I set foot here at the bishop's property—this pain? It's like a curse."

Sarah went to all fours again, this time with both hands digging into the grass as if she'd rip it out by its roots.

"Don't talk that way," Ella cried. "For some reason it—she—just started to turn now. There are no curses here."

But were there? Her near-drowning. Her panic attacks—and harassment by someone who must hate her. She tried to hold one of Sarah's hands but her friend gripped back so hard Ella feared her bones would break. "It's going to be all right," Ella told her, wincing.

"Ella, I just wanted to be near everyone, everything,

today," Sarah gritted out with tears dripping off her chin and nose. "I know I can't—can't be a part of things."

"You are always part of my life no matter what!" Ella heard herself say. "Hannah's too, even when we're apart. Do you have a cell phone on you? I can call Nate for you, the emergency squad. Don't be afraid!"

"Cell phone's in my car, over at your house."

"It's closer than the phone shanty on the road. I'll run over there, get it and make those calls. Is the car locked?"

"No, but don't leave me. And Gabe—he's growing so fast, still in love with your sister—ahhh!"

Running footsteps. Anna Kauffman, Sarah's mother.

"Mrs. Kauffman," Ella blurted out, looking up at the older woman's shocked face, "Sarah's six months pregnant, and she's having pain, like the baby's turning over inside and hurting her."

"My dearest girl," Anna Kauffman cried, and fell to her knees on the other side of Sarah. "That happened to me too."

"*Mamm,* I can't lose this baby. Nate's away. I just wanted to bring a gift for Hannah. I—"

"Mrs. Kauffman," Ella interrupted, "I'm going to run to our house for Sarah's cell phone where she left her car. Is Nate's number on it, Sarah?"

"You call the emergency people first, *ya,*" Mrs. Kauffman said.

"Yes, he's on quick dial," Sarah ground out. "Just turn it on, find his name on top of a list. You'll see."

"Ray-Lynn taught me to use one. I'll have help here soon," Ella cried as she pried her hand from Sarah's and got to her feet. "But can Gabe go get my mother, get more help? Should Sarah be in a bed?"

"Oh, no, in the bishop's house, I can't," Sarah insisted.

"We want to help. We will help," Ella told her, "and that baby will be fine!" She squeezed her friend's shoulder, lifted the hem of her skirt and ran behind the barn to start across the field.

Standing in the doorway of the crowded living room, Alex had never seen such cornball joking as went on after the cake was cut and eaten. Someone gave Seth a bull's ring to put through his nose; Hannah was given a rolling pin to keep him in line, on and on... But where had Ella gone? Surely, the fact she was unwed—a *maidal,* as they called it—hadn't gotten to her. Earlier she'd seemed to revel in her friend's and her brother's happy day.

He wondered if *maidal* also meant virgin. He'd picked up some gossip today that Seth had been wed before and his little girl was conceived before he was married, so premarital sex wasn't unheard-of around here. But, Alex supposed, many unwed Amish girls would be virgins, especially because they married so young. Ella was no longer young by their standards so was she a virgin?

"How do you like the Home Valley so far?" a voice in the doorway behind him—an English voice—asked. Alex turned and saw Ray-Lynn Logan, the woman who had showed up to help the night Sam Lee had his car accident. Alex had been told she was the sheriff's significant other, one he was partners with in the Dutch Farm Table Restaurant in town.

"Oh, *ya, ser gut,*" he told her. "The Lantzes are kind and the people very nice."

"Has your hurt ankle kept you from helping out?"

"For a few days. It was just twisted, not sprained. *Grossmamm* Ruth's cures fixed me up. I helped Ella weed lavender, but I'm about ready to work in the fields now."

"Your accent's really different from the others, even from some other Pennsylvania Dutch we've had visit family here."

Alex was getting annoyed. He'd thought he was doing a good job of imitating Amish English at least. Or could the sheriff have said something to this woman— pillow talk—and she was just testing him? He knew that Ella and, he'd heard, Hannah too, put great stock in Ray-Lynn's friendship. Maybe he was just overly sensitive after having gone through so many grueling interrogations over the economic espionage he was accusing Marv Boynton and SkyBound of committing.

"Oh, I know," she said, before he could think up an answer. "I'll bet, like Hannah, you've lived in the world for a while. She said her patterns of speech changed a lot the few years she was away too."

"You got me there," he said, trying to take the ambiguous way out.

"Or are you an Amish convert?" she asked with a little laugh. "There are those who have joined the Amish faith from the outside world, but they're few and far between. The Amish don't evangelize like other Christians, and obviously a person would give up a lot of life's luxuries to join them."

"But get something good in the bargain," he countered, surprised he'd said that. He'd love to keep her questions in check. Maybe the best defense was a good offense. "Your speech isn't like anyone else's around here," he said. "So, where are you from?"

He almost wished he hadn't asked as she told him about growing up in rural Georgia, about loving the big city of Atlanta. Not only did that make him a bit homesick for New York, but he didn't need any reminders of being shot at in Atlanta. He'd never figured out how his enemies—a hit man and whoever hired him—had found him there. And if they found him here…

He ended up walking Ray-Lynn, still talking, outside to her car. She said she needed to get back to the restaurant, and he just went along because Ella wasn't in here and he wanted to look for her.

"Easy to find your ride in this sea of buggies," he told Ray-Lynn as they headed for the only motor vehicle in sight. "So what's going on back behind the barn?" he asked, when they saw a group of women there, all looking in the same direction.

"Sometimes they decorate bridal buggies just like the English would do cars," she told him. "So maybe…"

But Hannah herself, with several of her female side sitters, rushed past, their faces worried. "Ding-dang, what in the world?" Ray-Lynn said, and skirted around her van where Alex had opened the door for her.

Ray-Lynn sprinted for the back of the barn; Alex did too. Could Ella have been hurt? He scanned the kneeling, praying Amish women surrounding a non-Amish girl on the ground. Who was she and what had happened? And with all these women here, even the bride—where was Ella?

As Ella emerged from the field, she was out of breath and had a stitch in her left side. Fields full of knee-high crops made for slow going. She could feel dirt inside her shoes as well as caking them, but nothing mattered except getting help fast for Sarah.

Sarah had left her car—really, it was a van—almost blocking the barn doors, so she obviously had not intended to stay for long. She'd just wanted to get the gift to Hannah, then, no doubt, get back to her worldly life. Yet she was still Amish at heart: the van was black, and she hadn't locked it. Even when she had valuable things inside—Ella could see the back was filled with stretched canvases—she knew to trust the area. And yet, lately, things had changed.

Ella opened the van door and immediately saw the cell phone. It was sticking out of one of the two small wells that could hold a coffee cup or bottle of water. Feeling too closed in by the van, she got out, shut the door, then hunched over the cell phone. She hoped she could recall what Ray-Lynn had shown her about how to use one, when Ella had to call Amanda Stutzman from the restaurant to say she couldn't get to the B and B that day.

Intent on her task, fearful for Sarah, Ella prayed she would not get another panic attack. She'd call 9-1-1 first, then get Nate's number to summon him home from his trip.

The small, flat phone shuddered in her hand when she turned it on. Although she was in the shade of the barn, she bent closer over it to see what was on the lighted screen better. What if this didn't work like Ray-Lynn's? What if she was taking too long? What if…

She heard someone behind her—just a few fast strides, around the corner of the barn. One of her brothers must have come over to check on the animals, or Andrew saw she was missing or was afraid for her

Before she could turn, something huge whooshed over her head, knocking the phone from her hand. Darkness. Thrown to the ground. A knee across her legs when she tried to kick, to struggle. Trapped in this huge sack. No one to help near. She opened her eyes to realize she was wrapped in a big quilt. She screamed but was slapped across her face, right through the quilt. And then another tie, tight like the one holding her ankles and her right arm pinned awkwardly to her side, the left bent up across her chest. Another tie—a gag—was fastened around her mouth, jamming the quilt partway between her lips. She tried to protest again.

"Shh! Or else," someone hissed, a sound like a snake's. Man or woman's voice? Not sure. Footsteps. Two people or one?

Whoever it was dragged her in the quilt, feetfirst, head down, around the barn, then uphill. Even nearly suffocated in the material with the gag across her mouth, she could tell she was being taken through her lavender beds, but for once, the smell did not comfort her as she panted for breath. She could not have a panic attack right now—could not, even though it sure was the time for one. She had to think—get away.

On, upward. The person was panting like a dog. Woman or man? If only everyone wasn't at the wedding. She prayed someone would see her being taken. How did her captor know she would be alone—or had she been watched all this time, just waiting for the right moment?

But why would someone kidnap her? The other signs

of being spied on—nothing foretold this. *Lord, please, please help me! Why? Why me?*

But even the answer to that was not going to save her now.

12

Word had spread that Ella had gone across the field to use Sarah's cell phone. Standing at the rear of the cluster of praying women, Ray-Lynn kept listening for the sound of sirens. Both fire and rescue squads in Eden County were volunteers, so they took a bit longer than in the big cities. Surely Ella must have called them by now, and Jack would be on his way too. Ray-Lynn had taught her to use a cell phone, but what if Sarah's was different or Jack's receptionist wasn't right at her desk when the call came in?

Ray-Lynn longed to comfort Sarah, but at least her mother and others she'd been estranged from were with her now. Of the many Amish women Ray-Lynn called her friends, Sarah and Hannah were the closest to her. Yet since their developing relationships were part of her memory loss, Hannah and Sarah had both explained how Ray-Lynn had encouraged Sarah to follow her dream to paint Amish scenes.

Ray-Lynn had been at Sarah and Nate's wedding too. She and Jack had been guests in their home. Since Sarah was shunned for leaving the Amish and wedding a worldly man, Ray-Lynn and Hannah had been the only two area residents who knew she was pregnant. They hadn't even told Ella, because she'd been so much against her friend's leaving the Amish. How Sarah had hoped, when she bore her child, that it would build a bridge back to her family and friends she missed so much.

Ray-Lynn startled when her cell phone sounded. She backed away and took the call before her voice mail kicked in. What if it was Jack calling to find out how Sarah was doing after Ella's 9-1-1 call?

"Ray-Lynn here!" she said, moving away from the women but speaking quietly.

"I need to talk to Andrew Lantz." It was a man's voice, but strange. Flat, tinny, like it was recorded.

"Who shall I tell him is calling, and how did you get my number?" she asked, craning her neck. She wished now she'd paid extra for caller ID, but she'd never needed it in Amish country.

She could see Andrew, pacing the yard, shading his eyes and looking across the field toward the Lantzes' house. A lot of the men had come outside too, as word about Sarah spread. Andrew was separate from the others who were milling around and whispering, but then he stood out to her as different anyway. She intended to ask Jack about that. Andrew couldn't be an imposter, could he, or some journalist or author who had wormed his way in here?

"I need to talk to Andrew Lantz," the voice repeated.

"Just a moment," she said, frowning. At a quick clip, she walked toward Andrew, even as the voice repeated again: "I need to talk to Andrew Lantz."

* * *

Alex saw Ray-Lynn approaching, just when he was about to have a panic attack of his own. He'd been told that Ella went across the field to use her friend Sarah's cell phone to call for help, but he figured she should be back by now. And the emergency squad should be here, the sheriff or his deputy at least. Alex was going to go across the field to the house to look for Ella, so he didn't need more questions from Ray-Lynn. Maybe Ella had had another panic attack. And why hadn't they just asked her to call from here on Ray-Lynn's phone to get help for Sarah when she became ill?

"This call is for you!" Ray-Lynn told him with a puzzled look on her face. She held the cell phone out, stiff-armed.

His insides flip-flopped. "For me? Andrew Lantz?"

"If that's your name, it's for you. Don't know who it is."

"Maybe Ella."

She shook her head. "A man."

"Thanks," he said, took the phone and walked away from her. Gerald Branin wouldn't call him through her, would he? Certainly his lawyer would contact him through Branin or the sheriff, not through the sheriff's very talkative girlfriend. Maybe the trial date had been moved up.

His stomach in knots, he said, "This is Andrew Lantz."

"Never mind who this is and tell no one. I have Ella. If you want her returned alive, leave the Lantz house alone after dark and start walking north on Oakridge toward County Line Road. Tell her family Ella said she needed time alone, you don't know where. We need to talk before she's freed."

"Listen, she has nothing to do with this. Let her come back now, and I'll leave here, walk like you said and th—"

"Never mind who this is and tell no one. I have Ella. If you want her returned alive—"

Alex swore.

"Never mind who this is, and tell—"

A damned recording, voice-reactivated. He was so freaked he could have thrown Ray-Lynn's phone down and stamped on it. He couldn't believe it had come to this, not Ella, not in Amish country! Despite someone trying to scare her, things had seemed so safe and serene—at least he had desperately wanted that. Now his enemies were using her to get him. They'd found him— that must be it—found him again. And when he walked down that road, and they took him or shot him, would they even give her back? What if she could ID them? Hit men didn't take captives. Was she even alive now?

He broke out in a sweat. His heart nearly beat out of his chest. He had to find her, fast. What was the common denominator, the link between Atlanta and here? Why didn't this bastard target him directly without using her, harming her? Not Ella!

He jerked around when someone touched his arm. Ray-Lynn, frowning, worried too. "Who is it? That voice—like a robot."

"A bad joke," he told her. "How they got your cell number, I don't know. Some Pennsylvania buddies of mine in their *rumspringa*," he said, hoping his voice wasn't shaking like his insides were. "My younger brother's friends from home, probably on a dare."

He was lying, but he had learned that from a master. All those years Marv led them all on at SkyBound.... "Thanks, Ray-Lynn. I'm sure there's no problem, but I'm going to go see what's keeping Ella. How about you try the sheriff, be sure she made the E.R. call." He realized too late he'd defaulted into executive mode and abandoned the aw-shucks attitude he'd tried earlier on her, but she probably just thought she was right about him once living in the world.

As he jogged away and then broke into a run through the field where Ella must have gone, he realized what Ray-Lynn or anyone else thought didn't matter. Finding Ella did. With all the weird things that had happened to her—and her cape—he felt frantic. He feared he wasn't going to find her and he'd have to do what the caller said to save her—sacrifice himself.

On and upward, her captor dragged Ella. She could not fight back, but she fought her growing fears. No panic attack! she told herself. Breathe, just breathe. Calm down. If he was going to kill her, he would have done it already—wouldn't he? Hopefully, he hadn't let her see his face, so she could be released without describing him. He had disguised his voice and said next to nothing, so she could not place that later either.

But that all meant something dreadful too. Surely, this man didn't think her family could pay a ransom. His target must be Alex/Andrew. He had been tracked down. *Daad* was sure something terrible had happened to their guest before and now it could again. Was she to be the bait? Did this man think Andrew would come looking for her, and he'd hurt him then? Her captor could have a gun. He already had the advantage of this high hill with a vantage point to shoot someone.

She almost wished he carried her, not dragged her, or at least pulled her headfirst. Thank the Lord, she was being hauled over grass, though the quilt was little protection from bumps and bruises. Nor did she have her bonnet on for protection. Her hairpins had yanked her braids loose. If she could only get her prayer *kapp* off to leave a clue—but then she didn't want Andrew following her trail. She prayed he would not see the drag marks in the grass. Was that the plan, to get him climbing the hill in the open so he could be shot?

She tried to think clearly but terror scrambled her thoughts. No panic attack yet but battered by this man's attacks on her. Dizzy…her head hurt… She kept seeing the black van dragging her cape…the tattered remnants of it nailed to the door over the disfigured scarecrow and lavender cross. This quilt, maybe snatched off a nearby clothesline. No, she recognized it now, an old one they kept in the barn for an extra lap robe. This man had been in their barn, maybe taken the telescope, who knows what else? A crazy quilt pattern…her life so crazy since Andrew came. If he was this man's target, she had to find a way to help him now. She had to get herself out of this.

Finally, they must have arrived at the top of the hill. The steep grade leveled out. He stopped and dropped her feet. She lay there, panting through her gag, afraid to move. Her captor kept silent, but she heard him move a few steps away. At least she was not being assaulted—not now—but she didn't think this was about rape, because he could have taken her into the barn. He must have known everyone was at the wedding. He'd been lurking, just waiting for a chance to snatch her. In her rush to help Sarah, she'd given that to him.

When her own breathing quieted, her ears were ringing, or could that be the buzz of *Daad*'s beehives nearby? That must be where they were, near the hives at the top of the hill where no one could spot them from the bottom. She must be fairly close to one of the sink-holes that opened up to a steep ravine. If he dropped her in it, she'd die for sure, and they might not find her for days—ever, if wild animals found her first.

Did she dare to move, to see if she could get the gag out of her mouth that made her feel she was going to throw up all that good wedding food? Whether he was watching or not, she had no choice but to try. At least her left arm had not been pinned full length against her like her right one, tied tight over the wrapped quilt. Her elbows and shoulders hurt; the back of her head ached. She fought the dizziness to make herself think.

Slowly, carefully she tried to expel the quilt gag from her mouth. It seemed impossible, but she used her tongue and lips, while inching her left arm upward. She prayed the left side of her body was away from where her captor had walked. Was he looking down the hill at the wedding? Could he see the women tending to Sarah?

A horrid thought hit her like a punch to her belly. Oh, no. Oh, no! He had grabbed her just as she'd started to call 9-1-1! No help was coming for her friend and her baby could die! And, if she herself wasn't careful, wasn't clever, she could die too.

Alex saw Ella nowhere around the parked, unlocked van, nor in it. He even popped the back hatch from in-side. Nothing there but artist's supplies.

Still out of breath, he ran toward the house. It was locked, but he knew where they kept the key. He opened the door with it and stuck his head in. "Ella! Ella!"

From the counter, he took her key to the smaller house, ran to it, opened the back door and yelled. Nothing, no one. His gut told him it was a waste of time to search inside. Her abductor would not keep her here. He tore toward the barn and saw, under Sarah's van, the cell phone Ella must have used because no one else around here had one, as far as he knew. Still, Aaron had told him on the sly that some of his buddies had ones they'd bought, even before their running-around time began.

He turned the cell on, checked recently made calls. No 9-1-1. He punched those numbers in. When he told the sheriff's dispatcher about the need for a squad next door, it took everything in his power not to scream for help for Ella. "We got that, thanks," she told him. "Ray-Lynn Logan called for one, and it's on the way."

He turned the phone off, wishing he could dare to ask for the sheriff's help, but he was coming to trust no one. How had his enemies found him here? Unless Ella had a stalker, he was blaming himself. He was the serpent in the Garden of Eden County. He'd tempted Ella, fallen for her fast. Someone must have observed that, decided to use her. Whoever had been watching her could have been watching him first, waiting for a chance to get rid of him.

Alex had no doubt that, if he followed directions and walked those dark roads tonight, he would disappear or end up dead. Eben Lantz had told him about hit men burying victims in other people's graves around here— that could easily be his fate. So he would expel himself from the Garden of Eden after he found and freed Ella.

But found her how? He'd be a sitting duck on that dark road. Here he'd been a situation analysis expert at SkyBound, a go-to guy for any crisis involving setting goals, psyching out competitors—and he had no damn clue who to blame or what to do here. But he did know that nothing mattered but saving Ella.

The barn door squeaked as he opened it and stepped into the dim, coolness. "Ella?" he cried, but only the owl that lived in the rafters answered, "Whoo-whoo."

Ella froze when she heard footsteps coming close. Her captor loosed the tie that was her gag but gave her a little slap across her face through the quilt with a "Shh!"

He was giving her a break, but she was not to talk. No one would hear her up here if she screamed anyway. Only trees and *Daad*'s bees. *Only trees and Daad's bees* repeated in her brain. If this man walked away or night fell, could she somehow get free by using trees or the bees?

Maybe she could find a rough-barked branch and saw through her ties, but that seemed far-fetched. If only she was closer to *Daad*'s beehives without that sinkhole in between, she could try to roll or scoot over there. If it was still there, he kept an old metal fishing tackle box with some tools in it, including the serrated kitchen knife he used to uncap the honey cells. He'd told her once when she watched him gather honey here several years ago that worldly beekeepers used electric heated knives, but his old knife worked just as well.

The ties on her ankles felt so tight, and her right arm was totally trapped and going numb. She had not managed to free her left hand all the way—if she could only pop her elbow free, that tie would go slack, but she was afraid to move too much. Breathing was easier at least. The quilt had been tattered in places. If her captor bent close over her, maybe she could catch a glimpse of him without his realizing it.

How much time passed, she wasn't sure. Minutes? An hour? Two? Had she heard a distant siren from the direction of the Esh farm? *Please, Lord, let someone have called for help for Sarah.* She prayed for her friend and her unborn baby, for herself, for Andrew/Alex, in case he was the real target.

Footsteps came closer again. The man retied her gag, but not as tight as before. He pulled her backward, sat her up against a tree and then walked quickly away. If she was oriented correctly, he was heading down the back of the hill, not the side that led to her lavender field and the farm. It was a shorter, less steep walk that way. She thought she heard a distant engine start. Unless it was a trick, he was leaving her alone up here!

Ella strained to listen. Squirrels chattered in the trees, wind rustled the leaves, and yes, bees buzzed.

She inched her left hand upward again, tugging harder now. It was tied between her wrist and bent elbow, but—no, she couldn't get it to her mouth to loosen the gag. But she could shake her head enough to get the top hem of the torn quilt to fall, allowing her to see.

The summer sun was low in the sky, so it was later than she thought. She could not bear the idea of being up here in the coming darkness. Surely, when her family came home and did not find her, they would be frantic. It was about time for the evening meal they, as the groom's family, had prepared for the wedding guests. *Mamm* would be upset, even angry that she was not there to help with it. Or maybe Sarah's situation had taken everyone's attention and disturbed their well-laid plans.

Ella turned her head as far as she could, right and left, craning to look around. Unless her captor was hiding behind a tree or had climbed one, she was alone. Blessedly alone, but she knew he'd be back. Had he gone to harm Andrew? She had to free herself, find him, tell him he had to run, get Mr. Branin's help, go hide somewhere else.

And the mere thought of that hurt so much. To lose him, to send him back to the world…

Stop it! she told herself. *Just get free. Get out of here, warn Andrew*—if she wasn't already too late.

Alex knew he'd never get out of here or have a shot at getting Ella back if he didn't obey orders and keep this dreadful secret from her family. Such a happy day, with their oldest son, Seth, wedding the woman he'd always loved, Ella's dear friend Hannah. And then, even in the potential tragedy of it, a reunion between Sarah, banned from her people and her mother.

How he'd loved his glimpse into all their lives, being a part of them even for a little while. He knew, if they learned what he intended to do, they'd try to stop him, to help him, even risking Ella, and he could not allow that. At all costs, he had to get "Ella enchanted" safe and sound and back to them. At least he'd heard a siren across the field and had seen a rescue squad turning into the Esh farm. How he wished he could call the cops, just be a normal person who needed help.

With his small satchel of earthly goods at his side, huddled by the open haymow door in the barn loft, Alex kept a watch out for the dusk to turn to darkness. He waited for the Amish and his enemy, wishing he did not have to lie to the Lantzes about Ella in the note he'd left on their kitchen table. Some of it was sadly true:

Dear Lantz Family: I can never thank you and your people enough for the care and concern you have shown me. However, I think my location has been discovered and I must move on. When I told Ella this, she went off angry, but I'm sure she'll be back soon. I hope and pray that someday I can get through my troubles, return to visit you and somehow repay your loving kindnesses.

—Andrew

He'd tried to keep the note calm and light, not to scare them and to give him time to bargain to free Ella and send her back safe to them. How he was going to do that he wasn't sure, but he did know it could cost him his life.

13

Ella knew she had to escape before her captor came back. Or would he return? Did he just want to get her out of the way until he could hit his target, Andrew? Had he somehow contacted Andrew to meet him? Or maybe he'd even sent Andrew a note and signed her name, for a romantic meeting. Would that mean her captor had been hiding in the barn the night she and Andrew kissed?

All she knew was that she could not stay here. She could not bear to be helpless while something terrible happened to Andrew—or rather to Alex. He was not who he pretended to be, even to her. Those good qualities she'd seen in him, the trust and sharing, the magnetic pull he exerted over her—were those real too?

She had only one chance she could think of to escape. With her left hand unable to grasp something unless she got close to it, she had to reach *Daad's* tackle box and pray she'd find his old serrated knife there so she could cut herself loose. And she'd have to get there by rolling down the hill, somehow avoiding the sinkhole between her and the beehives. She might annoy the bees, but that would be nothing next to the huge drop that meant injury or death below.

She shoved away from the tree and scooted around until she thought her path downward would be right. She would roll toward the beehives, then stop herself before the drop-off—how, she wasn't sure. Maybe by rolling at an angle, making a zigzag path downward. On the other hand, if she went too far left, she could roll all the way down and end up in the valley where she had nothing to cut herself loose.

Wishing she could breathe through her mouth, she said a quick prayer, then writhed and heaved herself over on her stomach until she began to roll.

Fast, faster—too fast! She fought to get her feet in front of her to stop her rotation. So dizzy again, her head bumping and hitting the grass. She had no choice, had to save herself, save Andrew. Had anyone missed her yet, with the chaos over Sarah? Maybe they would just think she'd gone off in a fret because she'd earlier criticized her friend for wedding a worldly man, for getting put under the *bann*. Maybe they thought she could not bear to see her other best friend's joy on her wedding day when she herself had no come-calling friend, no husband, no family of her own.

She stopped her rolling, breathing hard, fearing to go on, but she had no choice. Angling herself away from the sinkhole, she started to roll again. She tried to use her elbows to control her speed, but that only made the ride bumpier. She rolled over branches, even a small rock that hurt. Again, she stopped herself and set a new path, one that could take her to the beehives. Their base would stop her rolling, but she couldn't hit there hard.

If the worker bees got agitated, they'd dive-bomb her, and she'd never fend them off.

Sweating, panting, praying, once more, she stopped, then rolled again. Oh, no! As a beehive flew by, she hit her head on its wooden base, but then kept going!

No! No, she had to stop or she'd crash into trees at the bottom of the hill. She fought to turn her body, get her legs downhill, stop the whirling....

She came to a halt and looked dazedly up into the darkening sky. The clouds, streaked red by the sunset, seemed to jump up and down, but it was her eyes, her head doing that. Moaning, she looked up the hill. She was not far past the hives. She'd have to scoot up toward them, like an inchworm. Digging her heels into the grass, balancing, she started back uphill, bending, straightening, shoving herself, careful not to roll again. At least *Daad* never locked that old tackle box, but what if the knife wasn't there?

To be able to reach it with her partly free hand, Ella had to curl herself around the metal box. Lifting it a few inches, she jammed a knee between the lid and the box, forcing it farther open. Several tools in there—*ya,* the old kitchen knife. But she could not free her hand far enough to reach for it or grasp it.

The lid of the box flopped open. With her feet, she tipped it over, then writhed into position to grab the knife. But how to hold it, move it to cut her ties? So awkward, sawing this way, her other arm numb, her bruised body screaming...

Her left arm popped free! She yanked her gag from her mouth, then just lay there, gasping for breath, sobbing.

Stop! she told herself. Get up, get down the hill. She

had to find Andrew, tell him to flee or get him in the sheriff's protection. But then, once Andrew was safe, was gone, what if her captor came back for her? She would go crazy being afraid all the time, having to be a prisoner in her own home.

Ella cut and pulled herself completely free. And then she saw what she'd been tied with and gasped aloud. It was the silky, crimson cording, just like what the Lees wrapped their spa products in! She seized a piece of it, rolled onto her knees, then got unsteadily to her feet and, bruised all over, started down the hill.

Gazing out the haymow door, Alex knew he had to get out of here before the family came back and buggied into the barn. Maybe he could hide in a ditch down the road a ways, observe any car that came along. It was the only strategy all his agonizing had come up with so far. As dusk descended, he'd been watching the buggies from the wedding go by on the road. No doubt folks wanted to get home before dark. He pictured the Lantzes helping to clean up after the evening meal they'd provided for everyone and wished he and Ella were there to help them. He felt so conflicted, so damn confused about what to do, about everything.

Out of curiosity—he'd taken the flashlight Ella had used in the barn—he opened the trunk she'd said had been her grandfather's and shined the beam into it. A couple of carpentry tools, a map of Florida and shells. If he got out of this alive after freeing Ella, maybe he should head south, hide out until closer to the trial, tell no one. He had most of the cash Branin had given him. He could call Logan Reese, one of his lawyers, but was that wise? Could he even trust Gerald Branin? Sheriff Freeman?

The barn owl swooped past him, a silent predator, but the flap of its wings fanned the air. A human predator was out there too, a raptor looking for its prey—him.

He closed the trunk and, with his few Amish possessions and his cash in his bag, climbed down the ladder into the dark barn. He decided to keep Ella's flashlight. He'd left five twenty-dollar bills for the Lantzes, but he knew he'd never repay the kindness he'd experienced here.

Okay, he thought as he went out into the night and closed the door behind him, time to strategize again. He figured the reason his enemy had gone to all the trouble to take Ella captive was to force his real target away from the Amish. With the other things that had happened to her, he should have run before. It was one thing to gun down a man in a motel parking lot in Atlanta near an interstate freeway where something like that wasn't unheard-of, but it was a real risk to kill someone in the midst of quiet Amish country.

Rather than just shoot him down here, his enemy might think it was better to remove him, then get rid of him, maybe interrogate him first about what he'd told the feds so far. Though Bishop Esh, Eben Lantz and Ella had told him crime had been creeping into Eden County, a murder here would get a lot of media attention. Anything amiss in Amish America—arrests for the lack of safety triangles on buggies, an angry Amish man cutting off the beard of his rival—made national headlines. No way a hit man or his employer wanted that, not the murder of a star federal witness who'd already been in the headlines for whistle-blowing about economic espionage with the Chinese.

So Alex had reasoned that the brains behind the hit man would rather have him taken prisoner. That at least would give him some time to bargain for Ella's release. If his enemies had any smarts at all, and he knew they did, they should want to release her anyway. The kidnapping of an Amish girl—no way these guys wanted the FBI in on that. That is, unless someone who used to be with the FBI wanted to worm his way back into their good graces by finding and freeing her.

Alex started toward the fence. He did not want to be a sitting duck, walking down the road, but he would not run just to save himself. Not with Ella's safety at stake. Did her captor know that about him? Had they been followed and observed, maybe even in the barn that one time he'd kissed her? And as a result, she'd become the bait?

He ducked through the rail fence, but took one glance back at the now dark farmhouse where he'd lived so briefly, but had been given so much and had been so changed. Things he used to value, to crave, had faded in importance. He'd come to question his life of personal ambition, his professional aggression. His desires had changed....

But was that a lantern flickering in the kitchen of the house? He hadn't heard the buggy come in, but someone could have come across the field.

He hesitated a moment. What if her family finally realized they had to look for her and came back? Could it be that Ella had been freed because his enemy was so sure Alex was doing what he'd been told? Was he even imagining that lantern light because he wanted to so desperately?

It didn't seem to be in the kitchen anymore. Maybe the person holding it was moving around in there. He ducked back through the fence, bent low and ran toward the farmhouse.

Carrying a lantern, Ella ran upstairs to her old bedroom where she'd been sleeping lately. Her hair was loose, a mess. Aching all over, she longed to strip off her grass-stained, tattered garments and take a hot bath, but no time—no time. She was shaking, her teeth chattering. She was only going to grab a cape and bonnet, get some coins, then run out to the phone shanty and call the sheriff to report what had happened to her and have him find and protect Andrew.

The last thing she wanted to do was go out into the dark where she could be endangered again, especially if her captor found her missing, but she had to get help. Her family would be back soon, but what could they do to save Andrew? Hopefully, he had not already been contacted about her abduction or had gone to meet her captor.

She swirled the cape around her shoulders, then, under the bed, hid the piece of crimson cord she had tied around her wrist. It pointed directly to Connie Lee and her family, maybe to someone who worked for her, even to her husband. But then, spools of the expensive cord had uncoiled all over the road the night of the accident. Someone could have come along, even the next day and found some of the pretty stuff. At least the sheriff had seen it before. He'd know exactly what she was describing to him.

She froze as she heard a hall floorboard creak. But she'd locked the back door and had not heard the buggy come in. She watched in awed horror as the door she'd left ajar slowly, silently swung open.

She gasped and let out a little scream. Andrew! She flew into his arms.

"Oh, thank God, thank You, God," he was saying, the same as her very thoughts.

He crushed her to him; she held tight. He hugged her so hard she couldn't breathe. Her sore muscles screamed, but she only pressed closer to him.

"My fault, my fault!" he was saying, his voice choked with emotion. "What happened?"

"Someone—a man—put a quilt over my head—all of me. He tied me and took me up the hill and left me, but I got away. I'm calling the sheriff."

As he set her back, his eyes went thoroughly over her. "You're turning black-and-blue," he stammered. "He didn't—beat you or…"

"No—no. He didn't want me, just you, I think."

Tenderly, he stroked both her shoulders with the palms of his hands. She'd been cold, but now a heat wave hit her as his eyes traveled the length of her again. "Give me a head start before you call for help," he said. "Since I've been found again, I have to run, and I don't know who to trust. I was going to bargain with your captor, trade for you…"

"But I'm safe now. You can hide here again—"

"No! I can't endanger you and your family further. You've got to go somewhere else now, so they don't find you either. Can you ID him, or describe him?"

"He was careful about that, didn't even use his voice

except disguised. I'll be all right, but I see—that you have to go."

"Ella…" He kissed her, slanting his mouth hungrily against hers as if he could devour her. His cheeks were wet with tears. No, those were hers. He gave a shaky sigh and held her hard again with her head nestled under his chin. "I'll be sure you're safe with your family, then I have to go. But promise me you'll make plans to go somewhere else for a while."

And then she said words that astounded her as much as they obviously did him. "I should go with you— Alex."

His eyes wide, he set her back at arm's length. "The sheriff or Branin told you? Or that former FBI guy?"

"I overheard Mr. Branin talking to you outside the barn the other night."

"Did you overhear anything else?"

"Oh, *ya,* I heard you give him Connie Lee's name, and I think they're the ones behind this."

"You're on your Chinese kick again."

"But aren't you too? It's not just a crazy idea. Here," she said. She pulled away and bent to retrieve and toss the piece of crimson cord at him. It landed on the foot of her bed. He picked it up and stared at it, took it closer to the lantern, looking puzzled for a moment before he nodded. Ella explained, "Connie Lee gave me a sample box of one of their spa products tied with that same thing—their so-called signature wrapping ribbon. That's what I was tied up with, over an old quilt my captor took from the barn."

"This is the cord that was all over the road that night. It got thrown out of Sam Lee's car when he did."

"Right. Alex, I can help you—help you figure out who's behind this."

"I trust you to be on my side, when I don't trust anyone else. My—our enemy—has been lurking, no doubt took the telescope from the barn to keep an eye on us from the hill, when he wasn't hiding in the barn."

"That's why I'm going with you."

"Ella, I can't take you, even if I don't trust the authorities here to protect you!"

"Sheriff Freeman's okay, but what's he going to do, lock me up in his single jail cell to keep me safe? Or make me stay with Ray-Lynn, so she gets hurt with me? She's already been beat up and nearly killed."

He came around the bed toward her. "Don't talk like that!"

"Andrew—Alex, I've escaped and ruined the plan to be your bait. So my captor, someone the Lees or your enemies hired, could be furious at me and want revenge. They could try to take me again, even if I can't, like you said, ID him. You don't want to be a protected prisoner here and neither do I!"

"I don't even know where I'm going. You can't just run off with a worldly man."

"Then I'll run off alone. Do you think the Amish have some kind of witness protection program?" she challenged, grabbing her bonnet and jamming it on her head. "Like what, go live with some distant cousins in Pennsylvania, where our enemy would think to look first and get some other of our people hurt? I'll pack a few things and grab some money and clothes. I heard the buggy come in a few minutes ago. I'll run out and tell *Daad* not to unhitch the horse. As soon as I find out how Sarah's doing, he can call the sheriff while we head for a bus stop or hop a train."

A voice from the hall said, "I think a bus—the Pioneer Trails Bus, *ya,* that will be *ser gut.*"

Grossmamm! Andrew spun around, and Ella gasped. She couldn't have been standing there too long, could she? The old woman moved into the doorway, blocking it.

"The *what* bus?" Andrew demanded. "To where?"

"The one that goes to Florida," *Grossmamm* said. "You two can't run off alone even if you're both in danger. Ella needs a—what's that word—a champion."

"A chaperone?" Andrew asked. "Look, *Grossmamm* Ruth, you can't—"

She propped her fists on her broad hips. "I'm the one knows all about Pinecraft, Florida, and I always wanted to see it in the summer when it's a ghost town—folks not there, a good place to hide and be safe, *ya?* I came back early in a friend's buggy, but I'm not tired now, and if you two are going to yell at each other loud, you better know someone could hear you. I'll pack a few things, Ella too, but I'll talk to your parents first. Andrew's bag is already out here in the hall. I'll tell your sister to take care of the lavender while you're away, Ella, just that she should say you are sick and in the house to everyone. Bad to tell lies, but necessary. Right, Andrew, also known as Alex? *Ya,* all that will work *ser gut!*"

Ella and Andrew stood staring agape. The Bible said that people were sometimes visited by angels in disguise, Ella thought—but *Grossmamm?*

"Oh," the old woman said, turning back in the doorway. "Ella, I know you are worried for Sarah, and I hear you comforted her and tried to help. The baby was turning inside her—got stuck against her spine, hurt her nerves. She's in bed in her parents' house, and her husband sent for. The medic men said bed rest, see her doctor tomorrow, because the baby's heartbeat is strong. Hannah and Seth gone home to the Troyers for a few days before coming to stay here. Then too much of a crowded house if we're all here anyway."

"Sarah's at her parents' house?" Ella asked, because her mind had snagged on that impossibility. "But she's under the *bann,* and her father won't allow… And Nate's been sent for—to go there?"

Her own heart was beating so hard she shook. Would she soon wake up from all of this? But *Grossmamm*'s news about Sarah's being taken in by her family was a blessing.

"*Ya,* Nate McKenzie will be welcome there, for now. Sarah's resting good. She asked where you went, but I said I would tell her later. Now, it will be much later."

Grossmamm turned and walked away. Ella's head was spinning worse than when she rolled down the hill.

As Andrew went down to talk to *Daad,* Ella started to throw things into her little suitcase. *Grossmamm* popped back in one more time.

"And put in some of that nice lavender suntan cream too," she said. "We're not just going to hide out down there. We're going to enjoy life and see if we can save that man, save his life and save his soul."

14

So, Alex thought as the miles blurred by outside the bus window, he was playing Amish again. He was not only fleeing but with others to worry about this time, though they acted as if they were taking care of him.

Ella and her grandmother slept in their seats across the aisle. He'd insisted on sitting in the back of the bus so he could keep his eye on the few other passengers—eight Amish, two Mennonite and four English, nowhere near a full load. Somehow it made it all worse that it was the middle of the night and too dark to really observe people inside the bus or cars outside that might mean trouble.

Imagine, he thought, shaking his head, Alex Caldwell, executive director of a Manhattan-based international firm, a refugee riding something that resembled a Greyhound bus down Interstate-75 through the Appalachians, running for his life—and maybe now for Ella's too.

After convincing her distraught parents this was the best thing to do, after prayers, hugs and advice, the three of them had trekked over the familiar field between the

Lantz and Esh farms. In the early-morning hours the night of the wedding, the bishop himself had buggied the three of them a roundabout way into Homestead, where they'd roused an *Englische* driver the Amish often hired. He had driven them into Wooster where they waited hours the next day at a place called the Guerne Heights Drive-In to catch this Pioneer Trails bus.

Though exhausted, Alex had stayed awake until they'd bought their tickets and finally boarded. At least it was a luxury cruiser with a bathroom on board. Mrs. Lantz had packed them food, because there would be only one stop during the seventeen-hour trip, and that was for breakfast later this morning in Tifton, Georgia. Alex hated the idea of going through Atlanta, right past the motel where he could have been killed.

Now and then he leaned out into the aisle to see what time it was on the clock above the windshield at the front of the bus. Almost 4:30 a.m. His eyes had long ago adjusted to the dark, and he'd been watching Ella in the reflected lights of passing traffic. She looked so beautiful asleep. For a moment, he pictured her lying on the pillow next to him in a big bed, to have and to hold. But now her brow was furrowed, and she fidgeted as if snared in a bad dream, which, thanks to him, she was. He longed to comfort her but he needed comforting himself.

As a noisy semi passed the bus, her eyelids flickered open. She glanced over at him and gave him a sleepy smile that made his insides flip-flop like a sixteen-year-old's. She rose carefully from her seat beside her grandmother and came across the aisle to sit by him as he shifted over to the window seat.

"We could all spread out on our own seat and lie down to sleep," she said, stifling a yawn. "There's room enough, for sure." The hypnotic hum of the wheels on the road meant she didn't have to keep her voice down. Besides, *Grossmamm* Ruth slept like a rock. She'd been exhausted at the wedding but had put on a good front about being able to make the trip. He knew too that she was worried about her daughter in Pennsylvania, who had some sort of health issue she'd recently learned about.

"*Grossmamm* says these buses are loaded in the winter," Ella told him, "but I only counted seventeen passengers, including us."

He turned even more away from the window toward her. Their arms touched on the armrests, and it seemed so natural to be close to her. "One of the best things your grandmother said was that little Pinecraft would be almost a ghost town right now. It sounds like a good refuge until I can figure out what to do and it's safe for you to go home."

"I always wanted to see the Gulf of Mexico, walk the beach and gather shells, though I sure won't get in the water. When my grandparents told me years ago about how pretty it was, I thought it sounded like paradise. I've seen Lake Erie, but this is the farthest I've ever gone. See, something good comes out of something bad."

"That's what I'm hoping for in my life."

"Will you—I mean, now that I know your first name at least—will you tell me more about your life, about the real you?"

The seats around them were empty, and *Grossmamm* was still asleep. It scared Alex how badly he wanted to share everything with Ella when he'd tried to keep his secrets. He sighed and took her hand.

"My name is Alexander Caldwell, and I'm thirty-two, never married. My parents are deceased, and I was an only child—hardly an Amish-size family. I grew up in Fairfax, Virginia, went to William and Mary College where I played guard on the basketball team—my big passion at that time in my life."

"Guard. That sounds like your mission, trying to take care of others."

He smiled to keep from laughing at that. Better not to explain that his mission as guard was to take care of the ball, and his original mission in life was to just have fun, chase girls and take care of himself. It touched him how she gave him credit for what was a really selfish youth.

"So then what?" she prompted.

"I went to another college—Harvard—to get an MBA, which is a business degree."

"So then you learned all about the packaging, branding and promotion you said I should use to expand my lavender business."

She'd surprised him again, remembering all that he'd only mentioned once when he should have kept his mouth shut. "That's right," he said. "And I want to apologize for taking you away from your lavender in peak season."

"Barbara's helped me before. She and *Mamm* can keep it going, though I hate to think of Connie Lee coming around again with her fancy car, clothes and ideas, when she was probably just spying on us and you. And here," she said, with a sigh, "she was the main way I was thinking to expand."

"Once I—we—get through this, and we nail whoever took you and wants me, I'll help you expand. I owe you a lot."

She shook her head. "We were all glad to help you, take you in and tend to—to your wounds, like the Good Samaritan did to the man who fell among thieves. Is that kind of what happened to you? You got in with someone bad and tried to make it right and now they've turned on you?"

He gripped her hand. "Yeah, that's kind of it."

"Do you miss your other life a lot?"

"Some of it. But some of it seems—well, shallow and too rushed and—I don't know—pointless since I've observed and been a small part of your people's ways. But I've got to see all this through. Ella, there's going to be a trial where I'll testify against my former mentor and boss. Big publicity, things brought out into the light that will rattle a lot of cages, even affect some high-ups in the government of two countries. It's a Pandora's box."

"What's that?"

"Like a can of worms."

"Oh. And you will testify about man-made spy satellites and the Chinese?"

He reached out to cup her chin. "You aren't a spy sent to seduce me into telling you all my deepest, darkest secrets, are you?"

"I'm your guard. Like in basketball, only this is the game of life. And, Alex, there is a real paradise much better than sunny Florida beyond life. Facing death is terrifying—as I can testify—but there can be something wonderful beyond if you just trust Someone stronger than yourself, and I sure don't mean me."

"I've got to get through the here and now and keep us all safe," he insisted. "And part of my problem is you really get to me in all kinds of ways, and I don't want to hurt you."

"In all kinds of ways—I like that," she said with a pert smile as he reluctantly loosed his grip on her chin. "I want us to stay safe *for* you but I don't know if I want to stay safe *from* you. And on that, I'm going to get in my own seat, lie down and sleep until the Cracker Barrel Restaurant stop for breakfast in Tifton, Georgia. Do you think there will be palm trees there?"

"Not there, not yet."

He longed to pull her to him and kiss her, just a good-night and grateful kiss—or more—but she popped up and left him to his agonizing.

"I'm in shock," Alex told Ella and *Grossmamm,* as he woke up from a dead sleep and looked out the window.

"And you weren't when you first saw Amish country?" Ella asked.

"True, but this little enclave of Pinecraft—there's not even a sign labeling it, but I'm grateful for a well-kept secret."

The neighborhood was nestled on the east-side sprawl of busy Sarasota. Jets coasted overhead and cars were everywhere on busy, four-lane Bahia Vista Boulevard. Yet, down the grid of side streets and all around was a quiet enclave of what appeared to be a separate, sleepy village.

He admitted to himself he missed the hills, open fields and woodlots. Nothing looked Amish at first, until he saw a sign for Troyer's Dutch Heritage Restaurant and a couple of bearded men in straw hats. Except for that, this tidy community of trailer courts, small houses, bungalows and little shops could be any lower-class but neatly kept Southern neighborhood.

It was half past noon when the bus pulled up in front of the Tourist Mennonite Church and finally came to a stop. Alex felt dopey, as if they were still moving. They'd had the air-conditioning on ever since the Georgia-Florida line, so he knew it was going to be hot and humid outside, but that was the price to be paid for Pinecraft being a ghost town this time of year. Man, he needed a shower or dip in the Gulf, but *Grossmamm* Ruth had told him that Lido Beach and Siesta Key Beach were a city bus ride away.

A few folks greeted the bus with happy, noisy reunions when their fellow passengers got off. The three of them waited until the little welcoming committee had dispersed. Alex kept looking out the windows, all around, but saw no one suspicious, no one who didn't appear to belong. They disembarked and retrieved their bags from the driver who had stored them in the belly of the bus. "Hope you got three-wheeled bikes like everyone else around here," Lem, the driver said. "Always thought buggies would add something to the charm, but the horses would melt in this heat."

They thanked him and, blinking in the bright sun, trudged a few blocks to the Raber cottage, for that was *Grossmamm*'s married name.

Why didn't the Amish wear sunglasses? Wasn't that needful and therefore not prideful for eyes in this bright sun? Hat brim or not, he was getting a pair ASAP. He told himself to calm down: he was strung out physically and emotionally as well as still scared for himself and his companions.

"Good thing we didn't rent it out this year," *Gross-*

mamm said as she produced a key to unlock the door. "Next door, I see they rented again, though. That's where the Kurtzes from Sugarcreek live in the winter, real good, nice folks."

As they stepped into the dim, quiet cottage, Alex got hit with more surprises, welcome ones. The old woman clicked on an electric light, started a window air conditioner, and he saw a wall telephone. "Came with the place, got to have all that fancy worldly stuff to rent it," *Grossmamm* said only.

The narrow cottage had a small front room, two little bedrooms with a bathroom between and a tiny kitchenette. "Wow," he said. "The modern world."

"But we go to the beach on a bus and in the water dressed just like this," the old woman told him. "Does this place need cleaning! But not now. What you call this I have—jet lag?"

"Bus lag," Alex said, walking around quickly to look out all the windows. In the tiny, high-fenced backyard, trees were laden with citrus fruit, one with limes, one oranges. Off-season ghost town or not, she was right about someone living right next door. There were clothes hanging on the line, stranger than some of the things he'd seen on Amish clotheslines. Old-time police uniforms? Clown costumes?

"Ella and I will sleep in here," *Grossmamm* announced and went inside the bigger bedroom, followed by Ella with both their suitcases Alex had been carrying. He collapsed in a rocking chair in front of the air conditioner but started to sneeze when it kicked out dust.

"God bless you!" Ella said when she came back out and plugged in the refrigerator, closing the door on its empty insides, which reminded Alex he was starving. "I can't wait to look around this place and see the beach!"

"We'll head to the beach tomorrow, maybe eat at Yoder's tonight. I figure I can pretend I have a sore throat and you two can talk for me if the *Deutsche* is going fast and furious. But we are going to have to be wary and aware of our surroundings—of people. I don't think they, whoever they is, can track us here, though they found me twice before."

"I pray we will be safe. But even your Mr. Branin doesn't know where you are. Bishop Esh said he wouldn't tell. No one but my nearest family members and Bishop Esh know."

He sneezed again. "Speaking of God bless," he told her, "I'm praying He keeps a good eye on your family as well as us. As clever as our great escape seems, I'm still a hot commodity to someone who tried to kill me once before."

"But since I was just kidnapped," she said, "I was thinking maybe that's all they'd do to you—keep you prisoner until after the trial and then it would be too late for you to do them any damage."

He shook his head, got up wearily and went to her, put his hands on her shoulders. "It doesn't work that way. No Alexander Caldwell, no trial. Now that you know what kind of a target—and danger—I am, maybe I should leave you two here for a while and go off on my own—really get lost."

"No," she said, clasping his wrists with both hands so that it seemed they propped each other up. "They won't find you again. At least give it some time, get some rest. As long as you don't call in—call anyone— it's got to be safe here."

She looked as if she were going to cry. He kissed her cheek, turned her around and gently propelled her toward the bedroom door.

"I'll wake you both for dinner later," he said. "Table for three at Yoder's—very romantic."

She lifted a hand in a little wave, his Ella enchanted and enchanting, went inside and closed the bedroom door.

Alex checked to see the front and back doors were locked, then the living room and his bedroom windows. He carried his few earthly, Amish possessions into his tiny, plain bedroom. He hid most of his money under the pine dresser, now only about three hundred fifty dollars since he'd bought the bus ticket. He took his shirt and suspenders off, used the bathroom. He splashed cold water on his face and upper torso, then, leaving his bedroom door open, unlike the women's, stretched out atop the quilt on the double bed that almost dwarfed the room.

Being here with two Amish women, both of whom he admired, but one he wanted... So conflicted. What to do? What next?

His eyelids were heavy, but what was that strange sound? He could not let this place and Ella's confidence lull him into complacency. The bus could have been followed. Someone could figure out where they were... Would he ever be able to relax again, to be himself—whatever that self was now that he felt so changed after such a short time in the heart of Amish country, in his own heart, yearning... Situation analysis: goals, competitors, brand... Goals, to protect these women and live long enough to testify...competitors...captors, killers... brand upon his heart...Ella...

He jerked awake and sat straight up, his heart thudding. What *was* that sound? He rose, walked to the room's only window and parted the slats. A spear of sunlight shot in, almost blinding him. He couldn't believe what he saw. From behind a fence and their neighbors' clothesline, which was crowded with two orange shock wigs and floppy pants and jackets of two dark blue, old-time policeman costumes with oversize brass buttons, a man kept appearing, rising, falling. He made strange faces, weird posturing frozen in space for a moment as if he were chasing someone or running away. Then he disappeared downward again. Was he on a trampoline? Was he watching their house while pretending to practice some crazy stunts? No, Alex scolded himself, he was the one punch-drunk with exhaustion, but he was not seeing things. He shook his head and snorted a laugh. His life was in shambles, and he just might be going nuts. There was a contract out on his life. He had fallen for an Amish virgin. And his next-door neighbor was not an Amish bishop this time but a circus clown!

15

"I didn't know it could all look so big, the waves too," Ella said to Andrew—they'd decided they must still use that name for him—as he put the cooler on their blanket late the next morning at Lido Beach. They sat side by side about twenty feet from the surf rolling up on the slick sand. It was pretty obvious the tide was coming in. "I think I'll just look for shells in the dry part of the beach," she told him.

Grossmamm had been too worn-out to come with them on the city bus. Truth be told, Ella knew the old woman had been exhausted the night of Seth and Hannah's wedding when she'd urged them to flee to Pinecraft, despite her claims that she wasn't tired at all.

Ella knew *Grossmamm* had other worries besides keeping Andrew and her safe. Though *Grossmamm* hadn't wanted to put a damper on Seth's special day, she had recently received a letter that her only daughter had breast cancer. Ella's aunt Martha lived in central Pennsylvania and had two little ones, so she could obviously use some help. It sure said a lot about *Grossmamm,* Ella thought, that she was willing to try to save a man who had been a total stranger just two weeks ago, when her own daughter could use some help. Or was *Grossmamm* even more upset by the fact Martha had told her not to come?

"You've been so brave through everything," Andrew told Ella, leaning back on one elbow, facing her, soaking in the sun. He looked strange, wearing sunglasses he'd insisted on buying at a drugstore nearby. Ella knew they stood out around here in their Amish garb. Only a few other plain folk were on the beach, but it was a Monday and off-season. The *Englischers* basking in the sun and surf wore so little they looked stark naked to her. She just bet Andrew would like to shed his Amish clothes. If someone was a danger to them—and she knew Andrew feared that, since his eyes darted around behind his new sunglasses—would they be safer in modern dress—that is, undress?

"Are you sure it isn't time to conquer your past?" Andrew asked. "I'm working on mine, even if I'm doing a lousy job of it. I'm terrified half the time, but I'm still going to face my fears and testify."

"You mean for me to wade in?"

"I mean *go* in, all the way—with me, of course."

"Oh, I couldn't."

"As I said, you're a very brave woman. Isn't it time you put that drowning nightmare to rest and fight back like you did against your captor?"

"I didn't fight back. The Amish don't fight back. I just escaped. And you tricked me into coming here today to pressure me to go in!"

"You know you longed to see the beach and water. I'm not tricking you about anything, not anymore. I'm just hoping you trust me and want to get over your fear of water and drowning enough to go in with me. I think you said the fear of death is terrible, but you have faith the Lord will take care of you. He did, through Sarah and Hannah that day years ago, when you could have drowned. And now I'll be there with you, holding you up. I'm a good swimmer."

"Were you ever a lifeguard, like you were a basketball guard?"

"No, and don't change the subject."

"You're trying everything to get me to trust you."

"Please argue with yourself, not me. If you don't trust me, you are a crazy woman to have left Eden County with me. I'm going swimming, even fully dressed as a Pennsylvania country cousin who probably learned to swim in a local pond there. If you come in the water with me, I will not let your head go under. I will not even let you have a panic attack. That has to be part of the struggle too, Ella." He took off his shoes and hat, tossed his sunglasses on the blanket, squeezed her knee, got up and strode for the water.

Ella watched him go. Tears blurred her vision of him, of the beach with the scattered people who were here on this hot day. She was perspiring already, but that was partly because Andrew always made her feel warm. Gripping her hands together, she felt the beginning of a panic attack. Why did he have to mention that? Could getting over her fear of the water heal her dark drowning attacks too? They weren't caused by water most of the time. *Dear Lord in heaven*, she prayed, *if I don't swim with Andrew, will he think not only that I don't trust him, but that I don't trust You? I want him to learn to trust You.*

Her heart thudding in her chest, her hands shaking

so hard her fingers fumbled with the laces, she took off
her shoes and black stockings. Andrew was in waist
deep now. In a big whoosh, he left his feet and floated
on his back with his head still above water. She knew
full well from the way he always looked around, even
in Yoder's Restaurant last night, that he was fearful of
being watched, probably of being shot at again. He'd
quizzed *Grossmamm* about the couple next door, but
she'd said they were renting and she didn't know anything about them, except what they could see: one or
both of them were clowns.

"And I'll be one if I don't go in," she muttered as she
got to her feet and started across the sand. It was hot. It
burned her feet. Hotter than the hinges of Hades, *Mamm*
would say if she were here.

The wash of water was cool on Ella's ankles and feet,
so delightful, but the blood pounded in her veins. Trying to concentrate on the strewn shells washed up, she
fought the swirling blackness that always threatened her
when an attack began. Even in this bright sun, a panic
attack! But she could fight that. An attack came from
the outside, but she was strong inside. Andrew believed
in her, and she was certain that worldly Alex did, too.

He swam toward her as she went in, shin deep. Her
aqua skirts clung to her legs. Andrew stood about ten
feet away, the waist-deep waves cresting around him.
She almost bolted back toward shore. She could not do
this! He wasn't reaching out for her. He wasn't helping!

A wave buffeted her, and her terror surged stronger. But it was now or never for her, with this water
and with this man.

The force of the next cresting wave stunned Ella. It
was so different from the pond. But the water looked

beautiful, a dozen colors of green-blue frosted with white foam. She bent her knees and rode the first wave. It wasn't as high as some others. She still dragged her feet on the sandy bottom. Andrew came toward her, reaching out. She took his hand and held on hard, then his other hand touched her waist, helping to buoy her up.

"I want to keep my feet on the bottom!" she told him, realizing she'd been holding her breath.

"No fun that way. You'll float. We'll tread water. You've got to let go. Trust yourself—trust me."

"I do, or I wouldn't be in here—oh!"

Either the next wave lifted her or he did. Her feet—all of her—floated as she held on to the man she had not even known ten days ago but was now depending on with her life.

His hands on her waist, hers on his broad shoulders, out in deeper water, they rode the waves together. It was as if they were so safe here, in the Gulf under God's wide sky, but she saw Andrew turn to look ashore, scrutinizing the few others swimming, though none were near. He turned to frown at a man farther out, riding what she'd call a water motorcycle. He bounced along on the waves, straddling a machine that made a loud, grinding sound.

Despite Andrew's unease, feeling triumphant, Ella linked her hands behind his neck. That brought them closer together, rubbing against each other, up and down, around, pressed tight. Swiftly, Andrew's attention was back on her. His knee slid up between her legs, tugging her sopping skirt with it so she almost rode him like a horse. He lowered one hand to cup her bottom to slide her even closer. Her body, her entire being sprang instantly alert with heat. Yet she shivered and her nipples pointed against his bare skin as the water parted his shirt to reveal a chest with curly, brown hair, and she felt so open to him and…

Careful, Ella thought. Too easy to just let go, to pretend she was here with her Amish sweetheart, her husband, and that they had a whole life ahead to love each other in bed and out. To live in the Home Valley but visit here, to tend her lavender and sell it. To have children who would bless their home and—

She got a mouthful of water and spit it out, coughed, so he set her back a bit but still held strong to her. She tried to rein in her emotions. She'd always been careful and practical while Sarah and Hannah were the dreamers, so why were things different now? Keep safe, keep Andrew safe, then pray for him when he had to testify against someone he had trusted who was now his enemy and maybe had sent someone to hurt him, kill him. She'd always known that dreams were real close to nightmares.

What was that new sound? Not that same machine. They both turned to see a sleek, long-nosed boat bearing down on them, smacking through each wave. Had they floated too far out too? Surely the boater would see them in the water—or was that exactly what he had done?

Andrew started kicking to get them closer to shore. She tried to help. Pulling her right hand from clutching him, she dug into the water. Dog-paddling, Seth had called it when he'd taught her and Hannah to swim. But the boat was still coming so loud, so fast…

"Take a breath!" Andrew shouted.

She barely had time to suck one in. But they'd have to go down so far to keep from being hit by the boat!

What if a deep current held them under? She hadn't been afraid, since they were together, but—

Andrew jackknifed into the water, taking her under with him. The old terror, drowning, being pulled downward to death…

She held her breath, held tight to him, eyes closed against the sting of salt water and so she wouldn't see that monster hit them. She hadn't seen the other monster who took her captive. Andrew had said he never saw the face of the man in a black pickup truck who tried to shoot him in Atlanta. The black van that had pursued her: dark windows, so she hadn't seen a face. A faceless enemy but so very terrible and real…

Below the surface, a wall of water slammed them, but it wasn't the boat. In bubbling white foam, they surfaced, both sucking air filled with gas fumes. Andrew swore under his breath.

"Was that…" she choked out, gasping. "Do you think…they found us? Will they turn back for…another try?"

"Just some stupid kid, I think," he said, squinting at the boat as it roared away, spewing a big plume of white water. "Saw him—before we dove, but—I don't think—he even saw us. Let's get out. Salt water in the eyes or not, keep them open!"

Their feet touched bottom, and they staggered toward the shore. A tanned man in a tight swimsuit with a shaved head came up to them as they walked out of the surf onto the sand. Andrew thrust her behind him, whether for safety's sake or because her sopped clothes were clinging to her, she wasn't sure.

"Hey," the man called to them, "glad you're okay. I've seen that idiot before. I know you all don't hold

grudges, but you can report that to the Coast Guard. I'll
let you use my cell, if you want," he added, holding out
a thin, rectangular phone. "You just fill out a complaint,
give your name and contact info, get interviewed later."

"Thanks for your concern," Andrew told him, "but
we're fine."

Always fearful he would not sound Amish enough,
even speaking English, Ella put in, "We just hope that
bad boater doesn't hurt anyone else. We appreciate your
kindness, *ya,* we do."

"Sure. No problem," he said with a nod as he started
away. He called back over his shoulder, "I can phone it
in, not give your names or anything. That stupid dude
comes back, I'll get a photo of him too!"

They collapsed onto their blanket and began to dry
off with their towels. "If that kid's been around before,
it's hardly our enemy trying a new way to eliminate
me," Andrew muttered.

She shuddered, partly from being chilled, partly from
how matter-of-factly he'd put that.

She repinned her hair, even as she realized her prayer
kapp was gone. It was probably floating out there in the
waves, but at least they were back on solid land now.
And her thoughts about wanting a worldly, forbidden
man—she was surely back on solid ground with that
impossibility now too.

They decided not to tell *Grossmamm* what had happened, since it was an accident and not an attack. She
didn't need to be put more on edge than she already was
over their hiding out here and her ill daughter. She'd
been to the local store and had supper waiting for them
as well as three adult tricycles she'd had delivered.

Another blow to his ego and past life, Alex thought, as the three of them took a tour on the trikes around little Pinecraft that evening. In the prime of his life, Metro Man—who'd ridden in limos and loved big, solid cars—had been reduced to peddling a rented trike around like a kid or an old man.

Alex judged the Pinecraft area to be over a hundred acres. Spread out in an oval around its grid of little streets, it boasted a park, which seemed a magnet for the few Amish and Mennonite in the "ghost town" this summer. People played checkers, shuffleboard and boccie under huge old Florida oaks with gray Spanish moss hanging off them like twisted hair. The old Pinecraft water tower, even at a little distance from the park, looked like the next tallest thing to the modern buildings of distant, downtown Sarasota. They saw a pair of bearded women—freaks, he supposed people called them—walking a tall, French poodle that had less hair than they did.

"Probably retired circus performers," *Grossmamm* said as they pedaled toward home. "Got lots of them around in the winter, like dwarfs, one lady with leathery skin like a snake's. Sarasota was the home of John Ringling years ago, such a good place for his workers. The circus used to winter in these parts, then went up the beach a ways to Venice, but they're all over this area too, especially retired ones. Only some here, because in the summer the circus goes on the road."

"But the renters next to us look too young to be retired," Alex said. "And he keeps practicing, though I haven't seen her."

"Maybe she keeps the house and cooks real good—I smelled something baking," *Grossmamm* said as if that closed the conversation on that. Alex just nodded, but he winked at Ella as he caught the quick smile she sent him. He smiled back, but he couldn't help but think the way *Grossmamm* Ruth stared at those freaks was just the way some outsiders stared at the Amish.

He padlocked their trikes to the orange tree in their backyard, and they started inside.

"Janus, they're home!" came a woman's melodious voice over the fence they shared in common with the renters. "You can stop twirling that baton long enough to go over with me!"

Not too subtle, Alex thought. And the guy was twirling a baton now? But as a very attractive brunette, who, on closer range, he saw was heavily made-up with cosmetics, came around the end of the fence with a tray of something, Alex's gaze was not riveted on her but on the man behind her. Not only was he twirling what looked like the collapsible baton like cops carried but his face was more painted than hers. A clown for sure, with a bulbous, red nose, exaggerated eyes, black-and-white face paint and what looked to be an orange Halloween fright wig jammed in one front pocket.

"Sorry," he said, collapsing the baton and sticking it in the other front pocket of his jeans. He also wore a purple sweatshirt that read in big, white script, Foreman's Fabulous Circus. "I scare kids sometimes," he said with a little shrug, "but didn't mean to startle you or the ladies."

He swept Ella and *Grossmamm* an elaborate bow. Their neighbor thrust out his hand to Alex, who shook it.

"Janus McCorkle here, and this is my wife, Patricia, known as Trixie. We thought you two might be on your honeymoon until we saw your chaperone here. Pleased to meet you," he added with another bow as Alex introduced them all by name, trying to think how to explain their relationships and why they were here. Suddenly, the country cousin bit sounded all wrong.

"*Ya,* they've been married quite a while—a year," *Grossmamm* put in. Alex nearly fell over at her quick lie. "And they were nice enough to bring me along for a little while, but this really is my place here. I lost a good husband three years ago, but kept this cottage. Oh, what nice cupcakes, decorated for pretty, so good!"

Alex saw each one was frosted and sprinkled to make a clown face with two huge jelly bean eyes. While the women clustered together admiring the baked goods, Janus said to him, "I've been with the Foreman Circus, as you can see. Broke my leg in a fall, so had to sit this winter out, and Trix was sweet enough to stay with me, when they would have taken her—an aerialist, you know, trapeze artist," he said with a rocking gesture of both arms over his head as if he was being caught by someone else aloft.

"Oh, *ya,* sure," Alex said.

"But I'm literally back on my feet now, and using the Foreman winter headquarters to practice, not far from here. We just rented this place," he said with another sweeping gesture, "for a change of scene, since we miss the life—you know, touring."

"I saw your costumes on the clothesline," Alex told him. He was surprised how much he instantly liked the guy. Maybe it was the clown aura. Or maybe he was just plain starved to talk to a modern, as the Amish said, even one who was a huge stretch from anyone he'd ever known. The guy not only had a variety of facial expressions but several different voices he used, some low, some high. That alone make Alex want to smile.

"Oh, yeah, the Keystone Kops outfits," Janus said. "I like to clown for adults even more than kids, put a satirical bent on things, which is really easy to do in this day and age—politicians, financial disasters, corrupt bankers, Hollywood and government scandals." His voice was low now, almost menacing. "You name it, I try to parade it and deflate it. Hey," he plunged on, his voice more normal again, "I'd really appreciate it if you'd come see my new act tomorrow, Trixie's too— give us an outside opinion. We'd be happy to drive you."

Alex had promised himself he would not trust anyone, but these people—longtime locals and clowns? Maybe it would even distract *Grossmamm* from her worries about her daughter.

"If we wouldn't be gone too long," he said. "Things are tiring for my—my wife's grandmother."

"No sweat—except ours," he said with a smile and clapped Alex on the shoulders as if they were long-lost buddies. "It's a real nice facility we're hired to be caretakers of this summer, though I'd love to be out on the road. Just Corky the Clown—my stage name—in my costume and disguise, moving on, always moving on."

A fake name, costume, disguise, and the always-moving-on that Janus McCorkle, alias Corky the Clown, longed for, Alex thought, was exactly what he was trying so damned hard to survive.

16

"Sure 'preciate your coming along with me, honey," Jack told Ray-Lynn as they drove toward the Lantz farmhouse in his civilian car late in the afternoon. "I don't want to upset anyone or, in this case, tip them off it's official business. But I got word that Ella and their Pennsylvania guest have disappeared and that needs checking out."

"I can't believe the family wouldn't contact you if it was something unusual," Ray-Lynn said. "Maybe they just went to visit his people in Pennsylvania. But there's something strange about him, right? Like he's been put here to keep an eye on someone? Keep someone safe?"

"Now, Ray-Lynn, you gotta trust me on this."

"Right, but I thought something was fishy with him when I talked to him at the wedding reception. Jack, the guy just doesn't sound or seem Amish, and I've been up close and personal with enough of them to know. Now, I'm more than happy to help by coming along to the Lantzes'," she assured him since she could see him grinding his teeth, "but can't you tell me more? I wish I could be more a part of your work. I mean, here you own half of the restaurant and are in and out all the time, especially since you've got Win Hayes to help police this place now—which I'm happy about, and you sure don't need me for a sounding board, but—"

"Ray-Lynn," he cut her off, reaching a hand over the console to gently grasp her wrist, "I need you for lots of things. And when a contact I have asked me if I could check into the fact he hasn't seen Ella working her lavender or their cousin helping in the fields, I just figured if we went as a couple—no police car, no uniform and you bearing your usual gifts—it wouldn't alarm the family. Can we please leave it at that?"

"Just one more thing, then. You aren't still in league with that former FBI G-man Armstrong, are you? Ella told me at the wedding reception he had scolded and threatened her about getting in his way with Hannah and—"

"He did? Why in the Sam Hill didn't you tell me that? He has no right to harass her!"

"So it *is* Linc Armstrong who noticed Ella and Andrew might be missing?"

"I didn't say that!"

"Jack, I won't tell anyone else, so don't get upset. The Lantzes are a lovely family, and Ella's very capable of taking care of herself, though, compared to Sarah and Hannah—she can be a bit—well, prickly. You know, judgmental, set in her ways. But all right, I'll just go along, not ask any more questions. Besides," she added, twisting in her seat belt toward him as he withdrew his hand and turned up the lane to the Lantz farmhouse, "even if we're on official business, I love being with you in your regular car, with you out of uniform—"

"I can arrange to get out of uniform for you anytime."

"Jack Freeman! I am so *not* shocked!"

"And I'm just happy to have my chatty, sassy Southern sweetheart back," he said as he parked near the barn. She got out quickly and took the angel food cake with fluffy white coconut icing from its carrier on the back floor of the car.

"Opening your own car doors now?" Jack asked with a grin as his eyes went over her. "Guess that means we're not dating anymore but ready for the next step— the big time."

"I hope you mean more than asking me to help you with future undercover work—and never mind a flirty remark about working with me under the covers."

"Yeah, for sure, serious commitments for both of us. Soon," he vowed as they stood by the car staring at each other.

"Hello there, Sheriff, Ray-Lynn," came Eben Lantz's distant voice. "This is a good surprise. But we got three folks down with the flu, so best you not come in. I pray you not got something bad to tell me."

Eben closed the door behind himself and came down the porch steps. Ray-Lynn noticed Mrs. Lantz and her oldest daughter Barbara's faces at the kitchen window, and they'd passed the two Lantz sons on the road, driving a wagon loaded with spring wheat, so the ones sick must be Ella, the grandmother and their so-called Pennsylvania cousin.

"There's your answer to why some are missing," Ray-Lynn whispered out of the side of her mouth. "But flu this time of year?"

"Yeah. Strange. Just follow my lead, okay?"

"Don't I always?"

"Heck, no."

"Today, just call me deputy in disguise."

"Shh!" he muttered as Eben started down the walk toward them with a frown on his face. "The fact that he asked about bad news—I'll bet they're not here at all and he's worried. But for the Amish to lie—I don't like it. So, we brought you a cake, Eben," Jack said in a louder voice as he shook hands with the frowning man. "No bad news, though—not on our end of things."

After supper that evening, Ella was excited to be driven around Sarasota a bit and thrilled to see the big, high-ceilinged building where Janus and Trixie Mc-Corkle practiced their circus act. Janus unlocked a big building, turned on the overhead lights, then the Mc-Corkles left them to look around while they went to put their costumes on. High up, the huge room was strung with wires and a swing, which Ella soon learned were called tightropes and a trapeze. At least, she thought, a net stretched out below to catch anyone who fell.

"Even climbing in or out of that high net would take some skill and courage," she whispered to *Grossmamm* as the two of them sat in the front row facing a large asphalt floor edged by a raised rim.

"*Ya.* I wish the regular circus folk didn't take all the animals away with them this summer," the old woman whispered back. "Like to see an elephant up close, *ya,* I sure would."

Andrew was entranced, Ella saw, not by all the circus trappings but by talking to Janus, whom he seemed to like a lot. Now painted and costumed as Corky the Clown, he had appeared before Trixie. Ella was glad to see the odd friendship between the *Englischer* dressed up like an Amish man and the *Englischer* dressed up like a clown. Janus had explained his costume was based on some old-time movie policemen called Keystone Kops. Right now, that was probably the only kind of law officer Andrew wanted to trust anyway.

"I have to laugh just looking at him in that getup," Andrew said as he came over to sit with them. "I'm tempted to kid him back sometime by getting in that second identical costume that always seems to be hanging on the line."

Grossmamm put in, "Too hot and humid to dry things good on the line like at home."

Andrew went on, pointing upward, "But he sure knows his stuff about everything here—the rigging, the lighting. If I have to run away again, maybe I'll go join the Foreman Circus. They're in Minneapolis right now."

"Very funny," Ella said, hitting his shoulder lightly with her fist. "I can't see you as a clown."

They sat back smiling while Janus—that is, Corky the Clown—beguiled them with antics and explanations: "Okay, I don't talk in this gig, but without the clowns who play the bad guys I'm chasing, I'll have to narrate my shtick. Playing robbers, the other clowns steal a big wallet from the ringmaster's pocket—so big he'd never get it in his pocket in the first place—that's sleight of hand—and then I chase them around for a while."

"So that's what he was practicing in their backyard," Andrew said as Janus tore around the ring, bouncing high off several small trampolines, contorting his body into strange poses before bouncing down again. From somewhere strange music blasted over loudspeakers that went along with the pantomime. "Old silent film chase music," Andrew whispered.

Janus had to talk really loud to be heard over the music. Ella noted that, as well as being the clown of a thousand tricks, he was also the clown with different voices, some low, some high-pitched. That was really clever too, but he'd said he didn't talk during this routine.

Meanwhile, Trixie was climbing a rope ladder up to a small platform where a trapeze was attached. Ella's gaze bounced back and forth between her and Janus. They were both so wonderful to watch, she so graceful, he so crazy. Too bad the circus never came to the Home Valley. She was sure her people would think it was wonderful.

"Janus says he's what is called an Auguste clown," Andrew told them, though he didn't take his eyes off the performers either. "They have colorful clothes and makeup. They specialize in a certain kind of lawlessness and disorder—sounds familiar to me."

Ella said, "I just can't believe that some people have a fear of clowns. What was that he called it?"

"Coulrophobia," Andrew said. "I'm waiting for the satire part he promised, instead of his just mocking cops and robbers."

To their amazement, Janus—oversize shoes and all—began to climb the same rope ladder Trixie had used. As he started up, he called down to them, "Now the clowns who took the money—oh, by the way, they took it from a prop labeled 'Big Bank'—gave the money to me and I stuff it in my pockets."

"Cops being bribed?" Ella asked, but no one answered her. As Janus climbed, they saw, across his rear end, he had somehow attached a big sign that read FAN-

NIE, then under that, in slightly smaller letters, FAN-NIE MAE."

Andrew said, "That was one of the two government mortgage agencies the feds—the national government—took over when they got in debt, a real mess."

With Janus nearly to the platform, Trixie, in a skimpy, red outfit with sparkles all over it, loosed the trapeze from its hook and, hanging on by her hands below it, swung back and forth, pumping her legs to go faster and higher like someone on a swing. Suddenly popping out from beneath her was a bright banner that read YOUR IRA.

"Who's Ira? What's that mean?" Ella asked, feeling this was all above her—in more ways than one.

Andrew started to explain but he was laughing too hard, especially when Trixie, still holding her YOUR IRA sign, intentionally let go and took a big dive into the net below, which now had a notice, US GOV'T, which had magically appeared. She bounced wildly up, then down when she hit into the web of ropes.

Grossmamm, who had been transfixed, cried out, "Should we go see if she's all right?" But their attention was riveted on Janus, who had grabbed the trapeze as it swung back to him. Now, somehow, from the depths of his costume—or maybe from the platform—he produced a sign that had a tumbled-down wall painted on it. The drawing also had a big + and the word *STREET* on it.

Wall Street? Ella thought. What about Wall Street?

As he swung back and forth, big dollar bills began to drop from his pockets. He too took a dive into the net just as Trixie was holding on to its edge and doing a summersault to get back onto the ground.

Grossmamm and Ella clapped hard as Janus bounced a couple of times, then walked to the edge of the net, grabbed its edge and flipped over to stand on the ground.

Ella didn't get all the satire, but she could ask Andrew later. When she looked his way, tears were in his eyes but he was no longer laughing. His lower lip quivered. Oh, *ya*, this had gotten to him bad, because he really was crying and over some silly clown act about money and Wall Street.

The night of their visit to the Lantz farmhouse, which had gotten them nothing but the repeated insistence that Ella, Mrs. Lantz's grandmother and their Pennsylvania visitor, Andrew Lantz, had all caught the flu, Jack took Ray-Lynn into Wooster for dinner at an Italian restaurant called Little Italy. Wine, the works. They had gone in his unmarked car again and, as far as she could tell, he had no cell phone on him at their secluded booth, no pistol in a shoulder holster under his nice navy-blue suit jacket. He was dressed so spiffily, she thought, people would probably think he was a lawyer or a funeral director.

At that, a little chill shot through her, despite the fact she felt warm from the Montepulciano d'abruzzo and from just being the object of his riveted attention. Here they were on one of their rare real dates, she had him all to herself, he did not seem to be distracted—though he was nervous—and she was starting to get jittery. Maybe she just hadn't been able to shake the feeling that something was wrong about Eben Lantz's story.

Jack clinked his wine goblet to hers, and they lifted them together. "Gotta level with you, Ray-Lynn. I wasn't sure you—or we—were gonna make it, but I think we have. If you can just put up with how distracted I get sometimes, I—"

"And you can put up with my Southern flippancy and my *Gone with the Wind* collections all over the place, then I guess—"

"Will you just let me talk for a sec, honey? I love you, Ray-Lynn, and I'd like you to be my wife, and I want to give you this."

A red rosebud, she thought, as he extended the single flower to her. Now where had he been hiding that? But her hopes fell. With that pretty speech and his shifting around on his side of the booth, you'd think there was a ring in sight and not a red rose, however fresh and beautiful.

And then she saw it. The tight bud was wearing a diamond ring, which glittered in the candlelight.

She sucked in a quick breath and reached for the flower to touch the ring, to put it on. You might know she managed to snag a thorn getting it off, scratching herself, but that didn't matter.

"Does that mean a yes?" Jack asked.

"It means everything's coming up roses for you and for me," she cried—and, ding-dang, really started to cry as she jumped up and slid into the booth on his side of the table to hug him. Surely nothing in their entire lives could ever go wrong now!

Ella was indeed enchanted, just like Andrew sometimes teasingly called her. Janus and Trixie had brought the three of them to see the Gilded Age mansion of John Ringling, one of the founders of the so-called Greatest

Show on Earth circus in Sarasota. She was awestruck at the size and grandeur of the estate.

"There are other circuses with their home bases around these parts," Janus told them, as if he were the guide on their tour, "but no one can ever top this man! If he was alive today, no one I'd rather meet!"

Ca' d'Zan, or House of John, built in 1924, was the most magnificent building Ella had ever seen. Every inch of imported European furniture, even in the big bathrooms, was ornately carved or gilded. Its high ceilings were painted with patterns or scenes, and its black-and-white marble-tiled floors reflected their images as they followed their guide around. Such a huge place, fifty-six rooms! How could just two people have a home like this, for only John and his wife, Mabel, had lived here where they had copied or purchased furnishings and decor from many castles and palaces they'd seen abroad. So much money spent, Ella thought, and all for prideful show—for pretty, as her people would say.

As they traipsed along with others on the tour, she listened intently to the narrative about John Ringling's life. The fact he came from a large German family—she could relate to that. But when the tour ended and the five of them sat together in the beautiful gardens in the shade of a tree, and Andrew turned to her and asked, "So what do you think?" she could not help but tell the truth.

"I think it's an amazing place, and I thank you, Janus and Trixie, for bringing us to see it. But I can't help but pity the man."

"Pity John Ringling?" Janus asked with a gasp. Even when he wasn't in clown face, he had a habit of extreme expressions and wide eyes. "But he had it all!"

"He had no children to carry on his dynasty," Ella said, ticking things off on her fingers. "He lost four of his brothers when they were fairly young. His dear help-meet Mabel died and, when he wed again, it ended in domestic violence and lawsuits. We Amish just don't like or trust lawyers. He broke off with his only sister, Ida, and her son, who could have been an heir and solace to him in his old age. And he died with only about three hundred dollars in the bank. I can't help but think he sometimes thought he'd give up all this and his Greatest Show on Earth for a nice little house, his dear Mabel at his side and a big family of his own."

Everyone just stared at her, though *Grossmamm* solemnly nodded her approval. Trixie looked surprised, like such a crazy thought had never entered her head. Janus seemed thoughtful, though he was frowning. But what touched her was that Andrew took her hand and said, "I completely agree. People matter, not things, and your—our people—have that figured out just right."

Our people, Ella thought. He'd quickly corrected himself on that near slip. But he'd been through his own kind of hell already, cut off from his people, friends and home, just as the circus magnate must have been when he'd faced death. And, through it all, blessedly, Andrew who was once Alex was starting to sound just a bit Amish.

"Well, let's get back and get some homemade lemonade," Janus said. "It's hot out here. This time of year it's best to do things at night, but I wanted you to see this in case you have to leave—head back."

Ella saw Andrew's head snap around at that. They had not said anything to him about having to leave. Even with his friend Janus, was Andrew thinking he had to be more careful, less trusting? No, she thought, for sure these kind people were ones to be trusted. So what that the McCorkles had moved in just a day or so before they arrived here and, from the first, had kept a good eye on their Ohio neighbors? Both Janus and Trixie had mentioned they wished they had money to start their own clown and trapeze artist school they could retire to someday, but where would they ever get a windfall for that? So what if Ella was pretty sure that both McCorkles had a suspicion that Andrew wasn't exactly Amish? And did they believe the two of them were really married, especially when Trixie had asked to use their bathroom when they were visiting and probably noted that Andrew did not keep one thing in the bathroom, even though all three of them shared it?

But no, Ella scolded herself, she was being too nervous again, too afraid. Things had been going great here in this ghost town of Pinecraft. And with Andrew near, she was savoring each moment, more than she'd ever treasure a gilded palace.

17

That evening, *Grossmamm* insisted on taking Ella and him back to Yoder's Restaurant. Alex didn't argue, because he was low on cash and that was going to be a problem if he didn't contact his lawyers or Gerald Branin soon to have some money sent. But that was a big risk. Some insider must have been bought off or threatened to give up his location in the Home Valley. Would they eventually trace him here too?

He still wasn't sure who had found his location, evidently twice, and sent a hired gun, as they used to say in the old Westerns. He wished he could ask Janus if he could work for him for cash around the Foreman Circus practice grounds, but that might tip Janus off to things he shouldn't know. Again, he felt he was a failure at acting Amish: Ray-Lynn had guessed; Janus seemed a bit suspicious; and had Connie Lee known?

"Good food, *ya?*" *Grossmamm* Ruth interrupted his agonizing as she pointed at his roast beef and mashed potatoes. He hadn't realized he'd stopped eating. They'd already hit the salad bar where he and Ella had eaten heaping plates of everything from coleslaw to pasta.

Nerves, he thought. He knew people who quit eating when they were upset but he—and shapely Ella, so easy and natural with her beautiful body—reacted just the other way.

"It's all delicious," he said, digging in again. He had to stop frowning off into the distance, studying people who came into the room they were seated in. The place held six hundred, *Grossmamm* had said, so he couldn't check out everyone if he had a year here. Even though it was off-season in late June, the place was doing well with a mix of tourists and locals.

"Here we thought we'd find a ghost town," Ella said as she polished off her meat loaf. "I mean, the town is pretty quiet, especially in the evening, but the restaurants keep bringing outsiders in."

"Yeah," Alex said. "Good for Yoder's, but a concern for us. I'm still tempted to get myself a clown costume to hide out."

"Not for you," *Grossmamm* said as if he'd meant that. "You got a serious streak in you, I'll bet even if you didn't have current problems. You'd make a better Amish man than a clown."

"Actually," Alex said, lowering his voice, though the restaurant buzz would keep anyone from eavesdropping, "I don't think I'm passing myself off very well as Amish."

Ella put in, "It's just your talk and some of your beliefs, or lack thereof, which come out. After knowing some of us, you don't think we're all alike, do you?"

"No way. Different personalities, different preferences and desires."

"Right," Ella said with a decisive nod. "But built on our faith, so whatever happens, there is nothing to fear."

He sighed. "Ultimately, but that's hard to keep calm about when someone wants you dead and has the means to achieve it. Let's talk about this later, in private."

"Fine," Ella said. "Then let's go back to the fact that even though this isn't totally a ghost town right now, we're blessed to be here."

Man, Ella was tenacious, Alex thought. But she was right. Yet, if someone did find him again, the collateral damage could still be two of the dearest women he'd ever known, one who treated him like her own grandson and the other—damn, he wanted Ella desperately but had to protect her by just loving her from afar, not making love to her. Love! To even think that, was he absolutely, stark raving nuts?

"It's a ghost town for me, always," *Grossmamm* said with tears in her eyes. "Ever since he died, I picture my dear husband, Gid—Gideon, his name was—here with me. At Yoder's or in the square when we played shuffleboard, or walking the beaches, even just sitting in our little backyard under our citrus trees. Sure, at home in Ohio too, but there were so many others to care for around us then. It's here in Florida, which he loved so in the winter, that my memories haunt me, like he's a ghost here, even in this summer ghost town."

She sighed and her usual upright posture seemed to wilt. Ella reached out to take her grandmother's hand the same moment Alex grasped her other one. That was, Alex thought, the most at one time the old woman had said since the night she more or less ordered them to flee to Florida. Had she hoped to find good memories of her husband here but had found sadness instead? If he could go back to his past life, would it be that way for him, in the crowded streets of New York? He'd been changed forever. Would SoHo no longer seem like home? Would he be haunted by the ghosts of his past there—especially Ella?

"So, have we saved room for pie?" their petite Mennonite server asked with a smile, jolting them back to the here and now.

"Oh, sure," *Grossmamm* said, making an obvious effort to perk up. "I'll have strawberry, long as it's not made with that red gelatin stuff."

"No, ma'am, not here at Yoder's. All berries—with a bit of thickening."

"Cornstarch, flour or tapioca thickening?" the old woman asked. Alex saw Ella roll her eyes.

"I think cornstarch."

"Fine then, with whipped cream."

"That sounds good to me too," Ella said only.

Alex put in, "Make that three."

"See!" *Grossmamm* said, patting his hand as their server hurried away. "Sometimes you think just like us. Oh, *ya,* I think you would make a good Amish man, really Amish, not just in disguise. Then you could help Ella expand her lavender business, help small carpentry shops, our little bakeries, craft shops do better. Tough money times for the Amish too. Then, you could marry Amish."

Ella gasped, whispered, *"Grossmamm!"* and began a big blush. Alex, despite feeling so depressed and on edge tonight, choked, then bellowed a laugh that would have done Janus proud.

That evening when it was not yet dark and *Grossmamm* had gone to bed early, Alex and Ella sat out in the bungalow's small backyard sipping lemonade. Their old canvas and wooden lounge chairs were comfortable, their stomachs were full and the smudge pot to ward off mosquitoes hissed out a sweet, smoky smell.

"I just want you to know," Ella said, "I did not put her up to that you-could-marry-Amish comment."

"I know." He could have really teased her about that, would have if he wasn't still worried—fretting, Ella would say—about his finances and his future.

"But her point about you having good Amish qualities is true. Andrew, there's something different tonight. You're especially worried," she said, keeping her voice low despite the fact no one could hear them out here. "Are you getting itchy feet?"

"You mean to move on? This is the safest I've felt for months except for my first couple of days with your family. I just keep going over and over in my head who keeps fingering my locations so I can be traced and attacked. Atlanta, Amish country—hopefully, not here."

"Can you really trust your lawyers or the government? Over the centuries, my people have learned to trust neither. Not only did they help to condemn us when they were persecuted in Europe years ago but the Bible says, *'Woe to you, lawyers! For you load men with burdens hard to bear.'"*

"That's why I'm not contacting them until it's close to the time for the September trial. As for trusting my government contacts, I don't suppose you ever saw the movie *Witness?*"

"I never saw it, but all the Amish know about it. It was filmed in Pennsylvania, so it looked authentic. But we didn't like it—the scene where the Amish girl let an outsider see her naked—"

"Partly naked. She was washing. And maybe he just peeked in on her and she didn't set it up."

"And that movie showed terrible gun violence that came onto the Amish farm at the end, like it might give people ideas about how easy it is to hurt or rob our peaceful people. So see, I know about that movie."

"The reason I brought it up," Alex said, trying to get back on track, "is because the ultimate bad guy who wanted to silence the witness was a higher-up in a detective bureau, like a police officer boss."

She gasped. "You aren't thinking it could be Sheriff Freeman behind all this?"

"No, not him. But maybe Gerald Branin, my contact to WITSEC, maybe even that former FBI guy Armstrong who was hanging around Hannah and then you. It's not news to anyone that, even high up, the government and the police can be corrupted. I know you think the Chinese connection is the best guess but—"

"Don't you?"

"Maybe. But the wreck Sam Lee had wasn't staged."

"What if he'd been told who you were? Either sent by his parents or some Chinese officials, he intended to kill you in a hit-and-run, but his car got out of control? A so-called car accident like that would make your death look better than a direct murder, like with a gun."

"Yeah, you're right about that. The feds would be suspicious, but if it didn't look like a hired hit and they couldn't find another witness, they'd probably have to dismiss the charges."

"So maybe when Sam failed to hit you with his car and got hurt himself, then Connie Lee starts coming around with the excuse of buying my lavender, then hires another hit man because she's sent by the Chinese who stole your GPS stuff. And she tells him to kidnap me to get you away from the others, because if any Amish really got hurt, there would be a huge investigation."

"Possible," he said, rubbing his eyes with his index fingers while his palms massaged his face. "This whole thing—my life—is a mess right now."

"If it's not the Chinese, can it be your former boss you used to look up to and trust, who has turned on you? Besides the Chinese, he's the one who wants to quiet you, stop you, isn't he?"

Andrew's old canvas lounge chair creaked when he shifted his weight, leaned his elbow on one of its wooden arms and looked bleary-eyed at Ella as she stared at him.

"Sad but true," Alex admitted. "That's the best—and worst—theory, because it hurts so to believe, to accept that. Marv was my mentor, but he was also like a father to me when I first joined the company. He taught me, promoted me—trusted me. Even though he knows I turned on him, it's hard to believe he wants me dead."

"But maybe he was so kind earlier to rope you in," she whispered. "So, when and if you figured out what was going on, he gambled on the fact you wouldn't tell on him. But it was wrong, he was wrong and so—you did. You had to, so you could live with yourself and look others in the face and keep this country safe."

She sounded like a patriotic ad, he thought, although it was said of the Amish they lived *on* the U.S., not *in* it. She was so passionate to help him, and that really hit him in the gut—and the heart. As dusk descended, he stared deep into her eyes. This young Amish woman might be naive but she was bright. And she had read him, his thoughts and fears. She was like his conscience in a way, and that could be so bad when he wanted to grab her and crush her to him.

Finally, amidst cricket sounds, the whine of a mosquito and their own breathing in the silence of the night, she whispered, "I talk too much."

"But you talk true. It's just so hard to accept betrayal from him—but no doubt, that's what he thinks I've done to him. But I can see him hiring someone to do his dirty work for him. People at his beck and call—that's him."

"He's desperate enough to order the kidnapping of Amish girls or to hurt anyone else to get to you. My captor had such a strange whisper and hardly talked at all when he could have…"

"Don't get me thinking about that tonight, or I won't sleep. I stay awake too long at night as is, worrying, hearing every creak of the bungalow or shift of wind."

"Me too, worrying about you, just one room away," she whispered.

They stared deep into each other's eyes again, silently, for much too long. Finally he said, "I was going to say our worlds are worlds apart, but that sounded dumb. In the future, could you ever see yourself having a big lavender farm somewhere else, maybe not living as Amish but—"

"The big farm, oh, *ya*. The other, as much as it would give me some things I might want, *nein. Nein, danki.*"

"I knew that. You can take Ella out of Amish country but you can't take the Amish country out of Ella." He sniffed once hard and knew he had to change the subject. "Listen, Ella, advisor and friend, I'm going to have to get some cash somewhere, since robbing banks in a clown costume is not a good option. You know, I think there was a movie about that too, a comedy, no less."

"I can just see you and Janus in cahoots on that. But, Andrew, I brought cash with me I kept hidden under my bed, and *Grossmamm* has some too—"

"I cannot live off you two."

"But I know you would pay it back when you could. If you help me expand Lavender Plain Products someday, that could be part of your salary."

"I was thinking about asking Janus if I could sweep out the circus practice area, or do any sort of bookkeeping for him. I just wish I knew whether to risk that and some other things I'm longing to do...."

The darkness had deepened. He wanted to kiss and caress her, but if he did, he wasn't sure he could stop. And he had the strangest feeling that, unlike other women in his life he'd desired, even if he completely possessed Ella's body and heart, it would not slake his hunger for her, only deepen it. And, even on top of everything else, that scared him to death.

They both jumped at the voice from between the two houses. "Hey, there you are! Can't a clown get any help around here?"

Andrew swung his feet to the ground and turned to face Janus in full paint, costume and shock wig. "What kind of help do you need?" Andrew asked. "Looks like you're going full bore to me."

He didn't come closer. He seemed to be in a hurry.

"Some evenings I walk uptown just to practice my act on people who might need cheering up. You know, around the town park. I was hoping you could pull yourself away from the lady for a bit and come along."

The guy was still into voices. He was using another low-pitched one tonight.

"Why don't you go ahead?" Ella whispered. "We'll be fine. It would give you a chance to ask him about a job, if you're sure you want to do that, but the offer of a loan still holds."

"The missus says okay with her," Andrew said and stood up, then helped Ella rise. "Is Trixie staying here?"

"Yeah. A headache. See you later," he said to Ella.

They both owed a lot to Janus and Trixie, Andrew thought as he pecked a kiss on her mouth—well, it wasn't a peck. Even in front of Janus, it lingered. The McCorkles had kept their spirits up, taken them here and there, been real good neighbors. Andrew handed her his empty glass and followed Janus—that is, Corky the Clown—out of the backyard.

Once again, their favorite clown made him chuckle as he almost went off balance and bounced a shoulder off the fence. Both he and Ella laughed at the way Janus stumbled over his own big feet, when he was usually so smooth handling those bulbous orange shoes.

Ella went inside and washed their glasses. To her surprise, *Grossmamm* was up, sitting in the living room, slumped in a chair and crying.

"What is it?" Ella cried, rushing to her. "Are you ill?"

Grossmamm spoke in their *Deutsche* dialect, although they'd been using English among the three of them here. "Sick at heart. Got a phone call from your *daad*. Never did get good news by a phone. It hasn't rung once since we been here, now this."

"Now what? Something happened at home?"

"Your aunt Martha. She's going to have surgery,

going to lose a breast. This time, she says to tell me please come."

"See, she wants you there. She just didn't want you to make a trip for nothing earlier—not until she knew what was going on. You'll be a big help to her, get her through this, help take care of her children."

"Your *daad* also says she wonders what am I doing in Florida in the hot months and you during lavender time. He told her I just had to come back where your grandfather and I had happy days."

"First thing in the morning, we can ask Janus or Trixie to take you to the Greyhound station, get you on a bus to Pennsylvania."

"But I can't leave you and Andrew alone together. Where is he?"

"He walked uptown with Corky the Clown. I think he's going to ask Janus for a job to tide him over here. *Grossmamm,* I can't leave him."

"But if you ever have a chance to make him Amish, playing his wife here is not the way."

"A chance to make him Amish? You meant that tonight? You think a modern man, one who's had money and cars and a big, worldly job, would ever turn Amish?"

"With God, all things are possible. Could Trixie drive you uptown to look for Andrew, so we can decide what to do?"

"I don't think they'll be out late. Besides, Trixie has a headache."

"Then I got just the thing for her," she said, popping up from her chair. "Wish I knew something to fight breast cancer, but lemon juice squeezed into hot water will help a headache, a good home remedy, *ya,* it is. Here, I got a lemon," she said, and bustled to the refrigerator. "But back to Andrew," she said, suddenly switching to English, "I tell you, my girl, even though he cares for you and desires you, he will say you should go with me too. Just a minute now. I'll mix this in a glass and you run it over to Trixie. I hope she does not have one of those very bad migrant headaches."

Ella didn't know whether to laugh or cry. Maybe she'd get a migraine—or migrant headache too—over all this migrating from place to place. Just when she was certain things could not get worse, they did. Too many people dear to her were in danger. And she just felt she could *not* leave Andrew, even if he turned back into Alex!

She took the glass of hot lemon water from *Grossmamm* and headed over to give it to Trixie and to tell her *Grossmamm* might have to leave. She sure hoped the McCorkles could take her to the bus station tomorrow. As she went into their backyard, she noted that for once the extra clown suit was not drying on the clothesline.

Some people still didn't lock their doors around here, especially during the day, but, of course, they always locked *Grossmamm*'s bungalow. Trixie's back door was shut because their air conditioner was running—this close, it was so loud—so she knocked.

No answer, no movement, no sound. Had Trixie felt better and gone uptown too? If so, the door would probably be locked. She tried it—open.

She stuck her head in and called, "Trixie? It's Ella. I hear you have a headache, but Grandma's sent something over for you that may help."

No response. Ella felt bad. Trixie must be sleeping, and she had no right to wake her. She'd just leave the lemon juice here with a note, if she could find some paper. She clicked on the kitchenette light, stepped inside and put the glass down on the counter. It was really cold in here, so maybe they turned their air conditioner way up to sleep. Ella saw a notepad, so she scribbled:

> Heat and drink this to help headache. If you don't have lemons or lemonade, we have more. Need to talk to you early a.m. —Ella.

As she started to tiptoe toward the door, her feet stuck to the tile in something tacky. Had she spilled some lemonade? No, the splatters on tan tile were dark like cranberry juice or—blood? Could Trixie have cut herself?

"Trixie? It's Ella. Are you here? Are you okay?"

She peeked into the living area and clicked on a lamp. She gasped. A trail of blood, mostly drops but an occasional streak, led toward their bedroom.

"Trixie?"

Maybe she was in the bathroom with the water running, or was that just the whir of the air conditioner in the window of this room? Or was that someone's voice, distant, muffled?

Should she call the police? But that would mean giving her name, and Andrew said not to trust the authorities, even here. She could run uptown to find Janus and Andrew. It wasn't far, and if they stopped now and then so Janus could clown a bit...

Ella tiptoed to the closed door of their bedroom—the other smaller one was a workroom—and knocked. "Trixie?"

She heard a muffled sound within. What if Trixie had fallen, hit her head? Even had a stroke?

Ella turned the knob and pushed the door slowly

inward. Though she didn't snap on the bedroom light, the reflected glow from the living room lamp jumped across a messy bed. On it lay Trixie, struggling, gagged and trussed up with her wrists bound to the bedpost. The whites of her eyes gleamed as she turned her head toward Ella and tried to shout through her gag.

Even more horrifying was the fact that Janus's second clown costume lay across the foot of the ravaged bed and, with a bloodied head, looking like a corpse, Janus himself lay unmoving and tied on the floor.

18

Ella rushed to ungag and untie Trixie. That man with Andrew was not Janus! And he'd been watching them and McCorkles. He'd used the clown disguise. He was clever, demonic. Had he invited Andrew/Alex to his death, and he'd gone willingly, a sheep to the slaughter? Trust no one…trust no one. She had to run uptown, see if she could stop them, find them before it was too late. Or was Andrew taken or dead already?

She untied a knot to get the gag out of Trixie's mouth, then darted for a knife in the kitchen to cut her loose.

"A man—a thief!" Trixie yelled. "Hit Janus over the head and jumped me. Went into our bathroom. Dressed up, even face paint, like Corky the Clown, but he messed up the face!"

Why didn't they notice that? Ella thought as she cut her friend loose. She had to go, but Janus needed help. She thrust the knife in Trixie's hand. "Janus isn't dead— I saw him move! I think that man's out to hurt Andrew too. I have to go!"

"You know that man?" Trixie screamed as she slid off the bed and knelt over her husband.

Ella didn't answer but ran for the door. No, she didn't know that man, only what he wanted. She took a second knife from the drawer where she'd found the first one and tore out into the dark, humid night.

They'd walked almost to the park, passing a couple of people Alex thought would be good to practice what Janus called his shtick on. But he'd noted two things, even in the darkness. Not only had Janus put his bulbous nose on sideways but he'd done his face paint a bit different. Didn't clowns have a signature design, kind of like company branding or a corporate icon? Also, Janus was always talkative when the two of them were together, but he had said little after that initial spiel. Maybe he was worried about leaving Trixie behind with a headache. Alex knew lately how it felt to really care for someone and worry about them as well as himself.

"So are you looking for a particular group or place?" Alex asked, slowing his steps.

"Near the park."

Why the brusqueness, the tenseness that reeked from this man? The hair on the back of Alex's neck prickled. Was he crazy to think this might not be Janus? He was his friend's height and build, as best as he could tell, under that floppy costume. He knew about them and had come out of Janus's house. Alex had heard their back door bang like it always did when someone came out.

His muscles tensed. When they got just a little closer to the few people in the park, he was going to run. No way someone who meant harm wanted witnesses, despite a disguise.

"Let's set up over there near the field," the clown

said, and reached into the depths of his pockets. From that loose-fitting costume, Alex had seen Janus produce fake dollar bills, balls to juggle and a single flower that popped into a big bouquet.

Only this time, the clown produced a handgun and pointed it right at his chest.

Horrid scenes flashed before Ella's eyes as she picked up her skirts and ran toward town. It had never seemed this far on the trike. She was out of breath already, scanning each side street for a car or a dark van. What if the man who had attacked Janus and Trixie and had taken the other clown suit just disappeared—with Andrew? He had been right to be afraid, even here. Somehow his enemies—hers now too—had him again.

A few people were strolling, enjoying the night air, but Ella was slick with sweat. They had been watched! Instead of the clown, she saw the horrid scarecrow nailed to a lavender cross on her door at home. What if they tortured Andrew to make him tell all he knew before they got rid of him? And who had told that man where they were? Trixie and Janus had suffered because of them, yet they had to keep secrets, they had to protect Andrew! But now it might be too late.

She stopped at the fringe of Pinecraft Park, blinking in the lights there. A single elderly couple played shuffleboard on the farthest court. An old man rolled boccie balls by himself. Farther across the way, four teenage boys shot a ball through a basketball hoop.

But no clown. No Andrew.

She gripped her hands so tightly together her fingers cramped. Tears streamed down her cheeks. This

could not be happening. Bad dreams were one thing,
but this nightmare…

She gasped. She saw them, two tiny figures climbing the metal ladder to the water tower across the park
in a dark field. Was that man going to make Andrew
jump or push him off? Surely he knew the clown was
not Janus by now!

Having no idea what she should do, praying for
strength and help, shaking so hard her teeth chattered,
Ella ran around the edge of the park and took a shuffleboard stick from the box of them, then sprinted across
the dark field toward the tower.

A voice sounded in Alex's head: *Think! Keep calm!
Survive!*

This guy with the gun had not shot him point-blank,
a small reprieve. He felt not only panicked but so damn
dumb. This man had managed to sucker him into falling
for this clown disguise. But somehow he was going to
outsmart him, turn the tables, then get some answers.

Although Alex climbed the water tower ladder ahead
of his captor, he felt as if the muzzle of the gun were
still pressed against his chest. What to do? When to
make a move? He couldn't kick at the guy, because he
stayed several rungs below. He said he'd just as soon
shoot him on the ladder if he didn't do as he said. Alex
didn't believe for one second that the clown intended to
tie him to the walkway of the tower, as he'd said. He'd
even shown him the ropes he'd produced from one of the
deep pockets in the clown costume. But Alex had also
glimpsed a noose, so he'd figured out the real scenario.

Obviously, what Ella had theorized earlier was in
play here: an accident—or in this case, an apparent sui-

cide—would make his death look better than a murder. In the morning, someone would see a man, an Amish man at that, who had hanged himself from the town's water tower. Either that or this guy was going to shove him off as if he'd jumped. A clever way to get rid of the feds' star witness without having it appear to be a hit. Ella's beautiful face kept intruding in his terror, but he tried to thrust the thought of her away so he could make a plan.

He figured it would be important to fight back. Better to make the guy shoot him, so everyone would know it was a murder. Up here, high above the middle of the dark field, despite the glare of distant park lights below, he could see *SeaStar* satellite in the night sky overhead and the recon spy called *Lacrosse 4,* so beautiful. It was like a last-minute gift from God, one that should help to calm him. Would that stunning view be one of the last things he'd ever see, that and Ella's angel face?

An idea hit him. Talk. Keep this man distracted. Alex called down to him, "The American stealth satellite that keeps an eye on Cuba is that orange-red one there at ten o'clock in the sky." It was a lie, but what did that matter now? "Amazing what close-ups our government can see and record, even in the dark. You have seen videos of how the U.S. drones hit targets in the Middle East using GPS, haven't you? Did they tell you that's ultimately what this is all about, spy satellites and corporate espionage by the Chinese Communists who want to hurt our country?"

"Don't know or care about any of that. Shut up and keep climbing."

No attempt to disguise his voice anymore, Alex thought. The guy actually sounded as if he had a Jersey or Bronx accent, so was that the New York City connection again, which pointed straight to his former boss? Oh hell, the Chinese had visited there as much as he'd been to Hong Kong.

"Of course," Alex went on, "they didn't tell you how many billions of dollars are involved in the international espionage scheme either. Your employer's probably going to pay you a piddly one-hit amount, when you could keep me a prisoner like you did the Amish girl and hold out for much more."

"I said, shut up! I hear you're a smart guy, but nothing you say is gonna work."

"They always give prisoners a last meal. I'm just having a last chat. Unfortunately, it's with a lackey, a gofer with a gun, one they'll want to eliminate to cover their tracks. You're expendable too. They'll find you. Ultimately, the big boys take no prisoners and cover their tracks. They like to tie up loose ends."

"This isn't some damn TV show like *Criminal Minds!* You've slowed down. Speed it up!"

"So maybe with smart lines like that, you could be a real clown."

No answer. Alex still climbed as slowly as he could. Too late, he realized he should have just let go of the ladder near the ground, dropped into the guy and taken him to the ground with him—broken bone, bullets or not. But they were too high now, almost to the walkway that girdled the water tower.

Alex tried again to thrust everything away but an escape plan. No thinking about his past, his enemies. Sadly, no time to think about Ella and all she'd come to mean to him in such a short time. Thank God, she had not seen her captor back in Ohio, so he wouldn't try to get rid of her too.

But then, looking down, then quickly away, he both blessed and cursed her. Damn, if Ella wasn't running across the field where, if this guy looked down and toward the park, he'd see her too.

Ella's first thought was to scream up at Andrew and his captor to stop climbing, that she'd called the police, which she hadn't. But what if that panicked the man and he shot Andrew right then? The fake clown must have a gun on him or Andrew would not be climbing that high ladder. Was he going to push Andrew off, make it look like an accident—even suicide? With the strain Andrew had been under, some would believe that. Besides, if she drew attention to herself, the man might shoot her. The few people in the park were near the lights, whereas she'd been beyond when she spotted the men. Would outsiders even see them or come to help? So many moderns refused to get involved with others' problems.

Though she didn't want to panic an armed man, she was panicked now. An attack setting in, making her shaky, letting the drowning darkness in… But she had to go on, go up…

What to do with the shuffleboard stick she had grabbed? She still had Trixie's kitchen knife too, and thrust that into the top of her stocking, where it hurt her thigh with each step. Nothing would do any good against a gun, unless she could get close—surprise the clown. He must have hit Janus over the head with something; maybe she could hit *him* with this long stick. Trixie had said the intruder had jumped her. He had no right to harm innocent people, their friends! He had no right to try to kill a man he did not even know for money—and what if the clown was the same man who had held her captive? Somehow, she was going to stop him.

Do no violence...turn the other cheek... The thoughts danced through her panic. Her people were peaceful, but she was so angry she could brain that clown.

She fought to push back her terror as she thrust the long handle of the shuffleboard stick between her apron and her dress and started to climb. It was awkward with the stick, and the knife cut into her flesh. She shook so hard it seemed the tower was shaking and would topple. Her hands were wet with sweat. But up she went.

As they reached the walkway that circled the tower—the old metal bouncing under their weight—Alex knew he'd need to move fast, definitely before his man knocked him out or shoved him over. If it came to a struggle, would he have a chance? He dared not peer down to see if Ella was still below, because he didn't want to tip the guy off so he'd take a shot at her. But again, he was the one who had the pistol pointed straight at his chest. This time, though, the man kept out of his reach.

He tried to steady himself. The single guardrail was not quite waist-high. He put a hand on it. It seemed as shaky as he felt.

"All right," the clown said, gesturing with the gun from about six feet away. "We're going around the other side of this baby, away from the town."

Hoping someone might have left so much as a screwdriver up here, anything he could use for a surprise weapon, slowly, Alex obeyed, shuffling around the curve of the tower. Again the walkway shuddered under their feet.

"Believe me," his captor said as they walked into complete shadow but for satellite and starlight, "it's gonna be easier on you to cooperate. Here—put this around your neck and keep your distance, or I'll shoot."

Alex easily caught the noose the man tossed him, one connected to a rope he still held, but he did not put it around his neck. "Are your orders not to shoot me unless necessary?" he demanded. "You know, you're pretty good at disguises. I would have sworn there was a redneck in that truck in the Atlanta motel lot when it was an East Coast hit man. Then you adapted to Amish country and now here."

The guy snickered. "Atlanta, yes, Amish, no."

Alex gasped. Why should he believe this bastard? But he did. Why would he deny being the one after him in Amish country when he admitted the Atlanta attack? Someone else must have been responsible in the Home Valley.

"Since I'm going to die, who sent you?" Alex demanded. "Who's behind getting rid of the star witness?"

"I've got others above me. You think they're gonna send it down the line, who's the top guy? But you're right, I'm gonna kill you, and it's gonna be easier on you to have a drop and a broken neck in a noose than take a bunch of bullets. Get that noose on! Do it, and I'll leave the Amish girl alone. Otherwise, I'll get her too, and the old lady. I hear the little blonde came in real useful once before, so here's your chance. Save her and her mother by putting that noose on—now!"

Alex nearly complied. But he was as furious as he

was scared. He'd gotten himself involved but Ella was innocent. And the fact this guy thought *Grossmamm* Ruth was Ella's mother and seemed not to know Ella's name—it must be true that someone in Ohio had passed information on to this guy, but he had not been in the Amish area. Someone else had taken Ella and meant to kill him back there.

And could he believe this man when he said that he'd leave Ella and *Grossmamm* alone? Not if he stumbled on Ella when he climbed down. Alex had heard no police sirens, no shouts from below.

No! His gut told him he had to fight. Stand his ground, however shaky here, and fight!

"Obviously," he told the guy, "you win. I'm tired of running, tired of staying up at night waiting to be found again. I don't think I can trust the feds anyway. Okay," he said, keeping a tight hold of the noose. Praying he could stop it from being tightened, he lifted it around his neck. But when the guy reached into Janus's huge pocket to uncoil the rest of its length, he threw himself at the gunman.

He went in low, hit the guy's shins and ankles hard. The walkway bounced, the guy swore. The gun went off, a single bang! up into the air. Alex scrambled for the gun, punching, kicking. Where was it? Over the edge? The guy was a lot stronger than he'd guessed under that floppy clown suit. Alex was fighting for his life, but at least now they both were.

Ella heard the shot and felt the walkway move. She could see the men now. She had sneaked around the curve of the tower, her hand on the flimsy rail. Should she cry out, hoping to startle the clown? When she'd

reached the top of the ladder, she'd heard their tense
voices but not what they were saying. At least it told
her where they were. Besides, if she cried out, Andrew
could get distracted.

She heard a struggle now, then glimpsed it. The men
were flat on the walkway, throwing punches, grunting.
She could hear fist on flesh. She edged closer, her back
to the tower, still fighting her panic.

She saw they were wedged against the shaky guardrail, but it could break and they could roll right off. The
clown was on top of Andrew, the bulky clown costume
covering most of him. She saw a length of rope, so had
he been trying to tie Andrew up? If she shouted, she
could startle them, but the edge was so near…no room
to spare.

She pulled the shuffleboard stick free from under her
apron. It could reach them without her getting too close.
She had to try, because the clown was dragging Andrew
out from below him, shoving him closer to the edge.

Praying that a hard swing of the stick would not
make her lose her balance, she lifted it and swung it
at the man's head. He'd hit poor Janus with something
like that. What went through her head was not *Do no
violence,* but *Do unto others.*

The stick connected with the clown's head. Ella felt
it in her wrists, heard it. His head slammed into the
metal tower. He grunted, turned his head as Andrew
landed a blow to his chin and shoved him off to scuttle
away like a crab, taking a noose from around his neck.
As Alex got to his knees, the clown staggered to his
feet glaring at her, surprised and dazed. He roared in
anger like a beast, then, even as Andrew tried to grab
him, lunged at Ella.

She had no time to go for the knife. Backing up a few small steps, her back pressed to the curve of the metal tower, she let out a shriek. She tried to lift the stick to swing again, but the clown grabbed it from her and heaved it over the side. Andrew threw himself at the man but the clown tripped over his big shoes, hit his legs backward into the guardrail. With his arms flailing, he tumbled backward like some trick Janus could do from a trapeze—but there was no net below.

Neither was there a sound, even when the man hit the ground below. Nothing but the balmy breeze, Andrew's hard breathing and her sobbing. The walkway and railing bounced so hard from the clown's fall that Ella thought it would spill them both off or just give way. Trembling, kneeling, still unspeaking, they clung together, holding tight. Beyond and above, the night sky was vast and black.

19

Stunned and shaken, Andrew and Ella climbed down the ladder from the tower. Leaning against each other, hidden by one of the tower's big legs, they looked out into the dark field at the crumpled body of the hired killer. Ella shook so hard her teeth chattered, but she'd fought off her panic attack. She'd also fought back against an enemy instead of turning the other cheek but, strangely, she felt no guilt for that—only horror.

She tugged Andrew's arm and cried, "We have to get *Grossmamm* and flee before someone finds him here! Then we'd have to explain—it would get all over. We might be arrested. If Trixie makes a police report, she might give them my name and they'd want to talk to me—to us. Whoever hired that man could send someone else, then—"

"Shh! I know. I know!"

When she tried to pull him away again, he hauled her back, cupped her face with his hands and looked down into her eyes. "Tell me what happened. You went to McCorkles' and found what?"

"First *Grossmamm* got a phone call to come to Mar-

tha in Pennsylvania since she's having surgery. Because
Trixie had a headache—supposedly—I took something
over to her for it. She was tied on the bed, and Janus
was unconscious on the floor with a bloody head. I cut
her loose. She told me about this man—a thief, she
thought—attacking them, and I ran to find you—to
stop him."

He looked around, scanning the area, then back at
her. "We haven't been spotted. There's only one old couple left at the shuffleboard court. I've got to take a minute and check the guy's deep pockets. Maybe I can find
out who he is, who sent him. If he's got money on him,
we need it to run. We'll get *Grossmamm* on a bus for
Pennsylvania, then hide out somewhere far from here."

"She thinks I should go with her."

"But if they found and questioned you without me
there—so far you're just a means to an end to get me,
but now, whoever wants me knows to use you."

"Even if the police arrested me, the Amish won't
testify in court."

"The so-called authorities can be relentless. You'd
never be able to lie to them or stonewall them. Both of
our faces could end up everywhere in the media. Getting any publicity on this would be like putting a big
sign on our rears like Corky the Clown wore, only with
the words, *Come get us and kill us! Do it right this time.*
Ella, I'm so sorry you got in this so deep with me, but
I don't want you out there on your own where I can't
protect you! Wait here."

Her mind reeling at all he'd said, she hunkered down
in the grass under the tower that had almost been Andrew's tall tombstone. The fake clown had first meant
to hang him from it, then when Andrew fought back,

to push him over. Despite being slick with sweat, she shivered. She hadn't exactly committed murder, because the killer had stumbled on the stolen clown shoes, but if she hadn't hit him he would not have gone over, at least not right then.

A new thought came to her: She'd better get that shuffleboard stick. Not that she'd ever been finger-printed, but could that piece of wood hold clues to lead to her? What if someone saw her take that stick and described her?

How had it all come to this? Here she was looking out across a field of dark grass in Florida instead of her own lavender field at home. Her safety had been shat-tered, her Amish promise of no violence torn apart. And she was in love—*ya,* that was it for sure, *in love*—with a worldly, verboten man who had a price on his head, and now she was an accomplice too!

Keeping low, although, blessedly, no one else seemed to be in sight, Ella ran into the area where the shuffle-board stick must have fallen. She found it easily, took it, then made the mistake of glancing over at the clown. He lay sprawled in a grotesque posture, as if he was running. With his neck twisted at a terrible angle, he seemed to glance fearfully behind him.

"People will think it's Janus when they find him," she whispered as Andrew searched the man's pockets. "He is…dead, isn't he?"

"Very."

He stood and came over to her with something in his hands.

"Did you find any identification?"

"No. The guy's a professional killer and careful, but he thought he was clever and he was wrong. I did find a wad of twenty-dollar bills and a car key, and that may actually unlock some of his secrets." He showed them to her. It looked like a lot of money. "Man," he muttered, "I wish Amish clothes had pockets."

"Too worldly and—"

"Never mind." He shoved the key in his right sock and opened the roll of bills to fasten them flat between his suspenders and his bare skin under his torn shirt.

"Let's go," he said. "No running, just a walk around the side of the field and then back to the bungalow, two people out for a late stroll. *Grossmamm* will be worried, to say the least, and Trixie, I hope, has not called nine-one-one, because we'll be questioned about her thief then, especially you will be since you found Trixie and Janus. I hope he isn't seriously hurt, but perhaps she's had to focus on taking care of him right now, not on calling in the cops."

"When we get to the bungalow, maybe we should sneak in the back door, over the fence."

"Only if the cops are around. What's with that?" he said, pointing to the shuffleboard stick.

"It's what I hit him with that knocked his head into the tower. Then he tripped and went over the side. I didn't want to leave it here for evidence."

He nodded, but his eyes widened. She could tell he was surprised that she was thinking of not leaving clues.

"The guy mentioned a TV show called *Criminal Minds*," Andrew told her. "I hate the idea that you— my angel-faced Ella enchanted—are starting to think that way too. Let's lose the stick on the way and head back, but we need to look for his car, probably parked on one of the side streets near our place."

"What about the knife from Trixie's I have stuck in the top of my stocking?"

His eyes widened again and dropped to her hips and thighs. She guessed he was picturing her pulling up her skirts to place a knife against her bare skin. He raked both bruised hands through his mussed hair. "Unless we get a chance to return it, keep it."

They walked hand in hand to the edge of the field, wrapped the shuffleboard stick in Spanish moss and wedged it in the crotch of a huge ficus tree.

"We're both a mess," Ella said when they got back into the glow of streetlights near the park. "You've got a big black eye coming on and some of that clown paint smeared on you."

"And you, my Amish beauty—I know, nothing just for pretty—look like you've been through a tough time you don't deserve." He loosed her hand but put his arm around her shoulder as they walked. "Ella, I've got an idea to throw them off our trail. If we can leave Trixie a note, we'll mention that we're headed to Nassau—you know, in the Bahamas."

"But that's out of the country! We can't—I can't."

"But we're not really going there," he assured her as they stretched their strides, glancing down each side street. "I just think my—our—enemies might believe that, since I used to spend time there with my grandmother. They seem to have traced your grandmother here, so maybe they'd take that bait about mine. But if I can find the killer's car, we're driving north, not south."

"In a stolen car? To Ohio or Pennsylvania?"

"No, but—look! Just talking about it is good luck!" he said, and pointed down a dimly lit street at a lone parked vehicle, a sleek black car with tinted windows.

"That's a Lexus, and that's what the key is for. Wait a sec."

She gasped as he retrieved the key, merely pointed it at the car, touched a button, and the car's lights flickered on like magic. Then he punched the key again and the lights dimmed and went out.

"I'd love to go through the car right now," he admitted, "but we need to get to *Grossmamm* and get on the road. If she hears what happened next door, she might think you've been hurt by that thief too by now."

They hurried home, half-expecting to find a police car sitting in front of their house or McCorkles'. The lights were on in both houses, but they saw no sign of anything unusual.

"A trap?" she whispered.

"We have no choice but to go in. But you're getting as paranoid as me."

"And without even having a panic attack."

"Let's look in the window," he said and, keeping low, went into the small yard. She hurried after him. Inside, they could see *Grossmamm* kneeling in prayer, her elbows on the old sofa, her head down.

They hurried to the back door and knocked. "It's us!" Ella called.

They heard the lock turn, and the old woman opened the door. "I knew the Lord would protect you both," she said with outstretched arms that encompassed them both. She gasped when she saw their bruises and ripped clothing. "Trixie and Janus had a break-in tonight," she said as she shooed them inside. "Ella, she said you ran out to get me or Andrew but you never came back, and I knew something terrible happened."

"How is Janus? Are they home?" Ella asked.

"Still at some walk-in clinic where Trixie took him. Lots of blood, a concussion. I knew it could be those evil people who were after you again, but I told Trixie nothing. And here I was so sure today that nothing bad could ever happen in Pinecraft! Now we have to leave again, *ya?*"

"Both of you get packed right away," Andrew ordered. "Ella, we'll have to change clothes. Yes, we're going to have to run again—this time in a killer's car."

Alex regretted that they dared not leave an explanatory note for Trixie and Janus. He'd changed his mind about involving them in his lie about heading to Nassau. He promised himself that once he lived through the trial and could be himself again—if that were ever possible—he had a lot of explaining to do and repaying of people who had been kind. But before they'd locked the bungalow, he'd left a note on the table that made it look as if he'd called an airline to inquire about flights to Nassau from Miami. And as soon as he'd driven several blocks away, he'd disabled the car's GPS system in case it could track them as well as give directions.

"Any other hints of how Janus was doing?" Andrew called over his shoulder to *Grossmamm,* sitting in the backseat of the car as they left Pinecraft and headed northward on I-75.

"I saw him get in their car with his head wrapped in a towel. Hardheaded circus people, Trixie said."

"Did she say anything about calling the police?"

"No. I got the feeling that circus people trust them about as much as our Plain People do. But she's going to be mighty confused when someone tells her that man who stole Janus's extra clown outfit fell off the tower and is dead."

Alex exchanged a glance with Ella. Neither of them wanted this dear old woman to know all they'd been through tonight, but they had told her that much. She'd been as shocked as they were to realize the reach of Andrew's enemies: he had been tracked to quiet, little Pinecraft, spied on along with the McCorkles. His enemy had gone to great lengths to try to make his death look like suicide.

"It just might be your prayers that got us all through," Alex said. "Now, here's my plan. We're going to head across the state and put you, *Grossmamm* Ruth, on a bus to Pennsylvania to spend time with your daughter. Once you're there, you can contact your family at home, tell them where you are but that they should tell no one else. But I think both you and Ella will be safer if she goes with me."

"I talked to her about that. I suppose you think you can protect her, but can you?"

"She can't just go home or even to Pennsylvania, where a lot of people know who and where she is. I'm afraid there's someone local in the Home Valley hired to kill me. My captor tonight admitted he was the one who tried to gun me down in Atlanta, but he claimed someone else was the one in Ohio. I hate to say it, but I believe him. And since my enemies tracked us to Pinecraft, evidently through the fact you have a place there, *Grossmamm,* both of you could be hurt in Pennsylvania if Ella were there."

Silence from the backseat. Alex heaved a sigh as he turned onto the I-75 ramp and headed north. Finally, Ella said, "*Grossmamm,* we believe no one saw our struggle on the tower, but I hit the man with a shuffle-board stick just before he tripped over the clown shoes that had given him trouble from the first—and fell to his death. So someone might blame me as well as Andrew."

"Pride—and evil—goeth before a fall," *Grossmamm* said. "So you committed violence, just like Andrew—struck back?"

"Yes, and can't regret it because it may have saved us both. He was trying to shove Andrew off, then lunged at me."

"So, Andrew, you left behind in my place a note about flying from Miami to Nassau, but you are really going where?" *Grossmamm* asked.

"Best I don't tell you."

"Andrew Lantz, or whatever your God-given name is, you don't think you can trust me after all this?"

"It's just safer for everyone. For all I know, this car could be full of listening devices—as soon as we stop for gas, I'm going through it with a fine-tooth comb. I just think Ella's safer with me. She's a link to me now and even if they don't try to get rid of her, they could pressure her to tell where I am."

"All right then, I'm going to say my piece. If Ella goes with you without me, any good Amish man will not have her to wife. And she won't ever leave our people. I know our Ella! You, Andrew Lantz, need to get this all straight in your life, then come back to us and turn Amish!"

He almost swerved off the road. He shocked himself by not shouting, *No way!* Instead, he blurted out, "You can do that?"

"Oh, *ya!*" *Grossmamm* insisted, sounding more excited than angry now. "Not common but possible. Takes a year living among the people, join the church, turning your back against the world's ways, but look what the world has done to you."

"It would never work," Alex insisted, more to himself than to them. "I'm too—worldly, as you say."

"The reason I know you can is you were ready to lay down your life for Ella when she was taken at home, give yourself up for her, right?"

"Yes, but—"

"Same thing the Lord did, was willing to lay down his life for others."

Ella couldn't hold back longer. "*Grossmamm,* the point is Andrew does not want to die. I want to go with him. I'd be scared to go out of the house if I was home, afraid to tend my lavender until he can testify against evil men, see them sent to prison, and it's finally all over."

"And then you come home and face your people? I repeat, who will wed you then?"

"Who wants to wed me now? It might be as rare as someone turning Amish, but I would rather remain a *maidal* than marry someone I don't want or maybe marry at all. I'd be happy tending my lavender and building my business."

"*Ach,* I've said enough," *Grossmamm* muttered. "You put me on a bus to Pennsylvania, and I'll pray for both of you to find your way to green pastures and still waters, because it sounds like you been walking through the valley of death."

After that, it got quiet in the car as all of them agonized silently. At least he saw that, as upset as Ella looked, she wasn't going to have a panic attack. But he was considering having one of his own.

20

Alex stopped for gas shortly after they turned east on I-4 toward Orlando. He figured it would be easier and safer to get Ella's grandmother on a bus to Pennsylvania in the land of Disney. After he filled up the hit man's gas tank, paying with the hit man's money, and everyone used the bathroom, he pulled away from the gasoline bay and parked next to the building, where a light was shining. *Grossmamm* got back in the car, but Ella lingered while he opened the trunk.

Inside lay a small suitcase and a long, black leather case.

"Not a musical instrument in there, I bet," she said, pointing at the case. "Do you think it's a rifle?"

"Probably a high-tech version of one." Using his shirttail to avoid touching the handle and latches, he snapped the case open. Disassembled, each piece in its perfectly shaped section, lay an assault rifle with a long-distance scope. Two pistols were also snug in their foam pockets.

"All we'd need is to be stopped by police with no driver's license and this in the trunk," he said. "I'm going to deposit it in that Dumpster beside the station. I just wish I could have found his cell phone somewhere, so I could check who he's been talking to. He either hid it or it came out of his pocket when he fell. Or if it's in that suitcase, it's great evidence."

"Are you sure this gun doesn't have his name on it?"

"Look, Ella," he said, pointing at something she couldn't really see. "Even the ID numbers and brand name are filed off. No, a professional killer is not going to put his name on his gun."

"Oh, *ya*. Just trying to help."

"You do help. If there's anything personal of his, it's in his suitcase, but we're not going through it now. I want to keep moving, put a lot of distance between us and Pinecraft before dawn. It's nearly three in the morning."

Again using his shirt to avoid leaving prints, he snapped the gun case closed, hefted it, looked around to be sure no one was watching and carried it to the Dumpster she could see in the shadows of the gas station. The case made a thud as he dropped it in. When he got back to the car, Ella pointed at two extra sets of license plates from different states, shoved behind where the gun case had been.

"Those we can use," he said. "When we head north, we'll change the plates—if you're still going with me. She's probably right that you shouldn't," he said with a nod toward the car.

"I'm going, but *where* are we going? Will you tell me, at least?"

"I've decided the best hideout is the place my enemy probably had watched after I first disappeared, a place they think I'd never dare come back to. But I've thought of a way to survive there and be close to help if we get completely desperate. I've seen your world and now you'll see mine. Don't tell *Grossmamm,* but I'm going to take you to see New York City. Let's get going."

He slammed the trunk closed. His stalwart Amish girl nodded, but she looked as scared as she had when she'd been hit by her first big breaker in the Gulf of Mexico.

Ray-Lynn shot wide-awake and rolled over in bed. Ding-dang, that's right! Jack had stayed this time! She came instantly alert. Her too-bright, glowing-red digital clock read 3:00 a.m. She was so excited about their engagement she hadn't slept much, but then, neither had Jack. He'd been tossing and turning and hogging the covers, though she'd gladly put up with that to have him near.

"You awake?" she whispered.

"Yep," he replied, and reached out to pull her back against him so it was almost as if she sat in his lap.

"Regrets?"

"Not about us."

"About what then?"

"Just a feeling that I don't have my finger on the pulse of this place like I used to—the town, Home Valley, Eden County. I mean, with the Amish, you never quite know all they're thinking, but this is different."

"So what's different now—other than Eben Lantz probably didn't tell the truth about flu in his family? I think you're handling things well."

"I told Linc Armstrong not to get near Hannah again, but you heard he hassled Ella about her. Then earlier today, someone told me they saw him in the vicinity the day of her wedding. Yesterday, Connie Lee, whose family's building that big new spa, practically accosted me, all upset she wasn't allowed to see Ella. Ms. Lee wanted to take her and anyone else in the family who was ill to the Cleveland Clinic, so she'd get better and agree to some damn deal about buying lavender. It was like stopping a tornado to get the woman to back off!"

"Anything else?"

"Actually, yeah. My new deputy has not only become my eyes and ears around here, which I wanted, but in this short time he's made me feel he knows it all and I don't."

"He's just overeager, Jack, a real go-getter. I'll bet you were like that when you started out. I, for one, am glad you have Win Hayes so you have more time for me."

"There is that. Then to top all that off, I swear Andrew Lantz must be on the run again."

"The run *again?* I knew there was something strange about him!" she said, shifting in his embrace. "And you think he has Ella with him? But surely not the Lantz grandmother. What did he do? He's on the lam from the law, and you regret he slipped away?"

"Not exactly. I just blurted out too much of my laundry list of grievances. Honey, I know we're sharing things now, but I still can't explain except to say Lantz is not a criminal."

"Don't tell me he and Ella eloped? Not straitlaced Ella. They haven't known each other very long, and she never got over Sarah leaving for the world with Nate."

"I swear, you ought to write fiction, Ray-Lynn," he said gruffly, giving her ribs a squeeze. "None of that's true, far as I know. You've got an overactive imagination. You and that *Gone with the Wind* hobby of yours...."

"Just say it. I'm obsessed, a fanatic—obsessed with you too."

He squeezed her even tighter and ducked his head to press a kiss on her bare shoulder. "Glad for that at least."

"So what about my idea that we could dress kind of Civil War style for our wedding? Just rented things, of course, or maybe I could get one of the Amish quilters to make our outfits, though it would be a lot harder than sewing theirs. Could you get through the short service and reception at the restaurant dressed like a Southern gentleman?"

"If your stick-out skirt doesn't make me bounce away from you when I kiss the bride. And me as a gentleman? 'Let's think about that tomorrow,' said not Scarlett but Sheriff Jack."

She laughed, then sobered. "But I didn't mean to turn trivial when something's bothering you," she told him. "I'm glad it wasn't the fear of a fancy wedding costume keeping you awake when you've been so tired."

"I just don't feel hands-on enough with Win Hayes around, turning heads one way or the other." He sighed. "But I've wanted help here ever since the arsons and the graveyard shooting, so I'd better just shut up. Besides, I always feel hands-on with you, honey."

He slid his free hand down over her waist to her bare hip. He turned and tipped her so she lay under him. She saw, as she reached up to put her arms around his neck, her new diamond engagement ring glint a fierce red in the reflected light of the clock.

* * *

"It was hard saying goodbye to her," Ella said, wiping under her eyes with her fingers as they pulled away in the car from the bus station in Orlando. The Greyhound heading north to Harrisburg where *Grossmamm* would make a connection to Union County, Pennsylvania, had just left Orlando in a rush of noise and fumes.

Suddenly, Ella felt bereft and exhausted—and nervous on top of everything about being really alone with Andrew. It was nearly dawn, and the sky ahead of them glowed pink. She stretched her sore, weary body and leaned back in the comfy seat. Would he stop the car somewhere so they could sleep? It was roomy enough and the seats tipped back.

"She's been good to me, too, so I feel the same," he said after a pause, despite the fact she'd nearly forgotten what she'd just said. "Your entire family was kind, but Ruth Raber is special. Of course, she has an ulterior motive. It seems she's hoping to turn me Amish and into an honest man—marrying Amish."

"It's such a crazy idea. Impossible."

"What's that your *daad* told me? *With God all things are possible.*"

"True! After all, I've only known you for ten days and look at all that's happened. And now New York! But in these clothes?"

"You're one step ahead of me. As soon as I spot a Walmart or other all-night superstore, we're going to go modern, thanks to this money from our favorite hit man—or one of them."

"I'll be okay if I don't have to wear slacks and can get a conservative skirt. But I hate the idea of thinking, after we're rid of one killer, there's another one still out there. Did you actually believe the killer clown that he wasn't the one in Amish country—believe a man like that?"

"He had no reason to lie at that point. He thought I was going to die. He knew no details of the Home Valley, including your name. He copped to—that is, admitted—he tried to take me out—kill me...."

"You don't have to translate everything for me!"

"Right. Sorry. We're both exhausted and on edge. Go ahead and get some sleep until I find a store."

"But you're tired too, and you have to drive."

"I love to drive, even illegally in a borrowed vehicle without a license. It feels so good again," he said, flexing his hands on the steering wheel, "to control something. I've driven all night before. I'll get some coffee and be fine."

"I'm sure you've missed your car and your real life."

"Yes, but sometimes I'm not sure what is real life anymore. The Home Valley seemed real—authentic. It's like, for the first time in my life, I had time to smell the roses, or in this case, the lavender. Miss it?"

"I do. I can smell it now, see it in my mind and heart. But people are more important."

He reached over the armrest that separated the front seats and put his hand on hers. "I agree. Other people are key—not just the big I."

"Aren't you going to tell me that's spelled capital I and not *e-y-e?*"

"I like a woman with spirit. But, back to the clothes for a minute, you're going to stick out in New York if you look too conservative, at least in SoHo. And we'll have to hide or cut your long hair—"

"We don't cut our hair. It's important. It would dishonor us, and a woman's hair is only taken down for her husband at night when they go to bed—sleep."

"All right. But I'm hoping you'll be able to go out during the day to shop for us. I might be recognized but—unless you draw attention to yourself—I'm betting you'll get by."

She heaved a huge sigh. "I have learned in whatever state I am to be content," she said, not bothering to tell him that was said by a man in the Bible with the authorities after him too. Someone always wanted to get rid of the apostle Paul, and he was often on the run. But finally, he was caught and killed.

"Then I hope—and pray," he said, and squeezed her hand, "you will learn to be content in the state of New York." It was a feeble joke, but she smiled as she leaned back in her seat, then sat up. He was taking a brightly lighted exit ramp toward a huge Walmart guarded by a cluster of fast-food stores.

Well, she told herself, she would have to go along with new clothes and New York. She could face anything that might come her way except for another person trying to kill them. But she wished she hadn't fallen in love with a man who, despite *Grossmamm*'s bold ideas, she could probably have but never keep.

"Are you going to come out of there?" Andrew yelled into the hall of women's dressing rooms. At least no other customers were in here at this hour of the morning. "We have to get going!" he added, not in a quiet voice.

"Just a minute more!"

Ella looked at herself again in the mirror, a full-length one when her family usually kept their small one turned to the wall. It had even taken her a while to pick out things to try on because she had no idea of her sizes. Why would she, when her garments had always been hand-made and fitted just for her?

She pivoted again, twisting around to glance at the reflection of her backside in the mirror. This was the second pair of slacks she'd decided on, but, despite the fact they covered her waist to ankle, she felt undressed. She'd also picked out what was called a business suit, so she'd fit in, as Andrew put it. She wasn't sure she wanted to look like the moderns of SoHo, the neighborhood where he had some sort of apartment called a co-op.

But these slacks—just like men's pants, truth be told. They seemed to show off the curves of her legs and bottom, at least compared to what she was used to. She felt naked enough without her bonnet, prayer *kapp* and apron, but now this!

She threw the sweatshirt-type jacket over her T-shirt top and bra—she'd never had a bra on either—gathered up the other clothes and went out to meet Andrew. He stood there with a cart holding his new clothes, except for those he had on. As far as she could tell, he had nothing dressy like her navy suit and white blouse, but he said he'd left business suits at home. He wore jeans, a T-shirt with a big check mark on it that matched the ones on his running shoes. At least these weren't all scuffed up from a fight. She'd bought a pair of those too, her easiest purchase. She was pretty sure she'd never be able to walk far in her navy high heels, even though they were the lowest ones she could find. Worldly women were crazy to walk around in those tipsy things!

She also noticed Andrew had two big backpacks, four flashlights and a box of candles.

"You look great," he said. "Did you get something to pull your hair back in a ponytail or braid?"

"*Ya*—yes, that was the easy part. Why all the lights?"

"We won't be able to turn on the electricity at night at my place," he said. "Put your stuff in here, and we're on our way. I even got some makeup to cover my black eye."

"Won't they be upset we're already wearing one set of the clothes?" she asked as she added her things to his.

"I cleared it with the floor manager. Did you keep all the tags together so they can ring the stuff up?"

"Just like you said. All we need is to get arrested for shoplifting."

"Ella, I took care of it. I asked at the information desk near where we're going to check out. She got the manager and I told her our stuff was stolen, but I have a feeling she thinks we're a couple of hayseeds eloping."

"Hayseeds? Is that what the *Englische* really think of the Amish? And we're telling so many lies," she muttered, following him and the cart toward the front of the huge store. "Pretty soon we won't have any conscience left at all."

"I used to wonder how my boss managed that, the years of lies and cover-ups. But I like the idea the manager thought we might be running off together to elope instead of just hide out."

"You're starting to sound like *Grossmamm,*" she said, keeping close to him, though there were few folks in the store aisles now. She knew she was getting cranky, but she couldn't help it. Besides being exhausted and upset to be so dependent on him, she didn't like his attitude. But then, what did she expect? That he'd tell the store manager they were running from killers and had just avoided getting thrown off a tower?

She decided to change the subject. "I was thinking there might be something in the fake clown's suitcase you could wear or use," she told him.

He pushed the cart up to the only open checkout aisle. Ignoring her, but with a smile at the middle-aged, plump cashier, he said, "Lindsey over at the information desk got the manager and she told me it would be okay to wear some of the clothes out of the store. She said just give you the price tags, so if you need to ask her about th—"

"Oh, Lindsey and the manager already told me and described you," the woman said with a blush rising right through the rouge on her cheeks. "She said to take good care of the handsome man who got a black eye when he and his girlfriend got mugged and their suitcases taken."

The woman didn't so much as look at Ella, which was just as well, she thought, because she was rolling her eyes at Andrew, who was evidently starting to act like Alex. Clever and in control now, that was him. In his element, even though they were running for their lives. And smooth with the ladies. That made her wonder if he had someone back in SoHo in New York.

Had she been crazy to come along? No, she knew this man, didn't she? He'd been an *Auslander* in her world as she now was in his. Surely, Alex Caldwell could not be completely different from her thoughtful, caring Andrew Lantz.

Outside, as they carried their packages to the car, the sun looked balanced on the edge of the horizon like a big, red ball. "I saw a sign that there's a rest stop about twenty miles ahead," he told her as he unloaded their cart and handed her the things to put in the trunk he'd opened without even touching it. In the mingling of harsh parking lot lights and pale daylight, he pulled the hit man's suitcase over to the edge of the trunk.

"I was going to wait until it was really light for this, but I'm too curious," he told her, snapping it open. "No cell phone here either! Just clothes, clean T-shirts, a shaver. I wouldn't want to wear anything of his, so I'll forget you said that. And—more money! I guess they paid him up front for taking me out."

She stared at the packet of fifty-dollar bills Andrew was fanning through. "Maybe," she said, "he had double money because, after what happened to me in the Home Valley, he was paid to get rid of you first—then me too."

She peered down into the depths of the suitcase. There was something else still inside, something square and black.

"Look," she said, pointing, "a billfold. Even more money?"

"Here," he said, "hold this," and thrust the packet of bills into her hands.

He reached in and pulled the billfold out, one that appeared to be black alligator skin. Andrew flipped it open and, through a little plastic window inside, they stared down into the frowning face of Michael F. Moreland, of Atlanta, Georgia, born 04/06/65, the man who had tried to kill them, no doubt, for the money she now held.

Andrew said, "I'm going to email this info to Gerald Branin from a library somewhere he can't trace me. Either he'll use it to find who hired Mr. Moreland, or—if he's the one who's given me up—he'll realize I'm on to him and back off."

"Or get even more desperate to keep you quiet. Anything else in there—like a contact's phone number or name?"

"Not that I can see. Not even a credit card, insurance card, nothing. Have gun, will travel light. Divide that money up, and we'll put it in our pockets. You see, sweetheart, pockets come in handy, and I do like you in those jeans."

Pockets? Jeans? Sweetheart! As he opened the car door for her and she climbed in, she guessed it was official now. Like it or not, on the run or not, in love with Alex Caldwell or not, she had officially jumped the fence to the world. Could she ever find her way back home?

21

It was the first time she'd ever slept with a man—
that is, slept next to one. By the time they'd driven off
the highway to follow Route A1A through St. Augustine, even Andrew was starting to fade. He'd pulled off
the highway and followed the signs to Crescent Beach,
where they actually drove on the wide stretch of sand,
though he had to steer around a chained barrier. Hopefully no one would see or find them here. They parked
by some dunes where they could hear the steady sound
of Atlantic Ocean waves even through the rolled-up
windows.

Despite the fact that Andrew dozed instantly, Ella
was so wound up it took her a while to fall sleep…to fall
for Andrew…to fall from the water tower, but she didn't
hit the ground…kept rolling down the long, grassy hill
toward her lavender…

That rhythmic roar in her ears…her blood pounding? Was that the sound of the waves as she rode them
up and down with Andrew? Oh, no, it couldn't be the
panic pounding in her head, surrounding her with dark
water in the pond at home! *Help me, I'm drowning…*

She tried to swim, to keep her head up, to breathe. A scarecrow nailed to a lavender cross floated by in the flood, then a clown, a horrible clown with a big gun. Someone tried to put a mask on her face, tie her up so she couldn't swim. As tired as she was, she had to wake up, stop the drowning fears...*ya,* the man with the gun! He was going to shoot her!

Bang! Bang-bang!

With a gasp, Ella jolted wide-awake. Daylight, not darkness. Oh, she was in the car with Andrew! A white, green and gold car marked St. Augustine Beach Police sat nearby. And an officer was knocking on the driver's side window. Or was he really a policeman? If that killer could dress up like a clown, then who knew...

Andrew turned the key in the ignition and rolled the window down. "Yes, Officer?"

"You two all right?"

"Just driving north and didn't want to fall asleep at the wheel," Andrew said. "Is there a problem with parking here for a few hours of sleep?"

"Sign back there about restrictions, and you drove around a chained barrier that was there for a reason. Where're you from?"

"Atlanta, Georgia. I'm Mike Moreland, and this is my wife, Ellen."

That's right, Ella thought. Georgia license plates were on the car, but if the officer looked in the trunk, he'd find the other ones. Andrew had thought fast to call himself by the hit man's name because that was the only driver's license they had. But Andrew looked nothing like that killer. And he'd said, *My wife, Ellen.*

"How you doing, ma'am?" the clean-cut policeman

said and touched a finger to the bill of his hat. "You two don't like to take turns driving, huh?"

"Oh, he's much better than I am at that," Ella blurted. At least that wasn't a lie. She used to worry that Andrew didn't sound Amish enough, but now she had to worry about her own talk. She knew full well that her people, however good their grammar, had a particular cadence to their speech.

"You'll need to move on," the policeman told them. "I can lead you to a nearby motel or a store parking lot."

"I'm wide-awake now," Andrew told him. "Sorry about missing that sign, Officer. We'll be leaving town now. Thanks again."

He started the car. The officer followed them out. As they left the park, Ella glimpsed a wide strip of sand and whitecaps rolling in. She had to admit that some worldly lies had saved them again. And the biggest one was that she was his wife.

"Don't you think we should leave town since you told that officer we would?" Ella asked as Andrew pulled the car into the drive-through lane of a McDonald's and ordered Egg McMuffins and coffee for them. They were in a line of cars, since it was breakfast time. It was the first time she'd noticed he had stubble on his usually close-shaved face. Young Amish men looked like that when they first started to grow their beards. With or without facial hair, Andrew had a fine face, even if he looked tired and tense right now.

"I want to send that email to Branin from the library here before we head north again, and I'm starving," he explained, jolting her back to what she'd just asked.

"In Wooster, I think you have to have a library card

to use a library computer. And are you sure, just in case Mr. Branin's the one who has turned against you, that he won't be able to trace where you sent the message from?"

"That's my sharp-minded partner in crime! No, emails with phony addresses are untraceable if sent from libraries or internet cafés, especially if you don't use your credit card. It's called spoofing. And if he could trace it, he'd only know we were here and not that we're heading out. When we get our food, I'll ask where the library is. We're on a roll since that cop didn't ask to see my driver's license. Even frowning, I don't resemble Mike Moreland. We've been fortunate on the road so far."

"Not fortunate, blessed," she corrected him.

"Okay," he said, turning to look at her with the hint of a beguiling smile. "Blessed."

Midmorning, as soon as it opened, they went into the library just off Ponce De Leon Boulevard. Of all things, it sat right next to a merry-go-round. At least Andrew hadn't left her in the car, she thought, but he asked her to sit over in the corner while he headed for the library laptops. She could see him across the room, chatting and smiling with several people who were waiting in line to use them. Why didn't he try to keep what he'd called a low profile? Actually, he seemed to be concentrating on one woman, a blonde with a big laugh. Ella told herself she shouldn't be surprised that the woman gave Andrew her library card and let him step ahead of her to take her place.

In less than ten minutes he was back to Ella. "Let's use the restrooms and head out," he said. "Mission accomplished."

KAREN HARPER

She hurried after him, then slowed her steps. Alex Caldwell, alias Andrew Lantz, was sure good with women, even ones he didn't know, oh, *ya,* he was. So had she fallen for a man who was real skilled at his own disguises? Was she just another willing woman who was more than happy to go along with his wishes?

Ella banged the door shut to her restroom stall. Her only choice was to trust him now. But she was going to have to keep up her guard, not only in case another hit man found them, but because, in a way, the former Amish Andrew was a hit man of another kind.

The next day was a blur. Cars, trucks and highway I-95 seemed to roll endlessly past and toward them. Rest stops, fast-food places, gas stations, back in the car. She dozed sporadically, but Andrew seemed ever vigilant, uptight on coffee and whatever he was thinking.

"So how long will it take us to drive to your neighborhood in New York City?" she asked.

"We'll leave this car in Washington, D.C., with no plates on it or in it. We'll put everything we need in our backpacks and take Amtrak—that's a train—from Union Station into New York's Penn Station, about a three-hour trip. Then from there, a subway to SoHo. And we won't be going in my front door."

Her head spinning at all the places he mentioned— the capital of the country?—she said only, "I can imagine. But can you be sure your back door isn't watched too?"

"We won't use a back door either, not exactly."

He said no more about that. Was he keeping back something that would upset or scare her? At least he had it all planned out. But she felt even more distanced from him to realize that he knew all about these huge cities, so far in miles and mood from the places she knew and loved.

It took them almost a half hour of cruising to find a rare curbside parking space in Washington. They emptied out her small suitcase that had once been her grandfather's and put all their belongings into their two backpacks. She was in awe of what she'd seen in the short time they'd driven into and around Washington: massive white marble buildings, wide avenues, huge open areas with monuments to long-dead leaders, lots of drivers, tourist buses and walkers. And a glimpse of Capitol Hill not far from here, swarming with people even at this midafternoon hour.

"I know it's warm," he said, "but you'd better pull your hood up on that jacket to hide your long hair. No, wait—I have an extra baseball cap. Let's just stuff it up under this."

She had no idea who the Florida Gators were, but, with his help, she got her long, heavy braid up under the cap. How strange to wear something with a bill, but it did help shade her face just like the bonnet she was missing. To her amazement he whipped out a pair of sunglasses for her too.

"Got these at Walmart. I figured you'd refuse to wear them in the car, but we're going to be around a lot of people and, when my name went public about a big trial, there were photos of me in the papers. Both of us need to hide our faces somewhat and blend in."

She put them on, and this world went even darker. At least she agreed that the sunglasses, hat and backpack hid her a bit. She watched him as he removed both license plates with a screwdriver he'd found in the car, then threw all three sets of plates in a trash can. He wiped the interior of the car down with wet rags he'd picked up at a gas station to obscure fingerprints.

"You left the car unlocked," she said as they started to walk away.

"With the key on the dashboard. I'm betting someone steals it. If the cops find it first, I don't need them dusting it and IDing Moreland's or my fingerprints—and two pairs of mystery prints. You and *Grossmamm* were never fingerprinted, were you?"

"Not that I know of. We never trusted the government, and here you're just learning that." He only muttered something she—blessedly—couldn't catch.

Ella was amazed at the train and bus station with its people, noise and too many shops to count under a sky-high, curved ceiling. Union Station seemed more like a shopping mall where escalators connected three floors of stores with pretty, potted plants all over. That greenery was the only thing that reminded her of home. They bought sandwiches, root beers and their tickets to New York.

As Andrew had said, the Amtrak Metroliner they took north was a train, but a fancy one. The city, the river, then some rural scenes zipped past outside her window. She wanted to take it all in but a constant hum and the movement lulled her to sleep. She woke with her head on his shoulder and another train, a twin to this one, whooshing past in the other direction so fast it made her dizzy.

Another huge city, packed tighter and higher than Washington, appeared outside their window. It grew even thicker and bigger: bridges, tall buildings close together, streets clogged with cars, trucks and taxis.

Her stomach cramped. She did not know the distance in miles, but she was so far from home.

They put their backpacks on again, and she followed Andrew off the train and out through a turnstile into the flow of people. Down they went on escalators into the depths of the city. She soon saw that people who were in an extra hurry ran up or down the moving stairs. Others evidently expected it, because they moved way over to the right and let them charge past on the left. She had to be careful not to turn and slam the runners with her backpack.

Andrew bought subway tickets. They waited as a different kind of train without an engine whooshed in and out of the lighted area with sunken tracks. Looking down them, she could see an entrance to a dark tunnel. Amid a crowd of people, even with Andrew so close—he looked more excited than nervous now—she felt alone.

The second train that came roaring out of the tunnel was theirs. Amid the push of people, they got on but couldn't find seats. They had to hold on to a pole as the train plunged into the dark throat of the tunnel. At least the lights stayed on in here. When they went around a curve, Andrew put one hand on the back of her waist to steady her and she leaned gratefully against him. Another lighted station, then another flew by. They stopped at some, not others. The rhythmic clatter of the train was endless. She lost count until he said, "This is us."

Ella knew what he meant, but that was a scary thought: *This is us.* She tried not to judge too hastily, but so far, this was not her, nor could it ever be.

* * *

"This is not my usual subway stop," Andrew whispered as they got off the train and climbed stairs out of the station. "Too many people might recognize me there. We'll have to do some extra walking. Ella, I knew you'd have culture shock here and I'm sorry for that. I'm sure it's much harder to go from the peace of the Home Valley to this hectic pace than the direction I went."

"*Ya*—I mean yes. Thanks. I'll be all right."

When they emerged from the subway station, it was getting dark, which must mean it was around eight. "Okay," Andrew said, "we're going to need some food to take home with us until we can get a few groceries in, though I guess I left some canned and frozen stuff. I'm going to send you into that sandwich shop over there— see the sign Café Habana? I've been in there too many times to go waltzing in now. Take this thirty dollars— don't dig the stack of money out of your pockets anywhere around here—and get us a couple of roasted pork sandwiches and something to drink. Maybe a side of slaw or salad. I'll be right here. Here, let me hold your backpack. You'll have to stand in a line."

"They eat this late? Okay, like I overheard someone say here, no problem."

Again, feeling she was sleepwalking, Ella carefully crossed the street to the restaurant and got in the carryout line. The place was busy; it took a while to wait her turn. It smelled great in here. Her stomach rumbled so loud she hoped others didn't think it was thundering outside. She placed her order, paid what they asked, took the food and the change and went back outside.

Strange, but she felt a little thrill in her stomach to see Andrew—Alex—waiting for her. He helped her into her backpack and carried the sack of food as they walked down a street named—why, it was called Wooster, the same name as the city closest to Homestead!

And it was probably good too he'd brought them here, because again she noted that New Yorkers on the sidewalks didn't really look at or greet others like at home. They just kind of passed them by. She tried to copy that *I'm busy* inward look, but she still couldn't help studying others. Some folks looked happy, some sad. Most seemed in a huge hurry, maybe to get home after a day's work. It was pretty obvious that some were outsiders, probably tourists, as they gawked and slowed down to look around.

They walked several blocks, around corners. Hoping to see more familiar street names, she studied them at first then just gave up. As darkness deepened, lights popped on in busy stores and restaurants. There were fancy lampposts lit, ones shaped like a shepherd's crook. The cobblestones underfoot were charming too, so at least there were some things to like here. As for the buildings, many were amazingly ornate. Painted metal pillars and arches repeated over and over as they surrounded rows of windows. The buildings looked heavy enough to just plain fall down on them.

"My address is actually Wooster Street," Andrew said, "but we're going in a back way."

"That's a good sign, Wooster, I mean. I've been in Wooster, Ohio, plenty of times. It's a big city for Amish country, but nothing like this."

"It will be good to get away from people and have some peace and quiet—some sleep—so I can make some plans. Okay, we turn here on Broome, then down to Greene."

Now she noted he looked around more, even up at windows as they walked down a street that had fewer shops and restaurants but more buildings where people lived. "In here," he said. He led her down a dark passageway so narrow their backpacks scraped if they didn't walk straight. They emerged from between two buildings into a dimly lighted area with Dumpsters. They were between two blocks of buildings, each one with stories of metal fire escape ladders attached to their rears.

"Is there a back way into your place from here?" she asked.

"Not one the super—that's the superintendent of the building—doesn't control. We have to go up and over. I'd like to dig out a flashlight, but we don't need to draw attention to ourselves. I think there's enough reflected light here."

"And up on top, maybe we'll have the moon and stars—even your satellites—to see by."

"Don't know what I'd do without your spirit, Ella," he said, and pecked a kiss on her cheek that she felt clear down to the depths of her being. And here, she'd been trying to emotionally distance herself from him!

They went along the buildings until he found the fire escape he must estimate was on his building. "Give me your backpack," he said. "There's a narrow metal guard up above we'll have to climb through, and you don't need to be hauling the extra weight." He bent to put their sack of food in the outer section of his own pack. He strapped hers to his so both of them dangled from the back of his belt.

"I'll go up first," he told her. "You stay at least one flight of stairs below me in case one of these drops. You're not afraid of heights, are you?"

"I used to climb trees and was up on the roof of our house once to retrieve a baseball from the eaves. In other words, who knows?"

Her last words before they began to climb stayed with her and seemed to echo off the metal rungs and stairs: *Who knows?* She didn't know who was after Andrew-Alex, maybe after her too. She didn't know how long she could stand to be in this scary, foreign place, before she went screaming mad to go home. And she didn't know if trusting this man with her life was going to make or break her future. But she did know one thing and that was—risk and all, culture shock and all, as he'd put it—she was blessed to be with him to help.

22

They climbed five stories of the fire escape. Strange, but she thought of Janus and Trixie, climbing that circus ladder, then diving into the net. She prayed their Florida friends were all right. Andrew had said that after this was all over, he would contact them, explain and try to make amends.

From the flat roof, the highest Ella had ever been off the ground, other rooftops and lit buildings stretched as far as she could see. "Too bright in the city to pick out the stars," she said. "I wish we were on my lavender hill at home."

She followed him across the roof, one that butted up to other buildings on each side. Well, not quite butted. She saw a gap of about four feet between them.

"I was afraid of that," he said. "My building's the next one. I miscalculated, but I've never gone in this way before, only figured it would work. We'll have to jump, so I'm glad you're in pants."

"I was hoping we were going into your apartment from a fire escape through a window." She didn't budge as he threw the backpacks onto the next roof.

"We'll go down from the roof and in my door, even though a fire escape like the one we just climbed goes past one of my windows. I have the loft—top floor of an old artist's studio that's been redone. I know the roof entry because some of us used to sunbathe up there. After I got locked out on the roof once, I put an extra key in a magnetic box under the air conditioner. We'll just go down one flight of stairs and then in my door— that key's hidden too, if it's still there."

"*If* it's there?" she muttered. "Way too many *if*s."

The four feet of open air between buildings suddenly looked four miles wide to her.

"I'll go first," he told her. "Don't look down. We'll need to take a running start. At least there's enough light up here to see. The flashlights are for when we get inside."

He gave her shoulders a quick hug, went a few steps back and easily sailed over the space onto his own roof. How had it come to this? Ella thought, as she moved back a ways. Looking only at Andrew on the other side, she leaped over to him.

"That's my girl!"

"So much for me wearing that tight-skirted suit you had me buy, if I have to go in and out this way," she told him as they retrieved their packs and walked toward four lounge chairs set up around a table with empty glasses and two beer bottles on it.

"This is a great place to watch Fourth of July fire-works too," he said. "Hard to believe that's only three days away. I'll really celebrate an independence day when this is all over." He knelt and stuck his arm under what must be a huge air-conditioning unit that made a whirring sound.

"Bingo!" he said, and pulled out a tiny metal box. When he came closer, she saw he had two keys. Looking exuberant, he said, "I prayed they'd still be here, if you want the truth."

"I always want the truth."

"Ella, I've staked my life on revealing the corruption I found—the truth at any cost. I'm sorry I got you involved, but I felt so alone until I met you. I know it's been a dangerous ride so far, and I've got to reach out for help to someone else. I think—I hope—I can trust my lawyers. But let's go inside. I've got to figure out my next move, but we need food and sleep first. I'm like a zombie—the walking dead."

"You were doing fine until you had to define zombie for the naive Amish girl," she groused as she waited while he unlocked the roof door. He held it open as she stepped in, shut it quietly behind them—it clicked closed. Feeling their way along, they descended one short flight of stairs to a dark hall.

She heard him fumbling in his backpack. He turned on a flashlight and shot the beam toward a wooden door at the end of the short hall. She saw there was also a flight of stairs down from where they stood.

"Stay here a minute until I check inside," he whispered. "It might be booby-trapped, like to set off an alarm if the door is opened."

"Why didn't you think of that before?"

"I did, but I'm betting on the fact they don't think I'd dare to come back to my lair even if I am a hunted animal. That's the witness protection program's top rule—don't go home and don't contact those you knew."

"Oh, great. Thanks for telling me that now."

"Just wait here. I'll be right back. We'll have to walk

and move quietly up here, since people live in the co-op right below."

He left her in the dark and tiptoed down the hall to shine the flashlight beam all around his door frame. She watched him run his fingers around the edges and under the door.

He unlocked the door and went in. Standing there in a strange place, waiting for someone who'd called himself a walking dead man, made her insides twist with terror. Oh, *ya,* once again he'd left her in the dark all right.

Inside, Alex heaved his backpack in a chair and swept the light around the big room. At least the vertical blinds were down the way he'd left them, so no one would see a flashlight beam moving inside his big, high-ceilinged loft. He had no intention of turning a light on after dark, though with the heat, he'd chance turning on the air conditioner. All the co-ops in the building used the same big one on the roof. But he wasn't going to risk electric lights.

He hurried to check out the other rooms. They seemed strangely overlarge, even unfamiliar to him now. The open kitchen area, the hall, both bedrooms and their bathrooms. Like an idiot he even looked behind doors and in the closets, then rushed out into the hall to get Ella. His beam illumined two tear tracks on her cheeks.

"Sorry that took a while, but I needed to be sure. When I first turned my boss in to the feds, my lawyers hired a tech guy to sweep the place for bugs—that's listening devices—so I think we're safe." He took her backpack from her arms. "Let's go inside."

Though she wore thick-soled running shoes, he saw she tiptoed. He locked the door after them and dug out a flashlight for her.

"Are you sure we can run water and flush the toilet without being heard?" she asked, something he hadn't even considered. He thought a minute as she dug their beat-up sack of food from his backpack and carried it toward the open kitchen.

"I think, in the lower apartments, you can hear water running, but you can't tell which place it's from," he assured her, going to the sink to wash his hands just after she did. "People will assume it's any of the six places above. Water and the air conditioner, we'll use, but not the electric lights. This loft is the largest apartment in the building."

"Good for entertaining a lot of people, I guess," she said as he clicked on the cool air.

"I'm sorry we can't open the blinds so you can see the view."

He opened the fridge and found cans of soda, a bottle of wine and a couple of beers. It seemed ages ago he'd left in such a rush. His lawyers had been paying his bills from his checking account. They were his best bet for a contact here, but they'd pushed hard for him to trust WITSEC and he didn't need the firm contacting Gerald Branin. Still, maybe his lawyers could find another place for them to stay in the city. He was determined not to leave New York until the trial—but maybe not stay long here. And could he keep Ella with him? Would she be safer back in the Home Valley, if he wasn't with her? Should he send her home?

"Can we heat these in the oven?" she asked as she dug out their cold sandwiches.

"The microwave, except it beeps when it's done. Let's just eat them cold tonight and have hot food tomorrow. We can bring things in from a grocery a couple of blocks away and heat things on the stove or in the oven."

"I can bring things in, you mean," she said. "That's why I'm really still with you, right?"

He plunked two cans of soda on the dusty marble countertop and shoved the refrigerator door shut with his knee. He reached for her, pulled her into his arms.

"You're still with me because I was afraid they'd come after you too since you escaped in Ohio and helped me get rid of their man in Pinecraft. You're still with me because I want you to help me survive, yes, so I can get this over with and take you home. And you're still with me—I hope—because maybe you need me just a little bit as much as I need you."

Ella jerked awake, not sure where she was. Oh, right—Andrew's co-op in New York, a neighborhood called SoHo. After they'd eaten and taken showers, they'd fallen asleep talking on the huge, soft, beige leather U-shaped couch. She had only stretched out for a moment, and he had done the same, sprawled head-to-head with their feet in opposite directions. On his back, Andrew still slept, breathing heavily.

Should she get up to go sleep in the guest bedroom he'd showed her on his dim tour of this place? Though this loft had fancy, modern furniture, she couldn't get over the big white pipes that ran across the ceiling. She stared up at them. Rising quietly and taking her flashlight, she padded barefoot to the guest bathroom over the dusty, polished wooden floors, then came back into the living area.

Except for the two bedrooms and baths down the hall, this apartment was one huge space divided into areas by rugs and groupings of oversize furniture. Paintings—modern ones her artist friend Sarah would not like—adorned the walls, but there was not one living plant or small, cozy chair. She planned to dust the metal and leather furniture and run a mop over the wooden floors. Cook a bit too, if she could get some food in.

What had surprised her were the pieces of Chinese art in the room. A large, decorated porcelain vase. A one-foot-high statue of a Chinese warrior and his horse. A scroll on one wall with painted flowering plum trees on it. It both bolstered and confused her theory that the Chinese could be Andrew's enemy. When he'd shown her around, he'd said he'd made several business trips to China, and had either bought artwork there or been given it. So did those fond feelings keep him from realizing or admitting the Chinese could indeed be the ones after him?

Standing there, looking down at Andrew, she felt her nose tickle. She tried to jam her finger under her nose in time but sneezed.

"Ella, you okay?" Andrew asked, quietly lifting a hand to her, which she took, though she stayed standing.

"Oh, sure. Just woke up for some reason. It felt warm and at first I thought I was in Pinecraft."

"It can get hot and muggy here in the summer."

"In Ohio too. I guess, despite the circumstances, you're glad to be home."

"Not as glad as I figured. I thought I missed my space and my stuff, but now that I see it all—not so much. It seems changed when I'm the one who's different." He sat up and tugged her down to sit beside him. On the buttery-soft leather couch, she sank way back.

"I've been thinking," he went on, "that I'm going to risk contacting my law firm. I'll buy a cheap cell phone and make a quick call so it can't be traced. I'll set up a meeting with Logan Reese, the attorney I worked with most there. The thing is, they're the ones who set me up with the protection I had in Atlanta, where someone found me. I guess there's no way we can risk trying to stay here long, though, and the trial's not until September. It's pretty crazy that I'm trained to be a situation analysis expert, and I can't figure out what to do and who to trust in my screwed-up situation."

"I think you're right about not staying here long. We have the hit man's money. What if your enemies have this place watched or at least checked on now and then? Won't they look every possible place when they figure out you've escaped again?"

"And since I was tracked to the Home Valley and to Pinecraft, they're diabolically clever, but I still don't believe they'd think I'd come back here. But who's the link, who gave me away not only in Atlanta but in the Home Valley?"

"'Who's the link' reminds me of Linc Armstrong, the former FBI guy. He got disillusioned and left that job but now works for a security firm of some kind. Maybe he and your bodyguard in Atlanta knew each other or worked at the same place."

"Any theory's not too far-out lately. It was Gerald Branin who talked me into the WITSEC program, saying it was the only way to be completely secure until the trial. My former boss, the defendant in the case, has the most to lose if I talk. I know you're a fan of the Chinese theory, and they're in deep too, but—" He heaved a huge sigh. "I just don't know. I do know, though, how much you've come to mean to me."

He leaned closer, one elbow on the back of the couch, so close she could feel his breath. She tried to tell herself that this was really Alex, the man who easily convinced women he didn't even know to let him break store rules and hand over library cards. Here in New York, how much of Andrew Lantz was left in Alex Caldwell?

He held her hands in his, then ran his fingers up the inside of her arm, then caressed the curve of her throat and chin. With the tip of his index finger, he traced the trembling pout of her lips, then tilted his head to kiss her. Their kisses back in the barn had seemed forbidden, but now—now here in this worldly place, alone…

They stretched out on the couch with her pressed into the soft leather beneath him, though he kept most of his weight off her. Slowly and thoroughly, he kissed her mouth, cheeks, throat. His beard stubble was turning from prickly to soft. Mindlessly, she kissed him back. She held hard to him while his hands raced over her body, cupping, kneading until she thought she would go crazy. Bright colors danced before her eyes, even with her lids closed. Their tongues darted and twisted the way he'd taught her to kiss before. He rolled them over so they were side-by-side as he thrust a leg between hers and she gripped him hard with her thighs.

So this is what it was really like to desire a man… to love him and lose oneself in his hands, to surrender and take back. She had never wanted a man so desperately, never even knew the power of this. When he bent his head to kiss her breast through her T-shirt and bra, she heard her plead with him for what she wasn't sure. "Please, please, Andrew…"

Breathing even harder than her, he lifted his head. Even in the dark, his eyes were luminous.

"I won't. I'll be careful."

"No, I mean…I like it."

"I can tell. Ella, it's because I love you I can't just make love to you."

Love? The man had said love! Twice!

"Then maybe *Grossmamm* is right," she said, almost panting as he ran his hand from her rib cage to her flat belly and hips.

"I know. I promised her I wouldn't take you—this way, I mean. That's why we have to stop."

"I mean she's right about you should maybe turn Amish!"

He laughed once, then sobered. "To have you, possess you, I just might."

She exhaled hard as his hand stilled, gripping her waist while his thumb stroked her bare stomach under her shirt. "But that would be the wrong reason to change your life so much," she said as tears prickled her eyes.

"I promised not only *Grossmamm* but myself I wouldn't lose my head—but then," he said, sitting up, "when it comes to you, I already have. I don't just keep taking cold showers because it's hot weather."

She wasn't sure what he meant, but it didn't matter because he kissed her hard once again. Suddenly, she realized Andrew had ruined her life. It would never be enough to just love her lavender and breed and tend new plants anymore. She wanted to have *him* and breed and tend his children. She wanted Alex Caldwell almost as

KAREN HARPER

much as she wanted Andrew Lantz, yet she could never have them both—maybe neither.

But he'd said the word *love*. It might have just slipped out in the heat of the moment, but he'd said *love*.

Late the next morning, Ella walked through SoHo with two recyclable bags of groceries, from a store called the Gourmet Garage, no less—and what outrageous prices compared to the Kwik Stop at home! Alex had gone to buy a cell phone and use it to set up a meeting in a neutral place with his lead attorney, Logan Reese. Ella wore the jacket to her suit and its blouse, but not the skirt. She'd compromised with her dressier pair of slacks and her new walking shoes. No way was she going to deal with that tight, short skirt and heels on these cobbles and on the fire escape and roof. She wore her hair in a braided ponytail coiled on the top of her head, because it made her look so unlike herself.

She was gazing upward, admiring the elegant, historic buildings Andrew said were made of cast iron so they wouldn't burn like in the old days when this area was nicknamed Hell's Hundred Acres for its crowded slums and tendency to burn down. Despite the warmth of the day, she shuddered at the nickname "hell" and the memory of the arson fires that had consumed Amish barns back home. She prayed this escape would not turn into hell for either of them.

She consulted the little map Alex had drawn for her and stopped next at Balthazar Bakery. She liked the place instantly since it smelled as good as her mother's kitchen when she was baking bread.

She bought not only bread—something called baguettes—but homemade soup and half a coconut cake,

which she had a feeling would not be as good as the
Amish-made ones Ray-Lynn served at the Dutch Farm
Table. She realized that if Andrew wasn't back yet to
help, she'd have to carry her sacks one at a time up the
fire escape and over the rooftops. This was all so crazy
and yet she loved the challenge of hiding out with him,
just the two of them against the world.

Beyond the bakery, her eye caught a sign that made
her gasp. The Herbal Spa, it read, and painted next to
those words were spikes of lavender. She stared at some
of the products they had displayed in the window with
red, white and blue bunting and glittery stars since the
Fourth of July was two days away. Lavender toner, lavender massage oil with rosewood, wrinkle-relaxing eye
serum and—here was a good one!—lavender antiaging
capsules that supposedly released something called en-
dorphins for mood-enhancing ecstasy!

She pictured Connie Lee, so pushy to have Ella's
Lavender Plain Products for their Home Valley Spa,
but these were real fancy ones. Still, she could learn
something here that she could use later. She juggled
the sacks so she could shove her sleeve up to glance at
Andrew's wristwatch he'd insisted she wear, though it
hung like a big bracelet on her arm. He'd said not to go
back to the fire escape until eleven this morning because he'd be back by then and meet her there. Good.
She had a half hour. Though she had a few things that
might melt, she shifted her sacks, managed to open the
door and went in.

"Thank God, you're safe!" Logan Reese told Alex
as they met in the Rest Easy Café in the West Village.
Alex had set up their secret meeting here because he

could walk to it. He had to get back to the fire escape before Ella to help her with the groceries and since he didn't like her being alone in the first place.

"I may be safe but since my enemies have learned the third time's not a charm, they may attempt a fourth," Alex told him as they sat in a back booth. They ordered coffee before he spoke again, keeping his voice low.

"Number one, Atlanta. Two, the first place WITSEC put me, a quiet, rural area. Then, again, about a thousand miles away where I put myself when I went on the run. But I figured they'd never think I'd dare to come back here until the trial."

It made Alex feel really tense that Logan, who usually had nerves of steel, seemed uptight, but this was pretty cloak-and-dagger. Reese was around fifty with impeccably styled, silvering dark hair and wore contact lenses that made him blink too much. Usually he had a steady demeanor that went with his compelling voice and inspiring confidence, but not today. Hell, that's how he'd felt for months, Alex thought, like he wasn't his assured, in-control self anymore.

"Where are you staying?" Reese asked.

"I'd rather not say."

"If you can't trust me, you are a goner. You've dumped the WITSEC protection, right?"

"Right, because that all went wrong."

"Why don't I find you a safe place, close to the office? A busy, common place where we can meet to go over the depositions again, plan more of our attack."

"Because attacks on me are what I'm afraid of! At best, I tell myself that Marv Boynton—or whoever's after my head—just wants to scare me to shut up, withdraw my testimony. The thing is, after their first attempt on my life went wrong, I think they've decided to play cute. Kidnap someone close to me, so I give myself up to them. They'd make it look like I just disappeared and I'd never be found again. Or they plan to make it look like I committed suicide or had a fatal accident."

Alex was on a fishing expedition now to see how much this guy knew about what he'd been through. He'd love to know if he and Gerald Branin were still in touch. They quit talking when their server brought their coffee.

"I need more details on all of that," Logan insisted, leaning forward on his elbows. "We can use it all in court. But who could they kidnap to get you to surrender to them? You're not supposed to be in contact with anyone from your past."

"I have a friend with me, a woman."

"Are you nuts?" Logan exploded, dinging his cup down so hard he slopped coffee into his saucer. "You're on the run with a woman? From here? Okay, okay, I can see you're going to stonewall me. We can put her up, too, but how about adjoining rooms so you and I can work on things without being overheard—and you can keep her identity even from me if you're so paranoid."

"Yeah, that would be best anyway. And you think you wouldn't be running scared if you'd been a target, even a moving one?"

"Give me your cell number, and I'll set it up. The Grand Hyatt near Grand Central is so busy that no one pays any attention to anyone, and it's near the firm. I can send a car for you this evening. Where to and when?"

"No car, but call me when it's set. We'll get there."

"You're not—on the streets? Or at her place? Listen,

Alex," he said, punching the air between them with an index finger, "you realize Boynton and maybe the Chinese too could find out the addresses of both of the women you were dating here."

"More later," Alex said only, and downed the rest of his coffee. "And I'd appreciate it if you don't let Gerald Branin, WITSEC or that security firm you hired know I've turned up or even contacted you. What? Why are you looking like that?"

His stomach clenched. As stone-faced as this man could be, he looked like he'd swallowed hot tar instead of black coffee.

"Branin was in to see me just yesterday."

"He's here in town and not D.C.?"

"He told me you'd skipped out of where he had you stashed, as he put it. He said he wasn't sure you hadn't turned rogue, but he was following leads to contact you again."

"Damn, hope that wasn't contact me with a contract on me. He could have been bought off. With the money at stake here, as well as reputations and prison time, not to mention an international incident with the Chinese, I'm sure money's no obstacle. Look, I've got to go. It's probably a good idea to keep moving, so I'll take you up on the Grand Hyatt invitation, if you make the arrangements yourself with no middleman."

"You have my word. I'll arrange for you to get in by this evening without even checking in under an assumed name. See you there. I'll pay with cash to avoid even using my credit card."

"Call me when it's set up and the coast is clear."

Alex made for the door as he checked his second-best watch. It felt so strange to be able to glance down at one again. He'd given Ella his new one, under protest. The Amish didn't wear them, yet they seemed always to be prompt. Another mystery about the Amish, another admirable trait to show they could do without the time-and techno-run, selfish and screwed-up world. But damn, it was nearly 10:45 a.m. He'd have to rush to get there before she did.

23

The little store inside the spa entranced Ella. It seemed to have a lavender theme and it smelled so much like her field of flowers that tears stung her eyelids. She could probably find ideas here for her own shop at home.

Turning away from stocking the shelves, a beautiful Asian woman with shiny, straight black hair dressed in a lavender-hued blouse and skirt smiled and said, "Welcome! Are you here to make a spa appointment or may I help you with some products? Our herb of the month is lavender."

"Yes, I'm interested in your lavender products. I grow some lavender myself."

"Oh, where?"

"In the Midwest."

"We have a spa in Chicago and one in Pittsburgh. Are either of those near you?"

Ella wasn't certain how much to reveal, but it was a good thing she didn't say Ohio, because on the side wall, in a huge, slightly blurred black-and-white photo, almost like wallpaper, was a smiling Connie Lee! She'd walked into the spa that Connie Lee owned?

"That's our founder, Constance," the woman, whose name tag read Michelle, said, still smiling.

Ella's thoughts raced. Connie had told her from the first that she and her husband were from New York City and had a spa there, but Ella had never asked its name. The Home Valley Spa they were building out-side Homestead was the only name she knew, and, of course, that wouldn't be the same. As for the laven-der products, Connie had not been making it up that they were hoping for new ones. So maybe she had not just come to Ella to find out more about Andrew. But the fact that the Lees had so suddenly appeared in the Home Valley area—could they have been funded or set up there to keep an eye on Alex Caldwell? No, surely they were there before Andrew. But they could have been approached and hired to watch him then—hired by the Chinese because they were of Chinese heritage.

"Miss, are you all right?" Michelle asked, leaning forward across the counter.

"Oh, yes. Fine. That's just such a striking picture. They call what your founder is holding in the photo body candles, right? Good for the fragrance and then the massage."

"Absolutely. May I show you some of those, though I must admit we're still perfecting our lavender-scented ones."

Ella wanted to flee. What if Connie Lee was in New York or found out they were here nearby? The laven-der connection aside, she still didn't trust her. Was it coincidence that her store was just blocks away from Andrew's—Alex Caldwell's—home here? No, no. She was jumping to conclusions.

"The body candles are an innovation here at the spa,"

Michelle was saying when Ella had forgotten what she'd asked. "People are absolutely too stressed-out by technology and their schedules today—lots of issues and problems. I can show you those candles in several fragrances and you can use them at home, of course, not just in a luxe spa like ours."

At home. Where was home? Ohio? With Andrew? Anywhere they could be safe?

Ella cleared her throat. She had to say something so she didn't seem like the fool she felt she was. "I was so entranced by your lovely window, I forgot I have grocery items that will melt. But I will come back," Ella told her, forcing a smile. She started for the door. "So are there any more Herbal Spas being built in the Midwest?"

"Absolutely. Asian luxury for busy Americans. We don't like to announce new sites until the facilities are ready to take guests, but there is another one being built in a rural area, far from the madding crowd, so to speak. That area will be the perfect escape and hideaway spot."

But, Ella thought, that had not been the perfect escape and hideaway spot for Andrew.

"Here, let me give you a sample of our lavender and lilac bath salts," she said, and brought Ella a small silver-wrapped package tied with the same signature silken crimson cording she'd been tied up with when she'd been abducted from Hannah's wedding, the same stuff that had uncoiled all over the road the night Connie's son might have tried to run down Andrew.

"That ribbon—so distinctive," Ella said.

"Absolutely. Another marvelous product from the land of acupuncture. And there's a little trick about these ties that has to do with the innovative texture of them—see. If you pull it taut, then release it—just the opposite of trying to loosen and untie it—it comes free. But if you retie it again—*voilà!* Magic, just like the spa products beneath the wrap."

"Thank you. That's amazing, and I never would have guessed," Ella said, and put the package in the bakery sack.

Strange, she thought, as she hurried out the door onto the busy sidewalk, but the usually calming scent of the lavender in that store hadn't calmed her at all.

"So, how are you settling in here?" Ray-Lynn asked Jack's deputy Win Hayes as she refilled his coffee cup herself. The handsome guy sat at the Dutch Farm Table counter where he could watch who came in and out.

He smiled up at Ray-Lynn just as his eggs-and-ham special was delivered by Leah. "I guess telling you is like telling the man himself, right?" he asked. "Congrats on your engagement. The truth is, I like this quieter area a lot. Wooster was the big city compared to Homestead and Eden County. But this gives me more time to get to know people instead of rushing from case to case. And the sheriff thinks I'm good luck since there have been no bad crime flare-ups since I came, at least not like the serial arsons and the graveyard shootings."

"Or my being almost killed when my car was shoved off into the ravine," Ray-Lynn added with a shudder.

"But you've come back from all that just great," he said, salting and peppering his eggs. "It's pretty obvious you're one of the hubs of this community, an important lady to know. Of course, in my case, having more time for locals means caring more about them. Speaking of which, have you heard if the members of the Lantz family who were sick are any better?"

"Jack mentioned that?"

He shrugged. "Either he did, or I read it in his daily records. We both keep good track of where we go when. You better realize you're going to have to clock in with him when you two tie the knot," he said, and chuckled.

Ray-Lynn could see why people liked Win, despite the fact that his can-do, take-over nature was eating at Jack, however grateful he was for his capable assistance. She said only, "Enjoy your breakfast," instead of the other tactics she could think of to draw the guy out. For once, she would keep her mouth shut. Anyway, for claiming to be a people person, Win Hayes still seemed kind of a loner to her, someone who played his cards close to his vest, as her daddy used to say.

She was no more back to the front desk when Connie Lee came barging—ding-dang, that was the word for it, all right—in the front door.

Wearing canary-yellow slacks and a pale green frilly blouse, with high heels that looked like sandals and perfectly matched her huge purse, she was overdressed for around here as usual.

"Good morning, Mrs. Lee," Ray-Lynn greeted her, hoping she wasn't the one she was looking for as the woman's dark eyes lifted over Ray-Lynn's shoulder to skim the restaurant.

"I hope it's a good morning," she told Ray-Lynn, looking back at her. "We're having union problems, because we want to hire Amish carpenters to finish the interior of the spa. They work for less and refuse union membership. I swear they'd be hung out to dry in New York, but obviously that's the Amish way here, and the lesser costs coupled with excellent craftsmanship are fine with me. But the local unions are horning in, trying to make trouble for them and us."

"If you're looking for Amish builders or union men, I can tell you neither are in here, not right now, at least."

With a clatter of bangle bracelets, the woman's hand shot to her hip. "No, I'm looking for Deputy Hayes, but I don't see him."

"He probably sees you. He's at the counter, not in a booth."

"Oh, thanks. I want him to patrol our project, keep an eye out, the sheriff too, of course. Until we get this settled, I don't want any pro-union high jinks going on at our site. Excuse me. Oh—I see you sell Ella's Lavender Plain Products here," she said, gesturing at the small display of them. "I'm hoping to help her really build her business up, but I haven't seen her for days. Do you know how she is—or where?"

Ray-Lynn almost said that Win Hayes had just asked the same, but what was the point? She'd tell Jack, no one else, so she told the woman, "How she is—I hear she's been ill. Where—probably keeping to her bedroom and fretting she's not out tending her fields."

"Her sister and her mother seem to have taken over. I've dropped by but gotten nothing out of them. And that Pennsylvania cousin of theirs who used to help with the lavender seems to be ill—or missing too. I'm just hoping that he wasn't really someone trying to get a monopoly on her products before she signed with us. He seemed rather unfriendly and secretive to me."

So that was the big interest in Ella and the mysterious Andrew Lantz, Ray-Lynn thought. "Oh, the Amish won't sign anything like a contract," she assured her, "but Ella's word can be trusted. The word of the Amish is their bond, so they don't need detailed legal contracts. That's the problem between the labor unions and the Amish too, the same reason I don't have any sort of contract with my Amish servers here. It's all on the up-and-up, based on trust and being true to God's word to live honest lives."

"Thanks for the advice," Connie said. "I'm going to see that you and the sheriff get a family gift certificate if I ever get this project off the ground."

As Ray-Lynn watched her walk away, two things struck her.

Just like Win Hayes, Connie Lee seemed to know she and Jack were engaged. And she had the strangest feeling that Connie's quiz about Ella's location was part of the woman's real mission here today.

Ray-Lynn gasped as Connie dared to walk behind the counter, evidently so she could talk to Deputy Hayes face-to-face. They spoke quietly—he looked annoyed—but Ray-Lynn did catch the word *Lantz* again. Was she asking him what he knew about Ella?

Win was nodding now, so Connie had obviously gotten what she came for. But then, Ray-Lynn had a feeling that woman always got what she wanted, so look out labor unions and Win Hayes if he didn't cooperate. Ella too, and—if Connie's crazy theory about Andrew Lantz really being a competitor for Ella's lavender was true—that meant he was on her hit list too.

Ella was relieved to see Andrew standing near the fire escape when she arrived with her sacks of food. "Wait till you hear what happened!" she told him, out of breath.

Frowning, he took the biggest sack from her. "Tell me."

"Connie Lee's family owns a spa in this neighbor-hood! I went in because they had lavender products in the windows. The sales lady wouldn't say they were building the Home Valley Spa, but Connie Lee's photo was on the wall big as the side of a buggy. I didn't tell the lady I knew Connie."

"You mean the Herbal Spa on Wooster Street? Never been in there, but I can't figure how the Connie connec-tion can tie to me. But it's another good reason we're going to move."

"We're moving again? So soon? I mean, I guess I'd feel better somewhere else, but where?"

"Let's get upstairs and put what we'll need into my suitcase this time. We're going to a hotel arranged by my lawyer. I'll start working with him to prepare our case again. Ella, I want you with me, but I'm going to try to find a way to send you home soon."

There it was again. Home. Yes, she longed to go home, but to leave him, go to Ohio without him? Noth-ing would ever be the same there or anywhere for her.

She blinked back tears as they climbed the fire es-cape with her sacks. While he packed their things in a beautiful, leather suitcase, she fixed them a large lunch, trying to use many of the perishable things she'd bought. He'd said they were leaving here late afternoon for another part of town, just when she'd started to know this neighborhood. But she had to admit she felt pan-icked, even more than when she'd found out the Lees owned that spa.

At least her panic attacks were a thing of the past, but she was hovering close to bursting into tears right now. Too much change, too many wild emotions, too close to this man she had almost begged to possess her last night. And she didn't feel one bit ashamed, though she was sure she should, that he had been the one with the will to stop.

"We'll take some of the food you bought in a sack so we don't have to go out much," Andrew told her. He was so nervous, his mind obviously racing about working on his case again, that he wasn't picking up on how upset she was. Where was the old Andrew? Alex Caldwell was back again. "And until I can have my lawyer contact Sheriff Freeman and be certain he or Deputy Hayes can keep a good eye on you there," he went on, "you'll have your own room at the hotel, so don't worry about having to hide out when my lawyer and I go over the embargoed evidence, our case."

She jumped up to take the dishes to the sink. "Are we going in a taxi?" she asked, trying to keep the catch out of her voice. "I guess, except for an airplane I've been on about everything else around here."

"No, we're not going in a taxi, and I turned down a car he wanted to send for us. We're going to get there on our own, subway to Grand Central Station, which is right next door to our hotel."

"Getting there on our own—I wish we were still doing that."

"I don't know what I would have done without you, Ella," he said as he came over to stand behind her at the sink. He put his hands on her waist and bent his head to kiss the side of her neck.

"But from now on you will do without me," she said, not turning to cling to him as she so desperately wanted to do. "And you'll be fine, now that you have someone else to trust—Alex Caldwell."

His hands tightened. She'd never called him by his real name before, and she'd said it more coldly and harshly than she'd intended. They stood like that a moment, unmoving, hardly breathing. He sniffed hard once, almost as if he too fought tears, then gave her waist a little squeeze and walked away.

"Just when I thought I was used to New York—this!" Ella declared as they got off the subway on the lower concourse of Grand Central Station and took the crowded escalator up. A huge food court lay below them, packed with people.

"There's a common saying to describe a really busy place. Just say Grand Central Station," he told her.

He had to admit he was having second thoughts about how he'd decided to proceed now, but trusting Logan Reese and going back to work on the case in seclusion and, he hoped, obscurity was the best move he could make. He needed to get his testimony planned and rehearsed. He had no doubt that Marv Boynton and Chinese money would hire the best defense lawyers possible to cross-examine him. Someone had spent big bucks on a hired gun, even a second one. As much as it pained him, he needed to send Ella away and pray that she'd be safe at home, because he was surely still a target here, and he didn't want her standing next to him if he took a hit.

Besides, if he kept her close, he was going to make love to her, and then he'd betray some of the finest people he'd ever met, let alone Ella. Keeping her with him, seducing her would be like—like shredding a bouquet of fresh, fragrant lavender. The sweet scent would haunt him forever, but the plant itself would be uprooted. That is, unless, once he got through all this, they could be together. But Ella could never flourish in this world and, despite what *Grossmamm* claimed, he could never become one of them.

"So many people!" she said again.

"Coming in not only on subways but on trains. Over that way," he said, pointing at commuters hurrying toward doors to platforms lining myriad tracks. He pictured the labyrinthine tunnels that lay below. He'd had a friend once who was always talking about homeless people living on old, abandoned train platforms in dark tunnels—the mole people, he'd called them. Alex used to wonder what those poor souls were hiding from. Eventually, the government had moved them out to subsidized housing projects, just the way the feds tried to move him around.

He was finished being a mole person of a different kind. Surely things were going to be better for him from now on, for Ella too. He loved her in a way, always would, he admitted to himself. His Ella enchanted still enchanted him, right in the middle of evening rush hour in one of the busiest, noisiest places on the planet, just as she had in the quiet hills of her home.

As she gazed around—upward—wide-eyed, he felt he was seeing this familiar place for the first time. Looking at things through her point of view had often done that for him, often educated him, even when they'd looked at the stars together that night on her lavender hill. He could name the artificial satellites by name, but he'd never really appreciated their beauty. As they walked across the massive main concourse floor of polished white marble, for once, he too admired the lofty ceiling and high windows.

He felt a bit strange dressed the way they were, he back in a business suit, she finally in her suit and heels. He carried his suitcase into the hotel and saw Logan awaited them in a corner of the lobby. "Got you checked into adjoining rooms," he told them. Even after he was introduced to Ella, Logan kept stealing glances at her. He'd evidently expected one of Alex's "painted woman" friends. It reminded him again how Ella looked like a beautiful angel off some sort of Christmas card, untouched, even amid the fury and frenzy of life here.

Logan went back to his office just down the street with a promise to be back with Alex's deposition to review after supper. He'd even arranged room service for them. Ella became very quiet as their elevator ascended to the twentieth floor, but that was new for her too.

Their rooms overlooked the vast roof of Grand Central Station next door with its huge statue of Mercury with his stone wings, staring down onto busy 42nd Street.

"That's the Roman messenger god, Mercury, patron of travelers," he told Ella when he brought her things from the suitcase over to her room where she was still staring out the window. She'd changed back into her casual slacks and running shoes.

"That's us," she said, not looking at him, her voice wan and wistful. "We have stone wings that keep us from rushing off again. We're travelers who have been fleeing evil, travelers through life, but not together anymore."

"Sure we are. Even though I'm going to have Logan find out if we can arrange security for you back home tomorrow, we'll still see each other. As soon as I get through all this and the hoopla dies down, I'm going to make it up to Janus and Trixie, your family—and especially you. I'll visit, and we'll work on a marketing plan for your Lavender Plain Products."

"A fancy plan for what's plain. And never the twain shall meet." She turned to face him. She'd been crying again, and he couldn't bear it. He wanted to hold her, to comfort her, to tell her how much he admired and—damn it—loved her.

But, like a coward, he said only, "I'll give you some time to get settled, then we'll eat together in my room, if that's all right with you."

"Sure," she said with a little shrug. "What I want doesn't matter. Just keeping you safe and getting you through all this…that does."

A knock he could hear clear in here from his room's hall door gave him an excuse not to touch her, not to make love to her on that big king-size bed behind her as he so desperately wanted to do. Later, tonight, he'd try to explain his mixed feelings to her, how he both wanted her but wanted to protect her. But as he started back toward his room to see if room service was here already, he heard another knock, a loud one. No, that was more like the sound of his door opening, hitting back against the wall.

But did Logan have a key? And wasn't it too early for room service?

He held his hand, palm out, toward Ella so she wouldn't speak again. Partly closing the adjoining door between the two rooms, he peered through. A man with a gun blurred by, heading toward the bathroom. Stranger. Killer! Had Logan been the one who sold him out? Who else knew they were here and which room was his?

Not daring to close the adjoining door in case it attracted attention, Alex held his finger to his lips to signal silence. Her eyes widened, but she nodded. Alex moved toward her, took her wrist, made for the hall door of her room. It would make noise and take too long to phone for help or grab anything. They had to run again.

He unlocked and opened the door and peered into the hall. Another man stood a ways down the hall, looking the other way. Another assassin or someone innocent?

They walked to the turn in the hall toward the bank of elevators, then broke into a run. He glanced at the floors the four elevators were on: nothing close. He heard running footsteps as he pulled Ella to the emergency exit of the stairs. They banged through the door and started down, their footsteps echoing in the tall stairwell shaft.

He heard a man's shout from above and two pairs of feet thudding after them.

"Hey, Caldwell! We're security your lawyer Reese sent. Hey, wait up!"

He glanced at Ella. "No," she whispered, shaking her head so hard her hair braid came loose. "We have to go!"

He thanked God she agreed with his gut instinct. And that she'd said *we*.

24

Ella was instantly out of breath. Not a panic attack! Not now.

As they vaulted across a landing to head down another flight of stairs, she glanced up into the maze of railings and the concrete underside of steps. A man leaning over—she saw his face. His arm—a gun!

Andrew pulled her on. Her heart thudded so hard it shook her entire body. Her teeth chattered.

She slammed into Andrew as he came to a dead stop in the corner of the stairwell.

"Go on!" she whispered.

He nodded but opened the door labeled 14th Floor, then slammed it. The footsteps pursuing them halted. Holding his finger to his lips, Andrew tiptoed toward the next flight of stairs down. Slowly, quietly they made their way to the 12th Floor door—what had happened to the 13th?—then opened that door and ran down the long hall of hotel room doors, heading toward the elevators. None were stopped on this floor but two were near. Andrew pushed the down button, then punched it repeatedly. One elevator arrived, but its doors seemed to open so slowly.

"Here!" They heard a man shout that single word from down the hall. Muted, running footsteps, this time on carpet.

They leaped into the elevator, and Alex hit the button to close the door. They crammed themselves into the corner by the controls. Yet she glimpsed the same man's face as the doors nearly closed. He stuck the barrel of a black, squat gun between the doors to keep them open. Or would he shoot? Alex grabbed off one shoe and, as if he were hitting a baseball with a bat, swung its heel hard into the barrel of the gun. The shoe shoved it out; the doors closed and the elevator descended.

"Come on, come on!" Andrew muttered as he jammed his shoe back on. But the small room that people here rode up and down stopped at two more floors. It seemed to take an eternity. On the sixth floor, two women with large name tags got on. No one spoke. The only sound was a muted *ding-ding,* the hum of the elevator and her and Andrew's hard breathing. The younger woman grinned at them, winked, then looked away. Ella just bet she thought they were out of breath from crazy kissing in here.

The two women got off at the floor called mezzanine where the buzz of conversations and laughter floated in. People, lots of them, some sort of busy gathering. "Should we go too?" she whispered. "Get lost in the crowd?"

"I don't want to endanger anyone else if those idiots open fire. If they're watching where our elevator stops, they may look for us in this mess."

In this mess, echoed through Ella's stunned brain as

the doors closed again. In this mess at least they were together. And he was right: What if even a few people would be near and that man shot at them? She knew they were both his target now: She'd seen his face—twice.

Alex had been sure Ella was going to have a panic attack in the stairwell, but she seemed pretty steady now.

As their elevator descended, she asked, "Should we find a policeman?"

"I still don't trust Gerald Branin and the feds. That's where we'd end up if we ran to the cops. And I still don't believe Logan Reese sold me out, but he could have been followed and accidentally led them to me. We need to hide right now, then contact him. He was working on getting you sent home."

"But where are we going to hide that someone else won't get hurt?"

"We'll have to pass a lot of people, but we'll go someplace that must be deserted by now after rush hour."

"At Grand Central Station?"

"You are getting too good at reading my mind."

Rushing past and around people on the sidewalk, they hurried down 42nd Street and through the first door to the terminal. He was relieved to see the crowds greatly reduced, but people still rushed here and there. Yes, this movement and these numbers would obscure them until he could find a place to hide, then call Logan.

Retracing their steps earlier today, they went down the escalator to the lower concourse, always looking back and up over their shoulders. "We can identify that one man," she said.

"There were at least two. Ella, I'm so sorry it's come to this, that I got you in so deep with me. I admire you,

care for you and don't know what I would have done
without you. Now I'm afraid I won't be able to keep you
safe. I left my cell in the room, but I have money. After
we've ditched the hired guns, I'll contact my lawyers
somehow. Right now, we're going not only to ground,
but underground."

As they hurried past the food court, which was
partly closed up for the night, he thought again of the
mole people who had lived underground. He headed
toward the mostly deserted train platforms. Glancing
back again, he gasped as he saw two men, both of them
in business suits, running toward the food court as if
they'd miss their train.

He grabbed Ella's hand again and pulled her on.

"I still say—we need to—find a policeman," she argued, gasping for air.

"Too late. Besides, how many times have I heard
the Amish don't trust them?" He wanted to keep her
spirits up. "I'm sounding more Amish than you right
now. I think the police might patrol where we're going,
subway workers too. The gun guys will back off then.
Come on!"

Their pursuers had not yet turned into this hall of
the concourse. Alex tried the first door he found that
led to a train platform. Yes, unlocked! Although it was
deserted since the northern commuters had thinned out,
the area was well lit.

They tore across the platform to the far end where
it narrowed and darkened. Pillars there supported the
ceiling of the tunnel, lit by sporadic, dim lights beyond,
but no good just hiding there. The tracks lay below
them—three rails, the third one he knew could be live
and electrocute someone. Should they just wait there,

pressed against the wall? All was silent but for their slowing footsteps—until he heard a door open and then close with a metallic click and echo.

"Oh, no!" Ella whispered.

Alex sent up a silent prayer for their safety. Yeah, he thought, who was turning Amish now indeed?

Slow footsteps came toward them, a scuffling sound. "They must've come in here," a whisper floated to them. "Perfect place—no witnesses."

Alex edged back along the narrowing concrete above the rails with Ella tight behind him. The tracks turned here, out of sight of the area where the men stood. If he and Ella moved quickly, got across the tracks, he saw a doorway. Wherever it led, it was better than staying here.

He mouthed the words to her. *We're going down and over. Step only where I step—only!*

He got on his knees, hung by his hands and let himself quietly down the four-foot drop onto the tracks. He put his hands on her bottom, then her waist to ease her down. It was easy enough to miss the third rail that might be live, but he scraped his chin pulling himself up to the concrete platform on the other side. He lay on his belly, pulled her up, just as he heard the man's voice again: "Check down here!"

Pulling Ella with him, making too much noise, they darted into the narrow entry to the doorway. To his dismay, he saw the metal steps went only one way and that was down.

Ella held tightly to Andrew's hand, then had to release it as they descended the narrow steps, trying to stay as silent as possible. Yet the sound of their fren-

zied breathing seemed to echo in her soul. How had it
all come to this? From the heights of her lavender hill
at home and the water tower in Pinecraft to the depths
of this massive city, she had been in danger.

The words *Yea, though I walk through the valley of
the shadow of death, I will fear no evil* came to her. For
certain now, that's where they were walking, but she
did fear the evil. And yet, to be with Andrew, to help
him—that was worth the risk, wasn't it?

They froze for one moment when they heard the
clang of feet on metal above them. Their pursuers had
crossed the tracks!

From the bottom of the staircase stretched a dimly
lit concrete passageway lined by huge pipes about two
feet in diameter that shot out occasional puffs of scorching steam. Although it was a balmy night above, it was
horribly hot and humid here. They were soon both slick
with sweat. Sporadic, oily puddles lay on the uneven
floor, reflecting the wan lighting in lurid colors. Was
hell like this? she wondered, as they dodged another
hiss of steam.

And then, as the sound of footsteps descending the
metal stairs echoed even here, she felt the old terror, the
drowning darkness reach for her. She'd fought off panic
attacks for days and yet now, she saw again the water of
the pond reaching for her, pulling her down. She sucked
in a huge breath and held it, tried to steady herself, concentrated on putting one foot before the other, staying
right behind Andrew. She didn't want to die. She could
not let the swirling waters win!

It became so narrow and low ceilinged that he had
to walk bent over, and she had to watch hitting her
head. Though she tried to keep quiet, she panted like a

dog. Shaking, fearful she'd collapse, she concentrated on controlling her thoughts. The footfalls behind them were now on concrete. They heard the all-too familiar voice rasp the words, "Come on! The perfect place to end all this."

To end all this…oh, *ya,* she wanted it to be over, but not like they meant. Thank the Lord this tunnel curved and kept them hidden for now. Suddenly, Andrew pulled her ahead of him. She figured it was so he would take a bullet first.

Sopping wet, gasping for air, she kept going, clawing toward the surface, kicking her feet, but again, she was going under. Pond water—no, tears and sweat—burned her eyes. She blinked to clear them. Both of them jumped and dodged another scorching blast of steam. All was grime and soot here, dark like the waters of her death.

They came to a widening of the passageway. A maze of machinery, a workers' storage area. Andrew picked up a big wrench from the floor, but what would that be against bullets and a gun?

They turned into an even wider tunnel. "There must be an exit near here," Andrew whispered, and took the lead again. She held so tightly to his hand that her fingers cramped. Another curve, one they could not see beyond. Train tracks lay below them again, so that was a good sign, wasn't it? They hurried faster only to find the tunnel narrowed again. But it had a walkway on this side, so they followed that.

Then they heard it, felt it. A distant rumble shook the air, the very ground, the wall she leaned against.

"I thought these tracks would be deserted," Andrew said. He had to talk up now, because the sound came louder, clearer. "I hope it makes them turn back. Come on!"

But they'd barely gone a few more yards when the tunnel exploded with light and screeching noise. As a train careened around the bend, a blast of air slammed them, then nearly sucked them off their feet. Dirt, papers, pieces of grit pummeled them as the subway train roared past endlessly, then away. They kept their eyes tight shut against flying debris but then had to look behind for their pursuers again.

"It will stop them too—for a minute," Andrew said and yanked her on.

Ella fought her fears, pushed back the waters. She was not being sucked into the drowning depths but was fighting for her life with Andrew. They ran past signs of workers, a discarded orange vest, more tools, a hard hat and then a lit sign over a doorway: EMERGENCY EXIT ONLY: ALARM WILL SOUND.

The alarm for them had already sounded, Ella thought. And yes, an emergency. She felt hysterical. Andrew twisted the knob and thrust the door open; a beeping sound that would surely bring the men behind them. They pounded up the stairs, past an alcove with more machines and tools, then to a tiny hall where they could go right, left or up.

Footsteps behind them again. A man panting for breath.

"Up," she said, when Andrew hesitated. "Go up."

The metal ladder seemed endless. It was dark here, but they could see a rim of light above. Climbing Janus and Trixie's ladder at the circus…climbing her hill.

"Where the hell are they?" they heard a shout below. And then, "Up here!"

Ella expected a bullet. She was behind Andrew. If this was a dead end, it was her fault.

Andrew opened a round metal hatch or door above them a couple of inches. Blinking at the brightness, she could have cheered. He grunted, shoved at the heavy lid, which lifted farther. He banged it all the way open and scrambled out. He reached down for her, nearly yanked her up and shoved her away from the opening, slammed the hatch closed, then stood on it.

Ella saw they were in a dimly lit storage area with unhitched train cars on tracks, but it seemed glaringly bright compared to where they'd been. Once again, tools and machinery littered the area.

"Stand on this," Andrew ordered. "I've got to put something on it. If they shoot, it would only ricochet back at them."

She was certain, as she stood there, that she could feel the men trying to lift it—or was she shaking that hard? Andrew came back, lugging something that looked like an anvil; he put it between her feet, then carried other pieces of scrap metal over and piled them there.

He hugged her hard, then they ran again. Out a door, where another alarm went off. Maybe workers would come and find the men with guns trapped below. But they were not dead like the fake clown. They could try again.

The bright lights of the city startled her at first, just like stars had the time her friends had saved her from the depths of the pond. But she was all right, she told herself. Better yet, this time, she was with Andrew.

Though they were both exhausted and looked horrible, they walked for ten blocks until they found an all-night restaurant. They used the bathrooms there to clean up as best they could, including putting cool water on a few minor burns from scalding steam. He ordered them burgers, fries and chocolate malts—how normal, she thought.

"I'm not hungry," she whispered, though she was on her second big cup of ice water.

"You can speak up now, and you have to eat to rebuild your strength. I'm going to pay one of the guys behind the counter to let me use his cell phone so I can call Logan. I swear he didn't set that hit up."

"But we still don't know who did."

"Stay put. Eat and rest."

Andrew chatted with the men who had been speaking a foreign language to each other behind the counter. One of the guys nodded, took the five dollars Andrew offered and handed over his phone. At least, she thought, the Alex Caldwell brand of salesmanship and charm wasn't just for women.

She tried to eat and found she was hungry. Keeping an eye on Andrew as he stood by the door and made his phone call, she downed most of her burger. Andrew returned the phone to the counter man and came back.

"Logan offered to take us to his home, but I said no. He thinks his executive secretary took a call from the hotel checking on his reservation, so she needs to be questioned—or her phone could have been tapped. He never gave away our hotel or room number, but the hotel gave it to his secretary."

"I still think I should stay with you."

"I used to believe that was the best way to go, but I'm the magnet for the killers, not you. Logan's going to also disappear for a while too so we can work together.

First thing tomorrow, he'll call Sheriff Freeman to arrange to get you back home, then he'll find a place he and I can hide near here that can't be traced."

"I'm starting to think that place doesn't exist. Andrew—Alex, I've come this far with you, so I should stay with y—"

"Ella, no! It's because I care so much for you that I have to send you away. It was wrong of me to keep you this long, but I thought it could be riskier to leave or send you home. Obviously, that isn't true."

"It's nice to know you care."

"More than that. Much more. But I have no right to do anything but get you home right now. I told Logan to stress to Sheriff Freeman that it should be common knowledge that you're back without me and don't know where I am. If I'm here and you're in the heart of Amish country, where they evidently hesitated to just shoot me before, I believe you can be safe. With Sheriff Freeman and his deputy keeping tabs on you, the assumption will be I'm with the feds, which I won't be. My enemies don't want more light shone on this case by harming an Amish woman. They just want to quiet me for good, so they'll be concentrating on me, not you."

"But, knowing that, I can't just leave you," she said, and reached across the little table to grasp his hand. "I know it's impossible for us to be together in the future, but I need you. I—through all this, I learned that I love you."

When he blinked, tears in his eyes flew to his cheeks. He did not brush them away. "And I will always, always love you, my Ella enchanted. But this is the only way. It's going to help me so much not to have to worry about you, to have you watched over by the law and back among your close family and protective people. I have to see this through."

"Yes, I know. You would not be the person I admire so if you ran away from what was right. But will I ever see you again, except in my memories and my dreams, Andrew Lantz and Alexander Caldwell?"

"If—when—I get through this…yes, I promise. And maybe not just to help get your lovely Lavender Plain Products going again. Yes, I promise you!"

They held hands across the small table in the little restaurant she knew she'd never see again in the middle of the massive city that still felt so foreign to her, the place that was his home. But promises could be broken from within or shattered from without. She could not bear to leave this man, but he was not hers and could never be, not unless she changed so much she would not be herself. Never could she walk the path her friend Sarah had chosen, to leave her people, be shunned for the love of a worldly man and the child she would bear him. And yet…and yet…

"I'll hold you to that," she told him, biting back a sob. But how long—if ever, she agonized—before she could hold him again?

25

The next day was one mad whirl, but at least Ella no longer feared for her and Alex's life—not right now, at least. His lawyer's wife, Claire, took Ella to someone's apartment who was away at the time, so she could rest. Then Claire drove her to an airport in New Jersey where she would board a small, private airplane to Cleveland.

The Amish girl on a forbidden airplane! But Claire assured her the bishop had given his permission and that a policeman would be awaiting her in Cleveland with someone called Raylene.

"Her name's Ray-Lynn, and that must be Sheriff Freeman himself," Ella told Claire as they waited in the small terminal. "Please thank Mr. Reese for phoning him."

None of this seemed real. Ella ached all over, physically, but emotionally too. Her parting from Alex—she'd decided to call him that now—had sapped whatever strength she had left. She'd tried to stay brave, but she could not bear being separated from him, even if it was what had to be done.

"Ella," Claire said, jolting her from her agonizing.

It seemed the woman's voice came from far away. Ella turned to her. Claire Reese was probably in her mid-forties, a thin woman with red hair that wasn't quite its real color. The diamonds in her earlobes sparkled. "I realize you and Alex have a bond, but you're helping by allowing him to do this very difficult thing. I'm reminded of a poem I used to teach my high school English students, not that they got the impact of it. Its title is 'To Lucasta, on Going to the Wars,' and the soldier is speaking to the woman he loves and has to leave. Part of it goes like this, 'I could not love thee, dear, so much, / Loved I not honor more.'"

Ella nodded. She got the impact of it, all right.

"Alex Caldwell is a very moral person," Claire went on. "It would have been so easy for him to just keep quiet as some others did, to protect his on-the-rise career track at SkyBound, Inc., to continue to please the man who had been his boss and mentor, almost his father figure. Especially now, when he's found something and someone to really live for... Well, I've said enough, but my husband and I thank you for helping him to do what he must to remain true to himself."

Ella thought of Claire's words as she looked out the window at the blur of the ground beneath the wing of the plane. After all she'd been through, she was not afraid to fly, but she felt so numb inside that neither was she as excited as she should be. It would, no doubt, be the only time in her life she would ever soar through God's beautiful blue sky with its rows of clouds reminding her of a snow-covered lavender field. Below, the eastern area of the country with all the buildings and towns tight together passed away, and then the fields and hills stretched out, beckoning her home. But home would never be the same again.

Her thoughts returned to the few moments she'd had alone with Alex to say goodbye and wish him well in the backseat of Claire Reese's car before Claire drove her away and his lawyer took Alex in the other direction.

"I swear to you, Ella, I will see you again when this is all over. I have so many people in the Home Valley to repay—"

"Who don't want to be repaid but by your safety, happiness and good memories of us. If you did come to see folks, even to help me market the lavender, you and I might be together again, but we'll never be able to really be together to share our love, our bodies, our lives. I mean, it would hurt so much we could not be more to each other."

"You're telling me to stay away?"

"I'm just telling you I'm Amish and will always be. This must be your world now as you do what you must and even after. I saw that magazine called *People* in the grocery store. Maybe you can be the 'man of the year' or 'sexiest man alive' next year, because you are all that to me…."

Realizing she sounded incoherent, drowning in emotion, she'd burst into wild sobs. He'd held her, murmured his love, but that could never be.

"Sorry," she'd said, pushing him away and sitting back on the leather car seat. "Just exhausted…scared for you. Missing you already and always will. No—don't kiss me goodbye. Let's pretend everything will work out. I know it will for you. Go now, Alex, please, and stay safe!"

He'd pulled her to him anyway and kissed her forehead. He'd squeezed her hard, then opened the door and slid quickly out of the backseat. When the door had closed, she'd felt it in her very soul. She had covered her eyes with the palms of her hands so she didn't have to see him get in the other car and disappear into the night.

Ray-Lynn's welcoming hug brought Ella back to reality. Home. But home is where the heart is, and hers wasn't really here anymore. She would have to fight herself to get that feeling back. She'd seen too many people and places, when she only wanted one person and for him to be here.

"Glad you and Alex are both safe," Sheriff Freeman said, and patted her shoulder. "Lots of folks, including us, been wondering what happened, but Alex's lawyer filled me in some. Took me a while to get used to a WITSEC witness in our part of the woods. You got any luggage, Ella?" he asked, looking on the tarmac behind her.

"Nothing. Just what people call baggage, Sheriff, after all we've—I've—been through."

"Like to hear about the earlier stuff in Florida. I take it, Alex was a target there too."

"Now, Jack," Ray-Lynn piped up as she kept one arm around Ella's waist to steer her along through the airport, "you can see she's exhausted. There will be plenty of time for debriefing. And maybe she's not supposed to tell everything yet, not even to you, right, Ella?"

"I do want the sheriff to know something for sure. Alex is certain he's the focus of the attacks, but the person who kidnapped me the day of Hannah's wedding and wanted to trade me for him could have been someone local. I mean, it could be someone who just came in to do that, but in such a tight-knit community, we were afraid it might—well, you know, be one of us, someone we know."

"You tell me all about your being grabbed that day and your escape, and I'll do my level darnedest to track him down."

"Or her," Ella added as they headed out of the airport toward the parking lot. "Connie Lee keeps popping up at the strangest times. Oh—Ray-Lynn, you have an engagement ring!" Ella cried.

"Thank you for noticing with all you've been through!" she said, and broke into a tearful smile. "Light at the end of the tunnel of a long relationship, right, Jack? Why, ding-dang, when we first met, I never thought Jack Freeman would…"

Ray-Lynn's words rolled on as they went to the sheriff's car and Ella settled in the backseat. She was so tired her eyes kept crossing, and she was seeing double…the light at the end of the tunnel…a subway train rushing at them…clinging to Alex with the killer right behind…

And, for him, for her, was danger still ahead?

It was nearly dusk when the sheriff pulled into the Lantz farm with Ray-Lynn and Ella. Ella had drifted in and out of a half sleep most of the drive home, even while Ray-Lynn and the sheriff talked. She'd overheard that he and his deputy were going to make regular stops at the farm, not only so she'd feel safe, but so that their patrol cars would be a warning to anyone else who had criminal intent.

She'd heard them talk quietly about their wedding and reception too: small wedding in the community

church, big reception in the restaurant, with the Amish
invited to the latter too. And they were going to be
dressed like characters in a movie called *Gone with
the Wind*. Gone with the wind—was Alex gone forever from her?

The moment she was out of the car, everyone came
running from the house. Claire had given her a midcalf
denim skirt and blouse to wear, but at first her family
even stared at that. The baseball cap she wore backward
was hardly a substitute for a bonnet or prayer *kapp*.

Mamm and Barbara hugged her, then *Daad*. "We
thank the good Lord—and you two," Daad said to her
escorts, "for bringing our girl safely home."

The sheriff nodded. "Hear tell Alex, alias Andrew,
took good care of her, protected her when things got
bad."

Wiping away tears, Ella said, "He sends all of you
his thanks for the days he spent here. He said—after everything's over—he'll be back to thank you in person."

"Well, I'm just glad you're safe," Barbara said as she
put her arm around Ella and drew her away. "We've all
missed you, your lavender's missed you, and now you
can deal with that burr in the behind, Connie Lee."

Ella didn't know whether to laugh or cry at that. "She
does seem to pop up in the oddest places," she said only.

"At least she's not here right now. She had some sort
of big business back in New York. So what was that
like? You have to tell me all about it and—"

Daad's voice broke in behind them. "Your sister is
exhausted, Barbara. She can tell about things tomorrow."

"Danki, Daad," Ella told him. "But there is something I have to do," she added. Gently breaking free

from Barbara, she walked across the yard, past the side of the barn and into the fringe of her lavender field. She just stood there, tears in her eyes, breathing, just breathing. Barbara, who had followed her, kept quiet for once, but Ella wondered if the family had decided she would go nowhere alone when she was outside.

Night was thickening, but in her mind's eye, Ella could see the lavender, pink and purplish hues marching out in rows before her. The scent perfumed the July night air, delicate, yet strong.

"You and *Mamm* did a great job tending it," Ella said as she leaned over and broke off a spike to feel its distinctive, grainy bloom and textured leaves.

"Well, like I said, it missed you. At least Andrew had it pretty well weeded."

"Andrew is really Alex Caldwell, a New York businessman who will soon testify about and against all sorts of worldly evils. I'll never set foot in this field again without thinking of him."

"Will he—really be back someday?"

"I just want him to make it through the trial, stay strong to do what is right."

"*Grossmamm* always said he had an Amish backbone."

"Did she?" Ella asked, turning at last to her sister. "She said a lot of things. How is Aunt Helen and when will *Grossmamm* be back?"

"Aunt Helen's surgery went well, but I'm not sure about *Grossmamm*'s return. I'll still help you in the fields if you want."

"I'd like that, but if you have other tasks now, I can do it. I need to stay busy. But I can use your help making sachets for favors at Ray-Lynn and the sheriff's wedding, even if it's a ways off—October, I hear."

"By the way, Hannah came over to help too, more than once. She and Seth have been really worried about you."

"I can't wait to see everyone, especially little Marlena. I'd better thank the sheriff and Ray-Lynn again before they leave," she said, hurrying back toward the car. Somehow just standing at the edge of her lavender field had given her strength and purpose. The herb might be known for inducing rest and sleep, but she felt alert and energized now, despite her physical exhaustion.

Somehow, she was going to help the sheriff figure out who could have dragged her up that hill above the field. She was going to read the papers and even try to watch TV somewhere when Alex testified at the Sky-Bound trial. And she was—she knew not where or how—going to find the strength to hide and treasure her love for that man, even if she never saw him again.

"Okay, you got that all straight?" Logan asked. "You'll be cross-examined *ad infinitum* about the timeline, both what happened here and on your two visits to China."

They were in the second safe house Logan had found from rental apartments in want ads. Strewn all over the floor were their charts and prep notes for the trial. Every now and then they'd stop planning and Logan would grill Alex on different aspects of his testimony as if he were the defense lawyer. They'd been at this for the two weeks since Ella had left to return to Ohio, which seemed an eternity away from her.

Alex hit the bathroom and when he returned, Logan

had taken a call on his cell phone. He wondered if it was his wife, who called a couple of times a day on cheap phones she then disposed of. They always kept it short so the calls could not be traced. He wished he could talk to Ella. He missed her terribly, her common sense, her caring, her mixture of naïveté and savvy. He longed to hold her, finish what he'd started so many times in his heart and mind but never enough in reality.

"You won't believe this," Logan said as he punched off his phone. "Claire just got a call from my office. You're going to be subpoenaed to testify before Congress after the trial about economic espionage as it affects Chinese-U.S. relationships."

"Oh, great, just great," Alex muttered.

"I thought you'd be pleased. It will lend credence to your character and this case. I don't care if Boynton has pleaded not guilty to peddling trade secrets to the Chinese, this boost to your prestige is going to make him look guilty. And the government should get on this since losses from theft of intellectual property cost U.S. companies about four hundred fifty-plus billion lately! No wonder corporations are now hiring security firms staffed by former CIA or FBI agents."

"I know, I know, but a couple of things," Alex said, raising both hands as if to head off another lawyer's speech. "First, of course, I'll do my duty to testify before Congress. I was just hoping not to get this more strung out, that's all."

"Places to go and people to see, right? Alex, you're crazy if you do more than thank the Amish for hiding you."

He decided to ignore that. He lost most arguments with Logan Reese, which was why he figured others would too. It was part of the reason he'd hired him in the first place.

"Secondly," Alex went on, "that security firm connection is something I've been thinking about. A former FBI agent, disgruntled now, I hear, kept turning up in the Home Valley. Can you call Sheriff Freeman and see if he knows the name of Lincoln Armstrong's security firm? Maybe it had links to SkyBound or Marv in some way. If so, Marv Boynton could have hired Armstrong on the side to shut me up, in the Home Valley at least. He could be the one who abducted Ella. Armstrong knows the Amish area and the people, even threatened her once, although he made it sound as if she was just getting in his way of a woman he wanted."

"An Amish woman? Why do I think this is getting to be a plague that's spreading fast among us…what do they call us? Us British?"

"British? Oh, you mean English. The Amish call outsiders English from the old days when they were persecuted and martyred."

"Okay, English. That's their problem in a nutshell, though, isn't it? They cling to the past."

"It's their strength too, and they do know how to adapt when necessary, or Ella would never have gone home in a plane. Let me use your phone, and I'll call Sheriff Freeman, all right?"

"Sure. Then 'heigh-ho, heigh-ho,' it's back to work we go."

Alex took Logan's phone and walked into the other room. He'd ask Jack Freeman what all he knew about Linc Armstrong. And it gave him an excuse to learn how Ella was doing, because the Home Valley police had promised to keep a good eye on her. He'd have to keep the call short. They were paranoid about calls being traced, even hiding out like they were in Brooklyn right now.

The receptionist he reached said the sheriff was out on a call and couldn't be patched through but he could speak with Deputy Win Hayes if he wanted to leave a message right now. "Sure, okay," Alex said.

"Alex Caldwell? Deputy Winston Hayes here. This is an honor to speak with you, sir. We're all pulling for you. You're a hero around here. I was just at the Lantzes' earlier today, and they're all doing fine. Their grandmother's coming home by bus this afternoon, and they're excited about that. I know better than to ask you where you are, but what can the sheriff or I do for you?"

As Alex explained, the *what can I do for you* question kept rattling through his brain. He didn't want to be a hero to the Amish or anyone else. He wanted to do what was right and stay alive and see Ella again. *What can I do for you?* He longed to say, *Take care of my girl, keep her safe. And tell her I'd rather be with her and her family, instead of facing any congressman or -woman in the entire United States.*

26

Mid-September, two-and-one-half months later

"Hard to believe a lavender farmer has become a student of corporate and economic espionage," Ella told Barbara as they each carried a big box filled with nearly one hundred small lavender sachets from their buggy to Ray-Lynn's house. It was just two weeks before the wedding, a brisk early morning, but light outside, since Ella never went out after dark now. She knew Ray-Lynn would soon be heading for the restaurant.

"That trial Andrew is the key witness in is all too complicated and worldly for me," Barbara admitted, as she managed to juggle her box and ring the doorbell.

"Here are the favors for the wedding guests," Ella said, announcing the obvious as Ray-Lynn opened the door for them. The two of them had become close friends. Ray-Lynn had tried to keep an eye on her and lift her spirits. She'd received only two short handwritten notes from Alex, telling her he was all right and to take care of herself. One had been postmarked from North Carolina and one from California, no less, so she assumed they'd been mailed by lawyers in Reese Logan's firm who were traveling.

"Of course," Ella added, "if you have other copies of *The Plain Dealer,* I'll take them with me."

"Those smell heavenly, even in closed-up boxes!" Ray-Lynn said, inhaling deeply with her eyes closed. "And yes, I've saved you the articles, although it's only been a day since you picked up the last ones. Come in here, you two," she said, and closed the door behind them. "I want you to see my wedding gown. Sarah did a drawing for a tailor in Wooster, who made it for me. I got the directions online from a Civil War reenactment website. The petticoats alone may do me in!"

In a spare bedroom, they gasped to see a wire dummy dressed in a pale green taffeta gown with a tight bodice, puffy sleeves and huge skirts.

Barbara said, "Lots of legroom, but are you sure you can breathe in that?"

"I've been floating on air ever since Jack Freeman proposed, and I'll float down the aisle in this," Ray-Lynn said with a sigh. She launched into an explanation of corsets and crinolines, but Ella's mind drifted again.

She'd tried hard to keep up with Alex's trial, but she felt like that dummy: things hung heavy on her and she was empty without Alex. She struggled to grasp distant, detailed things like wire fraud, punitive tariffs, money laundering, intellectual property and illegal currency manipulation. Why did they use all that fancy talk? Perjury was lying, espionage was spying, it was all wrong, and that was that.

"I'll get that copy of the newspaper for you, Ella," Ray-Lynn said. "Any time you'd like to stop in here to watch the national news, fine with me, whether I'm home or not. I can give you a key, as long as I know to tell Jack or Win Hayes when you'll be here, so they'll be aware."

"They've been great, though all that attention makes me feel like *I'm* the criminal at times, instead of that terrible Marvin Boynton, the boss Alex used to trust."

"That's a hard lesson in life," Ray-Lynn admitted, still fluffing out the huge skirts of her gown. "You need to trust folks, but they can let you down and betray you. Hey, if you want to watch *Headline News* on CNN before you leave, maybe you'll see some coverage from yesterday's events. Come on back in the living room."

They stared at Ray-Lynn's big, flat-screen television as she clicked it on with its remote control. Nearly each time she'd watched the TV, Ella could see new coverage of the SkyBound, Inc., economic espionage trial. She'd sometimes neglected her early lavender harvest to watch a string of people Ray-Lynn called talking heads hash it all over after each person testified and the lawyers did their thing.

At least, Ella thought, Logan Reese seemed very sharp, but he was prideful about doing his job, as if he was actually enjoying all the attention. The trial coverage had almost made her wish she could own a TV. She had to admit there were some good things about modern inventions, that is, if you could cut the bad parts out.

When a close-up of Alex's face appeared on the screen, she clutched her hands tightly and pressed them between her breasts. Though two lines of words about other events crawled across the bottom of the screen, she kept her eyes riveted on him. So handsome, so— worldly, sitting there at a long table beside Logan Reese and two other men with aides seated behind them. She'd never thought to ask Alex what his hiring of the law firm would cost. He hadn't worked for months. Why, he probably hadn't really worked since he'd weeded her lavender.

She savored hearing his voice, even if briefly. She frowned when the commentator talked over him to summarize what he was saying. Ella's eyes caressed him—that is, the graven image of him on the screen. No Amish haircut growing out now, but a stylish trim. A navy business suit, pale blue shirt and navy-and-gold-striped tie. A gold watch peeked out from under his shirt cuffs, perhaps the very watch she'd worn in SoHo. How could it have ever been that he had walked the hills of the Home Valley, held her hand, relied on her, kissed her? If she could only lunge right through that glass screen and touch him!

Then the man Ella considered to be the villain came on the screen. Alex's former employer and mentor Marvin Boynton was a distinguished-looking man, but he always frowned and shook his head or rolled his eyes as if to dismiss or deny everything Alex had "alleged." Other times, he whispered to his lawyers. He was surrounded and backed by as many men in suits as Alex was.

"So how does the sheriff think the trial is going?" Ella asked when a commercial for car insurance filled the screen. "He said he records it and watches it later."

"He and Win both think it's going well," Ray-Lynn assured her. "Win keeps telling folks that Alex is a hero he admires for standing up for what's right at any cost."

Ella nodded but her stomach clenched. She still feared for Alex's safety and prayed that "any cost" would not be the price for all this. Surely, once this was over and Marvin Boynton went to prison—up to thirty years was possible, she'd read—and the Chinese were sanctioned—which sounded like something good and religious to her, but she'd learned was bad—that Alex would be safe and free at last. Each time he'd entered or left the courtroom, or she saw pictures of him getting out of a big car in front of the New York City courthouse, he'd seemed to have bodyguards and police around him. She prayed they would protect him as well as Sheriff Freeman and Deputy Hayes were taking care of her.

Though she kept busy, the days seemed to drag, so Ella was surprised when October finally rolled around. She had agreed to provide Connie Lee with flower heads to be distilled into lavender oil to make body candles. It took about five hundred pounds of the florets to get just one-and-one-half pounds of the precious, expensive oil, which then had to mature for a year—just like fine wine, Connie had said. And, she'd complained, they both cost about the same.

The increasingly frenzied woman had been flying back and forth between New York City and here. When she was in the Home Valley, she fought the delay over the finishing of the spa's interior caused by the carpenter union's protests when Amish men could have finished it beautifully in a week. And, wouldn't you know, she'd hired Linc Armstrong to protect her property during the upheaval! Connie Lee and Linc Armstrong—now that was a partnership Ella didn't like, and she knew Alex wouldn't either.

Ella had been cutting the flowers for the distillation since August. Connie had even bought her a small still and gotten permission from the sheriff's office for her to use it since a state permit was needed in case someone would try to make moonshine on the sly.

The small still reminded Ella of a generator-operated ice-cream churn. She ran it in the kitchen of the old house that was now her lavender store, since she yet slept in the farmhouse. Each time the steam passed through the still, vaporizing the oil from the plants, she remembered the steam hissing from the huge pipes under Grand Central Station. Again, her heartbeat kicked up as she recalled her days with Alex, remembered their parting, his promises. It was the day before Ray-Lynn's wedding, and Alex had finished the trial, though the judge's ruling and possible sentencing of Marvin Boynton was still to come. Alex was now testifying before Congress, and she had no idea how long that could take.

She jumped when a knock rattled the back door. Maybe Hannah was here with little Marlena. They'd visited twice last week, and it was wonderful to see them.

She rushed to the door. Deputy Hayes looked through the glass at her. He was getting to be a familiar visitor, stopping when he went by, sometimes, he'd told her, even watching the house and her fields from the hill above, since that was where her abductor must have spied on her. She was glad he kept her up on what he was doing, and it was good to have someone on her side up the hill instead of an enemy.

"Deputy, hello!" she said, opening the door.

"Hope the mad spa woman—or anybody else—hasn't been hassling you again," he said, removing his hat and stepping in. He extended a piece of paper to her.

Not bad news! He wasn't smiling, seemed too serious. Not something about Alex!

"What's that?"

"Oh, no sweat," he assured her. "It's the final permit for the still, that's all. A good excuse for me to make a visit. Here you go. Boy, it smells great in here."

She exhaled. The paper looked very formal with signatures, including Connie's and Sheriff Freeman's. It wasn't a contract, she assured herself, recalling how Connie had ranted about labor unions insisting on a contract, which the Amish avoided. But, in a way, Ella still regretted doing business with the woman. And, of course, she'd never told her she'd visited her SoHo spa.

"Thanks for making a special trip," Ella told Deputy Hayes. "I hear you will be at Ray-Lynn and the sheriff's wedding on Saturday."

"As a guest but a working one, crowd control." He shot a smile. "With the sheriff the man of the hour, I'll be in charge of the entire area, so I may be in and out of the wedding. You be careful now, since you were abducted on the day of a wedding. Don't be going off alone for any reason. As for me, I'm just glad to feel a part of the community now."

"So working security means you can't bring a guest? I believe there are some young ladies in town who will be glad to see you there, crowd control or not."

"Career first right now, time for ladies later. Maybe I'll find someone later in life, like the sheriff did. To his way of thinking, at least, he seems to have it all."

Ella thought that was a strange way to put it, but she nodded. "So, do you want to see how the still works?"

"Thanks, but got to get going, keep an eye on this area. I missed all the real action around here, the arsons and shootings. It's pretty peaceful but for some drunks, domestic arguments, a couple of pot fields and a meth lab or two to bust. And, oh, yeah, don't think I'm not watching Linc Armstrong. He's out at the spa site or uptown lately, driving in from a motel out on the interstate. He makes the sheriff nervous."

"He makes me nervous too, since he said he blames me for things going wrong for him here. He was sweet on my sister-in-law Hannah, and thinks I got in his way with her. She and my brother Seth more or less solved the crime he wanted to handle and then he got in bad with the FBI."

"Yeah, well, those big government agencies lord it over small rural authorities like me and the sheriff. Listen, you're not afraid Armstrong will really do something, are you?"

"I've gotten a lot stronger lately. Very few people know this, but I almost drowned in the pond between the three farms here years ago. My friends saved me. Since then, I've had panic attacks that are about as bad as drowning, but I've gotten over that too. I've learned not only to rely on the Lord but trust myself and my friends more—and that's where you come in. Thank you for your dedication and concern."

"That means a lot to me. I came close to death once as a kid too—an auto accident that killed my dad."

"No! I'm sorry to hear that."

"I dedicated myself ever since to being not only a police officer but rising far. I had it tough financially, could have picked some better paying job, but catching criminals—the guy who hit our car was a drunk driver—is what means the most to me. Thanks for the thanks," he said, managing a smile again, despite his frown. "See you later, Ella."

He started away, then spun back. "You haven't heard from Alex, have you? Man—testifying before Congress, no less!"

In the nearly three months since she'd seen Alex, she had trained herself not to answer questions about him to those outside the family. But she confided in the deputy, "No. And perhaps not likely to. I'm not sure."

"You never know about people. Okay, I'm out of here," he said, putting his hat back on.

The man always appeared cheerful and in control, even recounting that terrible loss of his father. Unlike Sheriff Freeman, Win Hayes seemed to have no highs and lows. Ordinarily, his mention of Linc Armstrong would have upset her, but she figured Win Hayes could handle that or anything.

The morning of the wedding, Ella was harvesting the last of her stragglers of lavender with her curved sickle. *Grossmamm* was sitting on the back porch, wrapped in her cape, cracking open walnuts but actually keeping an eye on her.

The reception at the Dutch Farm Table Restaurant was at two in the afternoon, so Ella had time before going in to clean up. Barbara was tending the last batch of florets going into the still. Seth and Hannah would be here with Marlena to pick them up in their new, large buggy—obviously, plans for more children were in the works. Sarah and Nate with their new baby girl, whose name was pronounced *Monay* but spelled Monet, would be there, so that was exciting. But Ella still couldn't shake feeling alone. She'd probably be that way at the crowded wedding reception too.

She sat down on the grass, which had seen its first frost earlier this week. With her lap full of late lavender and her knife at her side, she clasped her hands around her knees and surveyed the scene.

She sighed and turned away from gazing up the hill at the trees ablaze with autumn glory. It was lovely, warm weather for midautumn. The sky was a shattering blue, and the fertile valley lay peacefully below. But it didn't calm her. She had to find her heart again, her contentment here and gratitude to God. But her soul was restless now, not to travel, not to see the world, but to have the one person in the world she loved as a woman loves a man come back.

A car she did not recognize drove into the lane and came past the house to park near the barn. A black car, shiny, stylish, but solid-looking. A tourist who had seen the Plain Lavender sign? Connie Lee again, only in a different vehicle? Not Linc Armstrong!

But, to Ella's surprise, the man who got out of the car looked Amish, at this distance. He must be Mennonite since they drove cars, usually black ones. Oh, yes, someone local who waved to *Grossmamm*. But he started up the hill. He wore black jeans and a black denim jacket. Underneath, she glimpsed a white shirt and Amish-looking suspenders. He wore a broad-brimmed hat that obscured his face, but she could tell he was clean-shaven.

And then she knew.

She gasped and stood, spilling the pile of lavender. Frozen in place at first, she took two steps down the hill, then started to run. Alex strode upward, his arms spread. Near the bottom, she hit into him, but he only lifted and spun her with her feet and heart flying. She held on to him so hard she probably hurt him.

"Ella, my love!"

"Me too—for you. I was so worried! I missed you so!"

Who cared, she thought, that courting among her people was only done in private? They held and kissed and kissed, and Ella cried.

"You two best come inside!" *Grossmamm's* voice finally interrupted their reunion. "Some others like to say welcome back to him, *ya,* they would." Ella glanced over Alex's shoulder and saw her family's faces at the windows, all staring. "You'll be late for the wedding today and for your own, if you don't get busy!" *Grossmamm's* voice floated to them. "And Andrew-Alex, you'll have to go talk to the bishop about being dressed like that."

"You are always giving orders," Alex told *Grossmamm,* pretending to be angry. He gave her a hug too. "But you and Ella are invited to dinner soon at the old farmhouse I'm renting just down the road until I can straighten lots of things out. I need to hire someone to help me buy a horse and learn to handle it and get a buggy too. Can't see keeping my worldly gas guzzler much longer," he said, gesturing toward the car.

"Well, if that don't beat all," *Grossmamm* told him in a sassy voice with a big smile. "If that's the Stutzman place you're talking about, you're gonna need all kinds of help to fix it up, but that's what we do, help each other. You'll make a fine Amish businessman and husband, won't he, Ella?"

"What wedding was she talking about?" he whispered to Ella as *Grossmamm* went into the house.

"The sheriff and Ray-Lynn's. We're going to the reception at the Dutch Farm Table in about an hour."

"I can't just crash it."

"Everyone will be happy to see you, especially since you're now yourself again," she assured him. "That is, you look different, but you are yourself, right?"

"My new self. I want to try it here, learn the Plain People's ways, live simply and safely—and pray the woman I want will wait for me to be able to marry her."

"I bet she will, but for an *Auslander,* it can be a difficult road."

"It's the right road. I know that after what I've—we've—been through. Here's hoping I can find the bishop at home. Maybe your father will go with me. I don't want to keep anyone who's in love and getting married waiting."

It got quiet at the reception in the restaurant when the big Lantz extended family walked in with their guest. Alex had squeezed in a quick but good talk with the bishop about his sincerity to join the Amish, but he wondered if he'd overstepped with these people who had been so kind and gracious before. Was he being pushy with the clothes, the car, renting the farmhouse close to Ella—after having her with him in the world for a time, appearing on TV, sending a man to prison, a million reasons they could reject him and ruin all his plans?

But Bishop Esh came up and extended his hand in public as he had earlier in private. "The right hand of fellowship to a friend of ours," the old man said in a loud voice.

And then it started. The beaming bridegroom in an old-fashioned tux came up and clasped his shoulder. Someone in the room started to clap. Seth Lantz, Ella's older brother, shook Alex's hand, while Ella hugged her sister-in-law, Hannah. Other men came up to shake his hand, most of whom he hadn't met yet. It would take him weeks to learn all these names, years to know these people. But that was exactly what he wanted to do.

Over the din of welcomes, he heard his names, both Andrew and Alex, and the applause swelled. He glimpsed *Grossmamm* standing with a group of older women, smiling and crying at the same time.

Soon, he and Ella were holding babies or little kids as if they could bestow some blessing on them. "This is Marlena, my niece, Seth's girl," Ella told him, bouncing a beautiful child in her arms.

"I'm Nate McKenzie, married to Ella's friend Sarah," an obviously worldly guy told him and shook his hand with a nod and glance at a pretty woman, one half-dressed Amish. She even had her hair covered with a little lace cap, though it was a lot smaller than the many prayer caps in the room. "And this is our new baby," he added.

Alex was nervous about such a tiny mite being put in his arms, but he didn't have to hold that one, since Ella cradled the child while she and Sarah leaned their foreheads together and whispered. Ray-Lynn came over to give him a hug that made her massive skirt bounce out so far in back she nearly knocked the bishop over.

It might have been Ray-Lynn and the sheriff's reception, but Alex felt it was his.

27

Alex was late. On this first day of November, he'd promised he was going to walk to the lavender shop right after breakfast. He had yet to sell his car, though he didn't drive it and had borrowed a horse and buggy until he went with *Daad* and Seth to buy a mare at the Kidron Auction next week. But he'd said he'd give the horse a rest and just walk the short distance to her shop.

He and Ella were going to make plans to market the lavender next year, not only through the Home Valley Spa, which was yet unfinished, but through more outlets than the several Ella had in town. Alex even had plans to sell products to Connie for her New York City spa, but Ella wasn't so sure about that. Now that Connie knew who Alex really was, at least she'd been friendly to him, declaring more than once she was an American at heart despite her family heritage.

"Well," Ella said aloud to the empty room as she stopped restocking the shelves, "then I'll go meet my man on the road."

How wonderful, she thought, to think of Alex as

hers. Everyone knew it; everyone who mattered approved. He had helped other Amish businessmen to market their furniture or sausage or windmills more effectively. He was learning Amish *Deutsche*. He was being instructed in the faith. The church was supportive of him, though he could not formally join for nearly a year, and so could not marry her until then. But he was worth waiting for. Now that they were safe and no longer being watched by his enemies or their police friends, she could happily wait an eternity for Alex Caldwell, the name he and the bishop had decided he should keep among them.

She wrapped her cape around her shoulders, tied her bonnet over her *kapp* and cut kitty-corner across the field toward the side road that led to the old farmhouse Alex was renting. She supposed they could fix it up even more than it had been already, but they hadn't decided whether to begin their married life there next year or here in the upstairs of her house.

Ella hummed and quickened her steps around the base of the hill. It looked barren now. She could see all the way to the top where *Daad* had his beehives and she'd been kept as a hostage last summer. If she'd only known then how the scarlet binding cords had worked, she might have gotten free sooner, but the Lord worked it all out for the best. If she had not been abducted, Alex never would have taken her with him when he fled.

Even as she came around the hill onto the road, she didn't see Alex up ahead. It was unlike him to oversleep. Why, he'd recently gotten up before dawn to help *Daad,* Abel and Aaron bring in the first cutting of winter wheat. She walked even faster.

The house came into view. As usual, his car was parked outside and Bethany, his borrowed mare, must be in the barn because his buggy sat just outside. What if he'd fallen or was sick? He'd probably wish he still had a way to call for help. She knew he missed his cell phone and what he called his laptop, but then he'd teased that she was his laptop now, when he pulled her down onto his thighs. He'd tickled her at first but then, as usual, it had turned to crazy kissing and caresses she could feel even now.

Cutting across his small lawn toward the porch, she felt much warmer than her rapid walk had made her. Although Alex mostly used the back door, she knocked on the front one since it was closer. Her footsteps sounded lonely on the porch. "Alex!"

No answer. Silence but for the wind through the bare tree branches and the caws of distant crows. She twisted the doorknob. Locked, but that was best. Besides, he had some of the New Yorker in him yet. She jumped off the side of the porch and hurried around to the back door.

Oh, good, she thought, it was unlocked. She hurried into the familiar kitchen where they'd fixed more than one meal together, though he often ate with the family. *Grossmamm* still liked to spoil him with extra-large desserts.

"Alex? Are you here?"

Maybe he was in the barn. He sure fussed over that horse a lot.

She hurried through the kitchen, then the dining room where he had papers and plans laid out on a card table under an unlit kerosene lantern he sometimes lowered on a chain from the ceiling, then into the living area.

"I've been waiting for you," a voice—a familiar voice—said from behind her, and then everything went black.

Ella fought her way through the darkness. Her head hurt. Was she paralyzed? No, tied. Tied, her hands behind her back, her feet together, and curled up in some small, dark place. A nightmare that she was back on the hill again? No, because when she moved, her ankle touched another body—Alex? She tried to say his name but she was gagged.

She struggled to remember what had happened. Where was she? Had she fallen and hit her head? A vibration, a hum surrounded her. Not *Daad'*s bees this time—a car?

Was she—were they—in the trunk of a car? Surely, not Alex's! She recalled with a shudder the trunk with weapons in the assassin's dark car they had taken after he fell to his death in Pinecraft. Then she pictured the black-tinted windowed van that had cornered her in the field the day her cape was taken at the mill, the day Deputy Hayes had stopped her buggy. Now why had she thought of that?

She jerked so hard, she kicked the body next to her, surely Alex, who was either unconscious or dead, because he didn't budge. Blinking back tears, she tried hard to remember what had happened. Oh, *ya,* she'd gone to Alex's house to see what was keeping him. Someone had spoken from behind, then hit her on the head—and that voice—Win Hayes!

But—but she'd been so certain the deputy was on their side. He wanted to please Sheriff Freeman, didn't he? She'd believe Connie Lee or Linc Armstrong, if there was someone evil who was local, but Win Hayes?

Yet she pictured the way he always seemed to be two people, smiling yet frowning, protective yet overly watchful. And that hero worship of Alex—too over-done?

The vehicle jerked to a stop. A car door slammed, the trunk lid opened. No, not exactly a trunk lid in a van, but they'd been under a heavy horse blanket in the back part of the vehicle and the hatch was lifted away now. When the blanket was ripped away, blinking in the light, she stared up at Deputy Hayes—in casual clothes, not his uniform—glaring down at her. When her eyes adjusted to the light, she saw she and Alex both were tied with lots of the Chinese red cord.

"I swear to you, I'm really sorry about this, Ella," Win said, reaching for her and hauling her out of the trunk. He slung her over his shoulder, slammed the back of the van, leaving Alex. He hadn't moved; Was he dead? Win walked with her through a short stand of bare trees to—to the pond!

"Mmm! Mmph!" she protested through her gag.

"I took a lot of money and promises of promotion to get rid of Alex for my employer, and then you had to get involved. You should've stayed out of it. But now, I have a contract for double duty, double death—and I appreciate your giving me the idea for the drowning. Who knows what went wrong? Just a lover's suicide to the outside world, but for Marv Boynton, justice."

"Mmph!"

"The guy's amazing, powerful, charismatic. He may be going to prison for the rest of his life, but he wanted to be sure that he settled with the guy who ratted him out. And when he heard about you, he figured letting Alex know you were going to die with him—before his eyes—well, like I said, I'm sorry, but too late now for me to back out. I'll remember your contribution to my getting a big police department someday, Ella. Maybe I'll name my first daughter for you."

This man was demented—a demon from hell!

He put her on the ground near the fringe of the pond she had feared for so many years. He left her there. She watched him trudge back to his van through the trees. He had pulled way off the main road. With all the time he'd spent driving this area, he probably knew every back way around here. And, *ya,* the van that had followed her that day, tormented her, then just driven off, that's what he was driving!

It must have been Win Hayes working for Marv Boynton all along, and she'd always urged Alex to watch out for the Chinese! She would have bet on Connie Lee as a contact, but then that crimson cord had spooled all over the road the night her son wrecked his car. Ella never saw Win there, only the sheriff, but he'd probably come later to help write a report or clean up the mess—and taken lots of cord.

Quickly Ella tried to loosen her bonds the way the woman in the spa shop had told her. Why had she not paid more attention to it? She should have tried it herself. Now she had multiple strands of it wrapped around her, so would tightening it, then relaxing it even work?

She saw Win lugging Alex toward her. She had not cried, even in her fear and grief, until she saw that Alex was breathing, was still alive but unconscious. And he wasn't gagged. *Help us, Lord. We had a good life within our reach....*

Win put Alex down with his back against a tree and slapped both his cheeks. Alex opened his eyes and stared at Win, then at her with horror.

"It's part of the deal you're still alive, Caldwell," Win told him. "I have specific orders from Mr. Boynton to make sure you get what's happening and why. And I figured if I waited at your place long enough with you, Miss Ella might just come calling."

Win went to the pond, stooped and filled his baseball cap with water, carried it over and threw the water in Alex's face. Alex sputtered, then said, "Let her go."

"You know I can't now. Besides, my orders—which I'd like to change, really—are to get rid of her first so you can watch, then you. Mr. Boynton wants to remind you that you are taking his wife and family away from him for life, all he loves and enjoys, when you should have kept your mouth shut out of loyalty to him. So an eye for an eye."

"Vengeance, not justice?" Alex challenged. "You believe in that? And you don't think Sheriff Freeman will find out it's you—assuming he puts two and two together *before* Boynton tidies up this dirty business by getting rid of you too?"

Ella was glad he was trying another tactic. Anything to give her more time to loosen her bonds. It seemed to be working for the ties around her ankles, but her wrists were still immobile, and she felt the cord cutting into her skin there.

"Don't give me that stuff about how you know how Mr. Boynton thinks," Win insisted. "You don't, or you would have caught on to what he was doing sooner. I'm the one going places with his money and influence now, not you. I think two drowned bodies in the pond's much better than a fall off a high tower. Yeah, I've been told all about that, how the others failed to eliminate you. And I want to thank Ella for giving me that idea of this place for the ending of a sad story."

He looked at Ella, back at Alex again, then went on. "I'll no doubt be part of the death investigation, and chime in on all the gossip around town. A lover's pact? Or Caldwell couldn't hack it here, but he didn't want someone else to have her. So he drowned her, then himself," he taunted. "Hell, I don't have all day. Law and order calls—which is also why no one will suspect me, not Sheriff Freeman's golden boy. If this goes to a homicide investigation, I'll be sure they're looking for another anonymous hit man like the one you two dispatched along the way."

Ella's legs were almost free if she could just carefully kick the ties off without his seeing her. But he was going to drown her before Alex. She watched as Win shoved a handkerchief in Alex's mouth. He tried to kick Win, trip him, but Win easily sidestepped, then turned to her.

"Sorry, Ella. I'm not kidding I regret doing this to you. Let's get it over fast. Pointless to give you two time to say goodbye. You Amish are good at forgiving—so I hope you can forgive me."

But as he half lifted, half dragged her toward the pond, she managed to kick off her ankle ties. In those few yards to the water, frenzy flashed at her, that old panic she'd held in check since Alex had talked her through it. Fear of drowning, of the dark water...

"I kept you gagged, because a woman's scream might carry through these bare woods," Win was saying. The man was crazy, but at least he was guilt-ridden, so if she could only talk to him...

He stood her up at the edge of the pond. "Don't struggle. I know there will be ligature marks on your skin, but I've padded his ties so it will look like you're the only one bound. They'll assume he tied you. Couldn't bear to leave you for someone else to have, could he, when he changed his mind to go back to the world? Forgive and forget and just let go, Ella."

He put one hand on the small of her back to give her a shove. But she hooked her loosed feet around his, tried to throw her weight into him. To his shock—hers too—they both went off balance and hit the water hard.

It was cold! It shocked and immobilized her at first. She tried to recall how she'd kicked to keep her head up in the waves in Florida, but then Alex's hands had been steadying her, buoying her. The nightmare came roaring back, drowning her in the pond of her terror, pulled down, under.

Win was close, so she kicked at him underwater, felt her feet hit his groin. He sucked in a breath, water with it. He choked. *No panic attack!* she screamed at herself. But why not, because she was going to drown with Alex watching. He was rolling toward the edge of the pond, but he was bound hand and foot.

Fighting to get a breath, she lay on her back, wishing she could breathe through her mouth gag. She blinked and shook her head to clear water from her eyes. Her bonnet had come off. Its ties clasped her throat, but she bent her knees and kicked hard at Win again. She hit his chest. He thrashed, roiling the water. She felt it then, the swirling vortex under the pond, the stream-fed current from below that had almost pulled her under the day her friends had saved her. No friends now. Enemy.

Do not fight back, do no violence. But she wanted Alex
and children and lavender and life!

She kicked at him one more time. She missed but the
sharp movement propelled her away from him. Despite
tied hands, she kicked toward the bank. Alex reached
bound hands toward her; she thrust a foot at him and
he held it, then rolled over to pull her out, bit by bit, on
her back. Her sopping skirts rode up, her head scraped,
but she felt warmer—wonderful.

Her first thought was to roll away. That's what she'd
done when her abductor—it must have been Win—tied
her up on the hill. But no time. Win was still thrash-
ing the water white. Surely he was going to get out and
throw them in again. Then, as she and Alex struggled
to pull and roll her out, she realized the pond had gone
quiet.

Both of them still bound but for her feet, she turned
to look back. Win was farther out in the middle where
the cold current had pulled her under that day. He was
facedown, turning in a circle, rotating but not moving
on his own.

She screamed through her gag. Again, again, she
tried to release her wrist bonds and finally got free
enough that she could loosen Alex's. He pulled the
gag from her mouth, then his own. She knelt over him,
her loose, sopping hair like a golden curtain, dripping
water. She shook with shock. Somehow, she managed
to untie his wrist bonds the rest of the way.

She collapsed against him before she could untie his
feet. He rolled them over, farther from the water. He
kept an eye on the pond as he untied his ankles then
bent to hers. "It's finally over," he choked out, holding
her hard to him. "We're free."

"We have to fish him out, get him help, arrested."

"I think he's beyond that. Too bad, because I'd sure like him to testify against my former mentor and friend, whose long arm did all this. Since I'm striving to be Amish now, I won't testify against him again, but I'll make sure Sheriff Freeman takes care of this. I think he'll be hopping mad he's been played for a sucker too—just as I was with Marv."

"Ray-Lynn said it's a shame we can't trust people when we need them."

"I do know one thing. I'm going to protect you for the rest of my life—though you're the one who saved the day just now, as usual, saved my life and my future with you."

He was wobbly on his feet as he stood and found a branch to pull Win Hayes over to the edge of the pond.

"I don't want to get my prints in his car, so can you go out on the road and flag someone down and have them get the sheriff?" Alex asked.

"Sure, but I don't want to leave you with him."

"Ella—he's dead. And I think with this attempt on our lives thwarted, we can bury the past with him. We're only going to look ahead now," he said. "Here, put my dry shirt around you and ask for a cape or blanket when you flag someone down. I'll be waiting for you, Ella, always!"

She kissed him and saw a huge bump forming on the top of his head. Hers still hurt too. She was so cold, shaking all over, but she felt warm inside. As she walked away from the pond that had saved her today as it had once nearly taken her life, she went with a steady stride and her head up. All this, a terrible tragedy, lives lost, but Alex was right. Together, they could face their future now.

28

One year later

"I just hope they like the clowns," Alex said, as he reined in their buggy at the crowded field next to the Home Valley Amish schoolhouse. The field had become a parking lot today.

Hard to believe, Ella thought, two months wed already! The bishop had decided ten months was long enough for a public betrothal when Amish ones were so much shorter than that. Alex's converting to the church was the best wedding gift, but *Grossmamm's* present of the deed to the Pinecraft property was second-best. And they'd been so busy with Alex building up her Lavender Plain Products and his own Better Marketing business, which served both the Amish and the English. But they'd had time to make a baby!

Ella was newly pregnant and felt a bit like she was riding the waves in the Gulf of Mexico, not just a buggy. But queasy stomach or not, no way was she going to miss this benefit for a church family that had lost their home in a fire. It had not been arson, according to Nate

McKenzie, who was the regional arson investigator, but had been started by an untended kerosene lantern. You just never knew what life was going to throw at you, Ella thought, as she clutched the sack of sachets she'd made for the auction.

"Who could not like our favorite clowns?" she asked. "Now if it was Trixie wearing her skimpy outfit for her high-wire act, or Janus had signs attached to his rear, that would be a different story, but they've promised to behave—as best clowns can."

For once, Ella waited on the buggy seat for Alex to help her down. You might know, the first person Ella saw was her shunned friend Sarah. But now Ella understood and accepted what Sarah had gone through to be bold enough to wed Nate. The two women clasped hands, then Ella leaned close to hug Monet, whom she'd learned was named for an artist Sarah loved. Hannah and Seth appeared and all three friends, with their men behind them and little Monet and Marlena between them, stood in a small circle.

"We once vowed we'd stick together through thick and thin," Hannah said. "And—Ella, are you pregnant?"

Ella gasped and, behind her, Alex laughed. "Why, I don't even show yet!" she protested. "I barely figured it out!"

"It's just that I know the look, don't I, Seth?" she said, and turned to smile at her beaming husband.

The three women hugged, then stood in an even closer huddle, arm in arm as Ella and Sarah compared due dates. Hannah sure had a head start on her there.

"Not tears all around already on such a great day!" Nate protested, as Seth and Alex chuckled. "Come on, let's all go see the clowns! I'll bet that's a first for

Amish benefits. Okay, okay, you three need more time," he admitted when the women didn't budge, "so we'll see you over there." Alex squeezed Ella's shoulder and also walked toward the noise beyond the sea of buggies interspersed with cars. Seth bounced his daughter in his arms and said, "Come on, Marlena-Marlena. Your *mamm,* Aunt Ella and Sarah need some time to decide what trouble they'll get into next."

"*They* should talk," Ella said when the three of them were alone. "Here we are, no longer *maidals,* and we've each had our extended running-around time, one way or the other, thanks to our husbands. Me, especially. I feel like I saw half the country when Alex and I were on the run. Sarah, I know you're still under the *bann,* but I just want you to know, I'm sorry I was so stubborn about it all before. I want us to always stay friends."

"Me too," Sarah said, and held out her curved little finger, just as she'd done years ago. Ella linked her pinkie finger to it, then Hannah.

"Well," Hannah said with a tearful smile, "we didn't save you for nothing that day at the pond when you went for a swim. With the Lord's help, we pulled you out and lately, you pulled yourself out."

"You two never knew, but I—I suffered for years from panic attacks. Alex helped me get over that."

Realizing they still held their hands up in the air, they let go. "I'd never be the same without Nate," Sarah insisted.

"And Seth saved me as much as I turned my own life around," Hannah put in.

"By the way, I want to talk to Alex to get a broader base for selling my paintings," Sarah said. "My father says he's helping a lot of our people—and yes, they are still my people too."

"Seth's already using his ideas to get more jobs building barns and churches," Hannah told them. "Something about demographic assessments." They all started to talk at once, just the way they had years ago. They didn't stop until Ray-Lynn came along carrying three boxes of baked goods to sell.

"Ray-Lynn," Ella told her, "I think you're the only one I know who can outtalk all three of us."

"I'll take that as a compliment, you all. Ding-dang, I'm just gonna let you help carry these half-moon pies for me. As usual, the sheriff's off doing his thing. Let's just say we're sisters under the skin, because you all have sure adopted me. I guess we've all been through enough to find ourselves and find our men, and— What's that noise?"

"A roar of laughter," Ella said. "Alex and I have good friends who are clowns, present company excluded from that. They're touring in Cleveland and came to visit for a few days. Come on, let's set up the Dutch Farm Table booth, then go watch them. All that we've been through, laughter's got to be the best medicine."

"And prayer," Hannah said.

Sarah added, "And love."

Alex was getting better at letting Ella out of his sight without worrying. Marv Boynton's attempts to kill him and then her had hit the national media through Sheriff Freeman's report. Now his former boss had been sentenced not only for economic espionage but for murder-for-hire charges. He was fortunate not to get hit with treason too, because that could mean the death penalty.

Marv's sentencing, Alex figured, and all the publicity that went with it, were the best life insurance an Amish man and wife could have, especially since buying insurance was strictly verboten. Anyone dared to harm him or Ella now, and the feds—maybe Congress too— would be all over it.

Oh, sure, he'd given up a lot of worldly trappings and devices to become Amish, but Ella and her people were worth it all. It still amazed him how right it felt to him. He, who had worked so hard at being special, had fallen in love with a woman and a people who valued being plain and ordinary—and yet they were all unique. Here, he'd hidden out in a very foreign place and found acceptance, mercy and his way home at last.

"Okay, Ray-Lynn, I've got something to tell you that bet you can't guess," Ella told her after they laid out her bakery goods at the booth.

"Someone's pregnant? Well, it's for sure not me," Ray-Lynn insisted with a grin. "Hannah?"

"Guilty as charged."

"There, see!" Ray-Lynn told Ella. "Got it on first guess."

"You're only half-right," Hannah said, raising her voice to be heard over the hoopla.

Ray-Lynn grinned at Ella. "You and Alex never did waste time getting in one fix after the other. Let's toast the good news with a half-moon pie apiece, maybe two. And you all take some to the lucky men who—"

"Blessed," Ella put in. "Blessed men."

"Right, the blessed men who are lucky enough to have each of us!"

Ella took two berry half-moon pies, then carefully

hugged each of the women. With a quick wave, she headed toward the crowd.

She spotted Alex at once, though he blended in pretty well now. He was shaking his head and grinning up at Janus, who balanced on a swaying ladder and juggled three balls at the same time. And, that, she thought, as she worked her way through the crowd, was the way she'd felt ever since she'd laid eyes on Alexander Caldwell, alias Andrew Lantz—tipsy, crazy, but hanging on to balance his world and hers.

She stood still for a moment, savoring the moment among her people with a new life inside her. Then Alex's eyes met hers, and he hurried to meet her.

* * * * *

Author's Note

I have greatly enjoyed writing this *Home Valley Amish Trilogy* of *Fall From Pride, Return To Grace* and *Finding Mercy* with the three Amish friends at the center of the action. Each time I visit Ohio Amish country, I see new possibilities for stories. Even now, I am writing *Upon A Winter's Night,* a Home Valley Christmas romantic suspense which I hope you will watch for in the autumn of 2013.

Finding Mercy is actually the eighth romantic-suspense novel I've set among the Plain People. These also include *Dark Road Home, Dark Harvest* and *Dark Angel,* a trilogy; and two stand-alone stories: the novel *Down to the Bone* and an Amish novella "The Covered Bridge" in an anthology entitled *Dark Crossings.*

Special thanks for help with this novel goes to my friend, Mary Ann Manning, for finding a great lavender farm for us to visit in Ohio, and for her friendship and the loan of her beautiful book, *Lavender* by Tessa Evelegh (Lorenz Books, Anness Publishing, Ltd., London, 2002). Also, our appreciation to Roy Manning for driving us all over a part of Ohio Amish country we were not familiar with.

The farm we visited is Springbrook Meadows Lavender Farm, owned by Debbie Cook, who answered questions and gave us a lovely tour. Her website is www.SpringbrookMeadowsLavender.com. She has unique lavender products for sale such as Lavender Linen Water and Lavender Hydrosal, a relaxing spray. Debbie has also written a cookbook called *A Taste of Lavender,* the source for Ella's recipes for Cherry Lavender Nut Bread and Lavender Surprise Muffins. I have Debbie's gracious permission to post these on my website at www.KarenHarperAuthor.com.

I also appreciate advice from Michael Slyker, cofounder and proprietor of Daybreak Lavender Farm in Streetsboro, Ohio, about growing lavender in North American climates. His website is *www.ohiolavender-festival.com.*

Thanks to Bill Harper for sharing information on St. Augustine, which we love to visit, and for his and Sunny's hospitality there.

As is brought out in this novel, it is possible to become Amish, though not common, because moderns must give up so much to join the church and culture of the Plain People. But their ways certainly look attractive, especially when someone is stressed-out and too tied to technology. Still, we need to remember that the Amish themselves have a saying, "It's not all cakes and pies." (I've also heard, "It's not all quilts and pies.") In other words, there are challenges and problems in their seemingly simple and charming way of life.

I'm blessed to live just a two-hour drive from the heart of Ohio Amish country (Holmes County), which has the largest population of the Plain People in the U.S., including Lancaster County, Pennsylvania, which we often think of first when we hear "Amish country." I based the Home Valley and town of Homestead on the area of Charm, Ohio, which is, indeed, charming. However, I changed names and locations so that I could put buildings where I need them to be without receiving an email that begins, "Don't you know there's not really a store on that corner…" (But I do enjoy receiving reader mail at www.KarenHarperAuthor.com.)

I keep with me at my writing desk an Amish bonnet and a faceless Amish doll to remind myself of the core beliefs of these fascinating people. Once you've looked at the world from inside a black bonnet with a deep brim and neck flaps or observed the featureless doll, it is easier to grasp their humility and faith in cooperation rather than competition. Their sturdy furniture and stunning quilts, not to mention their down-home cooking, all speak to Amish talent and generosity. The Amish of the Holmes County area, who prefer not to be individually named or thanked, have been very helpful and kind to me.

Thanks as ever to my husband, Don, traveling companion, business manager and proofreader!

Karen Harper

REQUEST YOUR
FREE BOOKS!

2 FREE NOVELS
FROM THE SUSPENSE COLLECTION
PLUS 2 FREE GIFTS!

YES! Please send me 2 FREE novels from the Suspense Collection and my 2 FREE gifts (gifts are worth about $10). After receiving them, if I don't wish to receive any more books, I can return the shipping statement marked "cancel." If I don't cancel, I will receive 4 brand-new novels every month and be billed just $5.99 per book in the U.S. or $6.49 per book in Canada. That's a saving of at least 25% off the cover price. It's quite a bargain! Shipping and handling is just 50¢ per book in the U.S. and 75¢ per book in Canada.* I understand that accepting the 2 free books and gifts places me under no obligation to buy anything. I can always return a shipment and cancel at any time. Even if I never buy another book, the two free books and gifts are mine to keep forever.

191/391 MDN FEME

Name _____ (PLEASE PRINT) _____

Address _____ Apt. # _____

City _____ State/Prov. _____ Zip/Postal Code _____

Signature (if under 18, a parent or guardian must sign)

Mail to the **Reader Service:**
IN U.S.A.: P.O. Box 1867, Buffalo, NY 14240-1867
IN CANADA: P.O. Box 609, Fort Erie, Ontario L2A 5X3

Not valid for current subscribers to the Suspense Collection
or the Romance/Suspense Collection.

Want to try two free books from another line?
Call 1-800-873-8635 or visit www.ReaderService.com.

* Terms and prices subject to change without notice. Prices do not include applicable taxes. Sales tax applicable in N.Y. Canadian residents will be charged applicable taxes. Offer not valid in Quebec. This offer is limited to one order per household. All orders subject to credit approval. Credit or debit balances in a customer's account(s) may be offset by any other outstanding balance owed by or to the customer. Please allow 4 to 6 weeks for delivery. Offer available while quantities last.

Your Privacy—The Reader Service is committed to protecting your privacy. Our Privacy Policy is available online at www.ReaderService.com or upon request from the Reader Service.

We make a portion of our mailing list available to reputable third parties that offer products we believe may interest you. If you prefer that we not exchange your name with third parties, or if you wish to clarify or modify your communication preferences, please visit us at www.ReaderService.com/consumerchoice or write to us at Reader Service Preference Service, P.O. Box 9062, Buffalo, NY 14269. Include your complete name and address.

SUS11

FAMOUS FAMILIES

YES! Please send me the *Famous Families* collection featuring the Fortunes, the Bravos, the McCabes and the Cavanaughs. This collection will begin with 3 FREE BOOKS and 2 FREE GIFTS in my very first shipment— and more valuable free gifts will follow! My books will arrive in 8 monthly shipments until I have the entire 51-book *Famous Families* collection. I will receive 2-3 free books in each shipment and I will pay just $4.49 U.S./$5.39 CDN for each of the other 4 books in each shipment, plus $2.99 for shipping and handling.* If I decide to keep the entire collection, I'll only have paid for 32 books because 19 books are free. I understand that accepting the 3 free books and gifts places me under no obligation to buy anything. I can always return a shipment and cancel at any time. My free books and gifts are mine to keep no matter what I decide.

268 HCN 0387   468 HCN 0387

Name _____ (PLEASE PRINT)

Address _____ Apt. #

City _____ State/Prov. _____ Zip/Postal Code

Signature (if under 18, a parent or guardian must sign)

Mail to the **Reader Service:**
IN U.S.A.: P.O. Box 1867, Buffalo, NY 14240-1867
IN CANADA: P.O. Box 609, Fort Erie, Ontario L2A 5X3

ReaderService.com

Manage your account online!
- Review your order history
- Manage your payments
- Update your address

> ### *We've designed the Reader Service website just for you.*

Enjoy all the features!
- Reader excerpts from any series
- Respond to mailings and special monthly offers
- Discover new series available to you
- Browse the Bonus Bucks catalogue
- Share your feedback

Visit us at:

ReaderService.com

RS12